What's *This* Cat's Story?

THE BEST OF
Seymour Krim

Edited by Peggy Brooks
Foreword by James Wolcott

PARAGON HOUSE
New York

First edition, 1991
Published in the United States by
Paragon House
90 Fifth Avenue
New York, NY 10011

Library of Congress Cataloging-in-Publication Data

Krim, Seymour, 1922–1989
    What's *this* cat's story? : the best of Seymour Krim / by Seymour
Krim ; foreword by James Wolcott ; edited by Peggy Brooks.
      p.   cm.
    Includes index.
    ISBN 1-55778-470-1 : $21.95
    I. Brooks, Peggy. II. Title.
PS3521.R557A6   1991
818'.5409—dc20   90-26416
                                                                CIP

Manufactured in the United States of America
10 9 8 7 6 5 4 3 2 1

Executor's Note

We would like to thank all those friends who sustained and encouraged Seymour in his time of illness. This also includes those who helped to get this book to the world. Especially:

Peggy Brooks, James Dickey, Jack Dube, Eleanor Goff, Joanna Ney, Tally Richards, Tess Schwartz, Pam Walker, Dan Wakefield, Regina Weinreich, Richard Yates and James Wolcott; and from Paragon House: Don Kennison, Leslie Rowe and Ken Stuart.

Seymour's papers are being collected at the Special Collections Division of the Library at The University of Iowa, Iowa City, Iowa presently headed by Robert A. McCown.

The Estate of Seymour Krim

Donald Krim
Bruce Ricker

Contents

Foreword

I never met Seymour Krim. But when I was writing for *Harper's* in the early eighties, I began receiving brief communiqúes from the excitable owl. He was pleased that I had quoted him favorably in one of my columns. It made him feel as if his out-of-print books hadn't been buried forever in footlockers at the bottom of the sea . . . that somehow his thought-bubbles had surfaced. He didn't make dialogue easy, however. I had heard that he was a secrecy buff (translation: paranoid nut), and his postcards did seem to have been pushed through slits when no one was looking. They would arrive with only a mailbox number for a return address (as if including a home address would leave him open to hit squads), and many of them were signed simply, cryptically, "Krim." At the time his articles bore the same terse byline. But the communiqués themselves were anything but clenched. Like his journalism, they were funny, offhand, yet intensely felt. I remember one card asking me to check out the reruns of "The Dean Martin Show," which featured Dino (Ol' Hair Oil himself) crooning on the couch surrounded by the Goldiggers, a harem of go-go girls in white boots drooping beneath their huge, butterfly lashes. He wasn't recommending the show simply as candied kitsch. He found Dean Martin a hidden rock formation of fascination. Because Krim kept up his defenses, the two of us never got the cha-cha rhythm of a real correspondence going. But when I shifted magazines, the postcards followed me to *Vanity Fair*, one disagreeing with me over my rough treatment of Arthur Miller's autobiography, another kindly asking me to contribute a foreword to a collection of his best work that he was cobbling together. "Pleased to," I replied. It amused me, the idea of beating the bongos on his behalf. But I was also touched, since we were still technically strangers. I knew him only through his jamming prose.

As a critic Seymour Krim started straight, then went woolly. His skull housed a lot of criss-cross lightning. Born in 1922 and raised in Manhattan, he wanted to attend the rolling freight of the big American night. For him this meant walking in the big boots of Thomas Wolfe. He attended Wolfe's alma mater at the University of North Carolina for that very purpose, beating a retreat after a year.

Back in Manhattan, he straddled the market, editing a slew of cheesy magazines while publishing in the choicest literary quarterlies. He wanted to be both a conscientious caretaker of culture and a classic howl who couldn't be house-broken. In his debut collection, *Views of a Nearsighted Cannoneer*, he published both his earnest apprentice efforts at traditional litcrit and his crazy-leg runs toward daylight. As a Greenwich Village Jewish intellectual in the bohemian forties and fifties, Krim suffered the oppressive awe of the Modern Library Giants—Kafka, Mann, Joyce, Proust, Melville, Yeats—and their interpreters at the *Partisan Review*. It was an intimidating period. You couldn't get by with being a small original bullet. Your talent had to have scope. You had to have a handhold on the seven types of ambiguity, plus an ability to spot the columned ranks of historical inevitability streaming like ants out of *Das Kapital*. Sheesh! "I knew gifted, fresh, swinging writers who told me in moments of confidence that they knew they weren't 'great' or 'major' and their voices were futile with flat tone when they confessed this supposed weakness: As if the personal horn each could blow was meaningless because history wasn't going to faint over them." They were all sucked-dry supplicants to the "self-deceiving chic snobgod of genius." Krim couldn't keep up the gladiator pose. He lay down his armor, though not his sword.

What Krim's criticism has is a frank absence of game-face certainty. Many critics treat their minds as a cloud of steel wool fixed for all time. They've long since squeezed doubt from their mental makeups. Their books are walled fiefdoms. The *Partisan Review* crowd aspired to be commissars. F.R. Leavis maintained his authority by laying down permanent tracks for his disciples to follow, allowing no deviation, even when he himself deviated (reversing himself on Dickens, for example). Edmund Wilson regarded his own growls as law, even when he was farting around with eugenics in "A Piece of My Mind." Most of their literary work offers a sound legacy of integral reading and thinking. It exalts literature to the utmost power. But for that reason it also can be killingly correct. "Life is greater than literature, and the man who enriches life is greater than he who enriches literature," Krim wrote in honor of Thomas Wolfe. As a critic Krim comprehends that even the most word-mad among us can't spend all of our time craning up at monuments. Consequently he doesn't build his essays on a classical pyramid of thesis-evidence-conclusion, QED. He jawbones like a jazz soloist, jumping right into the frenzied rush, springing a punchline or a major perception in the middle of a sentence, as much a practitioner of spontaneous bop as his other great hero, Jack Kerouac. (About Kerouac—"a White Storefront Church Built Like a Man, on wheels yet"—no one has written better than Krim.) The hubbub he created was his alone. For a critic to establish a school and train disciples, he has to have a settled body of opinions that can be transmitted. With Krim nothing could be settled, because he was always staring at *himself* through a kaleidoscope. He couldn't pretend to be disinterested, in the

Matthew Arnold-Lionel Trilling tradition. It was his own psyche hanging by a thread on the suicide hotline.

As Krim argued in *Nearsighted Cannoneer*, the creative self could no longer be a mere faithful recorder of common reality. The outer bombardment of stimuli was too big, the inner hungers for recognition too raw. The nervous breakdown and suicide attempt he describes in "The Insanity Bit" represented an inability to ride herd on these bursting galaxies of new sensations and formulate an artistic response. He didn't suffer the steady drip-drip-drip of depression. It's as if the stitching in his head unraveled as the ball was in flight. He needed to reconstitute himself. Years later in the collection *You & Me*, he wrote, "Our secret is that we still have an epic longing to be more than what we are, to multiply ourselves, to integrate all the identities and action-fantasies we have experienced . . . Let me say it plainly: our true projects have finally been ourselves." And what better assembly plant than New York? "Throughout the jumping metropolis of New York," he writes in the essay "Making It!," "one sees vertical fanaticism, the Thor-type upward thrust of the entire being, replacing pale, horizontal, mock-Christian love of fellow Christian love of fellow-creature; the man or woman who is High Inside, hummingly self-aware, the gunner and gunnerette in the turret of the aircraft that is Self, is watching out for number one with a hundred new-born eyes."

High Inside is where Krim aspired to be. He wanted success to massage him with a mink glove until he spurted gold. Crown me king, kiddo! But he was barely able to put one soiled foot into the penthouse suite. Although an early advocate of the New Journalism, he never found a nonfiction project to bring his giant lens into focus. His career became a long vagabondage, a thing of threads and patches. Perhaps the low point was when he was sued by Jimmy Breslin over an article he wrote for *The New York Times Book Review* and fired from the copy desk at the *International Herald Tribune*. A telex from Breslin sitting in the Trib office read, SEYMOUR, WHO DO YOU THINK YOU ARE? YOU'RE A LITTLE, RESENTFUL FAILURE, GOING AROUND JUDGING EVERYONE ELSE'S LIFE AND ABILITIES AND YOU HAVE NONE OF EITHER. Krim considered suicide again, but snapped out of it when James Jones offered to loan him the gun. There are slower ways to go. He indulges in self-pity and petty feuds. In a couple of his books he even reprints his letters to the editor, a sure sign of a crackpot. He cultivates the image of being an overgrown dropout. On the cover of his collection *Shake It for the World, Smartass*, he's photographed (by Diane Arbus) as a bedbug, sprawled under the covers in a one-man sleep-in. He found himself fighting the glare of Mailer's fame and forced to digest the realization that it was Mailer who'd seized the reins of sky chariot over America, not him. A decade later Krim wittily rues that no writer now holds the reins. Our age belongs to bummed-out actors who can barely avoid bumping into the walls. "Yes, the 'player,' whom muttering writers for the past zillion years have usually treated like an infantile textbook case, your ultimate ditzy narcissist, has walked right into history with the authority of a new nose job." Tough enough competing with Mailer. But these cream dreams from central casting! To be a word man in an image age is to be farmed out to the minors.

Failure to reach the majors is the great refrain of Krim's writing. Failure to become a star slugger, a literary stud, a Modern Library Giant. Failure still seems a taboo subject, despite *Sister Carrie* and *Death of a Salesman*—it has a foot-odory pathos right out of the poorhouse. America the Beautiful is based on positive thinking and material reward. His effort to emulate the epic mileage of Wolfe, Whitman, and Kerouac and encompass America the Blemished in his mammoth prose poem "Chaos" (excerpted here) became an ode to futility. Despite brilliant passages, its inner rhymes take on a finger-snappin' daddy-o syncopation that isn't sustainable for a longer stretch—symphonies require fuller orchestration. And yet his willingness to face failure first thing in the morning is what gives Krim's writing its tremendous tender sense of fraternity. After all, most people aren't favored by the gods to drip with pearls and drop *bon mots* as Superman holds our coat. It may be lonely at the top, but it's crowded at the bottom. There are millions more in the trenches than in the penthouse suites. One of Krim's *You & Me* essays was titled "For My Brothers and Sisters in the Failure Business," which found him huddling on the sidewalk, fingering the holes in his pockets, trying to figure out where his promise went. There was something Old World about Krim with his cloth cap and kvetching. He had an immigrant's soul. A man whose mother and father died young, he would always crave body warmth.

As I say, I never got to meet him. It wasn't until his death in 1989 that I realized that he and I lived within hollering range of each other in Manhattan's East Village. If only he hadn't been such a Secret Agent Man, obsessed with maintaining his cover! With the simplest exchange of words, we could have met for egg creams at the Gem Spa, haggling over writers and writing in person instead of postcards. Like you, I have to make do with his written words. What joyous, fighting words they are. In this collection we can hear him stepping up to the typewriter and taking his best cuts. For all his flopsweat, Krim was furiously funny, which is no small matter, and no small reward. Wisdom is for statues. Humor uncaps our inhibitions, unleashes our energies, seals friendships, patches hurts. Laughing is probably the most alive you can be. The happy kick that comes from reading Seymour Krim is irresistible, unless maybe you're a statue. If so, move aside, baby—you're blocking traffic!

James Wolcott

Editor's Preface

My friendship with Seymour Krim goes way back and I owe him a lot, personally and professionally. He introduced me to my husband (a story he tells in one of the pieces in this book) and, when I was an editor at E. P. Dutton and he became Dutton's literary scout, he brought me two of my favorite writers—John Clellon Holmes and Charles Simmons. I was also the editor of record on the Dutton edition of his first book, *Views of a Nearsighted Cannoneer* (1968), but the choices are more his than mine. I mainly encouraged him to put in a lot of the pieces he'd had to leave out of the Excelsior Press edition (1961).

Sy moved on to other publishers and other editors with his second and third books, and though we kept in touch, and he continued to send writers to me at whatever publishing house I was then working for, we weren't so close any more. Then, in 1987, he was hospitalized for a serious heart condition. When he was well enough to come home, he asked me to help him with this book. I was very happy to work with him again.

The first step was for me to reread the three published books—all by now out of print and almost impossible to find in libraries or secondhand book shops—and suggest which pieces I thought must be included in any new collection. Sy wasn't strong enough to make this list on his own, but he had very clear ideas about what he wanted in and what he wanted left out. We argued about the list a lot, as well as about proposed titles for the book, how much editing to do, which uncollected pieces to include. There is no piece in this final collection that Sy didn't want to have here, though the list also reflects my choices and those of his executors and his publisher as to what is his "best" work. I took four uncollected essays from a folder Sy gave me of his favorites among the short articles written since the last book.

Chaos was a ten-year project for Sy. In it he was feeling for a new form which he termed "total imaginative writing." It was written to be read aloud, so he knew it would need a special kind of editing for its first appearance in print. After considerable discussion we agreed on what this should be. Sy chose the section of *Chaos* he wanted to appear in this book. It is from the slightly longer part recorded by the American Audio Prose Library in 1984.

Sy had spoken to James Wolcott, whom he thought would be right for the foreword. He'd decided that footnotes should be added to "Making It!" and "Who's Afraid of the *New Yorker* Now?" The only aspect of the book we hadn't really talked about was what order the pieces should take. Simply putting them in chronological sequence as written didn't seem to be the solution. Because most are autobiographical, I decided to arrange them in a way that told his story. The narrative progression is occasionally circular but the self-portrait is there. Seymour drew from his life for his best pieces, and here it and they are.

Peggy Brooks

Acknowledgments

"What's *This* Cat's Story?" appeared in slightly different form as the introduction to the original edition of *Views of a Nearsighted Cannoneer* (New York: Excelsior Press, 1961), and to the new, enlarged edition of the same title (New York: E. P. Dutton, 1968).

"The American Novel Made Me" appeared in *Playboy* magazine, June 1969, as "The American Novel Made Us," and under its present title in *Shake It for the World, Smartass* (New York: Dial Press, 1970).

"Making It!" appeared in the *Village Voice*, September 9, 1959; in the original edition of *Views of a Nearsighted Cannoneer* (New York: Excelsior Press, 1961); and in the new, enlarged edition of the same title (New York: E. P. Dutton, 1968)

"The Insanity Bit" appeared in *Exodus*, 1959; in the original edition of *Views of a Nearsighted Cannoneer* (New York: Excelsior Press, 1961); and in the new, enlarged edition of the same title (New York: E. P. Dutton, 1968).

"Ask for a White Cadillac" appeared in *Exodus*, 1959; in the original edition of *Views of a Nearsighted Cannoneer* (New York: Excelsior Press, 1961); and in the new, enlarged edition of the same title (New York: E. P. Dutton, 1968).

"Milton Klonsky" appeared in shorter form under the title "Two Teachers—Nuts, Two Human Beings!" in the original edition of *Views of a Nearsighted Cannoneer* (New York: Excelsior Press, 1961), and in its present form in the new, enlarged edition of the same title (New York: E. P. Dutton, 1968).

"The Kerouac Legacy" appeared in slightly different form as the introduction to *Desolation Angels* by Jack Kerouac. Copyright © 1960, 1963, 1965 by Jack Kerouac; reprinted by permission of Coward-McCann, Inc., New York. It appeared with the introductory paragraphs added here in *Shake It for the World! Smartass* (New York: Dial Press, 1970).

"Who's Afraid of the *New Yorker, Now?*" appeared in slightly different form in the *Village Voice*, November 8, 1962; and with the introductory paragraphs and Part 2 added here in *Shake It for the World, Smartass* (New York: Dial Press, 1970).

"The Newspaper As Literature/Literature As Leadership," appeared in slightly different form in Evergreen Review, August 1, 1967; and in Shake It for the World, Smartass (New York: Dial Press, 1970).

"Joan Blondell: The Last of the Great Troupers Teaches Sadness to the Literary Kid" first appeared in the Soho News, January 3, 1980.

"My Sister, Joyce Brothers" first appeared in the Soho News, April 9, 1980.

"How I Hated London Before I Got to Like It a Lot and Then Had to Go Away," appeared in slightly different form in Nova, November 1970; and in You & Me (New York: Holt, Rinehart & Winston, 1974).

"Son of Laughing Boy" appeared in London Magazine, December 1973; and in You & Me (New York: Holt, Rinehart & Winston, 1974).

"For My Brothers and Sisters in the Failure Business" appeared in slightly different form in You & Me (New York: Holt, Rinehart & Winston, 1974).

"Notes Toward My Death" appeared in American Journal, December 1, 1972; and in You & Me (New York: Holt, Rinehart & Winston, 1974).

The excerpt from "Chaos," an unpublished book-length prose poem, was included in the section recorded by the American Audio Prose Library, Inc., New York, 1984.

"The 215,000-Word Habit: Should I Give My Life to The Times?" first appeared in the Nation, April 23, 1988. It was reprinted in Best American Essays 1989, edited by Geoffrey Wolff and Robert Atwan (Boston: Ticknor & Fields, 1989).

"The CAT Scan of Our Era: Actor as Incarnation" first appeared in the Nation, November 14, 1988.

1.
What's *This* Cat's Story?

1

Let me start at the beginning. I had always wanted to write ever since the age of 13 and followed the usual pattern gone through by a dozen of my friends in the same line. Namely writing for the highschool magazine (in my case the DeWitt Clinton *Magpie* up in the Bronx), co-editing a mimeographed literary sheet called *expression* (man, were we swingingly lowercase back in 1939!) because of the kid-stuff in the official one and getting temporarily kicked out of highschool for selling it in the john, then going on to college (I deliberately followed Thomas Wolfe's big romantic boots to the University of North Carolina) and writing for the magazine there. Then after quitting college I returned to New York and had the usual erratic round of uptown editorial jobs: editing a Western pulp magazine, working as a snotty silly kid reporter on *The New Yorker*, ducking the war in the OWI,* writing publicity for Paramount Pictures, writing the commentary for a newsreel (a job handed to me by the stylish poet-painter Weldon Kees who is presumed to have committed suicide in San Francisco several years ago although his body was never recovered from the Bay) and living off the advance for a novel that I never finished in the posh 1947 days when Don Congdon was giving away Simon & Schuster's money to young writers. He had come over from *Collier's* as their whizbang boy editor and I plus a few of my friends managed to get in line for the $1200 advance-money handout.

In case you know little or nothing about how American writers live (which includes the various art-sanitariums or retreats like Yaddo and the Huntington Hartford Foundation where I and my brother pack of hungry art-wolves made the free scene for wasted months at a time) the above is average until the writer unwinds and starts turning out the novels and stories that he presumably wants to. But I never unwound. I had natural sock as a storyteller and was precociously good at description, dialogue and most of the other staples of the fiction-writer's trade, but I was bugged by a mammoth complex of thoughts and feelings that prevented me from doing more than just diddling the surface of sustained fiction-

---

*Office of War Information—Ed.

1

writing. Much of this was personal; some of it was due to the highly critical (how can you write when you haven't read *Bartleby the Scrivener*? etc.) period I came of age in; and some of it was due to grave troubled doubts I had that the novel as a form had outlived its vital meaning and was being perpetuated by the dishonesty and lack of imagination of its practitioners. Taken together all these facts threw me off the narrowly uncertain balance I had to begin with and sent me shuddering down the tunnels of introspection and cosmic-type thought that more or less paralyzed me for a decade; until I finally vomited up my wretched life and found myself no longer even an amateur writer but a bona fide all-American-1-out-of-every-16 psychotic.

During this period of so-called paralysis—for it was that as far as the no-crapping-around, basic, definite creative birth of an *object* was concerned—I sought out the best intellectual minds I knew and absorbed, absorbed, argued, learned, was criticized, and finally found myself turning to literary criticism as a way of writing and thinking. Behind this choice-necessity (for I desperately needed some way to express even a little of myself and with it a mental center from which to operate) lay my painstaking conscious effort to think through literary problems that before I had instinctively sensed. But by now my self-conscious intellectual glands had become immensely swollen as a result of the people I hung around with and at the age of 28 or so I could no more go back to my former glorious naive conception of "the writer" than to knickers.

My most articulate friends were Jewish intellectuals (I'm Jewish but not a card-carrying intellectual) and they made me toe the ideational line like a spinster aunt going over her maid's cleaning with a white glove poised for dust. I was not permitted the excesses or romanticism I had kidded myself with before and if life were eternal this education would be recommended by me as a must for any kind of mature achievement. But life is lived in time, time is short and the burden of mortality is heavy, and a writer has only so much to say and should get to it without wasting his precious (to him) hours with scanning the heavens when his fly needs buttoning.

I didn't know this during those days in the Village in the early 1940s when I was part of a highly intellectual but not necessarily artistic group of brilliant minds which roved with barely believable and almost illegal freedom over the entire domain of the thinkable and utterable. Some of these minds—like Isaac Rosenfeld, Dave Bazelon, Manny Farber, Weldon Kees, Willie Poster, Chandler Brossard, Anatole Broyard (plus the occasional appearances of Saul Bellow, Delmore Schwartz, Alfred Kazin, James Agee) and the inimitable Milton Klonsky—were in literature partially or completely; some—like Will Barrett, Herb Poster, Clem Greenberg—were more interested in "ideas" than expression. All of us were broadly part of the *Partisan Review* and *Commentary* worlds where ex-Trotskyites, ex-anarchists, ex-Stalinists (everybody seemed to be an "ex" something) mingled with fancy Ph.D.s and metaphysical poets to produce that modern eclectic monster who is as much at home with surrealist poetry as British radical politics, with baseball and boxing (the big sport for intellectuals then) as the foolproof technique for banging a girl. There was a tremendous charge in all this to me when I was accepted into the group and soon I was trying to graft this interstellar burst of new ideas onto the emotional–instinctual drive of my being that had originally led me to want to be a writer.

Ideas are wonderfully fecund but they can be bait for ruin and the most miserable self-deception unless the party involved is modest and selective; I was neither; I wanted to swallow the entire fucking world and spit it out again not merely as an artist but as some kind of literary-human-intellectual God. What had happened was that my imagination, which coupled with experience is the source of fiction, took the implications of these (to me) new ideas and lifted them within my mind to extravagant heights buoyed up by the very helium of fantasy and inventiveness which—if channeled differently—could have made a modest career for itself writing novels. I had come from an entirely different background and self-taught tradition when I got my intellectual initiation in the early 40's; I was intelligent enough but my touchstones until then had been strictly literature and, humanly enough, American literature (because that was what I wanted to write).

But overnight it seems I became internationalized. I saw how parochial my small Hemingway-Wolfe-Dreiser-Faulkner standards were in the midst of these swinging world-dominating intellects and I was put in the impossible position of trying to write a piece of emotionally real description about some homely thing that happened to me and relate it to the interplanetary discussion I'd had the night before (tea-high, shouting, yelling, laughing, ideas zooming, then falling into Ratner's at 3 A.M. for chopped eggs-and-onions) on Joyce, Trotsky and (yeah my dear Klonsky!) the poetry of Marvell. This contradiction between my own small hut of experience and the skyscrapers of new thought obviously cut deeper than just literature. Soon I was spinning like a human top as a result of this fantastic dazzle of diamond-bright gab and revelation and almost every standard I had previously thought was impregnable began to crumble the longer I looked at it. I didn't know then that this is the fascinating, tempting, delusory (I'm learning! I'm growing! I'm developing!) thruway to nowhere and that self-providential man was made to draw the line when common sense flashes its light.

Some of this interpenetration of ideas into literature now seems to me inevitable in this high-questioning time of ours but its accommodation in the mind and the relating of its parts will faze even the most selective intellects, let alone untrained ones like mine was; it is inhumanly tough to think your way through the skein of the world today; but what I didn't know in the early 1940s is that nothing valid or true is ever cancelled out—you can add to it or increase its significance with resonant symbolism if you know exactly what you're doing, but even the most peasantlike or humble truth remains a grain of gold and therefore a plus factor in the world. I had stubbornly hung onto my faith in basic truths all through this tour of the upper atmosphere but I recognized many new truths as well that had been offered me through electric interchange with more refined and knowing minds, and the tragedy as I see it was that I was helpless to put them together and too proud to do the menial work I was sure of until I realistically outgrew it.

2

The phantom of great European-inspired ambition drove all of us in my group to the most miserable heights and voids of despair, like Hitlers in our own mad little Berchtesgadens; the reader shouldn't forget that the casual small talk of the people I greedily learned from was Kierkegaard, Kafka, Melville, Blake, Lawrence (Joyce was considered a misguided second-rater) and with such standards running wild and demonic in our lusting heads there can be little wonder that some of us cracked under the intense pressure we placed on ourselves or died (perhaps there is no direct provable connection but the deaths included Isaac Rosenfeld, the very well-thought-of Bob Warshow, my editor at *Commentary*, James Agee, Kees's and just recently his good friend Willie Poster's suicide) or sucked nightly on Christ's vinegar sponge because we could never attain the impossible.

Driven by this illusion of great power and omniscience—getting daily more intoxicated by handling the tools of thought which made mincemeat out of famous names admired by the square public—I aggressively moved over the line into book reviewing. Marjorie Farber, a peripheral member of our group and then an assistant editor of the *New York Times Book Review*, eased me into the Sunday section in 1947 and I showed off in print like a cramped colt led out onto a fast track. I was never completely at home in book reviewing and literary criticism during my 12 years doing this kind of writing (although I think I brought to certain novelists the insight that could only have come from a constipated brother) but it became an ego-habit. Having tasted the blood of print I couldn't stop; criticism was very much in the air, was hip, impressive, the sign of rank, fiction was for brainless impressionists (thus ran my snobbery), and even though I felt split about reviewing from the start and kept telling myself it was only a temporary filler the drug of seeing my glistening thoughts in print hooked me and I didn't have the courage to stop.

I felt I had to keep writing for publication (you've got to be printed no matter what or how!—young writers will recognize that junkie urgency) while I sweated out the private war of trying to reach a unity between my experience and the murderously suggestive new ideas that were being fired at me and even beginning to shoot up of their own accord in my head. My dream was to make a peace finally between my imagination-experience and these foaming ideas and out of

this come forth with a high art of my own making which would combine the
sensuousness of great literary style with the startlingness of an unprecedented
approach. It would come, it would come—I *knew* it (in my blindness). Meanwhile reviewing was the only way I could almost consistently get printed although later on I was to experience, along with others, the regarding of a book
review as a finely wrought poem by neurotic and snob-conscious editors: this
made and makes reviewers overwrite and overstate their case to glitter more
flashily than the competition and I too was to be such a shameless shimmy-
dancer after suffering my share of rejections.

But at this point I moved on to the *Commonweal* because they then had a
tolerant and sympathetic book editor named Bill Clancy, who sensed I was not a
native or orthodox critic but nevertheless brought out of me some of the best I
could do because he had a taste for fullness of expression rather than the
narrower, stricter conception of criticism then at its height (more or less going
back to T. S. Eliot and made into a very subtle instrument by the scholarly
Blackmurs, Tates, Ransom, Trilling, so forth). Along with the *Commonweal* I
began to hit *Commentary* and had one small piece in *Partisan Review*—both
places then giving the avant young writer the most superior feelings of having
made it for keeps when actually he was copying his elders' manner in most cases
and being dishonest to himself and his own generation in the way he expressed
himself.

I was never comfortable at *Commentary*, which I felt then and feel today can
be no true ally of literature because it has to watch its step like a nearsighted
cripple with asthma, as far as what it publishes; it is sponsored by and beholden to
the American Jewish Committee and tries to navigate a course between the
impossibles of freedom and a cautious, worrying, ingroupy conception of "responsibility" (translation: the current line of the New York radical-highbrow
corporation which loves to be sentimentally eloquent about avantgarde heroes
after they're dead and helps freeze them out when alive because their black
charm never fits the latest abstract recipe for profundity). Even writing for a
Roman Catholic magazine like the *Commonweal* I literally had much more
freedom of expression than in *Commentary*, where I and a number of writers I
know have had their most felt thoughts squeezed into grey lines of qualification,
humorlessness, overediting, unoriginality, by the staff's tiptoeing fear of making
a booboo. It took the *life* out of a young American-Jewish writer to do a piece for
them—the ton of worry that preyed on you when you sat down to the machine
made sunny days automatically gloom-ridden—and the eventual non-you solidi-
ty that could ultimately be wrung out (after 6 rewritings) by knowing their
Teutonic idea of a distinguished piece of work was not compensated for by the cru-
cifixion of self and the joylessness of the writing. It was truly immoral to the whole
act of writing. *Commentary*, taking its cues from the universities and the various
respectable academic and/or ex-radical pros like Richard Chase, the Trillings,

William Phillips, Leslie Fiedler, Dwight Macdonald, became a suburb of *PR* in literary evaluation and both magazines were sewed up with *reactionary* what-will-T. S. Eliot-or-Martin Buber-think timidity as far as the natural roaring young independent went. I feel sorry (premature as it may read to some who feel only the competitive sweat and panting breath of the race) for the hotshot young critics today like my friend Podhoretz, Steven Marcus, the various smoothie sons of the older literary generation who were taken or foolishly slicked their way into the smart-money fold. Unless they chafe now and discover their own style, thoughts, even magazines, they will not speak to me or for me in the wideopen days of the future that lie ahead. And it will be our mutual loss for we are of the same generation and face the same problems as their benefactors do not.

As for the influence of *Partisan Review* on American writing during this time in which I was trying to establish myself assbackwards I will say nothing: it has lost its impact today for the whole beat shocktroop of young expressors, as historically it had to and humanly it was fated to, and tried to span the world at the dreadful cost of patronizing (not caring enough, being too snob-clannish, overcerebral, Europeanish, sterilely citified, pretentiously alienated) its own country and the terrific reality of our life here. Factually it led writers to more disappointment—overevaluation of themselves, illusion, smugness, fancying they were extraordinary philosophers or prophets when they were just ultra-sensitive Americans who didn't always write well in their own language—than it ever saved or gave a point of view to. But it was the creation of a monstrously inflated period wherein it thought it had to synthesize literature and politics and avantgarde art of every kind, with its writers insanely trying to outdo each other in Spenglerian inclusiveness of vision. Yet it obviously printed many significant things and there was no place quite like it; and in my circle it was a hip badge of prestige and real in-ness to appear in its elephantinely big-gun pages. For people of my age and bent however the whole *PR* phenomenon along with the *Kenyon Review*, the *Sewanee*, the *Hudson Review* (to be discussed more closely) and all the others unfertilized into being by the Anglo-Protestant New Critical chill was a very bad, inhibiting, distorting, freakish influence. It made us ashamed to be what we were and the cruel acid of its standards tore through our writing and scarred our lives as well; in our prose we had to put on Englishy airs, affect all sorts of impressive scholarship and social-register unnaturalness and in general contort ourselves into literary pretzels in order to slip through their narrow transoms and get into their pages. Sometimes I got the impression that the editors of these magazines wanted to relax the entire torture-chamber that literature had become but didn't know where to begin. Whether I was right or wrong this masquerade obviously prevented direct writing for most of the perspiringly overwrought contributors and became a weighty, suspicious bore for the normally intelligent reader who couldn't rationalize it the way the insiders did.

By now as far as my so-called career was going in my late 20's and early 30's I was publishing an occasional short story and gaining a small steady reputation as a good critic—not a brilliant textual beagle or a conceptual Coleridgeian literature-shaker but unanonymous enough for a few party-met strangers to know my name and work. In spite of the kick of this I hated the critical reputation (a kid in the White Horse Tavern one night shouted out in a beer-voice that "Krim is one of the best critics in America!" and even though I knew this was a tight-type exaggeration meant to please me I suddenly felt that my very being was a sham) because I knew it was horribly unfair to my truer, realer imaginative bounce as a writer; what I didn't know was that each time I dug into myself to try and write an "important" piece of criticism—and even succeeded to some extent in pieces on Wolfe, Dreiser, Hemingway, Edmund Wilson, Whitman, etc.—I was committing myself to impossibly high standards that made me feel less like giving out with my own untested jazz than ever. I was weekly and monthly killing the best part of myself; setting up endless self-defeating dialogues and fancy but illogical rationalizations within; squirming always in the pain and defensiveness that goes with cheating the self of what it really wants and all for the perverted boot of being a small Name on the scene and keeping your hand in the pussy of even petty success, no matter what. Seen coolly it was disgusting self-murder but there was no one to tell me this because almost all of my friends were caught up in the same narrow pocket, becoming increasingly more exacting, fussy, competitive, fanatical, less human in their writing and standards.

3

I should have gotten out of criticism, said to hell with it, but one turned scared at the thought because where could you go? Until the beats came along and revived through mere power and abandonment and the unwillingness to commit death in life some idea of a decent equivalent between verbal expression and actual experience, the "serious" New York literary scene was becoming a prison, to the point of shutting off the real, gamey, lowdown communication that must go into writing if it's to have even as much meaning as the telephone. But such obvious realism was of no interest to me then. I was hooked in the life, as hustlers say, and even though I knew it was fundamentally wrong for me I felt I had to follow through until my creative work "matured" (illusion! perfumed bullshit!) and swept me off the bed of nails that criticism had become.

I was afraid to quit because then I would have nothing except the crumbs of the very few short stories I had managed to grind out. Thus I graduated to the *Hudson Review*, the very latest and coolest and most technical of the swank highbrow quarterlies. My editor was Fred Morgan, Park Avenue and Princeton, and even though the money-family thing is not one of my comes I strutted a little within to find myself in such *Fortune*-acknowledged (the name, the loot, the leather-binding-monogrammed-cocktail-glass-old-print montage) company and able to hold my own. On the cover of the *Hudson Review* were the names that impressed all of us (Yvor Winters, R. P. Blackmur, Ezra Pound, Robert Graves, Wallace Stevens) and I was now to be among them. So I punished myself to produce a couple of critiques that whatever their merit had no relationship in the pain of composition to what I could have said given the encouragement to loosen up, be real, fail richly rather than succeed as a miser and a tightrope-walker. I succeeded and became one of the *Hudson's* second-string boys until I lost favor, but in so doing I again made a cramped miniature of my spirit, chorus-lined my self-respect, tidied up my originality, emasculated my real iconoclasm. I was sucking the sugar-tit of local snob success and didn't want to let go for nothin, momma, not even the cry of perplexity and sadness that came up from the being of the man who had once wanted to be a big stubborn writer in the grand tradition that laid waste to crap and lying everywhere.

Fred Morgan, co-founder and editor of the *Hudson Review*, was and is a formal decent guy (approximately my age), particularly so in view of the heavy-moneyed life he had to duel with to find a way of his own; but his allegiance to his near literary fathers—Blackmur, John Crowe Ransom, Eliot, Pound, the whole over-studied list of recent saints who are not guides for *today* and should never have been sanctified since literature is no church—made him uneasy among the very equals in age and experience whom he should have embraced. The young need the young more than they need the old and honored: great writers take care of themselves and don't need monuments and schools since their influence is always present; but the brilliant kid writer can be crushed or turned into a foolish acrobat unless he gets an enthusiastic response from his own contemporaries, not elders whom he has sensible mixed feelings about no matter how concerned they are. Love your own kind and the love and faith of even your enemies will eventually come to you! But if you choose instead to rely on the judgment and values of another generation as I think Morgan did—out of caution and over-respect and measuring his qualities against theirs as if they were the standard—you will inhibit your most vital contemporaries and get their most studied showoff writing, not their best. An editor's spiritual job (and I have had two excellent ones, Bill Clancy and Jerry Tallmer of the *Village Voice*) is to inspire the writer to top himself with each new effort and this is done by the writer's knowing the editor has complete confidence in him. An editor who has no confidence in a writer should tell him so very early in the relationship so that both can relax. Tact in this very close business is much less important than faith and eventually degenerates into hostility and an insecurity that ruins the writer's relationship to his work: show the writer you are completely behind him or very early in this tight intimacy have the courage to be frank. But all of this implies a security of belief and a personal four-squareness (or four-hipness) which in this time of upset and fear and daily reversals of personality is uncommon.

In this way did I fitfully work, masochistically and unjustly spending whatever was precious within me on criticism—I'll show these intellectual pace-setters I can lick them at their own game!—when I wanted desperately to return to the blast-furnace of open creativity. But, went my inner monologue, what *is* creativity in this time? Semantically the word means "to bring into being, to cause to exist." Didn't an insight—ah how we loved insights and illuminations in my old gang!—bring a new thought into being, wasn't a thought a window into reality, and didn't ever new truths about this vast clutch called existence mean that you were doing the holiest work you could? It was not only rationalizations like that which kept me and mine ("I write criticism like hammered steel," one poet who wrote comparatively little poetry told me proudly) chained to critical-analytical prose; it was basically a passionate sense of *intellectual superiority*, a fanatical personal pride that used the mind and its accomplishments as the test for true aristocracy in the modern world. I formerly had believed in the aristocracy of the novel; but in this community of hip intellectuals I was justly in their eyes a naif. I reformed to my ultimate personal unhappiness. I fell in stride, saw or tried mightily to see a more subtle and extensive creativity in criticism, shaped and directed my protesting mind into abstract ideas and became another of the young avantgarde gigolos who moved with patent-leather nonchalance from French symbolist poetry to philosophy to psychiatry to—you name it.

I had become a contemporary intellectual in the eyes of my pleased older friends, which meant in the scheme of values implicitly held by us a suave masterspeaker (and theoretically thinker) in practically all literary and ideological fields. In simple actuality I didn't have the formal training for this glib seasoned role nor could any of my friends have had as much background as they would have needed; yet when we picked up a copy of *PR* and saw (or wrote!) an essay on Toynbee next to one on Wallace Stevens, followed by one of Robert Lowell's obscure early poems, it was necessary to keep up both to oneself and the killing standards of the superintellectual community by patiently tackling and understanding each of these works. I drove my mind to *inhuman lengths* to absorb and make mine each of these different offerings until I later sounded and sometimes wrote like a bastard encyclopedia. In the meantime my brain had the impossible task of trying to integrate this deluge of suggestive, often profound thought with my personal experience and the vivid fantasy-life of the potential novelist; because I was stubborn I kept adding the one on top of the other without restraint until I too thought I carried the entire world in my head and felt that I was the living embodiment of the modern god-writer, the omniscient one, the heir of all the ages and the true king of the present—out of my way slobs!

I now come to an unpopular topic but one that has to be opened up. Most of my friends and I were Jewish; we were also literary; the combination of the Jewish intellectual tradition and the sensibility needed to be a writer created in my circle the most potent and incredible intellectual–literary ambition I have ever seen. Within themselves, just as people, my friends were often tortured and unappeasably bitter about being the offspring of this unhappily unique-ingrown-screwed-up breed; their reading and thinking gave extension to their normal blushes about appearing "Jewish" in subway, bus, race track, movie house, any of the public places that used to make the New York Jew of my generation self-conscious (heavy thinkers walking across 7th Avenue without their glasses on, willing to dare the trucks as long as they didn't look like the caricature of the Yiddish intellectual); thus the simple fact of being Jewish when fused to the literary imagination gave a height and fantastic urge to our minds which outran reason. I may be reducing the many causes for the terrible display of intellectual egomania to a too-simple basic source—for surely the overworshipped genius-standards of the literary climate as a whole goosed the entire phenomenon—but if I can generalize on the basis of my own experience it was the ceaseless knowledge of knowing you could never erase this brand of being that drove us mentally upward without rest.

We were Americans who loved our country and its experience (being writers who thrive off the real) but we were also Jews who because of Christian society's traditional suspicion and our own heartbreaking self-awareness became almost fanatical within ourselves to try and triumph over this blotch of birth by transcending it in brilliant individualism. It was an immodesty born of existential necessity and it was reinforced (as I've said) by the constant references in the conversation of my group, in *PR*, in *Commentary* and the other reviews, to none but the highest figures in Western literature-art-thought. When I relive it in my mind now it seems like a hallucination but it was a specifically real personal and cultural fact; and it is being carried on to this very day in determinedly intellec-tual New York quarters that seem ultra-responsible from the outside but in fact are crippling natural genuine expression by their cruelly ambitious standards—born in this case out of the soul-pain of a hooked beak and a dead uncaring Jewish God who left the mess stamped on our faces and beings, and neurotically spread from there into a grim literary puritanism that uses the name of reason but not its pure spirit.

4

It is ironic that what was once an unquestioned good—such as the highbrow magazines printing nothing but the best, most honest, most imaginative non-commercial literature and criticism—became a 90 percent disaster. It encour-aged, not fulfillment of writing ability on the just level that the guy had in him, but a competition with the heroes of the past and present that placed inhuman pressure on the vulnerable young writer. If he couldn't be "great" in the sense of the over-reverenced Eliots, Yeatses, Prousts, Joyces, Kafkas (the chief figure in my group) he felt like a failure in the airless climate in which we all sweated. I knew gifted, fresh, swinging writers who told me in moments of confidence that they knew they weren't "great" or "major" and their voices were futile with flat tone when they confessed this supposed weakness: as if the personal horn each could blow was meaningless because history wasn't going to faint over them. History, the god of my grotesque period, the pursued phantom, the ruby-circled mirror of our me-worshipping egos which made monomaniacal fanatics out of potentially decent men! I found in my group that this sense of measuring yourself against history prevented the best talents from opening up and developing as only the practicing writer can—by publishing and exposing his work to other human beings, the public so-called. The self-deceiving chic snobgod of genius— reinforced as I've said by obsessive references to only the giants of literature and thought—grew like a tumor in the minds of myself and my friends and infected us in a sterile self-deifying way. In many cases including my own it prevented the writer from penetrating his own special vein of material, developing his own point of view, becoming adult and realistic about the tangible earthly tricks of his craft. Much of this fundamental understructure was snottily put down and dismissed next to the tremendous ego-thrilling zoom of loading one's work with "great" or hidden meaning. Atlas-like trying to lift the most commonplace material to an almost religious or epical height.

I can't stress strongly enough the insecurity that was put *into* the naturally talented writer with a feeling for people and story and good dialogue by such a Kafka (scripture)-quoting, perfectionist environment as the one I both wrote for and lived in. To be profound was not only a value in this world, it was almost a necessary card of admission; it was as if a person who had the wit to be intelligent should realize that the age demanded nothing less than genius as the bare minimum, and good taste itself required at least brilliance. As I look back on it now from the vantage-point of what I have been through it seems that our demands on life itself had gotten dementedly out of hand, for even a half-dozen of the most original works of the century—which my group did not and will not produce—could not have justified the height of our arrogance or the depth of our frustration which was caused by this sleepless mental anguish (like a drill on a New York street) to produce works that would shake the world and crown ourselves. The conceit of man, I have reason to know, is boundless. A naivete about the limits of human nature plus a riotous intellectual ambition— encouraged by the top-heavy literary reviews who with each issue salted the bitter wound that Man wasn't yet God, what a drag!—helped cook more lives and work during this period than it ever aided or inspired. In fact it uninspired, depleted, broke down, de-balled the very work it was theoretically supposed to encourage.

Concentratedly put, what had happened was that each outstanding single achievement of the recent past—by a D. H. Lawrence, Picasso, Stravinsky, Gerard Manley Hopkins, Melville—was linked with the other to create a vocabulary of modernity; familiarity with great work was as casually expected of a person as familiarity with the daily paper; combined with stitching-together of extraordinary achievement provided the background for all conversation, friendships, feuds, affairs, and such things as status in a livingroom or victory in argument were dependent on one's knowledge of the new Hip Bible of greatness. In other words, this acquaintance with greatness was turned into serviceability; and this serviceability took the form of coming out of the mouth at gatherings where it was used as a weapon for personal advantage by highly articulate and severely critical intellectuals. And in this arena I nursed my private dreams of writing—not talking. Yet verbal aggressiveness, mental agility in conversation, knowledge and insight as shown by the deftness with which they sprang to the lips, were actually much more valued among my friends than literary originality, which took grubby hard work and had to be done without glitter in private. The stuttering crudenik who couldn't come on in public and didn't understand or like Kafka—but who had a small, hard, true American imagination of his own sans the big-city vocabulary of genius—would have been slaughtered if he stuck his head in a jumping livingroom where my teachers and I mapped and remapped the world by the second.

To make an enormously charged, complicated, dizzying long story short, mine was as severe a critical-intellectual environment as can be imagined and being without true shape or definition as a writer (except for my stubborn urge to weave a unity between my actual experience and these new dimensions of abstract thought) I was strongly influenced by my friends. I put aside and did not develop my storytelling abilities—in fact they began to seem as I've said simple-minded to me—and got in ever deeper into the speculative manipulation of ideas. In the meantime, in the hours before sleeping so to speak, I would torment myself with those vain attempts to make a bridge between my newly found critical hipness and the emotional–experiential material that was begging for release and could only get out by working its way into my criticism—sometimes rawly. If I had been more restrained in my own ambition and more sure of the worth of what I had to communicate as a mere human-type writer, I would have been less knotted and uncertain about what to do. But all of the minds I most respected were almost without exception (one was the writer Michael Seide, not a member of my "group") as omnivorous in their intellectual greed and *not one* ever bothered to take me aside and say: "Why not be truly original Krim by cultivating your own natural garden and doing some accurate limited work that is right under your nose."

It wasn't until I was 33 and had to scream my way to the inevitable climax of all the foregoing inner-wrestling, doubt, confusion, backtracking, fantastic imprisonment, the me-self dying for release—not until I spewed up every hunk of undigested matter in my psyche and bloodily broke through to my own raw meat via the whistling rocket-ride of what is called insanity—that I began to think for myself because I had to. Man, this wasn't any bullshit about beautiful words and dream-masterpieces anymore—this was life and death and all that cellar-deep jazz! It was difficult to swallow the fact that I probably would not be a great writer because not only had I envisioned (in fact known!) that this would eventually come true, a few people had even used the magic word during my 20's and I graciously took it in stride. It was just a question of time I then thought, and in the meantime Time was ticking away and I was caught in the same vapor of twists and doubts that I'd been in since my early 20's: imagining a revolutionary prose in my mind while doing criticism for my ego's bread. But when I almost threw the switch during the suicidal depression that followed the revolt against my frustrations—then pulled myself out of it—it seemed stupid from that time onward to revert to such hypocrisy as keeping up an act as far as writing went. The criticism I did after this was much more straight and finally led to the series of controversial but definitely more initiative-taking articles which I did for the *Village Voice* (1957–1959) and *Exodus* (1959–1960). The cover-up of a stilted conception of writing always rips under the unshavable hairs on the dogged face of life.

5

I stand now at the end of any pretense with formal literary criticism (even if busted in pocket and adulation and blocked on my own road) but I will carry with me always the infection with ideas that no one in my environment escaped. When today I feel overextended and almost drowning in the sea of speculative thought—hangover from endless nights spinning the world with my brother-gods in the most brilliant untaped talk of the century—and know I must call a halt for my own preservation, then does the commonsense of Gertrude Stein's shrewd remark strike home every time.

> I know that one of the most profoundly exciting moments of my life was when at about 16 I suddenly concluded that I would not make all knowledge my province.

But this kind of focused chastity can only be a pastoral memory for me and mine—the seeds of oceanic thought were sown too beautifully in the ripest season and we must struggle with the bastard harvest in our heads. It is too late to duck the responsibility for what we so superhumanly craved; to wipe out the engrams grooved in our brains would need a Frankenstein-type operation. We became what we admired, in that joke of jokes always heaped on sinners who now pray for a leaner diet. Yet should such a communication as this be dug up in a future period I would insist that the reader try and appreciate how extravagant the whole conception of making volume-long outsmarting footnotes to the writings of others became, how superior to the unclothed novelist or poet the shrewd parasitic critic normally felt because of his safe armchair perspective (*sub specie aeternitatis* my ass—he was wielding power and making the law!). It was a period and still is in some dated quarters where the display of Mind—disembodied from its blistered feet, overloaded, speaking a language unlike the language of regular life—snubbed the value of imagination and offbeatness and found it juvenile or irrational because it met no preconceptions. The haughtily articulate became a hard iron criterion to hang onto because of the threat of the unknown in a time that was subterraneanly groaning in labor; university-groomed fraidycats clutched this rehearsed script with fear or at least insecurity and defensively called it Reason; and those of us who finally rebelled and refused to punish our beings any longer in imitation of this perversion of truth became ultimately what we had always secretly wanted to be—individuals thrown back on our own clumsy resources, free to err, live, die, speak the truth or a half-truth or a lie, but free baby free!

In the world I lived in the greatest applause went to those critical writers who traced out what were called original ideas; the entire notion of originality was drained out of explicitly creative writing and put into under-glass exegesis, where the critic could fly to the moon without risk or croon masturbatorily over the courage and demonism of a Dostoevsky but jump five feet if he met it in present-day life. (It was peculiar but sad: originality was the big kick, it was worshipped because of the gallery of approved modern heroes and the critics tried to duplicate it in the realm of ideas, but it was feared and dismissed close up if it was *unfamiliar* as it had to be.) Meanwhile in this artificial reality-denying paradise mere Somerset Maughamish competence in writing was looked down upon as a value crappily pedestrian and unchic. Mediocrity became the most disgusting enemy of this highly cerebral avantgarde *in theory*, with few realizing that they were installing a gorgeous new mediocrity (or orthodoxy) of the so-called alien-ated modern saints which inhibited and killed the genuine if crude life-reaching around them.

My style as man and writer was shaped by the prevailing superior tone of this straining decade and even the swinging creative work that I hope to do will never entirely shake off the odor of condescension and literary verbalism that was the norm in my circle. It is a fairly subtle distinction that I would like to make here—but the fact is that even if one of us self-chosen brillianteers wasn't natively the most gifted mind or writer ever to land on earth the *style* we expressed ourselves in *had* to be extraordinarily intelligent-sounding as a matter of duty. If you see it through my eyes for a moment you will realize that this injunction to be brilliant meant that natural flashes of illumination had to be hardened, that the posture of abnormally high intelligence had to be maintained at all cost if you were to hold your head high to self or others.

But what ultimately happened was that this emphasis on rare theoretical intelligence lost its value under the impact of life itself. Men and women who had trained themselves to be profound found in later years that they did this at the sacrifice of their total personalities and had repressed certain urges and over-evaluated others to their final literary frustration and personal unhappiness. Real life as it is lived in this time must inevitably influence those who would shut it out and *all of us* from my group have been justly lowered in our appreciation of ourselves and—if my experience is any judge—more respectful of the power of brute 1960 human reality than in its fancy intellectual transcendence. If extreme cerebration was part of the mental manners of my period, one shouldn't forget that a needy and sometimes adolescent romanticism was hidden beneath this fascinating agility with ideas; the desperate and often simple needs of the soul went on as they always do, under and quite disproportionate to the big ideas that were borne aloft on the fuel of fanatical ambition. I found in myself that I gave mental size to emotions that in themselves weren't worth it out of a need and desire to impress my Village scene with the image of my worth—converting bits of trivia into big-sounding phrases that used our mutual vocabulary and hence were kosher, no matter how intrinsically minor or childish the emotion was in itself. I'm sure my friends were guilty of the same distortion to some extent.

The path ahead is hardly an easy one for me now. Nor would it be for anyone who came from the intellectual-literary electric chair that high-voltaged me or had for years (as I did) judged and fantasied himself in the platinum currency of literary greatness that was tossed around like pennies by my friends and the magazines we wrote for. In a real way—assuming I had the choice which I don't—it is not greatness that I want now; my heart and mind are tired of the inhuman selfishness and egomania that I associated with its self-conscious quest. In itself it has lost its value for me, completely unlike what I would have imagined 10 or even 5 years ago. I realize of course that the choice is ultimately nature's and not one's own but having lived among superlatives for so long I am weary of pursuing what is not necessary. The talking and thinking in nothing but extraordinary, grand, complex and mentally suffocating terms for so many years has taken away my appetite for self-willed genius and made me doubt the value of the entire genius-concept for this time—which reeks with such self-idealization because of *personal identification* with the stars who make up the avantgarde constellation. I can never forget that so much of the pompous inflation of myself and my literary buddies came from just this injustice to the present by injecting the most pretentious traditions of the past onto a scene that is made on a different scale and should have been treated in a more direct, informal, speedy way, without the stiffness and Europeanisms that exaggerated the self-evident and prevented sexy vital American pace from busting out. (Nothing can speak for itself like what is, with the exactness, punch and accent that an unbugged, unproving-anything natural writer can lay down.)

The writing I want to do now is inspired by the pertinent, the immediate, the actual of this very minute; that would be sufficient greatness for me if I can give it full voice. My longtime secret dream of a consciously heroic style and attitude toward American experience which I envisioned as being legendarily all-inclusive and Proustian-Whitmanesque (a conception of mine for one monumental-type grand work which I lovingly nursed through the years) has been ground down by the steel heel of present-day necessity into a keener point and I am grateful now to be given a second chance to gun out some leveller messages about reality. It's the old story: the overthrow of unattainable or perfectionist ambition is the most freeing thing that can happen to a writer for it unlatches him to write what he believes in without strain and with humming conviction.

I believe my imagination is still my most unique possession as a writer and I want to use it to its uttermost to make such creations out of the life of my time as I am particularly geared to do. The critical form which I forced myself to approximate over the years has left its cast on my mind for good, but I have learned or am learning how to cut its magisterial bondage to "judiciousness" and "responsibility"—believe me there is deeper responsibility in the human soul than playing supreme court justice and that is to make the things that others can judge!—and use whatever organizational, reasonable, analytical powers it brought out as the mere mucilage to hold living thoughts together. I remember the ironic inner laugh I had recently when a good but literarily unsophisticated friend defined me to my face as a "Jewish intellectual" rather than a Jewish *writer*—ay, the stamp has probably taken permanently despite all of my protests and the attempt I have made here to show the way in which my innocence was raped (willingly) by the obviousness of intellect instead of the subtlety of soul. We violate ourselves ultimately and much as I can point factually to the historical period that over-evaluated abstract articulateness and lured me into imitating its way (thank stubbornness my voice had its own concrete human sound at times) it was the mush of my own being that permitted this plastic surgery in the image of what was outwardly impressive.

I can only trust now to remake myself as a writer in the light of the truths that I can clearly see are *mine*, won by experience and temperament and personal vision, without forcing myself to engorge the thoughts of a thousand other minds or mind-binding myself in the suicide of absolute perfection. There has always been a place in writing for candor and frankness, for real personal honesty, which I would like to extend with my actual American experience (Whitman, Dreiser, James T. Farrell and Henry Miller have already hewed this most marvelous trail over here but it can be taken into exciting new country) and a higher one for the imaginative emancipation of life based on this same ruthless love for what is. I am now committed to trying to combine the two, to creating a reader-participating living experience about our mutual days with my certainty that the foundation is real because I have lived it, not merely thought it.

All this assumes there is time. And yet time is just what I don't have, what is an uncertainty, what becomes more uncertain with each day. The years that have been wasted in living for the future when the great work would come and one would just have to transcribe it are never to be recovered; it is a bitter thought but one that I and my equally grandiose friends will pay for with increasing remorse as *The September Song* plays on the juke in the background. The trivial literary deeds (shreds of stories, memoir, unsatisfying critiques, a miserable few over-elaborate poems) that were to be a prelude to chords unheard on earth before may be all that many of us will have to show when the time comes for us to justify our presumption. My tears (both for myself and my brilliant friends) must turn to ice however when I consider our ease of opportunity as contrasted with the struggles of the men we quoted and the oceans of spirit we squandered in vanity that called itself by other names: exploration, speculation, experimentation, High Art, etc. That time is dead! We killed it! It can only return in the immense concentration of all this lost mortality that one of us can get into his work and unlike what I once would have proudly hissed out, that person is not likely to be myself; and even if this past is recaptured in words of eternal life can they compensate for the waste that the rest of us squatted in while competing with God? I saw what I used to think was the cream of a generation get increasingly sour because it talked more than it worked, criticized more than it praised, and not only demanded but accused life for not giving it the key to the universe—with the tacit encouragement of their unrealistic, too-haughty elders who flicked off a Thomas Wolfe for being a greedy romantic and could tell you in a flash what *hubris* meant but sinned quite as much as Wolfe. Not in the bad-boy area of sensuous excess but in the much more arrogant and sinister and fatal realm of mind, where vices are perpetrated that make those of the flesh mere child's play.

I must end this introduction to my first somewhat bloodstained collection (and it is curiously remarkable to me that in the middle of the weirdness that frankly describes my apprenticeship into the hip modern writing life I got this work done) with some simple logic. The world and living are obviously much more difficult than they appear and ask by their very nature for our fighting intelligence and full humanity; if we don't give proper moral payment the just angels of retribution squeeze it out of us when we are begging on our knees and all the literature we mouthed so fancily degenerates into a few humble words. What I am trying to say is that my period and its spokesmen used too many words to say too few things that matter today to young life-bombed kids; theirs was the elaborate rhetoric of ideas but when in time of crisis one went to grasp them for human use there was nothing specific and tangible which you could hold onto. I resent as a person as well as a writer having been misled by such a self-congratulating, aloof intellectual bazaar that failed to direct its statements to each very real individual who comprised its audience. Or as Tolstoy might have said with the simple nerve of greatness, what good was it? It is no longer enough in my opinion to deal in truths that are not directly related to the people who eagerly read you and take seriously what you say. Published writing is becoming increasingly a crucial public act in our stripped-down pressurized environment and its immediate goal should be to penetrate like a bullet the mind and emotions of each contemporary who reads it. This is basic in a time when people are hungry and desperate for straightforward communication about the life we are *all leading in common*; inflated or overwrought theory becomes an almost self-indulgent luxury— perhaps even a crime—under the hammer of the world we live in.

I was confused and torn apart by the amount of material I was expected to absorb reading the more abstruse literary quarterlies, I who wrote for them, and if this was true for a "professional" avantgarde writer like myself what can one say about (1) the bewilderment (2) the lack of human time to pit against the obscurity of much of the work (was it worth it in the mortal countdown?) (3) the lack of everyday experiential clues (4) the feeling of being a thick failure unto self of the unprofessional intelligent reader who wanted to know and experience this "apex" of modern writing but most often felt ironly left out in the cold? Literature is not worth the suffocation of life and the unnecessary alienation of your public if you have any respect for being alive yourself; it can't possibly be superior to existence and yet we often wrote about it as if it were separate from its living source. No single person can waft aside the chain of history and what I have described in these pages is now a historical accomplishment, with the overtones of the highbrow era having been filtered down to thousands of college students throughout the U.S. who read the magazines I used to write for and who will soon begin the same tortuous journey as myself if they want to be serious writers or even serious humans. I pity them. No, we cannot dispose of history; but we can change it by a recognition of where it has led us. In fact change only occurs I believe when we stand against the ultimate wall and realize that there is no place else to go except in a totally different direction. By the value of one man's life to himself and his conviction that others must feel comparably he has said goodbye don't bother getting up I can find the gate myself. I'm going out!

1960

2.
The American Novel Made Me

1

I was literally made, shaped, whetted and given a world with a purpose by the American realistic novel of the mid to late 1930s. From the age of 14 to 17 I gorged myself on the works of Thomas Wolfe (beginning with *Of Time and the River*, catching up with *Angel* and then keeping pace till Big Tom's stunning end), Hemingway, Faulkner, James T. Farrell, Steinbeck, John O'Hara, James Cain, Richard Wright, Dos Passos, Erskine Caldwell, Jerome Weidman, William Saroyan, and knew in my pumping heart that I wanted to be such a novelist. To me, an isolated, supersensitive N.Y. Jewish boy given the privacy to dream in the locked bathroom of middle-class life these novels taught me about the America *out there* and more than anything I wanted to identify with that big gaudy continent and its variety of human beings who came to me so clearly through the pages of these so-called fictions. I dreamed southern accents, Okies, bourbon-and-branchwater, Gloria Wandrous, jukejoints, Studs Lonigan, big trucks and speeding highways, Bigger Thomas, U.S.A., U.S.A.! Nothing to me in those crucial-irredeemable years was as glamorous as the unofficial seamy side of American life, the smack, brutality and cynical truth of it, all of which I learned from the dynamic novels that appeared in Manhattan between 1936 and 1939.

They were my highschool, my religion, my major fantasy life; instead of escaping into adventure or detective fiction—there were no groovy comic books then, such as Pete Hamill writes about 10 years later when Batman flew into his head over in Brooklyn, or if there were I was already a kid snob tucked into my literary American dreamscene—I escaped into the vision of reality that these fresh and tough pioneering writers were bringing to print from all corners of the country. In an odd way, even though most of these books ended bitterly or without faith, they were patriotic in a style that deeply impressed my being without my being able to break down why: they had integrity to the actual things that people did or said, to the very accents of frustration or despair voiced by their characters, they were all "truthful" in recreating American life. This was a naked freeshow about my real national environment that I damn well did not receive at

19

home—a home full of euphemisms and concealments, typical, with the death of one parent and the breakdown-suicide of the other hanging over the charade of good manners—or in the newspapers, radio or at the movies. Except for the fairy tales read to me as a bigeyed child and an occasional boy's classic like *Robinson Crusoe* or *Treasure Island* or the Tom Swift books this was the first body of writing that had ever really possessed me and apparently I would never (and will never) get over it.

How can I communicate the savage greenness of the American novel of 30 years ago as it was felt by a keenly emotional teenage boy?—or girl, I guess, although it was primarily a man's novel but certainly not totally. I and the other members of my generation who were given eyes and ears and genuine U.S. lifestyle by it knew nothing about its father, Theodore Dreiser, and his beautifully pensive younger brother, Sherwood Anderson, until we became intellectually smartassed and history-minded 10 and 15 years later. We lived in the perpetual present created by those men named in the first paragraph and were inspired to become prose writers because of them. It wasn't really a question of "talent"; if you responded to the leaping portrait of American life that these craft-loving realists (superrealists in actuality) were showing with professionally curved words you created the talent out of yourself; at first in imitation of what you creamed over in their style, point of view and impact, then later in painful effort to do equal justice to your own personal test tube of experience.

The deservedly legendary American novelists of this raw-knuckled period before the war (they were *our* celebrities, on high!) encouraged an untested, unformed young guy to dig into his own worst personal experience and make something exciting out of it in the form of a story. The whole movement was in the finest and least self-conscious sense the story of myriad personal lives in this country, it encouraged everyone caught in its momentum to look hard at the unique grain of his or her life and its interweave with other lives. None of us who in the late 30s were swept up into the romantic-heroic fantasied career of novelists were in any sense fated for this role, in my opinion; we were baited beautifully by the gusher of skilled novels—Maritta Wolff, John Fante, Dorothy Baker, Bessie Breuer, Daniel Fuchs, Pietro di Donato, Josephine Herbst, (the early) Robert Paul Smith, Tess Schlesinger, Frederic Prokosch, Gladys Schmidt, Irving Fineman, Gale Wilhelm, Albert Halper, Nathanael West, Oakley Hall—that seemed to be goosing each other to shine more truly than the next. To a young, hungering mind once hooked by the constantly fresh stream of national lives that made their debut in these novels—characters from all parts of the country, waitresses, fishermen, intellectuals, lesbians, truck drivers, salesmen, alcoholics, nymphomaniacs, jazzmen, generals, athletes, everything—it was impossible to call it quits; once the "real" American scene entered your imagination through the eyes of these standup individual recorders and native consciences who seemed to loom up, suddenly, hotly, with a rush before the 30s decade ended in World War II, there was nowhere else for the youthful truth-maniac to go but to the new novels hurrying each other out of the New York publishing womb. New fiction was the hot form, contested, argued, encouraged from *Story* to the *New Masses* to *Esquire* to the (then) *Saturday Review of Literature* to *The New Yorker*; the city buzzed with the magazine-unveiling of any new talent, it was news that traveled with enthusiasm (Irwin Shaw in *The New Yorker*, Di Donato in *Esquire*, James Laughlin telling it like it was down at his family's Pittsburgh steel works in *Story* before he became publisher of New Directions).

It is very true that as the 30s drew to a vicious close with the Spanish Civil War and Hitler's preparations for the new blood-and-iron stomping of Europe, the politicalization of the U.S. novel became more acute and the bleak international scene seemed to throw its heavy shadow over our comparatively virginal literary pinethrust. But all of this is seen from the cool view of later years whereas if you were just coming alive as a human being in the late 30s it all seemed like one nonstop fictional ball. As a highschool boy, although I bought my *New Masses* every week because the Communists were truly involved with fresh fiction (O Meridel LeSeur, where are you now?) no matter how slanted their typewriters, I found the political-propagandistic implications of the new novels much less important than the powerful concrete punch they delivered. Each of the exciting 30s novelists, it seemed to me inside my comet-shooting young head, were pioneers; they were tackling unrecorded experience in each hidden alley and cove of the country that I wanted to be a part of, bringing it to ground for the first time, binding it up and sending it East for exhibition before the rest of the citizenry. Certainly their moral flame was ignited and burning steadily or they would not have gone to the huge labor of making almost the entire country and its people accessible to fiction; but apart from the explicitly political base of men like Farrell and Wright (and the poignant Odets in drama, although his politics was a left cartoonstrip compared to the flashing originality of his voice) this flame was used to warm their faith in the value of writing truly rather than held aloft as a defiant gesture.

Their moral integrity—Weidman to his New York garment center, Saroyan to a Fresno poolhall, Faulkner to his luxuriant decaying cottonwood swamps (of the soul)—was concerned with how to verbally break the back of unarticulated and unacknowledged truth, that which has been seen, smelled and suffered but never before written. They were to my imagination outriders, advance scouts, and what they brought back from the contemporary American frontier was as rare and precious to all of us who were waiting as the information now hugged to earth by an astronaut.

I saw it in even more private terms; as a boy of 10 or 11 I had wanted to be an explorer, my fantasy-life taking off in the magic snowtracks made by Robert Peary and F. A. Cook who fought over discovering the North Pole and Admiral

Byrd and Roald Amundsen who independently reached the southern one. It was no accident, I believe, that the American novelists of the 30s took over the explorer's role in my mind after the merely geographical aspects of exploration had faded into the bottom drawer of childhood. Who else but these self-elected—self-taught—self-starting—gutsy men and women with the sniff of glory in their proud nostrils were the real explorers of this country's unadvertised life? The novelists who electrified me and hundreds, perhaps thousands, of young kids like myself between 1936 and the outbreak of the war were idealists in the most adventurous sense no matter how stained their material seemed to be on the surface. If you said to somebody, as I soon began to after breaking into print in the DeWitt Clinton highschool lit. magazine, that as an adult "I wanted to write" it could only mean one thing: the novel. A bigness impossible to recapture in 1968 attached to those three power-words, "wanting to write." One had the image of climbing the jaggedest of the Rockies alone, flying solo like Lindbergh, pitting one's ultimate stuff against all the odds of middle-class life and coming out of the toughest kind of spiritual ordeal with that book-that-was-more-than-a-book, that was the payoff on just about everything, held in your hand. It was heavenly combat the way I pictured it, self-confrontation of the most hallowed kind, and if my vision of it was ultra-ultra then the legendary American Novel itself at this time was the most romantic achievement in U.S. life for the dreamer who lived inside everybody with a taste for language, style and—justice!

To have wanted to be a writer in this country in the late 30s had about it a gorgeous mystique that was inseparable from the so-called American Dream on which every last one of our good writers was first suckled before being kicked out in the cold to make it come true. If that phase, A.D., American Dream, meant going all the way, that the individual in this myth-hungry society had the option to try and fly above the skyscrapers, then writing toward "the great American novel" was not only an act of literature but a positive affirmation of the dreamdust that coated all of us born under the flag. All the driving personal ambition, energy, initiative, the prizing of individual conscience and courage, that operated or was supposed to operate in every other branch of national life entered strongly into wanting to be a novelist—but with a twist. The act of writing a novel made use of all these widely broadcast qualities, yes, but the reward one sought in it was not palpable gold; bestsellers as such were sneered at unless they occurred by accident; the goal was one of absolute truth to the material, to make a landmark on the unmapped moral and esthetic landscape of America that would somehow redeem the original intentions of the country and the selves made by it and represent the purest kind of success story for the person who brought it off.

This meant that being a typical good American novelist in the 30s, even wanting to be one, was *not* finally dependent on having an extraordinary gift for telling a story in print. Certainly there were narrative and stylistic "geniuses" like

Faulkner, Hemingway, perhaps even the early O'Hara, James Cain, Djuna Barnes, each buff and lover of the period will name his or her own, and their overpowering skill with the craft produced virtuoso performances that set standards and became models to aim at. But the American novel only became a great art in its outward finish and skill, in the 30s, because of the internal spiritual motivation that made wanting to write it perhaps the sweetest gamble in national life. You might almost say that the romantic promise of the country as a unique society of total justice for all, pegged on the limitless possibilities of each individual—all the raging hope that the American Dream meant to the imagination of its most ardent dreamers—was all part of the religion of wanting to be a novelist when I got the call while in highschool. If the idea of the mystical American novel had not been bound up with all of these big national feelings and aspirations that writhed around in the direct center of one's being, if that novel had not been more than "literature," I doubt if I and so many prose writers my age would have chosen the written word as our badge.

It was the ambition (when the time came at 15 or 16 to tell yourself what you "wanted to be") chosen in the pride of the secret imagination by rebel fantasists, now in their 40s, who believed they could rebuild reality closer to the American soul's desire by writing in the light of a final faith that would transform their portraits of frustration or injustice into the opposite. By this I mean that because they wanted to believe in the promise of the country, were inseparable from its myth, were tied up emotionally and psychologically and every other way with "America" almost as if it were a person—with their own fulfillment as human beings actually dependent upon the fulfillment of the nation at the poetic height at which they conceived it—they felt they could let go in the novel to the full extent of their negative imagination. Everything bad, awful, unjust, painful, stupid, outrageous in their own lives or theirs in relation to the lives around them could be discharged at full intensity in fictional form with the underlying implication that it was just and right to give such ferocious bite to negative expression because it was all an attempt to redeem an invisible, psychic Bill of Rights. Towering idealism, paradoxically shown by the extent of the dark "realism" in the characteristic novel of the time, was the climate in which the fictional life of the 30s grew to bursting; the more the novelist envisioned The Way Things Should Be the more he and his readers felt he had the duty to show the ugly side of the land, the failure of the ideal, the color of the pus, the company goons beating down the strikers.

We kids who wanted to write the American novel knew without analysis, responded totally with our sharpened feelers, to the unspoken values that lay behind any particular book in question; if Weidman's *What's in It for Me?* or O'Hara's *Hope of Heaven* showed heels and weaklings with special corrosiveness of scene, dialogue, action, nailing them to the wall with the brilliance that comes from a mixture of contempt and pity, we shared enthusiastically in the experience because we knew that in writers of O'Hara's and Weidman's stripe the moral judgment was implicit rather than explicit as in a Steinbeck or Wolfe or Wright. It didn't matter to us, implicit or explicit, because we were instinctively clued in to the intention of all the late 30s novelists just by wanting to make the same nittygritty comment on our own experience; we knew by feel that even if a specific book baffled our haughty teenage heads it thrust at us a segment of the country's experience, it was criticizing America under the table in order to purge and lift it, it was forever encroaching on the most taboo, subtle and previously undefined aspects of our mutual life to show a truer picture of the way we lived.

Those of us, then, who couldn't forget what we had already been through— who remembered each hurt, black skin, Yiddish nose, Irish drunk, wop ignorance, too short, too tall, too poor, afraid of girls, afraid of boys, queer, crippled, sissies, young-bud neurotics/psychotics, the most vulnerable and stung of the new generation who could fight back with words—it was we who thought that being novelists would heroically reclaim us by recreating the bitter truth about our personal lives and our environment. Obviously it took sensitivity of the most piercing kind to provide the openings in the personality where painful experience could lodge and stick, so that one day it would all be poured forth in answer against frustration (personal and social both); you must never forget that we who wanted to be novelists not only thought it was the most free and ultimately ethical means of American expression, we were also squeezed by the very existential nuts into *needing* fiction in order to confess, absolve and justify our own experience. The majority of us who "wanted to write" were already middle-class losers who couldn't make it inside the accepted framework; the thinskinned minority who were set apart in our own psyches to observing when we wanted to act and to thinking when we wanted to participate—the kids who were constitutionally unable to do the saddle-shoed American Thing during the smoking acid-bath of adolescence.

Do I therefore mean, to hit it squarely, that writing fiction for me and my breed was a pimply kind of revenge on life, an outcast tribe of young non-Wheaties failures getting their own back, all the shrimpy, titless, thicklensed, crazyheaded dropouts and sore losers of American youth resolving in the utter misery of the dateless Saturday nights to shoot down their better-favored peers in the pages of a novel? Yes, I flatly mean that in part; the mimetic ability, the gift to recreate lifelike scenes and dialogue, to be good at acute description, even to have one's moral perceptions heightened, is spiced and rehearsed by unhappiness. Wasn't the novel to those of us caught in the emotional hell of American teendom a wish-fulfillment device for would-be lovers banished from the sensual playland that taunted us via radio, billboard, movie marquee and our own famished unconscious? From (in my case) the big, smooth, "in" gentile world of blue eyes and blond hair and supple tennis-racket bodies that I felt I could never be part of and that then seemed like the top of the heap?

Yes, the American novel for those of us who were precocious outsiders—and there were a thousand reasons why each one of us failed to measure up to the gleaming Robert Taylors and Ginger Rogerses who star-touched our Loew's Saturday afternoons and made us silently weep into the bathroom mirror on Sunday—was a magic, lifelike double in which we thought we could work off our private griefs, transform them into messages of hope and light, and remake our lives themselves by the very act of writing. This artform, then, for us, was *many things:* the freest and most total kind of expression for reality-loving idealists; the place where "truth" could be told as it could not in real life or in any place but one's mind (psychoanalysis was still a decade off for most of us); and a form so close to living matter itself that the illusion of personally controlling experience instead of being its fallguy or victim could not have been stronger. Sure, the novel was a legitimate "artform" even for those of us who wanted to use it for the redemption or glorification of self; but it was a yielding female art that was responsive to the most private subjective needs and it provided the only complete outlet for the being that was choked and distorted in our waking relationship to society. To us it was the golden cup of a modern fable—one which we could fill to overflowing with all the repressed hunger in ourselves and also one which could announce our fame, toast us to the sky because of our verbal triumph over the weights that near crushed us, make come true in imagination what could not be realized in the bruising action of daily life.

Of course it *was* action on a literary level, action with words, but in the final sense it was substitute or dream-action carefully clothed with the wrinkles of a photographic realism. The façade of the great realistic style of the 30s was documentary, bang-bang-bang, everything as hard and metallic as the shiny unyielding materials turned out in our most modern factories; swift as a biplane, lit up like a radio tube, driving as a racing car on the Salt Lake Flats ("James Cain's style is like the metal of an automatic. You can't lay his story down."— *Saturday Review of Literature*). But this was only the outward enameling that we swung with and mentally caressed because it was all so new, fresh, a prose like the artifacts of the country itself—streamlined. Our stripped-down, whipped-down appreciation of power loved that clean line bulleting across the page. Yet behind the lean, aware, dirty knowingness we were stylistically tuned in to was that assumption, as if by divine right, of impossible freedom—the novelist working out his total hidden life before our eyes—which made novel-writing in America such a tremendous adventure no matter how pinchingly personal the original motives might be that drove you to your desk.

I am certain that those of you reading this who came of age in the same late-30s period recognize the excitement about the novel that I am trying to recapture because it made me what I am essentially. Can you imagine a human being actually molded by something as abstract as a literary form? Yet it was quite real, not only in my case but in that of the vulnerable cream of an entire generation who graduated from highschool when the U.S. novel had grown so big that it literally stretched us with its broadshouldered possibilities. Our values, coloring and slant as people were dominated by the overwhelming idea of being novelists, the beautiful obsession that kept us secretly, spiritually high like early Christians. It puffed us up with humility, humbled us with pride, made us into every character we imagined and put us in every story we could cook up; but within, not outwardly as an actor might express it (and there were strong correspondences although we novelists-in-embryo toughly put down actors as childish narcissists) and we coolly loved ourselves for the infinite range of life that easily gave itself to us and you could be god-damned sure to no one else. When I flunked out of college in 1940 a year after finishing highschool, for example, this was not even remotely seen as a failure by me and mine but rather as a new and soon-to-be-significant phenomenon which I would be able to write about from firsthand experience. The first time I got laid, drunk, smoked "tea," shipped out (and jumped ship before we left Sandy Hook), saw death, spent the night in a hospital-clean Pittsburgh jail, masturbated over the fantasy of going to bed with my sister, put on women's panties and silk stockings for kicks, got into my first adult streetfight and almost had the mortal shit kicked out of me—all of these "firsts" and a hundred others were special, fated, grand experiences for me and those like me because I was a novelist-to-be and I was on a special trip!

What a dream it was, what a marvelous hurtproof vest we all wove in the name of the novel (which was another name for religion or faith in the nonchurchly modern sense).

2

I did not, finally, write novels as anyone familiar with my output knows; but I was made as person and mind and writer in their image, just as a newer generation (and even my own exact contemporary, Tony Curtis, *né* Bernard Schwartz) has been created by the movies. The reasons why I never added my own byline to that passionate list are many, some personal as well as cultural; I may not have had the "talent"—although I published my small share of vivid short stories—or what is more likely the needs of the post-World War II period *shifted* in my eyes and those of my friends and we put much more importance on trying to understand the new world zooming up around us than expressing what we already knew. We became, in manner, crisply intellectual instead of openly lyrical but much of that same apocalyptic sense of possibility that we once felt in the U.S. novel now went into its examination (the name of the game was literary criticism) until the work of fiction became for us a means to examine life itself. Wasn't that what it was all about anyway?—at least so ran our sincere and often troubled rationalization at the time. But even though the form began to slowly change in the late 40s and the early 50s for a radar-sensitive minority of us, nonfiction instead of fiction, the goal remained essentially the same: the articulation of American reality by individuals who really, personally cared because their own beings were so helplessly involved in this newly shifting, remarkably unstable, constantly self-analyzing and self-doubting society that had shot up after the war.

I sweated the national anxiety out in myself, what direction was I going to go in?, the idea of the novel still hanging over me as a kind of star but getting further and further distant as my ignorance in other areas—politics, poetry, sociology, history, painting, etc.—was exposed and I tried powerfully to educate myself now that as a non-novelist I was being challenged socially and even in print. The dream of being a novelist, the dream that being a novelist had been in this country, had kept me warm for 20 years; now I was torn from this sustaining fantasy by my failure to act and was forced to fend for my self-esteem in a hardboiled intellectual community (the literary-political magazines where I published) that had no sympathy for my little inspirational couplet on What The American Novel Means To Me. They either thought it was a put-on, because I had written none myself, or a sentimental indulgence. Therefore whether it was because I temporarily allied myself with the so-called New Criticism in its more cerebral search for reality—and there were a number who had wanted to be fictionists (even wrote their one or two novels) who took this further crook in the country's prose road along with me—or because basically I did not think "novelistically" which in all honesty I am forced to doubt or else all my former covetous years were pitiably unreal—or as I believe because "truth" no longer seemed to *me* to reside in my beloved American novel as it had in my young manhood—I began in the mid 50s to regard the novel as a used-up medium.

For a person like myself, confessedly given great hope and direction by this medium, justified in all my agonizing human goofs by its very existence because I thought I could one day redeem them through it, the beauty of knowing the novel was there like a loving woman for me to go to when beaten to my knees, it wasn't an easy emotional matter for me to say in my mind, "It doesn't sing for my time the way it once did." But I said it—at least for myself. What had happened, not only to me but I'm certain to others who came from my literary environment, was a fundamental change in our perception of where the significant action lay: the fictional realism on which we had been shaped seemed to lead almost logically to that further realism which existed in the world of fact; we had been so close to the real thing with the *style of* superrealism that it was now impossible to restrain ourselves from wanting to go over the edge into autobiography, the confessional essay, reportage, because in these forms we could escape from the growing feeling that fiction was artificial compared to using the same novelistic sweep on the actual experience we lived through every day.

In other words the very realistic 30s novel that had originally turned us on made us want to take that giant step further into the smellable, libelous, unfaked dimension of sheer tornpocket reality—my actual goodbye-world flipout in

1955—James Agee actually pounding on his small car in Santa Monica a year before he died and telling a friend of mine who had casually quoted a line from Agee's first and only book of poems, "I wasted it! I should have written only poetry!" sobbing while he banged on the hood with his fists—Elia Kazan looming tightfaced over Paddy Chayefsky and me at the Russian Tea Room saying moodily that he had to see the isolated Clifford Odets, Golden Boy with cancer, who had crept back to New York to sniff the ozone of dead triumphs before perishing on the coast—my remembering while Kazan spoke with disembodied flatness how I had met Odets at 17 at the U. of North Carolina and how he had taken me for a drive in his fast Cadillac (?) and switched me on so that I rapped pre–*On the Road* about speed and how the strange iodine odor came from his antiseptic-smelling body and wiry brillo hair—all these once-reportorial facts now became the *truer* story for those of us whose appetite for what is had been built up to a point no longer satisfied by fiction.

In addition to this feeling of irrelevance that I increasingly had about the novel as a meaningful statement for the late 50s and 60s, the audience for it in America was no longer as loyal and excited as it had been (as *I* had been!) when we were first mentally-emotionally bowled over by its momentum. TV, movies, electronic communications of every sort were cutting into the time that people who were totally alive to their era could spend on prose fiction; if it was *story* you wanted in the old *Saturday Evening Post* sense, you could get that dramatized for you on the Late Late Show while you did a multimedia thing with your companion in bed, and it was only the specialists, critic-teachers, the people in the book trade, who seemed to me to hold out strenuously against admitting that the novel's dash was being taken away from it by the new media. These electronic whispers of tomorrow could in a momentary flash do what Flaubert and Conrad spent their lifetimes trying to achieve with words: "Above all to make you see."

Of course, you can say that the post-Faulkner U.S. novel was no longer sought out for story-values per se but rather for radical insight into existence; that the form provided a framework for an attack from a completely different "existential" or "absurd" quarter than the realistic 30s novel; granted—and also more than granted that extraordinarily talented writers were opening up this form and "making it as limitless as the ocean which can only define itself" (Marguerite Young), writers such as John Barth, Young herself, Ralph Ellison, William Burroughs, Joseph Heller, Norman Mailer, Hubert Selby, Donald Barthelme, etc., the list is big because there were and are that many highly imaginative writers who have been doing remarkable things with fiction during these last 15 years. (Ironically, as the novel has shed its effectiveness in our society, there has never been since the 20s such a yell of native talent, wild originality, deadly challenge.) But the basic fact I noticed as the deluge of new fictional expression increased and readership became a frantic duty rather than the great thrill it once had been—and the practical impossibility of keeping up with the diversity of new books (new lives!) became obvious—was that the impact of the novel on our beings, on my being, was no longer as crucial as it had been. From my own changing point of view tremendous stateside writers could still appear in what was loosely called a novel—and what form has become looser?—but I felt that the entire role of the American novelist as I had originally heroized it had to be transformed into something entirely different if it was to be as masterful to the imagination of the 60s as it had been to me in the 30s.

In this sense: writing fiction for me and my breed was not an entirely realistic, naturalistic, rational human enterprise in spite of the authentic-seeming imitation of reality on which we were indoctrinated; underneath the accurate surface it was all bathed in dream or myth; we who wanted to mythologize ourselves and America (and they were inseparable) were trying personally to lift the national life into the realm of justice, we were attempting to use the total freedom of our imaginations to rearrange the shitspecked facts of our American experience into their ultimate spiritual payoff. We wanted to "build Jerusalem" (Blake) out of America's "fresh, green breast" (Scott Fitzgerald) and the novel was our transcendent, our more-than-could-ever-be vehicle for fulfillment of both ourselves and the national seed that had begotten us. In other words, *our* novel was a form of imaginative action. If you, the novelist, couldn't make it to the height of your vision in so-called straight or nonliterary life because of one handicap or another, then you did it through your books even better; but the goal was the same as the man of action's, your books were deeds that came out of your mixture of vision and moral commitment (Hemingway, Farrell, Wolfe) and they stood as the seal of where you were humanly at as clearly as if you had sewn your psychoanalysis into the binding. There could be no faking about taking a stand and you were measured every step of the way by readers who took your fictions as acts that influenced the world of the U.S. spirit until they were outdistanced by new and more penetrating fictional commitments. It was a soul-contest of the keenest kind, with the country as beneficiary.

But the effectiveness of such "imaginative action" today seems to have been reduced to mere toenail-picking by the tornado voices of the massmedia. Whether you and I like it or not we have all—novelists as well as readers—become pawns in the newscast of each day's events. "Our" novel can no longer affect these events in even an indirect sense: almost every ounce of my energy (for example) is used in coping with my own life, things happen too fast for me to be affected by the stance of some protagonist in a fiction, I am spun around by each latest threat to my survival, and what was once the charismatic lure of the American novel now becomes for me and countless others an extravagance instead of a necessity. But isn't that what makes artforms change—when life leaves them in the lurch? When concern moves away from them, not by design but by a gut-barometer whereby we seek out what is most vital to us and jettison the rest? Because of my existential impatience with fiction as it related directly to my life—and I concede that this could be a flaw of temperament although it is backed up by my professional work as an editor of new writing—I was and am forced to believe that in varying degrees my experience is true for readers all over the country; and I felt and feel that prose must find a form that can meet this reality and win readers back to the crucial excitement that I experienced when the novel was more than a novel and evoked a mystic response that molded being itself as well as an author's reputation.

But what happens then—I have had to ask myself—to our significant writers who are still either in love or "imprisoned" in a traditional form that is losing its cultural importance in spite of their brilliant personal fights? What happens—I must ask myself again—to that awesome authority of the imagination that encouraged, demanded, people who called themselves novelists to create human beings (like nature itself) and dictate their lives and fate (like gods or supreme justices of the universe)? What happens, further, to that great ton of submerged American experience locked inside themselves, more raw, subtle, potential human riches than the combined knowledge of sociologist-psychiatrist precisely because it was garnered by their blood as well as brain? What happens, in short, to that special mission, what to me for many years was almost a holy mission, of making an imaginary American world that would be more real than the actuality itself?

And where, as a final question, does the legendary U.S. novelist go when except for a handful of individuals* he is no longer a culture-hero in a radically new environment, when his medium is passing into the void of time, and when he is still stuck with a savage inner need to speak, confess, design, shape, record—the whole once-glorious shmear?

3

There is one drastic way out and even up, as I personally see it now, and that is for the American novelist to abandon his imitation or caricature of a reality that in sheer voluminosity has dwarfed his importance and to become a communicator directly to society without hiding behind the mask of fiction. (I must make it

---

*William Burroughs, Norman Mailer, Joseph Heller, Ken Kesey and possibly a few others are novelists who recapture some of the old tribal magic for their followers; but even more significant are the non-novelists like Allen Ginsberg, Tim Leary, Lenny Bruce (before he died), Jimmy Breslin, David Amram, Eldridge Cleaver, Abbie Hoffman, etc., who are setting the current trend of the action-involved Personality who speaks through writing. It seems plain to me, at any rate, that the literary microphone through which you can talk most directly to the most people is no longer fiction even though this doesn't rule out an occasional exploding star. The important point is that it is now the man and not the medium; and what the man who was trained as a novelist, or always wanted to be one, can do through nonfiction today is the whole thrust of the last part of this article.—S.K.

clear that what follows represents my own need and desire imagined out of the confusion of our time and my unwillingness to accept a literature that is primarily a reflection of our era's helplessness; committed novelists, and some very sharp ones too, will doubtless block me out of consciousness and continue to make an ever wilder art of their materials to match the nuttiness that fevers our days; I will always be a sucker for their spirit and bow to the new images they will offer us, but my compelling feeling that now as never before is the time for writing to become direct action and cause things to happen makes even potentially great novels grow small compared to what I can envision if the novelist puts his power into speaking straight to his audience.)

The American novelistic imagination as I received it with open heart and mind 25 and 30 years ago was really the most fully human expression of this society at that time; and it is the new humanizing of American writing by the boldness of direct communication, the revolutionizing of the writer's relationship to his reader, that seems to me tremendously more needed right now than the pale echo of fiction. Instead of "novelists" I believe we now actually have only literary individuals themselves, men and women struggling with their own destinies as people in relation to other people and with the problems that threaten to swamp us all—emotional, sexual, political, racial, artistic, philosophical, financial—and that these should be stated to the reader as candidly as possible so that he, too, can be brought into the new mutual non-novel of American life and make possible a truly democratic prose of total communication which can lead to new action in society itself.

I believe the ex-novelist, the new communicator that we can already see in the early and various stages of his making (Mailer again, Tom Wolfe, Norman Podhoretz, Dan Wakefield, Willie Morris, Frank Conroy, Jan Cremer, Erje Ayden, Fielding Dawson, Irving Rosenthal, Ned Rorem, Taylor Mead, Frederick Exley, myself*) should speak intimately to his readers about these fantastic days we are living through but declare his credentials by revealing the concrete details and particular sweat of his own inner life; otherwise he (or she) will not have earned the right to speak openly about everything or be trusted. He should try and tell the blunt truth as in a letter and this includes the risk of discussing other individuals as well—no one should be immune from the effort to clean

---

*Here are the books where you can check this out: *The Armies of the Night* plus *Miami and the Siege of Chicago* by Norman Mailer, who is in transition from the novel to the inchoate new form; *The Electric Kool-Aid Acid Test* by Tom Wolfe; *Making It* by Norman Podhoretz; *Between the Lines* by Dan Wakefield; *North Toward Home* by Willie Morris; *Stop-time* by Frank Conroy; *I Jan Cremer* by Jan Cremer; *The Legend of Erje Ayden* by Erje Ayden; *An Emotional Memoir of Franz Kline* by Fielding Dawson; *Sheeper* by Irving Rosenthal; *The Paris Diary of Ned Rorem* by Ned Rorem; *Anonymous Diary of a New York Youth* (Vols. 1, 2 & 3) by Taylor Mead; *A Fan's Notes* by Frederick Exley; *Views of a Nearsighted Cannoneer* by Seymour Krim.—S.K.

house, undo bullshit, lay the entire business of being an American right now on the public table without shame. So that the new communicator's statement—about himself, his friends, his women (or men if he's gay), people in public life, the cities, the war, his group therapy, wanting secretly to be a star, wanting to sleep with Mamie Van Doren (or Susan Sontag), still hoping to love and be loved, putting his being directly before the reader as if the page were a telephone and asking for an answer—will be evidence of the reality we are *all* implicated in, without exception, and be in itself a legitimation of this reality as a first step to changing it.

How can we suffer from too much truth? Who isn't heartened to see it when an author respects us enough to tell us where he really lives and by the very nature of his writing asks us to reciprocate? But there is a more significant reason for total leveling than moral straightforwardness in a time famous for its credibility gaps, and that is the power that can return to literature as a daring public act which has to be respected by even those pragmatists who habitually reduce words to playthings. If I write about my own being in relationship to other, real, named, social-security–numbered beings and present it to you, the reader, it is inevitable that you too will be pulled into the scene (at least a few hundred of you will know either me or one of my real-life cast of characters) and must take up an involved position about what you're being told and experiencing. You are interacting with me and my interactions with others so closely—assuming I have the ability as well as the stomach for truth—that you have become part of the experience whether you seek it or not. You Are There, now included in the network of my life as I am included in yours, and what you have seen and heard and identified with in my communication will not be put aside like a "story" because it is an extension of the same reality that unites us both; I will have established a sense of community with you about the destiny of both our lives in this uncertain time which becomes as real as if we were communicating in the flesh—and as existentially suspenseful. Reading then becomes a crucial event because something is *really happening* in existence and not in "literature" alone; due to what I have written our very lives will touch, the reader is just as much a participant as the writer, your isolation or indifference has been penetrated by reading just as mine has by writing and the alienation of our mutual situation has been broken through by my need to make you experience what I have and share my consciousness.

In other words, I want American prose to again become a potent force in the life of the individual in this country and not just his novelty-seeking mind; I want it to be necessary and important once again—even more important, since I see its purpose as having changed—as I knew it when it shaped me; and I want this selfishly because I have devoted my dreams to this business of words, and my own self-respect as mere human refuses to accept that what I once took vows for can be written off as a second-rate art, which "madeup" and irrelevant writing often seems like now in the aftermath of the electronic-visual explosion. But apart from my own investment in literature—and I can't rationalize and say that the source of my ideas doesn't spring from my own unappeasable imagination as a would-be American novelist who was once promised the world and shall never forget that fact—who can deny that once a gifted writer tells it to his equals exactly "like it is" we are moving into a new dimension where writing is used to speak directly to being? And where the talents of reporter and pamphleteer are now usurping those of novelist to awaken individuals to the fact that we all share a common bag as probably never before?

It seems plain to me that the man we used to call the American creative writer is now beginning to express living history through himself so urgently that he is becoming its most genuine embodiment. The imagination that once led him to build a stairway to the stars has been forced into coping with his own imperiled life on the same quaking ground that holds us all. Out of necessity he is being pushed toward a new art of personal survival and as a result he must move ever further into the centers of action to fight for his fate; if he left the crucial decisions of our time to The Others while he concentrated on his "work," as in the old days, he would be living a lie because he is now too personally a part of each day's events to pretend they don't shake him and dominate his existence. His only choice is to insert himself into these events through his writing, to become an actor upon them instead of a helpless observer, to try and influence the making of history itself with his art so that he can save himself as a man. His driving need for direct participation in our national life *now* makes the new communicator want to change America in a pact with his readers, and to begin by changing his own life in the commitment of laying it on the line.

For myself time has shown that the vision I saw or read into the American novel which immediately made me a character in it, the "hero" who wants to be a novelist, could only be fulfilled if the novel was real and was acted out. Perhaps—in the light of this late recognition of my own need to personify what to many others existed solely in the imagination—I was scheduled all along not to write novels, as I always thought, but to try and put their essence into action. If this is so, I embrace it willingly as the more exciting and now necessary of the alternatives; for just as I once believed that art was the highest condition that a person could attain to, I now believe that if this is true it is the duty of those who conceive such an ideal to use it on society itself and take their literary lives in their hands, if need be, in the dangerous gamble to make The Word deed. That's where the new prose action is 30 years after I got hooked—for real, chums, for deadly real.

1968

3.
Making It!*

When has an inside phrase like "making it" or so-and-so's "got it made" shot with such reality through the museum of official English? In this terse verbal shorthand lies a philosophy of life that puts a gun in the back of Chase Manhattan rhetoric and opens up, like a money-bag, the true values that make the Sammys and Susies of modern city life run today. *You've got it made.* How the words sing a swift jazz poem of success, hi-fi, the best chicks (or guys), your name in lights, pot to burn, jets to L.A. and London, bread in the bank, baby, and a fortress built around your ego like a magic suit of armor! *You've got it made.* Royalties pouring in, terraces stretching out, hip movie starlets strutting in butt-parade, nothing but Jack Daniels with your water, your name in Skolsky's column, Tennessee for lunch, dinner with—somebody who swings, sweetheart! And tomorrow the world (as a starter).

Middle-class ideals of success once curled the lip of the intellectual; today he grins not, neither does he snide. Columbia professor, poet, painter, ex-Trotskyite, *Partisan Review* editor, G.E. engineer, Schenley salesman—they all live in the same world for a change and that world says, go! The Marxist, neo-Christian, romantic, humanitarian values of 20 years ago are great for the mind's library and its nighttime prayer mat; but will they fill the cancerous hunger in the soul for getting what *you* want today? Softies become tough, toughies get harder, men dig that they'd rather be women, women say to hell with lilacs and become men, the road gets rougher (as Frankie lays his smart-money message on us) and you've got to move, hustle, go for the ultimate broke or you'll be left with a handful of nothing, Jack and Jill! What happened to the world out *there*, the one you always thought you loved and honestly-couldn't-get-enough-of-without-wanting-a-sou-in-return for your pure and holy feelings? *Baby, that world went up in the cornball illusions of yesterday! Forget it just like it never knew you were alive. This bit about being a fine writer, a dedicated actor, a movie-maker with Modern Museum notions of heaven, a musician because you truly love it, a*

---

*This article was published in the *Village Voice* nine years before the publication of Norman Podhoretz's book, *Making It* (New York: Random House, 1968).—Ed.

34

painter because you die when you smell the color? Don't make me laugh—it's not good for the stitches, dad. This world (nuts, this rutting universe!) is a Mt. Everest, kiddo, and you've got to start climbing now or the dumbwaiter of this age will slam you down into the black basement. Use whatever you've got and use what you ain't *got, too!*

Throughout the jumping metropolis of New York one sees vertical fanaticism, the Thor-type upward thrust of the entire being, replacing pale, horizontal, mock-Christian love of fellow-creature; the man or woman who is High Inside, hummingly self-aware, the gunner and the gunnerette in the turret of the aircraft that is Self, is watching out for number one with a hundred new-born eyes. He or she has been slicked down by the competition to a lean, lone-eagle, universe-supporting role. Hey Atlas, did you ever think that common man and woman would be imprisoned under the burden of your heroic weight and find it the ultimate drag rather than the ultimate godlike stance, without value, nobility or purpose? The ancient symphonies of Man have lost their meaning. It is hopeless-ness that drives the modern whirlwind striver to put such emphasis on personal achievement.

In every brain-cell of intellectual and artistic life the heat is on in America today no differently than it is in business. Values? Purpose? Selectivity? Princi-ples? *For the birds, Charley! I want to make it and nothing's going to stand in my way because everything is crap, except making it! I want my ego to ride high, my heart to bank the loot of life, my apartment to swing, my MG to snarl down the highway, my pennant to wave above the scattered turds of broken dreams for a better world! Why don't you level and say you want the same, you hypocrite? Be honest for Chrissakes!*

With the blessings of psychiatry, enlightened (so-called) selfishness has be-come the motto of hip city life; the once-Philistine is admired for his thick skin and wallet, the poor slob who translates Artaud but can't make his rent, a girl, or hold his own at a party is used as a dart-board for the wit of others—not by the "enemy," either, but by his very Village brothers who have forsaken a square idealism for a bite-marked realism. The only enemy today is failure, failure, failure, and the only true friend is—success? How? In what line? Whoring yourself a little? Buttering up, sucking up, self-salesmanship, the sweet oh-let-me-kiss-your-ass-please smile? *Don't be naive, friend. You think this halluci-nated world is the moonlight sonata or something? You think anyone cares about your principles or (don't make me puke!) integrity or that they make the slightest ripple in the tempest of contemporary confusion? Go sit at home, then, you model saint and keep pure like the monks with your hands on your own genitalia! Because if you want to make it out in the world, baby, you have to swing, move, love what you hate and love yourself for doing it, too!*

The one unforgivable sin in city life today is not to *make it.* Even though the cush of success may seem hollow to the victor as his true self sifts the spoils, alone and apart from the madding cats who envy him, he knows that his vulnerable heart could not bear the pain of being a loser. Wasn't success drummed at him every day in every way in relation to women, status, loot— Christ, the image of himself in his own eyes? Didn't he see those he admired in his tender years flicked off like so many flies because they'd never made a public victory of their talents? My God, man, what else could he do except be a success (or kill himself)—the world being what it is?

For *making it* today has become the only tangible value in an environment quaking with insecurity and life's mockery of once-holy goals, which the bored witch of modern history has popped over the rim of the world for sport, like an idle boy with paper pellets. *How can you buy grand abstractions of human brotherhood for that daily fix needed by your ego when Dostoevsky and Freud have taught us we hate our parents, brothers, sisters, and wives, as well as friends? Oh, no, you can't snow us, you peddlers of fake hope! We know you for what you are: Vaseline-tongued frustrates who wanted to make it and lost. Man, how the wound shows behind your pathetic rationalizations!*

The padded values and euphemisms of a more leisurely time have been ruthlessly stripped away under the hospital light of today's world; honesty, integrity, truthfulness, seem sentimental hangovers from a pastoral age, boy-scout ideals trying to cope with an armored tank of actuality that is crumpling the music-box values of the past like matchsticks. It is not Truth that is pertinent today, in the quaint dream of some old philosopher; it is the specific truths of survival, getting, taking, besting, as the old order collapses like a grounded parachute around the stoney vision of the embittered modern adult. *What is left but me?* mutters the voice of reality, *and how else can I save myself except by exhausting every pore in the race with time?* We see in America today a personal ambition unparalled in fierce egocentricity, getting ahead, achieving the prize, making a score—for the redemption of self. Are the ends good? Does it matter to the world? Will it pass muster at the gates of judgment? *Such questions are ridiculous: they presume a God above man rather than the god of life who thumps within my chest for more, faster, bigger, conquests for me, me, ME!*

As the individual stands his lonely vigil in the polar night of the desolation of all once agreed-upon values—as they have receded like the tide, rolling back into the past—where else, he cries, can he turn but to his own future? Who else will help him? What can he or she do but mount the top of personal fulfillment in a world that has crumbled beneath the foot? Upon the neon-lit plains of the modern city comes the tortured cry of a million selves for a place in the sun of personal godhood. As one by one the lights of the old-fashioned planets Peace, Love, Happiness, have flickered and gone out, plunging all into the spook jazzglow of a new surrealist dawn, the only believable light comes from the soul-jet of need that burns in the private heart. *Let the lousy world crash like a demented P–38! What can I do about it? I'm merely a pawn of this age like you.*

Man, my only escape-hatch is making it at the highest pitch I can dream of! An individualism just short of murder has replaced the phantom of socialism as the idols of the recent past shrink into mere trophies on the mocking walls of history. In an existence so dreamlike, uncertain, swift, the only nailed-down values that remain are those that can be seen in the bankbook of life. *Can honors be taken away from me? Fame? Money? The beauty I can possess (by name or dollar) in both flesh and leather? No! Don't croon to me of art or soul in a world that has flipped loose from its moorings, seen the futility of truth, the platitude of spiritual hope, the self-deception in innocence, the lack of discrimination in goodness, the pettiness of tears! You live only once, Jack, and if you don't swing with the fractured rhythms of this time—if you hide behind the curtains of a former, simpler, child's world of right and wrong—you condemn yourself to the just sneers of those who dig the real world as it is! Baby, there is no significance today but you and the sooner you wake up to the full horror of this fact, the better!*

By time-honored esthetic and moral standards the knowing modern man, and woman, is a barely polite gangster; his machine-gun is his mind, ideas his bullets, power and possession his goals. The reduction of the real to the usable has been whittled into a necessity by the impossible number of potential choices within himself: he knows, after juggling more thoughts than he can reach conclusions about, that he must snap down the lid on fruitless speculation and use the precious energy for making warheads on the spears of practicality. Victims of their own subjective desperation, pygmies under the heavens of thought that dot the roof of their minds with a million perverse stars, converge upon the external prizes of life like hordes released from prison: eager to bury the intolerable freedom of the mind's insanity in the beautiful sanity of—making it! *Yes, yes, I will convert the self that bugs me into an objective victory in the steel and weighable world! I will take the scalding steam of my spirit and hiss it outward like an acetylene torch upon the hard shale of life, and cut diamonds for myself! You say this therapy of mine adds brutality to the gutter of modernity, that I care only for my private need at the expense of the world? That my fuel is desperation and that I'm marvelously indifferent about adding my shot of cruel self-interest to an already amoral environment? I don't deny it. Survival at its highest conception means making it! To live you must conquer if you're normal enough to hate being stuck with your futile being and smart enough to know you must trade it for success!*

For what else is there? Dying at parties, as I used to, when I saw some headliner bring the fawn out of even the best people, who swooned around this living symbol of magic? Eating my heart out because I didn't have the admiration, the quiff, the loot, the attention *I and all human beings demand out of life? Suppose I do know how cheap and unlike my original ideal it all is? You want it too, you envious bastard, you know you do! Spit it out that the ego is the world today for all of us and that without its gratification living is a hell, a roasting on the skewer of frustration as you watch others grab the nooky! Jack, life is too far gone—too man-eat-man—for your wistful moralizing and pansy references to the cathedrals of the past. It's only the present that counts in a world that has no foreseeable future and I'm human enough to want to swing my way to the grave—sweetheart, you can have immortality!*

In an age that has seen the abandonment, because they are too costly, of cherished political and personal hopes, hypodermic realism inside and businesslike efficiency outside becomes the new style. The address-book replaces the soul, doing is the relief of being, talking of thinking, getting of feeling. *I've got to numb myself in action, exhaust this inner fiend, or else all the hopelessness of this so-called life of mine will come bursting through its trapdoor and overwhelm me! I've got to swing, plan, plot, connive, go and get and get some more, because what else is there, Buster?* The frenzied tempo of achievement is matched only by the endless desert within; the futility-powered desperado drives himself ever forward, trying to find in action some publicly applauded significance that is freezingly absent in solitude. Does it matter that he finds his buddies who have made it as rocket-desperate and unsatisfied as himself?

Hell, no. Doesn't the world admire us and isn't it obvious that it's better to be miserable as a storm-trooper than as a Jew? Wasn't my picture in Look, *wasn't I on Mike Wallace's show and didn't I turn down an invitation from Long John? Doesn't my answering-service hum with invitations, haven't I made it with that crazy-looking blonde who sings at the Persian Room as well as that distinguished lady novelist who lives near Dash Hammett's old apartment on West 10th? Don't I jive with Condon as well as Wystan Auden, Jim Jones (when he's in town) as well as Maureen Stapleton, Bill Zeckendorf, Bill Rose, Bill Styron, Bill Faulkner, Bill Basie, Bill Williams, Bill de Kooning, Bill Holden—just on the Bill front? Don't I get tips on the market, complimentary copies of* Big Table *as well as* Holiday, *didn't I put down Dali at that party for being square and get a big grin from Adlai Stevenson for doing so?*

Man, I know what I'm doing! I'm swinging instead of standing still, I'm racing with a racing age, I'm handling 17 things at once and I'm scoring with them all! Life's too wild today, sonny, to worry about the fate of the race or private morality or nunlike delicacies of should-I or should-I-not; anyone with brains or even imagination is a self-driven marauder with the wisdom to know that if he hustles hard enough he can have a moat full of gravy and a penthouse-castle high over life's East River! I'm bartering my neuroses for AT&T (not crying over them to Beethoven's Ninth like you, you fake holy man!) and bemoaning my futile existence with Mumm's Extra Dry and the finest hemp from Laredo and my new Jackson Pollock and my new off-Broadway boff and my new book and my new play and my new pad and this TV show they're gonna build around me and— Jesus, I've got it made!

. . . .while down below the lusting average man and woman sweats in jealousy at the sight of these Dexedrine angels, the very inspiration of what he and she can become if only they too can put that last shred of shame behind them and swing, extrovert yourself, get with it, make that buck, make that chick, make that poem, make this crazy modern scene *pay off.* O my heart, so I too can sink my teeth in the sirloin and wear the pearls of hell!

1958

4.
The Insanity Bit

1

Until this time of complete blast-off in seemingly every department of human life, the idea of insanity was thought of as the most dreadful thing that could happen to a person. Little was actually known about it and the mind conjured up pictures of Bedlam, ninnies walking around in a stupor, a living death that lasted until the poor damned soul's body expired and peace tucked him or her away for eternal keeps. But in this era of monumental need to rethink and redefine almost every former presumption about existence—which has inspired a bombing way of looking at what once were considered the most unbudgeable rocks of reality— the locked door of insanity has been shaken loose and shall yet be hurled wide open. Until one day the prisoners of this definition will walk beside us sharing only the insane plight of mortality itself, which makes quiet madmen of us all.

Every American family has its "psychotic" cousin or uncle; every friend has wept, prayed, hoped (and finally slid into indifference) for another friend sweating it out in insulin or electric shock behind the gray walls (public institution) or beyond the clipped roses (private sanitarium). Although my brother, Herbert J. Krim, was institutionalized when I was barely in my 20's—and I cosigned the certificate for a prefrontal lobotomy which ended with his death by hemorrhage on the operating table at Rockland State Hospital—I still had the conventional ideas about insanity that are shared by all "responsible" readers of the *New York Times*. It is true that as a serious writer I had inherited a great tradition of complete independence and honesty to my actual experience, regardless of what I was supposed to feel; but this was sabotaged by my youth, my ignorance, and an inability to separate my own personal life from a responsibility to question the cliches of experience to their ultimate depth. Like most American writers, from would-be's to celebrities, I was intensely preoccupied by my acutely painful and highly exaggerated subjective image—the Jewish cross, looks, sex, masculinity, a swarm of fears and devices for concealment that were secondary to my decent abilities and serious obligations as a writer intent on telling the truth. In other words: I was too narcissistically and masturbatorially stuck on myself to appreciate the horrible waste of my brother Herbert's death; and with the snotty sense of

40

superiority usually felt by the young American writer, I thought *I* would be forever immune to the judgments of a society which I loftily ignored, or nose-thumbed, without ever coming to grips with on the actual mat of life. Like every creative type of my generation whom I met in my 20's, I was positive I was sanctified, protected by my "genius," my flair, my overwhelming ambition.

I was as wrong as you can be and still live to tell about it. In the summer of 1955, when I was 33, the thousand unacknowledged human (not literary) pressures in my being exploded. I ran barefoot in the streets, spat at members of my family, exposed myself, was almost bodily thrown out of the house of a Nobel Prize–winning author, and believed God had ordained me to act out every conceivable human impulse without an ounce of hypocritical caution. I know today that my instinct was sound, but my reasoning was self-deceptive. It was not God who ordained me, but I who ordained God for my own understandable human purposes. I needed an excuse to force some sort of balance between my bulging inner life and my timid outer behaviour, and I chose the greatest and most comforting symbol of them all. He was my lance and my shield as I tore through the New York streets acting out the bitter rot of a world-full of frustrations that my human nature could no longer lock up. I was finally cornered on the 14th floor of the St. Regis Hotel by two frightened friends and another brother; and with the aid of handcuffs seriously-humorously clipped on by a couple of bobbies I was led off to Bellevue, convinced all along that I was right. I tolerated those who took me away with the kindly condescension of a fake Jesus.

From Bellevue I was soon transferred to a private laughing academy in Westchester and given insulin-shock treatments. No deep attempt was made to diagnose my "case"—except the superficial and inaccurate judgment that I had "hallucinated." Factually, this was not true; I did not have visual images of people or objects which were not there; I merely believed, with the beautiful relief of absolute justice which the soul of man finds when life becomes unbearable, that God had given me the right and the duty to do everything openly that I had secretly fantasized for years. But this distinction was not gone into by my judges and indifferent captors. They did not have the time, the patience, or even the interest because work in a flip-factory is determined by mathematics: you must find a common denominator of categorization and treatment in order to handle the battalions of miscellaneous humanity that are marched past your desk with high trumpets blowing in their minds.

Like all the other patients, I was considered beyond reasoning with and was treated like a child; not brutally, but efficiently, firmly and patronizingly. In the eyes of this enclosed world I had relinquished my rights as an adult human being. The causes for my explosion were not even superficially examined, nor was the cheek-pinching house psychiatrist—with a fresh flower in the button hole of his fresh daily suit—truly equipped to cope with it even if he had tried, which he did not. Private sanitariums and state institutions, I realized much later, were isolation chambers rather than hospitals in the usual sense; mechanical "cures" such as the one I underwent in a setup of unchallenged authority, like the Army or a humanitarian prison, slowly brought 75 percent of the inmates down to a more temporarily modest view of reality. Within nine or ten weeks I too came down, humbled, ashamed, willing to stand up before the class and repeat the middle-class credo of limited expressiveness and the meaning of a dollar in order to get my discharge.

In three months' time I was out, shaken, completely alone, living in a cheap Broadway hotel room (having been ashamed to go back to Greenwich Village) and going to a conventional Ph.D. psychologist (I had been to three medically trained therapists in the preceding decade) as a sop to both my conscience and family. I had broken beyond the bounds of "reality"—a shorthand word which is used by the average psychiatrist for want of the more truthfully complex approach that must eventually accommodate our beings' increasing flights into higher altitudes—and come back to the position I was in before. But once again the causes that had flung me into my own sky continued to eat me up. Sexually unconfident, I went to whores, ate my meals alone, and forced myself to write a few pieces in that loneliest of places, a tiny blank hotel room in the middle of nowhere. For the first time in my life the incentive to live, the isolation and frustration of my existence, grew dim; while the psychologist smiled and smoked his pipe—and did the well-adjusted, tweedy, urbane act behind his tastefully battered desk as he ladled out platitudes—I was saving up the sleeping bombs, and when I had enough to do the trick I burned the letters I had received through the years from the several men and women I had loved, destroyed my journal of 15 years' standing, and one carefully chosen night went to a hotel in Newark, N.J.

My plan was to take the pills and slowly conk out in the full bathtub, ultimately drowning like Thomas Heggen; if one missed the other would work. I splurged on a beautiful death-room in a modernistic hotel, one that included a bathroom with the biggest tub in the house. But it was too small to fit my long body. The idea of not being able to drown and of surviving the pills afterwards, perhaps to become a burden or an invalid, began to scar what seemed like a paradise of suicide. I went instead to a Polish bar in downtown Newark, vaguely seeking the eternal anodynes of snatch and booze while I mentally played with my fate.

I found the booze and saw a coarse, ignorant Polish girl do such a life-giving, saucy, raucous folk-dance (on the small dance floor to the right of the bar) that I broke into loving sobs like prayers over my drink. The sun of life blazed from her into my grateful heart. I went back to the beautiful hotel room, poured the pills down the toilet, and went to sleep. The next morning I returned to Manhattan a chastened man, shaking my head at how close I had come to non-being.

When I told my tale to Mr. Pipe, my psychologist, he speedily hustled me off to a legitimate head-doctor who doped me until a private ambulance came. Very much in my right and one and only mind but too paralyzed by drugs to move, I was once again taken on the long ride—this time to another hedge-trimmed bin in Long Island. I was helpless to protest, mainly because of the shame and guilt I felt for even contemplating suicide. Obviously I was not crazy, mad, psychotic, out of my mind, schizophrenic, paranoid. I was simply a tormented man-kid had never steeled himself to face the facts of life—who didn't know what it meant to have principles and live by them come grief or joy—and who thought that human worth and true independence comes as easily as it does in the movies we were all emotionally faked on. As a sputtering fiction writer and fairly active literary critic, I had had occasional peaks of maturity and illumination, but as a man I was self-deceptive, self-indulgent, crying inwardly for the pleasures of a college-boy even while in my imagination I saw myself as another Ibsen or Dreiser. Ah, the extraordinary mismating of thoughts in the mind of the modern American literary romantic, as fantastic and truly unbelievable a stew of unrelated dreams as have ever been dreamt, believe me!

Once again I was on the human assembly-line: electric shock clubbed my good brain into needless unconsciousness (and I walked to my several executions like a brave little chappie instead of questioning them) and unquestioned Old Testament authority ruled our little club. Good-natured, but mostly cowlike and uneducated male orderlies carried out the orders from above; and apart from the mechanical treatment and the unimaginative grind of occupational therapy, each patient was left completely on his or her bewildered own, a sad and farcical sight when one considered the $125 per week that their frightened families were paying.

I saw now that nine-tenths of the people I was quartered with were not "insane" by any of the standards a normally intelligent person would use: the majority had lost confidence in their own ability to survive in the world outside, or their families were *afraid* of them and had palmed them off on "experts," but positively no serious effort was being made to equip them to become free and independent adults. This was their birthright—beyond country and society, indeed an almost religious obligation—but they were palliated with pills or jolted with shock, their often honest rage echoed back to them as a sign of their "illness." Some of them must have been "sick," you say. I answer: Who can not be conceived as such in a world so complex ("The truth is there is a truth on every side"—Richard Eberhart) that each group has its own method for judging manners, behavior, ideas, and finally the worth of human values? What was more important was that I, a person from a hip milieu and with a completely opposite set of values, could see their so-called sickness with the human sensibility that an immersion in literature and experience had given me—rather than as a clinical manifestation. When I later recognized the objective provinciality of many psychiatrists in precisely the humanistic areas that could cover the actions of the majority of the inmates without finding it "psychotic," I realized that the independent thinker and artist today must learn to be resolute towards a subtle, socially powerful god-father who often drips paternalism: namely, the newly enthroned psychiatric minority that has elevated itself to a dangerous position of "authority" in the crucial issues of mind, personality, and sanity.

I now began to fight persistently—but still with shakiness—for my release; my life was my own: it did not belong to the cliches of the salesman-aggressive, well-barbered, Jewish-refugee (my brother, my enemy!) house psychiatrist or to my smiling, betweeded nonentity of a psychologist, who paid me diplomatically inscrutable visits like a Japanese ambassador. Even if I had been or if there were such a reality as a "raving maniac"—which, perhaps childishly, I implore the over-imaginative, zeitgeist-vulnerable reader to believe is an impossible conception today—I would and should have fought for my release. What the institution-spared layman does not realize is that a sensitive and multiple-reacting human being remains the same everywhere, including a sanitarium, and such an environment can duplicate the injustice or vulgarity which drove your person there in the first place. By this I mean that a mental hospital is not an asylum or a sanctuary in the old-fashioned sense: it is just a roped-off side-street of modern existence, rife with as many contradictions, half-truths and lousy architecture as life itself.

Both of the sanitariums I was in were comparable to Grossinger's, in that they took in only financially comfortable, conventionally middle-class, nonintellectual people. By every human standard my being there was life's sarcastic answer to whatever romantic ideas I had about justice. Since the age of 19 I had deliberately led an existence of experimentation, pursuit of truth, bohemianism, and noncommercialism: fate's punishment for my green naivete was for me to recover my supposed mental health in this atmosphere of uncriticizable authority, air-conditioned by just the whiffs of truth that are perfumed and bland, and based on a pillar of middle-class propriety with the cutthroat reality of money underneath. Could I accept my former life, which had produced some good work, as a lie to myself—which the house psychiatrist wanted me to do (in effect) in his one psychotherapeutic pass at me (he left me alone after this)? I could not and never would: not only for myself but for the great principles and accomplishments of others, both living and dead, which had been my guide throughout my adult life. I might fail—but why go on having an identity at all if in a crisis you will throw away not only your past years, but the moral achievements of rare souls who have shared in your emotional and intellectual experience and whose own contributions to existence are also at stake?

When I heard this second house-psychiatrist literally equate sanity with the current cliches of adjustment and describe Greenwich Village as a "psychotic community," I saw with sudden clarity that *insanity* and *psychosis* can no longer be respected as meaningful definitions—but are used by limited individuals in positions of social power to describe ways of behaving and thinking that are alien, threatening, and *obscure* to them. (A year later when I took a psychiatrist friend of mine to the San Remo, she told me with a straight face that it reminded her of the "admission ward in Bellevue," where she had interned. This was her analogy on the basis of accurate but limited experience, that increasing chasm which separates intelligent people from understanding each other. I realized with a sense of almost incommunicable helplessness that the gap between her and the well-known poet with whom I had had a beer at the Remo two weeks before was tremendous, and that between these two poles of intelligence the neutral person—who could see the logic of each—was being mashed up with doubt and conflict. The poet was at home, or at least the heat was off, there; while the psychiatrist felt alien and had made a contemptuous psycho-sociological general-ization. There was little bond of shared values and therefore genuine communi-cation between both of these intelligent and honest human beings, each of whom contributed to my life.)

To finish with my four months in the sanitarium, I argued and reasoned for the basic right to the insecurity of freedom, and finally a good friend did the dirty infighting of getting me out. Had I to do it over again, I believe I would now have the guts to threaten such an institution or psychologist with a lawsuit, ugly as such a procedure can be to a person already vulnerable with the hash-marks of one legally defined "psychotic episode" and the contemplation of the criminal act of suicide. But I had been—as so many of Jack Kerouac's subterraneans are when faced with the machinery of official society—milk and sawdust when, in such situations, you must be iron and stone in spite of your own frailty. It is not that the present-day authorities of mental life want to railroad anyone as in your Grade C horror movie; it is merely that as one grows older it becomes clear that there are almost irremediable differences between people in the total outlook towards life.

Mine had hardened as a result of my experiences, and I realized it was better to die out in the world if need be than be deprived of the necessity to confront existence because of the cheap authority of a lock and key. The majority of people who stay in mental institutions for any length of time do not want to return to the uncertain conditions outside the wall: which in our time spells out to emotionally anarchic, multidimensional, brain-trying, anxiety-loaded, and—O hear me mortality, from the Year One—ultimate and divine life.

2

I returned downtown—to the very Village that I heard the psychiatrist place deep in Freudian Hell, with that pious overextension of terminology which reveals a limited private morality behind the use of so-called scientific language—and tried to tenderly pick up the threads of my former social life. I saw that my closest and most brilliant friends did not really understand, or were afraid to understand, the contemporary insanity bit. Almost all of them had been soul-whirled by psychotherapy at some time, and each had the particularly contemporary fear of insanity which has become the psychological H-bomb of city life; in theory they may have granted that insanity was no longer the uniform horror it seems to the inexperienced imagination—like a spook in the night—but centuries of inherited fear, plus the daily crises of 1950s living, made them emotionally cautious about seeing my experience as merely an *extension* of their own.

One, a poet-philosopher whom I admire, clapped me on the back and said with some literary awe that I had "returned from the dead, like Lazarus." This struck me as greatly melodramatic, untruthful, and saddening because intellectuals and especially artists should be the very people to understand that insanity today is a matter of definition, not fact; that there can no longer be a fixed criterion, just as there is no longer a reality like that described by Allen Ginsberg in "Howl" (an exciting achievement), where he sees "the best minds of my generation destroyed by madness."

I believe this is lurid sentimentality. Ginsberg may have seen the most gifted people of his generation destroyed by an *interpretation* of madness, which is a much more real threat in a time of such infinite, moon-voyaging extension to experience that the validly felt act is often fearfully jailed in a windowless cell of definition by hard-pressed authorities, whose very moral axis is in danger of toppling. Madness today is a literary word; insanity is a dated legal conception as rigid as an Ibsen play; and "psychosis," the antiseptic modern word that sends chills down the ravines of my friends' minds, has become so weakened (despite its impressive white-jacketed look) by narrow-minded, square, and fast-slipping ideological preconceptions that it must be held at arm's length, like a dead rat, for any cool understanding. When this is done, I believe you will see that the word and state of mind it tries to fix are subject to the gravest questioning; much of which centers around the amount of freedom either permitted to human expression or, more important, what it must take for itself to live in this time when such *unfamiliar* demands are made on the being. Norms crack when they can no longer fight back the content that spills over cookie-mold conceptions of "sane" behavior—and they must be elasticized to stretch around the new bundle of life.

Two weeks before I was back walking down 8th Street a gratefully free neurotic, I had been thought of in the minds of compassionate but uninformed friends as a fairly wild-eyed psychotic. The mere fact that I had been in a sanitarium had pulled a curtain of emotional blindness down over my friends' vision; and yet I was the same person I had been when I entered the happy-house. The unexamined fear of an "insanity" which no longer exists as a framed picture conventionalizes the very people who should view this now only *symbolic* word with clear, unafraid, and severely skeptical eyes. I had not been among "the dead"—unless killing time looking at "Gunsmoke" and Jackie Gleason on TV, playing bridge, and reading Tolstoy and Nathanael West is considered death. I had not been "destroyed by madness," Mr. Ginsberg!—in fact, the act of incarceration made me realize how significant (indeed indelible) individual freedom is, and thus helped brick-and-mortar my point of view rather than destroy it. When I was once again semiknit into a way of life in my new Village home, I discovered that other writers and intellectuals whom I knew had also undergone the sanitarium or mental-hospital holiday, but had kept mum because of indecision as to how frankly one should confess such a stigma.

I understand their practical caution, but discovered that they lived in a sewer-light of guilt, fear and throat-gagging anxiety, instead of openly and articulately coping with the monster of doubt. "Do you think I'm sane?" is the question I ultimately began to hear from these brilliant people (one scarred tribesman to another!) who had been intimidated into denying the worth of their most pregnant ideas, the very ones that create *new concrete standards of sanity* or *sense* in a time that has emotionally, if not yet officially, outlived the abstractions of the past. For myself—although uncertain as to how expressive I should be, even with the very intellectuals I had always considered my brothers in a completely free inquiry into every nook and cranny of life—the problem was suddenly answered when a gifted young writer told a charming hostess I had just met that I had been in "two insane asylums."

I was pierced and hurt, not because I actually considered my supposed nuttiness a yellow badge of dishonor, but because the writer in question had ducked out from under his own experience (which I instinctively knew included some of the crises which had launched me upon the streets like a human missile) and pretended such melodrama was foreign to him. I was appalled because I thought that of all people my fellow highbrow writers should be the first to understand and concede the universal nature of the blows that had felled me in the eyes of official society. But I was wrong. There are spikes on the truth which are so close to the slashed heart of contemporary mortality that men and women will lie and refuse acknowledgment, even when it is necessary to the survival of others; they forfeit their humanhood and final worth to life by doing this, but even in the small band of the avantgarde the pursuit of the truth is given up with that weak excuse: "a practical sense of reality."

After this turncoat put-down by a member of my own club, so to speak, there was no longer any issue for myself. I could not live with the squirming burden of secretiveness because my personal history had become public gossip in the small Village group I traveled with. After snakebitten laughter at my own romantically cultivated simple-mindedness in thinking my fall would be taken with the hip sophistication I had truly expected, I was glad I had become a stooge or victim; because I basically knew that I had played a juicy part in a contemporary American morality play that is going to do standing-room nightly until its implications are understood. We live in what for the imaginative person are truly hallucinated times, because there is more life on every side—and the possibility of conceiving this surplus in a dizzying multitude of ways—than our inheritance and equipment enables us to deal with. My type and perhaps your type of person only *acted out* what other less passionate people feel, but do not express. A "breakdown" such as mine can therefore be learned from:

The first thing one can see is that the isolating of a person saves his or her friends and family from being embarrassed (trivial as this seems, it is a nasty factor in institutionalization), perhaps hurt, and theoretically stops the "sick" person from doing something irreparable while in the grip of the furies. Seen this way, the enforced shackling of an individual seems sad but reasonable. But contemporary adults, however disturbed (often with justice!), are not children; there is doubt in my mind whether we have any right, other than blunt self-interest, to impose our so-called humanitarian wishes on another to the degree where we jail them in order to save them. I must illustrate this with my own case. When I was considered out of my mind during my original upward thrust into the sheer ecstasy of 100 percent uninhibitedness, I was aware of the "daringness" of my every move; it represented at heart an existential *choice* rather than a mindless discharge. It could not be tolerated by society, and I was punished for it, but my "cure" was ultimately a chastisement, *not a medical healing process.* In my own exhibitionistic and self-dramatizing way, when I flipped, I was nevertheless instinctively rebelling against a fact which I think is objectively true in our society and time: and that is the lack of alignment between an immense inner world and an outer one which has not yet legalized, or officially recognized, the forms that can tolerate the flood of communication from the mind to the stage of action.

Traditionally, it was always taught that the artistic person could work out his or her intense private life by expressing it on the easel or typewriter. In faded theory this seems reasonable, but with the billionaire's wealth of potential human experience both fore, aft and sideways in the world today, it is abnormal not to want to participate more Elizabethanly in the overabundant life. The hunch-backed joy the artist once may have had in poring over the objects of his interest, and then putting the extract into his work, can no longer be honestly sufficient to the most human hearts today. There has arisen an overwhelming need for the highly imaginative spirit (based on the recognition that the mere mind of man can no longer lock up the volume of its experience) to forge a bridge so that the bursting galaxy of this inner world can be received in actual public life. But there is such a time-lag between our literally amazing subjective life—which has conceptions of a powerful altitude equal to the heaven-exploring freedom of privacy—and the mummery of outer behavior, that when the contemporary imaginator expresses his genuine thoughts in public, he often feels that he has exposed himself beyond redemption. Room has not yet been made by those who dominate social power for the natural outward show of the acrobatic thinking that ceaselessly swings in the surrealistic minds of our most acute contemporaries. Put crudely but simply, a bookish notion of what constitutes "normality" in this supremely a-normal age drives the liveliest American sensibilities back into the dungeon of self—creating pressures which must maim the soul one way or another—rather than understanding that the great need today is for imagination to come gloriously out in the open and shrink the light-years that separate the mind from external life. (Trying to fill this need is, hands-down, one of the significant accomplishments of the beats—in my opinion—no matter what defensive moralists say; the raw junk that they have peddled occasionally under a Kotex flag of liberation is a different matter, which doesn't rightly fit in here.)

It was trying to close this distance between Me and Thou, between the mind and externality, that I was instinctively attempting when I cut loose with my natural suffocating self in 1955 upon the taboo grounds of outer life. I could stand unfulfilled desire no longer. Thus it is my conviction today that ideals of social behavior must squat down and broaden to the point where they can both absorb and see the necessity for "aberrations" that were once, squarely and Teddy Rooseveltianly, regarded as pathological. The imagination of living human beings, not dead gods, must be openly embodied if there is to be some rational connection between what people actually are and what they are permitted to show. But as with every significant change in meaning, such acts of expressiveness will cost blood before they will be tolerated and understood by psychiatrists, sociologists, the law, police, and all other instruments of social force. Ironically, it is the very "psychotics" in institutions who have unwittingly done the most to initiate a bigger and more imaginative conception of what constitutes *meaningful* behavior. By dealing with people imprisoned in this category, the most perceptive laymen and psychiatrists are beginning to see symbolic meanings where before they saw flat irrationality, because their approach was literal (as if anyone who had the imagination to go "mad" would be stuffy enough to act in prose!). It is then borne in upon them, out of common sense and humility, that a much more expanded conception of what is "sane" is a prerequisite to doing justice to the real emotional state of human beings today; not the abstract theorems of a clean Euclidian conception, but the real, harsh, multiple, often twisted, on-again, off-again mishmash of the so-called normal mind. One can say without pretense that the pioneering "psychotic" is the human poet of the future; and the most imaginative, least tradition-bound psychiatrists are now playing the role of New Critics, learning to closely read the difficult and unexpected meanings of what formerly were thought of as obscure—in fact off-limits—warpings of humanity.

3

In my own case I was brought face-to-face because of my trial by shock (both electric and the human aftermath) with a crucial reality which I had long dodged. It can be put approximately this way: A serious artist-type must in the present environment, as always—cliches have a way of becoming profundities when you have to live them!—literally fight for survival if he or she is going to embody the high traditions that originally made the hot pursuit of truth through art the greatest kick in their lives. But to follow this ideal today is tougher than perhaps it has ever been before; and there are specific reasons why. Foremost is the increasing loss of position for the poet (the artist incarnate) as "the unacknowledged legislator of the race" in a period when the terrifying bigness of society makes the average person resort to more immediate and practical oracles (psychiatrists, sociologists, chemists) than to the kind of imaginative truth that the artist can give. Secondly, the artist-type in our mass society is no longer "privileged" in any way, if indeed he ever was; by this I mean that the laws and shibboleths of the huge democratic tribe judge him as severely as they do the shoemaker next door. Whatever pampering the serious artist once received has become a laugh in our time, when everyone is hustling on approximately the same level for success, lovers, status, money, headlines, thrills, security—for everything.

The emergence of an emotionally mutinous democracy has upset the old categories and cast us all into the boiling sea of naked existence, without the props of class, or profession, or the certainty about one's worth as judged by the seemingly clear-cut hierarchies of the past. While, in my opinion, this should be sizzingly beautiful to every true artist-type, because it is adventurous in the highest conceivable and most mortally dangerous sense, it is also full of the most sinking fears and doubts. For example: can the intelligent writer, painter or composer—the individual with a view of life all his own, which he believes to be true—be indifferent to the prevailing social climate and risk everything by sticking to a viewpoint which will bring him into conflict with the most *normal* (shared by the most people) human emotions in a mass society? (Tag him with the label of "insanity," estrangement from the tempting pie of regular-guy and regular-gal American experience, bring him the isolating fate of being misunderstood even by the "enlightened," and regarded as a personal challenge by others who have made an uneasy truce.)

This is a very serious problem and entails a bigger threat than in the past. Since the artist-type can no longer be realistically considered as being "outside" our definition of society or human nature—and must in this country above all others be seen within the circle of a mass-democratic humanity, for that is where his final strength probably lies—his defections will be judged by those in positions of social power as fluky aberrations *no different from anyone else's*. He will be judged and penalized by the same standards; and in a majority of cases, from what I have seen, his will and stamina are broken (or rationalized into loose harness) and his point of view changed. Frankly, for the artist-type in our environment there is no longer any solid ground whatever under his feet— anything solid he possesses must be won from air and shaped by fanatical resoluteness. For all is open to question today, is a gamble, and has none of the "official" security of the acknowledged professions or even any semblance of unity within his own field. It is for such reasons that the genuine artist-thinker is in such an unenviable and peculiar position in America right now. He is of society and yet, by instinct and inheritance, apart from it: therefore he has to clarify his position in his own mind to a menthol-sharp degree if he wants to survive with intactness, because, as I've tried to show, he will be crushed subtly or conclusively unless he separates his eternal role in society from the onrush of personal doubt that every human being worth the name lives with today.

I learned as a result of my far-out public exhibition, and the manhandling that followed, to distrust the definitions of crude social authority as they pertained to myself and my friends, who share a generally akin point of view and are all either professionals or semiprofessionals in the arts and intellectual life. We can not be skimmed off the top and bracketed as thinly as I had been diagnosed at Bellevue; and the psychiatrists who impatiently felt for the bumps within my head, while presumably competent at a human-machine level, are not as a group sensitive, informed or sympathetic enough with my purposes in life to be of help. In fact, in a basic way they must be my defining opposition in history (daily life) while my friends beyond time (the ideal)—if that doesn't read too pretentiously. It was a sharp revelation for me to learn this as a result of my on-your-hands-and-knees, boy! defeat with authority. As I confessed before, like so many confused young Americans puttering around in the arts, I had phonily pumped into my serious intentions the gassiest dreams of what the struggle for ideas truly is, of false and sentimentalized views of authority (both bowing before it and blowhard defiance), and in general acted more like a Hollywood caricature of a "genius" than a person with the ballbreaking desire to uphold the immortal flame of art in his smallish hand.

I found after I had been handcuffed, ambulanced, doped, needled, marched in formation and given a leather belt to make as if I were in my dotage rather than the prime of life, that I *had* to disagree basically and deliberately with the cowardly normal notion of what constitutes insanity because it is only by *the assertion of the individual spirit that we can change definitions of reality that are already losing their hold on the conceptual imagination.* In other words, if a majority of people agree that what was once confidently called insanity no longer exists in its traditional sense, can not truthfully be a determining measurement in a time like this where each good person in the reaches of his mind is often an amateur lunatic by older slogans of "rationality," then the enslavement of the word and meaning are broken. Not only was I forced to this simple attitude because my human spirit refused the reduction of my total self to only one exaggerated aspect of it—namely the pathological label—I saw in both sanitariums no consistency in what was thought of as "sick."

In short, I could no longer afford to think of contemporary insanity as an exact objective phenomenon, like thunder or cancer, but rather as an interpretation of human thought and behavior conditioned by inherited prejudices, fear, questionable middle-class assumptions of the purpose of life, a policeman's narrow idea of freedom, and dollar-hard AMA notions of responsibility and *expediency* ("1. Apt and suitable to the end in view; as, an expedient solution; hence, advantageous. 2. Conducive to special advantage rather than to what is universally right."—*Webster's New Collegiate Dictionary*). No longer could I see any true authority or finality in a conception that could be too conveniently tailored to fit the situation. I knew then that anyone who dares the intellectual conventions of this local time must be prepared to have "psychotic" or any of its variants—paranoid, schizophrenic, even the mild psychopathic!—thrown at them. The pathological interpretation of human nature has become a style in our period (overemphasized by the junior science of psychiatry) and has come to mirror the fears, anxieties and values of those currently in positions of social authority more often than the person who is being gutted. Within the iron maiden of this fashion—which undeniably hurts, right down to the roots of the soul—the independent person and the artist-type have no choice but to trust implicitly what they see with their intellect and imagination; for when the climate changes, only the individual vision will stand secure upon its God-given legs of having had faith in actual experience.

I therefore believe that the fear and even the actual living through of much that used to be called "insanity" is almost an emotional necessity for every truly feeling, reacting, totally human person in America at this time—*until* he or she passes through the soul-crippling (not healing) judgment of such language and comes out of the fire at the point where other words and hence different conceptions are created from the wounds. The psychiatric vocabulary and definitions, which once seemed such a liberating instrument for modern man, have unwittingly woven a tight and ironically strangling noose around the neck of the brain; contemporary men and women—especially intellectuals—tremblingly judge themselves and others in the black light of psychopathology and shrink human nature to the size of their own fears instead of giving it the liberty of their greatest dreams. But we can be grateful that the human soul is so constructed that it ultimately bursts concepts once held as true out of its terrible need to live and creates the world anew just in order to breathe in it. One final thought: should any readers see this article as an effort at self-justification they are right, as far as they go; but they should remember that it is only out of the self and its experience (even if I have failed here) that new light has ever been cast on the perpetual burden of making life ever more *possible* at its most crucial level.

1959

5.
Ask for a White Cadillac

1

After I wrote an article on the white jazz hipster and novelty-digging people of every stripe who imitate the Negro's style I came in for biting criticism in Greenwich Village, where I live. Friends of mine, and newly made enemies as well, accused me of being anti-Negro; the influx of tense, self-conscious, easily offended Negroes who have recently hit the Village has made any frank statement about colored life extremely delicate and often full of double-jointed guilt feelings; in fact I myself began to have grave doubts as to the truth of what I had written when I saw the reaction.

I now believe (a year and a half later) that my comments were essentially valid—in spite of my own, and every man's, limited angle of vision—and therefore of value, since any ounce of truth that can be dug out of the world and placed on the scale of justice wins you a moneyless prize, but one that gives point to your days. To ask for credit for trying to tell the truth, however, is the naivest kind of romanticism when you finally realize that the balance of life is maintained by cruel necessity. Truth is a bitter mirror to a humanity limping with wounded pride toward the heart's blind castle of contentment; those who would fool with it must be prepared for the worst, for in their zeal they are lancing the most private dreams of the race. After the anger, sentimentality and truly hurt communications that I received after my original piece, I felt compelled to investigate the whole bruised subject in more depth and background, to search for my own true attitude in relationship to the Negro. More than most white or non-Negro men I have haunted colored society, loved it (and been stomach-kicked by aspects of it), sucked it into my marrow. I aim here to tell as much of the truth about myself in connection with Negroes as I am capable of, with the knowledge that while it will no doubt expose my weaknesses of mind and temperament it will be another small step in destroying the anxiety that makes us try to balance on eggshells and bite our tongues and souls for saying the wrong thing. Complete equality for Negroes (and more subtly, for whites in relation to them) will only come when writers and speakers level down the whole dirty highway of their experience—level all the way.

53

Having been born in New York City in 1922—Washington Heights, to be exact—the image of the Negro first came to me through jazz and a colored maid (how proud young Negroes must burn at that—I would!) who took care of me as an infant. As to the maid's influence, it is unconscious but surely present; I remember nothing except for the dim feeling of warmth, big soft breasts, perhaps honeyed laughter with the head thrown back in that rich queenly way of buxom Negresses which has been typecast to death but is too vital to succumb. But I do recall vividly the beat of jazz rippling through our household from morning until night. My mother played Victor Herbertish light classics on the piano and my father sung them in a proud-peacock way, but my older brother and sister, during the 1920s, got right on board with the new jazz music and the big beat pounded away from both the bedroom (where my brother blew his tenor sax) and the livingroom (where my sister edged my mother off the piano seat and made the keys hop). What fascinated me as much as the music itself, even as a boy, was the verbal style that accompanied jazz; the easy, informal play on words that instinctively crept into the voice of people who spoke about or sang jazz. This was a Negro invention quite as much as the music itself, a wonderful, melodic, laughing camp with the hard white words that took the lead out of them and made them swing.

But it was translated into white terms, or middle-class lingo, by the easy-throated, golden-rhythmed Bing Crosby, whose voice dipped and flirted and slurred with great beauty to my 12-year-old ear when he introduced a tune over the radio or played with some lyrics while singing. It always seemed to me that Crosby had a powerful effect on the lovely small-talk of this country, its inflections and casualness, and that this came from The Groaner's being the almost unwitting ("I was a wheel that rolled uphill"—Crosby) ambassador from the black-belt to the white. He dug instinctively and with great fluid taste—in spite of his collegiate front—what lay behind jazz: the good-natured mockery of stiff white manners by Negroes and the sweetening of dry attitudes into rich, flexible, juicy ones.

The Negro to me, then, in my kid-ignorance, was jazz and fun; this was due to the accidents of my personal history—the fact that I came from a northern, comfortable, Jewish middle-class family and was shielded from any competitive or side-by-side contact with Negroes. Colored men and women were exotica to me during my childhood, magical, attractive aliens to the normal rhythm of the world. I take no pride in saying this. But because of my background and that of thousands like me, we couldn't know Negroes as the rounded human beings they are but saw them through a particular porthole of wonder and odd fascination. Unfortunately, Negroes were thought of as being the servant class by people of my economic bracket; but because my family was Jewish and in some ways (in others not) compassionate because of the endless history of trial of the Js, Negroes were never mistreated in my home. To be fair, however, I have heard numerous

Jews from lower economic groups—not to mention people from every other race in America—heap verbal scorn on the *schvatsa*, even at this late date. It goes without saying that such people are bucking for a future red harvest of bloody noses, both for themselves and more thoughtful people.

When I was about 15 the Negro came into my life with a wallop directly connected with the sex drive. It should be no secret that until the war the colored girl was the great underground sex symbol for the U.S. white man, the recipient of his trembling mixture of guilt, leer and male-sadistic desire. Feeling inferior due to what I thought was my physical unattractiveness (where have you heard that before?), I had never been able to make it with the pretty, aggressive Jewish girls of my own environment; not only was I an awkward, fear-haunted, savagely shy kid, my ego had been blasted full of holes by my being orphaned at the age of 10 and my having lived in a state of psychological panic all through my adolescence. I took refuge in heartless masturbation (yes, in technicolor!) and the Negro chick in all her stereotyped, Cotton-Club majesty became my hot partner for imagined sex bouts of every exciting kind.

There should be nothing shocking in your reading this. Thousands of white American men have done the same, I'm positive, and the reason why they selected Negresses hinges on the double taboo of both sex (long explained and still life's quivering ice-cream) and physical intimacy with a colored person. Together, the behind-the-shed appeal to a *timid* and therefore *prurient* white kid like myself was dynamite. Thus it was that the Negro girl became my jazz queen, someone who loved (in my imagination) to ball, could never get enough, was supreme physically, rhythmically, ecstatically—"Oh, baby, give it to me!" I know only too well that this is a standard cliche and that my blunt picture of it might be offensive; I also know that for historically and psychologically understandable reasons there was, and still is, some truth in this stereotype.

My love of jazz and raging enslavement to sex came together and focused burningly on the colored girl, but it wasn't until I moved down to the Village— already violently pro-Negro-radical-crudely Whitemanesque—in my early 20's that I first slept with a Negro chick. This baptism was a nothing experience: the girl was Villagey, neurotic, affected, unswinging, among the first of the colored pioneers to make it downtown. In those, my early Village days, she was just one gal among several whom one made and then lost in the merry-go-round of kicks that whirled me and my buddies. Days and nights were lost to us in an almost fanatical pursuit of pleasure during the war-ruptured mid 1940s, with booze, tea (pot), literature, psychiatry and sex leading us headlong into the foam of ever-new experience. But this wild hedonism played itself out in time both for me and my friends. We had to cope with our private selves. Weaknesses in each separated us from the pack, and our lives became more private, secretive, smaller, pettier. Things we had hidden from one another and from ourselves began to obsess us, and I in particular found that I had no genuine confidence toward women and could only make them (or so I thought) by not wearing my glasses and not being myself. I could no longer go on the charm and boyish good looks—as synthetic as not wearing my specs, since I'd had my nose "fixed" when I was 17—that buoyed me up when I first climbed aboard the Village kicks-train. I was becoming lonelier, more introspective, and hung up to the ceiling in my relationships with women. But my hunger for sex (warmth! light! life! the complete holy works!) was as cancerous as ever, and I craved, needed, burned for the gratification. It was then that I first began to go up to Harlem and really see dark society in its own hive.

2

I naturally went to prostitutes in Harlem, but I eased my way into this way of life—for it became that—by enjoying and digging the sights and human scenes of Harlem for their own sake. Here was the paradise of sensuality (to my thirsting eyes) that I had dreamed of for years, but had never gotten to know except for fleeting, half-scared trips through this no-man's land. Now, nerveless because of the heat of my desire (and even when this hot temperature in me waned I never once felt the anxieties on Harlem streets that my white friends tell me is a normal fear) I began to sidle up to my quarry from several sides—listening to jump music from the fine box at the Hotel St. Theresa bar, seeing the show in the small room at the Baby Grand on 125th St., going to the Friday night stage shows at the Apollo, getting the rhythm and feel of the place by stalking the streets and being perpetually slain within by the natural style of the men, women and whizzingly precocious kids. Harlem to me, as I got to know it, was a mature wonderland (until I saw the worms behind the scenery). Not only was the sex there for the asking—provided your wallet was full, Jack—but the entire place was a jolt to anybody with a literary or even a human imagination. The streets hummed and jumped with life right out in the open, such a contrast to the hidden, bottled-up phobias that I knew so well. You can't hide your life if you're a poor or scuffling Negro and live frankly among your own people. Jesus, it broke out everywhere, the cripples and amputees I saw begging or laughing or triple-talking someone out of bread (loot) on street-corners; the high heel-crackling (with metal plates so they can be *heard*, man!) sleepless hustling chicks on some money-goal errand in the middle of the afternoon, wearing shades against the enemy daylight and looking hard and scornful of tragedy because they knew it too well; the go-all-night male cats gathering around some modernistic bar in the late afternoon, freshly pressed and pomaded and ready to shoot the loop on life for the next 20 hours, crap-shooting, card-playing, horse-playing, numbers-running, involved in 15 mysterious and button-close deals with women—either girls working for them in "the life" (hustling), as I got to say, or sponsoring them in some gambling bit or this or that. The whole teeming place was alive to me in every foot of every block, for there was everywhere a literal acting-out of the needs and desires that all of us are condemned to cope with until we quit the scene, but here in Harlem there could be no false pride about doing your dirty-work behind a screen. Even when I cooled my sexual heat there many times—in a cellar near a coal-bin, lying on a pallet, or in a room with four other men and women pumping away on three cots barely separated from each other—I felt little or none of the shame I would have had in downtown Manhattan doing the same thing. On the contrary, I began to think that this was more real, natural and human, given the situation of Harlem as I knew it and as people had to live it out to *make* a life for themselves.

I began to feel very much at home uptown—and felt thunderbolt excitement, too. As a writer as well as a frustrated, needy man, I could never get over how Russian the amount of dramatic life I saw was. Here were the same radical contrasts of money and poverty, of tremendous displays of temper and murderous emotion, of hustlers and johns making their arrangements next to funeral parlors where last night's balling stud had perhaps just been laid out. (I obviously mean Russia before the Revolution of 1917.) Humor, the most quick and subtle shafts of wit, shot like sabre-points of Mozartian sparkle across street corners and bars where hostile or drink-angry people were mouthing the favorite Harlem curse for all frustration, "Motherfucker motherfuckin motherfucker!" And through all this street-embattled life ran the perpetual beauty of clothes, threads, duds!—bold, high-style dresses and appointments on the girls (flashing jewelry, dyed platinum-blonde hair over a tan face, elbow-length white evening gloves handcuffed with a fake black-onyx bracelet) while the guys were as button-rolled and razor-sharp as hip clotheshorses stepping right out of a showroom. Certainly I saw poor, frayed, styleless people and outfits: but the percentage of sartorial harmony and inventiveness was keener, perhaps out of the need to *impress*, than I had ever seen in any other single New York City community.

In fact I learned about clothes in Harlem—more than I ever had in college or fancy midtown Manhattan, when I worked on the *New Yorker* surrounded by smooth Yale-Princeton-Groton boys. Clothes merely seemed an external decoration to me then, and the pork-pied smoothies often seemed like phantoms with little or no personality. But in Harlem clothes literally make the man and woman: every hair of imagination, flair, nerve, taste, can be woven into your garb, and the tilt of a hat on a hustling, attractive spade cat will be pretty nearly an unerring clue to the style you'll run up against when you speak to him. The girls love a big approach in dress, stagey, rich, striking, and when you consider the color they have to work with you understand the way they'll pour on reds and yellows that smite the eye and make the average white girl seem mousey and drab by comparison. My own style of dress when I first hit Harlem was the casual approach which I wear in the Village and also uptown in the 40's—shined loafers, button-down shirt with a decent, perhaps regimental-stripe tie, a suit jacket and odd slacks (mostly the GI khaki type that can creep by as smart if the crease is truly alive). When I made my opening passes at the whore bars in Harlem—which you get to know by keeping your ears open, following a smile, seeing the number of chicks lined up at the mahogany—I felt embarrassed by my outfit in contrast to the tailor-made cordovan-shoed jazz that the bar-jockeys were showing. My embarrassment was correct to feel, for one or two of the frank hustlers I ran into soon after I made my play—within the first week—wondered "why the hell don't you dress, man?" (I later found out that in Harlem there are three gradations of male dress: clean, pressed, and "dap"—for dapper. Everything can be squeezed into these three categories, and by Harlem standards I was barely clean for any kind of swinging night-life.) After I had been properly put down about my clothes, which were slightly insulting to the dress-tight colored hustling chick and the sharp male studs, out of misunderstanding, I had to think about drapes in a new way.

I was taught that in Harlem if a man wants to make out with women he has to behave like a man, not a boy or a half-vague intellectual: he has to dress like he knows the score, is not afraid to be bold and flairful in the eyes of women, and wears a slick, capable look about him. Probably Negroes who have scored with money uptown wear the insignia of it on their back as a sign of pride or superiority; certainly some of it is narcissistic strutting and over-obvious, but in a rough community like Harlem there is nothing wrong in proving who and what you are by your appearance. You can't be a self-effacing Shelley or a Chopin— even the homosexuals in Harlem, which is bursting with them, are brash, daring, cop-baiting individualists—when you're competing with other lean and hungry cats for the sweet cream of life. After I was given a fishy eye because of my dress a number of times, my refuge in casual Village-type clothes underwent a change, and I dressed as rifle-hard and classy as I could when I later did my uptown balling.

What had happened inside me was this: I realized that downtown, in white society, especially the knowing, introspective, intellectual-literary kind, we put much value on "good looks" in the sense of paying excruciating attention to wart-tiny details of face and figure, and going into a tailspin when someone has facial one-upmanship over us. But up here in Harlem, where everyone is sunburned for life and can have little of that false self-love in what a blind fate has dealt them, good looks are *earned* by the way in which you bring art (dress, a cool mustache, the right earrings) to shine up an indifferent nature. The Negro has been and is an artist out of necessity, not necessarily a fine artist but a human one; and if you want to score in Negro society you have to compete within the rules that an *original* kind of tough life has laid down. I wanted to score. The romantic-fantasizing me had lain flabbily undeveloped on its Villagey couch of yearning for too long, and I knew that if I wanted the chicks and the heart-deep kicks I had to get with it in a hurry.

I learned not only to dress, but to bargain with hustlers, keep my appetite in my pants and not show it, and develop all of the masculine wiles that I had once attributed to philistines with grudging acknowledgment of their effectiveness, but scorn as far as I was concerned. I became careful about money after I had been suckered out of perhaps 50 dollars, either by girls who promised two tricks and gave only one (or none) or "guides" who maintained they knew great flesh-parlors, and then disappeared over the squeezed-together Harlem roofs after letting me wait on a fourth-floor landing while they made the "arrangements." I was being shaped by the environment in which I was trying to make it, and while I never yielded up my total personality I cut out many of the affected, indecisive mannerisms that almost seem to be the norm in bookish white society.

Pleasure was my business in Harlem and I had to approach it like a business-man; I had to control my wandering kicks and appreciation to a technique for getting what I wanted. Along the way I picked up, almost without knowing it, a hundred small bits of advice and know-how: never turn your back on a bar when standing there, it makes you conspicuous and is in bad taste; come on slowly and coolly with a hustling girl after looking them *all* over (Negro bar-buddies hammered this home), since you're a man and have the good money in your pocket or you wouldn't be there; ask for no favors, butt into *no* fights or arguments ("You might get hurt bad, Dick!"), show courtesy and good humor when put down by some h-high or drunken chick climbing a peak of meanness within herself; always buy a bouncer or bartender a drink when you can afford it; remember that music, sports and money are driving, magnetic topics in Harlem and will always get you an interesting conversation if you're hung up or ill at ease.

I had come uptown with a predisposition. Not only did I love the girls and the music—which reflected each other in warmth, drive, flashing humor, lusty beat—but my eye and heart had always been a pushover for the stylish, spirited Negro ace as well. It was therefore no strain on my grimly introspective makeup (a complaint I heard from several other isolated white writers who were drawn to Harlem but felt hurtingly awkward when they tried it) to make my way into colored society, to dig the tasty food, kibitz easily in the luncheonettes, listen to the finest and hippest jukeboxes for hours and be a happy addict with my quarters. I felt I was being educated and given a human feast at the same time; nor did I prey on it. I gave both spirit and gold and the greatest appreciation for what I got, and can say now, without self-consciousness, that the human exchange was equal. Most of the Caucasian men who come to Harlem to get laid are looking for easy eats, and carry their stiff marriage of caution and superiority so squarely that they are verbally speared in a dozen ways without knowing it. All they hear is laughter and they wonder why. The other greys who come, includ-ing myself, are the imaginative, sensitive, troubled, daring kicks-seekers who the hipper local Negroes take to without any break in stride, recognizing masculine brothers in the eternal war with fate, chicks and George Washington's dollar. There was no segregation once I got in. The masculine brother idea, like the female sister one, is a reality in Harlem, not just words; broke and drunk I found no trouble or shame in borrowing money for carfare back to the Village, which I repaid the following week, or even getting my ashes hauled on credit (which is difficult and embarrassing to set up with the average, where's-my-next-movie-money-coming-from hustler unless she digs you in the boy-girl moonlight sense).

But I also saw by about my third month in Harlem the low, cruel, ignorant, selfish, small-minded side of uptown life. I was first cheated out of money by lies and juicy come-ons which never matured. O.K., one expects to be played for a sucker in the tenderloin unless one keeps one's wits, and I learned what every pilgrim through the thighs and breasts of Fleshville and Champagne Corners has had drilled into his bank account since man first sought pleasure. I accepted it. But my finer senses, if after all this I can legitimately use the phrase, were humbled time and again by the sight of men beating women, hustlers drunkenly cursing and clawing each other, friends of mine (Negro men and women both) boasting of how they had cheated Con Ed out of money by fixing the meter or how they had boosted goods from Macy's and Bloomingdale's, or how some date I was out with was afraid to go home to her old man (the pimp she lived with) because he'd take three-quarters of what I gave her and beat the living jazz out of her if she held out. (This particular girl once hid in my apartment for three days out of fear, narcotizing herself among other ways with watching Darren McGavin as Mike Hammer on TV and impatiently waiting for Darren to "get to that dirty fighting, man, cause it's *too* much!")

I saw the most fantastic lying—not the exception but the rule with the gang I traveled with—to get money for H (heroin), jewelry, clothes, whisky, pot, the latest Big Mabelle record, money out of a sucker, stranger, relative, brother, mother; it made no difference. Yet side-by-side with this I saw the human good that lay just an inch away from its flip into unarguable nastiness. For example the great naturalness and wit of most of the people I got to know—their fluid ease, generosity, life-shrewdness, laughing philosophical fatalism—when taken a notch to the left became recklessness, hostility without restraint, the pettiest haggling over coin, the most sullen selfishness. The qualities I dug in Harlem nighttime Negroes often became, in other words, the viciousness I repudiated in all human beings who were bent on degradation of another, the violence of those who whined, fibbed, stole, backed out of jams, played others for fallguys, the gold in their teeth and back pocket. Apart from my jazz and sex self-interest—my plain thirst—I came to Harlem with an open mind that was ready and willing to find beauty in much that the squares, or engineers as we called them, backed away from. I found that I, too, backed like a trooper. I should have realized that I couldn't get my kicks, my needs fulfilled, without a corresponding loss on the other side of the human balance sheet. *Was it, then, people like myself who helped degrade the Negro by coming to his community in order to cut myself a piece of the pleasure pie? Was it my needs of ear and flesh that helped make some of the colored whore themselves, and understandably cheat and con on the side, because they knew why I was there and laughed up their mutual sleeve at my so-called decent ethical standards?*

These were rough thoughts and I had to try and face them. I came to the conclusion that we fed each other, the Harlem nighttime Negro and myself, but that the revulsion and often amazement I felt at the lying and cheating couldn't be my responsibility because, what the hell, I wasn't God. It went on when I and no white spy was present, in this Lenox Avenue hot-box, not because of any Gene Talmadge bullshit about colored inferiority but because the people were dollar-hungry, haphazardly educated, often ignorant (hardly stupid—I've got the scabs of many a mental thrust!), street-Arab tough, and ruthlessly indifferent or *foreign* to middle-class morality. They lived by night, in the old movie title, and they hustled their bucks and jollies any way they could; they had lied, spat, fisted, grabbed their way up from five in a room, rats, bugs, the unflushable toilet and the leaking ceiling, the misery-drowning bottle and the magic needle, mama doing the two-backed bit to make the rent and new-compact money ("I'm the third generation of prostitutes," a businesslike Negro mother told me with flat dignity) and their attitude towards getting what they wanted was the hardest, most selfish, screw-the-ethics approach I had ever been up against.

3

I was hypnotized by it for a while—the way the sheltered sissy-rich kid in movies always is by brushes with the underworld—but after a year of hitting Harlem three or four times a week, day and night, the fascination wore itself down and hardened into skepticism and suspicion. My heart no longer winced at the sights of misery and humiliation that I saw on the streets; I looked for the further truth, behind the too-glib appeal to my humanity, where before I accepted hard-luck stories on their running-sore face value. (As James Baldwin and Richard Wright have both pointed out, the Negro's suffering has been so full that it's often hard for him to refrain from using it, actor-style, to make it pay off. And who's to blame him from the distance of this printed page—while, similarly, who wants to be suckered and played the jerk close up?) I got to know, by my uptown education, something of what it's like to be an average Negro in any of the big-city ghettoes, how you harden your heart, your jaw, your stomach, take what you can get away with, spit at fate, laugh at wounds, conceivably dance at funerals to keep your own spirits alive. I appreciated the life-induced toughness of the hustlers I knew, by the dozen, even while their callousness and ignorance never failed to scrape against my upbringing like sandpaper. They had begun life, before American society had been wrenched open to make way for the man of color, as the very social garbage of U.S. existence; and if they didn't nastily laugh or scornfully sway with the right-is-white whip the very humanity in them would have said nix, nix, this can't be, and they would have used razor or gas to find pride's haven. And I, also a poor up-against-it mortal (but in a different way) had once too been ripe for the big sleep when my hope of happiness had fled, and here I was trading on the dirty pleasure streets with these my sisters and brethren in hardship!

Even after I had lost my girlish, milky notions about the natural greatness of Negroes—a defiant liberalism and sense of identification stemming in part from my being the unreligious modern American Jew who feels only the self-pitying sting of his identity without the faith—I was still haunted by Harlem. True, irony and slitted eye had replaced to some extent my former urge to dig all the sights and sounds. I was more realistic, cynical, harder and even nastier on occasion with the hustling girls than I would ever have dreamed I could be when I first entered paradise. I would no longer allow myself to be taken for quarters or drinks by one-armed and one-eyed beggars and bar-jockeys (who were actually less handicapped with the facts of life than yours truly). The promise of a wild blow-job by some outwardly gorgeous mulatto chick was now tempered by experience, by the coldness that could freeze the bed once the money had been paid, the quickness, indifference, cop-out; I could no longer sweepingly arc my dreams of sex and desire on to a Harlem that I had gotten to know from the spare-ribs up. I was more like Sam Spade now than Stephen Dedalus, or his crude U.S. equivalent. But even so, I still got a special boot out of walking the streets of Harlem, of mingling in its life to the depth I did (which went beyond the whore and bar-type acquaintanceships to two fairly solid friendships with working-class Negroes) that I never received downtown in white society.

This next is an uncomfortable point to write about: but it's true that when I strode the Harlem avenues I not only had an absence of the physical fear my buddies tell me they feel above 110th St., I had a sense of *security* and well-being precisely because of my color. For the first time in my adult life I felt completely confident and masterful in my relationship to both sexes because society judged me the superior, just as in a different, Irish-bar–type scene it made me stand out unto myself because of the Yiddish bit. In other words, I was the human worm turning; even more true and paradoxical is the fact that I was a better, more capable, objective and gentlemanly person among Negroes (for the one big reason that my security could never be threatened) than I was among whites. So oddly enough my Harlem experience made me feel both how and why many uptown Negroes act as they do and also made me feel like a southern white, understanding for the first time the tremendous psychological *impregnability* to the cracker (every white man has a built-in colonel-kit!) in having an "inferior" class beneath him. It was an astonishing revelation to realize that you could be a better person—more attentive, calmer, happier, and that last word is the truth—for the *wrong reasons*, that is by realizing that the people in Harlem wanted you to like them, and that if they permitted themselves any expression of hatred it was clear that it was an aspect of themselves they were crying out against rather than you.

I am not proud to write this: but it's true, or was in my case, and since I like you am wantonly and unmitigatedly human, I took advantage of this psychological reality to give myself the basic happiness I wanted. It brought out my best as a person among other people, and yet it's likely that my very security helped reinforce the *insecurity* of many of the Negroes I knew towards whites! (Thus does one human being use another for reasons that are deeper than morality—because of our inconsolable life-needs as individuals.) I was the predatory male in Harlem, which means the true male, refined, amiable, sure-footed and sure-minded because I knew that fulfillment of my needs (not downtown blockage and anxiety) was right around the corner whenever I wanted it. In the Village I always felt, like most of us, that I was in equal competition so intense that it brought out my worst and made me want to withdraw rather than come out in all my potential manhood and therefore complete humanity. I can only justify this Harlem-using by my need as a human being, and if I didn't know how desperate the necessities of life can be—to the point where the impossibly jammed-up contemporary person must hunt in every offbeat street and alley that the mind can conceive to assuage them—I would feel more guilt than my picture of total justice says is right.

4

It is unrealistic to think the same attitude holds in Harlem that exists downtown in the Village, or in midtown, or any of the new mixed housing projects, where Negroes are increasingly your neighbors, friends, lovers, wife, husband, landlord—Christ, your goddamn analyst! Harlem is Harlem, the brutal, frantic, special scene of the big-city Negro in America until this time, and the white–black contrast still maintains its unique, soon-to-be-blended (as Negroes increasingly crash out) charge for the pioneering ofay who crosses the line with nerve-ends humming. You are entering Negro America, man, and you carry with you—despite your personal courage or lack of it—an unspoken message stamped on your skin, Jim! You are there for a reason, as are the second-rate white dentists, real-estate finaglers, jewelers, optometrists, pawn-brokers, and so are the colored, because until recently they were hemmed in as neatly as an enemy. Why dodge the sociological exoticism in your being there? But why, also, dodge the needs that led you there? If you love music, beat, chicks, color, barbecue, wild inventive humor with the stab of truth in it—why shouldn't you be there when your own life has denied you these things? But, hungup human that you are, you can never mate the pleasure of Harlem with the pain; your mind doesn't want to see that the kicks you love breed in a white-ringed pesthole (I exclude the secret few upper middle-class hideaways) whose stink offends your very soul, like an unaired bathroom. I could never immunize myself (nor should I have!) to the garbage in the streets, the obsessive ads and shops for hair-straightening and beauty treatments (not so unlike my own nose-bobbing, is it, in the attempt to gleam like a clean-cut White Protestant beauty?), the pawnshops five to a block, the rat-infested tenements, the thousands of dollars spent on TVs and radio-phonographs at the sacrifice of medical aid and sanitation, the feverish traffic in drugs, the hordes of sullen-faced, corner-haunting hustlers, the waste of money on adolescent trinkets, the wild red rage on the broken-beer-bottle 5 A.M. streets and the ceaseless stealing (how many times have I had my change stolen from bar and lunch-counter while I was feeding the juke and trusting my nighttime friends!). And yet, my conscience sneers to me now as I write this, what did you expect, what could you have rightly expected—a heaven of sensuality without the pissmire of sociology?

I sincerely doubt that even God could marry the discrepancies: namely, the boots and joys of Harlem life for soul- as well as penis-starved human beings like myself, who could get the needed equivalent *nowhere* else in this greatest city on the globe, along with its ugliness, .45-calibre toughness, and kick-him-when-he's-just-getting-up attitude (not when he's down—that's too easy). The life-scarred pavement that reaches from 110th and Lenox to 155th breeds the one intergrown with the other. And yet if you look at Harlem without any attempt at morality at all, from a strictly physical and blindly sensuous point of view, it is the richest kind of life one can ever see in American action as far as the fundamental staples of love, hate, joy, sorrow, street-poetry, dance and death go. The body and texture of its solid reality is a 100 times stronger, sharper to the nostrils, eye, ear, heart, than what we downtown greys are used to. And within a decade (some say two) it will probably end as Negroes become increasingly integrated and sinewed into the society around them. I will truly hate to see Harlem go—where will *I* seek then in my time of need, O merciless life?—and yet I would obviously help light the match that blows it out of existence.

At a buzzing bar I used to go to on Lenox between 110th and 115th Streets, where the bait paraded boldly, drunkenly, or screw-you-Jack around the circular wood, wanting your wallet but trying to size you up as a plainclothes cop or not, the makers of Hennessey Whisky had put up a sign which I'm sure was designed for the neighborhood trade all over Harlem. It said: "Ask For A White Cadillac." This bizarre drink was just good old Hennessey along with milk, mixed together in a highball glass. But the name, the music and color and swing of the image, was a laughing ball to these pleasure-bored sports and duchesses, who were belting White Cadillacs (and perhaps the cat next to me was an off-duty chauffeur) at 3 A.M. while the rocking box dealt out sounds like hip bullets, and the entire bar shrank into a black-and-tan fantasy of booze, wailing laughter, the crack of palm on face, tears, the bargain of bucks for ass, and the lusty, caressing accents of "You can take your motherfuckin drink and stick it in your motherfuckin ear, darling!"

So long, dark dream mistress of my adolescence and educator of my so-called manhood!

1959

6.
Milton Klonsky

1

I first met Milton Klonsky in probably the early spring of 1945. I had inherited a (to me) charming small apartment at 224 Sullivan St. from a girl I had been dating who suddenly winked at me in bed one morning and said with a smile that she was getting married. She had realistically been cheating on my remarkable self-conceit that I was irresistible and had nabbed herself, while I was absorbed in making love to me, a guy much more of this world and less mirror-riveted than yours truly. So she moved out in a bridal rush and I moved into this clean swinging little hideaway with a feeling of delight (once I told my bruised ego it had no case). What the hell, women were replaceable but groovy apartments were something else!

I didn't know then as they say in the old stories that my 2 to 3 years at 224 Sullivan were going to radically change my formless young life, but they did. I was wide-open for it though. Full of bounce, full of fanatical seriousness about writing and ready and willing for every mother-loving experience—"black, white, a zebra or anything new they can invent!" as a laughing call-girl once nailed it to the door—I was able to overcome my native shyness and redhot anxieties and blossom to the point where my clean little pad became a nest for Vassar-Bryn Mawr chicks to make fairly happy weekends for me. I got mostly literary types when secretly I thirsted for expensive, well-stacked, fine-assed royalty, but I had no kicks coming since I knew how half-man I was in the deep dark cellar of psychic me. Not that I was queer, baby, but that I often felt as unreal as Kafka and neurotic as Proust and shaky as a leaf in the privacy of my own head. I take little pride in spelling it out but I was bugged, fearful, "sensitive as a baby's ass" (as Klonsky once described me with that fearlessness of intellect that could allow you to take a personal insult and not flip because you saw the truth-clicking mind behind the words) and at the mercy of a fireworks-livid imagination; but the big thing was that I was a kid, 23, and in spite of everything, the world and Eternity were just ripe dandelions waiting for me to pluck. Everything lay before before me, I felt (what 23-year-old globe-eater hasn't?) and now that I was out of the rooming-houses and chance 3-week flops in friends' apartments and the whole general weirdness of living that made the war years over here a night-and-day rollercoaster I was feeling feisty and ready to ride herd on everything that plagued me. Man, the world was going to part and bow low for me! Neuroses look out, cause Krim's gonna boot you puny little assassinators right out of his life! I had never really had my own adult-decent place before and I took tremendous pride in keeping it shining and kept clapping myself on the forehead, in effect, and saying over and over to myself, "You don't believe it but it's yours, yours!"

Billie Holiday blew her blues from my new record player (I took over my ex-girlfriend's first-rate modern furniture and equipment, too, when I moved in and still owe her $48 on the deal although I haven't seen her in 15 years), Miro prints danced on the wall, a lovely pungent undefinable furniture-and-straw-rug odor smelled through the place, and the optimistic merriment of having this nice new apartment really picked me up high. I had made the Village scene 2 years before, but in a much more squalid depressing way. I had lived with the first important girl in my life, Connie S————(now just out of a midwestern brain-lockup, as I served my time in a Manhattan one, having gone back out of awful need to a convent-girl brand of Roman Catholicism and following priestly bluntness after being one of the Village's most wide-open soul-sisters) in a lousy one-room bohemian fantasy on Cornelia Street. I had felt excited about it all when we took the place because Jim Agee had lived on Cornelia when I first visited him while in highschool (he was now down on King Street), and I was a book-hugging literary romantic who got high inside identifying with my crushes, but Connie's and my little stint on Cornelia was a savage bust. Nothing worked for us. I was scared of the Italian street-threat that used to psychically de-ball all us violin-souled Jewish boys who had fled downtown, I was wildly insecure and neurotic as was Connie, and together we managed to stagger through an unreal man-wife life for about a year before it became a comic tearful enraged nightmare and she pulled out (for she had personal integrity, God bless her).

But here I was now in my new Village cozy-pad on the second floor of F Building overlooking the clean-swept courtyard—there were and are 5 small buildings built around a courtyard sporting a concrete goldfish tureen in the center and the whole scheme is protected in a Shangri-La kind of way by a big gate which locks out the Sullivan Street strongarm locals—and it was a pleasure to get up in the morning these days, leg-tangled or alone. I was pulling down nearly $85 per week at the OWI writing war news, going dutifully to an analyst with the usual boy-scout dreams of solving all my "problems" (the echo of Klonsky's chanting quotation of Blake's "O why was I born with a different face? Why was I not born like the rest of my race?" coming back to me as I write this, for he had a profound sense of tragedy and wasn't snowed by pleasant theories of mortal amelioration) and I was full of the immense future-kissing conviction of glory that your average U.S. writing nut of 23 usually glows with.

Going in and out of this lovely courtyard I used to see with increasing regularity—since I had my eyes peeled for it by now, especially when I was wearing my glasses (for I used to wear them and not wear them in the usual nearsighted hangup that is almost a universal small symbol of uncertainty and shame among the boys and girls of my generation)—a strange shortish lithe dark-looking cat who would brush by me at the entrance with brusqueness and what seemed like hostility, but also looking me over in a grudging way. There was an under-the-rock air of furtiveness, reptilianism, about the guy; his eyes would never meet mine, never signal hello, but out of their squinting holes they'd flick off my buttons so to speak in one razor-swipe and then stare stonily beyond. Frankly, I'd feel like melting sheet every time I ran into this dark trigger-man and it jarred me—*me*, brilliant, handsome, proud, a Beethovian earth-shaker missing heart-beats because some dark snot didn't know who I was and stared through me! I resented this creep and steeled myself when I had to walk past the inhuman guns of his eyes, but even then—in spite of myself and my pride—I thought they were great eyes, green-grey, catlike, opaque, the possessors of some secret knowledge of mystery which later reminded me almost exactly of the hypnotizing eyes we see in photographs of Rimbaud.

This was Milt Klonsky, although I didn't know his name at the time. I also didn't know that part of the deadly looks he'd shoot me there in the courtyard-entrance was due to his own myopia and the accompanying bitching pressure of having to squint and almost bore holes in the air in order to see clearly—or else be forced to wear the anti-heroic, anti-moviestar, *anti-chick* glass over his unusual eyes. (He was and is less nearsighted than myself and has never fully resolved the problem downward as I have had to do because I was fingered by that dear old maniac, Mother Nature, as Dr. Chandler Brossard once dubbed her.) I knew nothing about Klonsky except that I was scared of him, aware of him, the cat was creepy—where did he get off acting so stony, rude, the hard-guy? I was mattressed sweet right then in my own terrifically self-important world—new pad, fears held at bay, fawncy-voiced eastern college pusserino tumbling (some), me not getting killed in the war and also living out an old newspaperman-dream via my OWI trick, some prose steaming in the Remington Portable at home and great-writer fantasies gassing me even as I shaved in my new hospital-slick john—and I didn't want some alley-hustler off the streets, some foreign-looking Mafia slitter, threatening my ego this way goddamnit!

There was no doubt after a couple of weeks of these minor eye-crises at the doorway to 224 that the two of us had sniffed each other out, the way hipsters or Beards or Negro chicks who refuse to get their hair conked will get animal-feelers toward a member of the same club walking down the block. We knew, baby! I don't remember exactly how it happened, whether it was a muttered defensive word (both of us shy) exchanged near the mailbox or a mutual friend like the now-gone Isaac Rosenfeld who placed a hand on both our shoulders and drew us together (although I doubt it), but soon, unexpectedly, easily, we were speaking and digging each other. Even though he was only about a half year older than myself, Klonsky immediately (the classic take-over guy) buttoned up the role of older brother and with good reason: he was wiser in the ways of the world—although a consummate practical fuck-up like myself—wiser about women (he was then in the process of teetering on the brink with Rhoda Jaffe Klonsky, his first wife who has long since split with him and remarried), wiser, in fact, period. Once I was able to penetrate the hard shell he grew for the world and swing with him I confirmed that there was nothing a hair's-width false in this wisdom except for the occasional high parabolas of thought, as in all under-30 visionaries, not backed up by enough experience to give them the body needed to support such rarity. Other than that the man was a masked literary marvel. He had matured much earlier than myself, especially in the minds he had trained with—difficult English poets like Donne, Marvell, Christopher Smart, his much-quoted Blake, the French Symbolists, Rimbaud, Baudelaire, Valéry, Laforgue, all the way up to Michaux; plus the most formidable of the contemporary headache-makers like Kafka, Eliot, Pound, Auden, Joyce, Yeats, Stevens and critics like Coleridge, Blackmur, Tate, I. A. Richards (with a Trilling read for mere entertainment like a mystery). Klonsky's mind seemed to contain the *entire* hip literary-intellectual university and closely grasped with an IQ that could stutter your butter too. When we got more relaxed and informal with each other after the initial feeling-out sparring—"Whodya like in prose right now? Chicks: Bennington or spade? Dig a tenor or a trumpet? You a Giant fan? What about Matisse?"—I got the downhome gooseflesh warning that I was on the way in for the most significant human and intellectual experience of my life up to then.

I wasn't wrong. Klonsky's personality was a subtle, forceful and, later I was to recognize, deeply profound one and it entered my being—tore through it actually—like a torpedo into the unguarded gut of a battle-innocent smug cruiser. I had never met anyone even remotely like him nor could I have conceived him in my imagination. Instead of being direct (my holy-grail kick at that time, encouraged by the prose of Hemingway, Eliot, Pound, which made a glistening literary virtue of straightforwardness and which I translated into an ethical ideal—even then trying to convert beauty into life-action!) he was indirect, elusive, paradoxical, frowning, iceberg-cheerless often. And yet one always had the impression, felt the impression I should really say, of a fine and deep mind that was fixed like a rule beyond every flare of mood, behind his furrowed swarthy face (now Roman-looking, now Jewish, now Spanish) and in back of those special catlike eyes. The guy's strangeness, uniqueness, was heaped further on my barometric apparatus by his style: although quotations from Blake or Hart Crane or Wordsworth—in fact most of the whole noble repertoire of English-speaking verse—sprang to his dark purplish cracked lips at appropriate moments, he electrically bit out the language of the ballpark and streets too. The combination was fascinating to me, jazzing my ear and mind with such new contrasts and perspectives on reality that I felt my simple-minded conceits blushing out of embarrassment. When I later found out that Klonsky was a hard-driving stud also, a refined digger of modern painting, a rigorous ace at mathematics and logical thinking (I know this sounds too good to be true but it *was* greased perfection), I willingly doffed my inner fedora all the way. I had never met anyone my own age before Milt who I didn't think I could top as a writer and ultimately as a man—a psychotic piece of egomania (shared by you too, my self-worshipping pals!) to set down yet true; but with Klonsky I had more than met my match and although I felt that hard lump of frustration at his being better and righter about so many things, something I was to feel at different times angrily or casually over the next 15 years, I was able to leash in my envy at his more perfect image and become a happy sidekick and admirer.

2

I've got to explain this. I'm afraid (pretty damn sure, in fact) I early wove a passive style out of a fear of being ego-licked in competition, a female (yes, say the hurting word shmuck!) containing absorbing quality which lived side-by-side with my "manly" or active self; it almost asked I be exploited, yet permitted me to suck life in like a plant does water, to be stationary and easy and gentle and quiet in a *huge bid for harmony and peace after the violence of my growing-up years*; I also have a strong dynamic charge which exists in opposition to this controlled homemade Buddhism and chances are that in spite of my life-long wrestling I'll never make groanless harmony between the two. In Milt's case my sense of reality told me with no tinted lights that here was a man better than myself—how we U.S. obsessionists measure ourselves tirelessly against the surrounding flesh, no?—and that it was a testimony to my own manhood to acknowledge this fact instead of taking refuge in the sealed tower of would-be greatness which I had built up in my head. So he became my great pal, I his more youthful greener gunsel, but my boy was always the leader in either the itching hunt for pleasure (meeting new chicks, going down to Bleecker St. to slurp up cool clams and hot sauce, getting high and taking a doubledecker 5th Ave. joyride up to the Modern Museum to dig the new shows) or in literary-intellectual discussions where the bastard invariably knew more than I did and could lucidly back it up down to the final comma. But being a superconscious writer-type—being always first a writer-man, a coldblooded Associated Press eyewitness of the reality around me—I could tolerate this superiority of his because I was always trying to learn more about life and transform it in my mind into miles of literature. A defeat, a put-down, another person's being sharper than myself was usually redeemed by me into a triumph for knowledge about existence (the human is a great and devious animal, daddy!) and in those days when I hung as closely with Milt as man and his shadow I felt I was living within at the top of my speed. I was swinging inside, learning, absorbing the brilliant angles of thought that K.'s mind created as naturally as most East Side tenement-hipsters scratch. There was nothing second-rate about my role to me, I was getting more out of it than when I'd been the power-boy in other relationships.

Klonsky at this time was finishing up his master's thesis on Metaphor at Columbia (a paper I understand that is still used as a model in the English graduate department) and ready to tear the last remaining fabric of his marriage with Rhoda. He had been catting around with various stuff as the marriage rocked on its last legs and now when I often came up to his little pad diagonally across from mine—across the courtyard in A Building—he and Rhoda would be in the midst of some shrill argument over his passion for stray pretty nooky. He wasn't like me in this very important, as-long-as-you-live hard-on of male being. I had kidded myself along, brought myself up with the typical (every young guy's autobiographical novel up to World War II) ultrasensitive, unaggressive, slightly-trembling over-romanticized attitude toward girls that I hoped could make it as a style because I was a spiritually "noble" literary type. But Klonsky, and I admired him for it, was much more of a tricky swinging operator with women and moved right in with dark cocky evil; he had his blushing hangups too (after all he was a poet and he knew the deep freezes of outer space, I had seen it in his eyes) but he would corner a chick the way a cat does a mouse and at a party it always gave me a feeling of reassurance, of the world spinning right, when I looked over my shoulder and saw Milt stroking a soft palm and purring out his line of mesmerizing jive. There was no nineteenth-century poeticizing for him as far as yon fair skirts went, at least nothing like my tense and elaborate literary-man come-on. I got my share of the good cush of course—and I always loved sex like a monster, which made my "gentle" approach that much more of a lie to myself when I really laid it on the line to the naked me—but it always seemed to me that I play-acted and almost stood on my head to get it, unlike Milt, and slowly I borrowed as much of his thrust and deviltry with pussy as I could to charge up my own style.

At any rate, I would go up to Klonsky's little one-room-and-kitchenette oasis and Rhoda would cook a knocked-out Yiddish meal for us all and then Milt would get the pot and Zigzag papers out and roll those marvelous tight joints with his meticulous alchemist's attention to every grain of gage (always rolling sticks over a white piece of typing paper and then carefully hand-sweeping the leftover grains back into an envelope or a tiny pill bottle—a pleasure for me to watch because of his absorbed concern with each microscopic detail) and soon we would all get easily, nicely, groovily high. This was our Hip Century after-dinner brandy and it warmed our modernistic freakish heads the way juice once carved slight heaven in an English lord's belly—just the same, kicks won and scooped off the knifeblade of being alive. These were wonderful moments for me up there in Milton's pad, no matter how commonplace they seem to any brother-sister hipster who is high right now while his-her eye snags these words. I had never had a true family scene (pop died when I was 8 and my mother killed herself roof-wise just before I turned 10 and at this time—The Time of Milt—I didn't have the security or ability to make a family-type situation for myself. But these dinners up at Milt and Rhoda's had for me all the warmth, goodwill, informality—since by now I was completely accepted by both of them as a kind of naive lovable shnook—of the most swinging kind of family setup, the kind where you really enjoy your own flesh-and-blood and share your precious mortal breath and laughter with them. Oh what a lovely, unplanned-for, forever-stamped gas it can be when it happens!

After dinner with the lights low, the food warming the gut, the pot working, the pad cozy, we would stretch out on the floor or bed and give laughing play to whatever came into our minds. Milt was always the leader in the thoughts we gave expression to while Rhoda and I chimed in at appropriate moments with our own giggling two-cents' worth. But even while I was stoned, jelly-relaxed and happy, I could never get over how unself-conscious Klonsky was in expressing himself; even while high and floating (probably even more keenly then) I could appreciate more than ever the lack of decoration in his thinking, the pointedness, the quick catlike way his brain would leap from silence and meditation into some clearly conceived picture or thought that had taken invisible birth within his mind. It hit me at these moments that this was truly what was meant by creativity, the ability to conjure up out of nothingness a pearl of thought that *no one else* could conceive. It was magic, man, and at the same time—as with all of Klonsky's far-out imaginings—there was nothing whimsical, cute, one-legged about it (as every pot-smoker knows imaginative types try to vie with each other when high to see who can cap who with new visions and often slay themselves with the novelty of their thoughts instead of the devastating beams of reality); Milt's ideas even when high could stand up under M.I.T. scrutiny and if I had taperecorded them (what an all-time goof that I didn't) they would have rung every bell even in the unwashed-dishes sobriety of the next morning.

We had wonderful fun on those strictly ad lib nights—ideas and warm love commingling in that tiny box over at 224 Sullivan, with the dangerous black night shut out and a million miles away—and I will never be able to forget them. As you can see Klonsky had already become my hero, the person I would think about when I couldn't sleep (his fantastically dominating image once rose up in my brain while I was in the saddle and I began worrying how *he'd* go about getting further mileage out of the party I was balling—and I'd been content as hell until that black presence of his scorned my easy unimaginative ride and burnt away my paradise!), the person I measured myself against in every way: measured my reading, my writing, my thinking, my style as a human being. No doubt he torpedoed into my life with such great power because I still had a kiddycar need for hero-worship, was more deeply uncertain about life than I would admit to myself, was coltish and goggle-eyed and impressionable as wet cement—at least that's what my analytical sense tells me and the beautiful irony is that it was from Klonsky that I learned to wield natural unsparing analysis, so even this explanation of his effect on my being owes itself to him.

I had almost willfully avoided cold and unpretty analysis before he pried his ideas into my head by sheer steel of logic. Certainly I was capable of spotting faults and holes in things, people, ideas, but my deepest feeling was in giving life an upward lift instead of reducing it because my fantastic ego-hopes couldn't bear shrinkage of any kind. I identified my own future so completely with the life around me, saw the world as the mirror of myself, that any acid undercutting of even the outer scene toppled my happiness-craving heart within myself. To be honest, I was a tremendous self-intoxicated idealist who often perfumed the reality around me as an *extension* of my own inner needs (fears!), who shaped and reshaped the girders of actuality to fit my hungry dream, and now Klonsky moved into this myth-building factory of mine carrying the hard club of impersonal truth. It smashed without meaning to—his sense of its weight was not mine, my universe quivered under its most casual swish—and bang! a vase of my most hoarded moonshine would topple to the floor and spill sadly, floodingly, over my entire being. But it was then, on my mental hands and knees picking up fragments, that I began the long arduous work of trying to integrate my spirit with the heartless real world, it was then and through Klonsky that I ultimately realized I had been living in a self-made diving bell where everything was just the way I wanted it instead of the way it more truly, cruelly was.

Milt was to drum away at me all through our friendship that I was an enthusiast, a rhapsodist, a jazzer-upper of reality and the constancy of this anti-lyrical vigilance of his beat so put-downishly into my mind that I became five-headedly aware of each exuberant yelp I uttered or even thought. What is fascinating is that Klonsky, schooled and fashioned by anti-Romantic verse from Marvell to Marianne Moore, became the living embodiment of poetic reason while I, identified in my heart with modern American prose literature which is both romantic and lyrical from Dreiser to Kerouac, was the opposite embodiment of vitality and excess. But just as I thought that poetry was a higher form of expression than prose—because I could never enjoy or want to understand it in school (it seemed like punishment compared to the groove of prose) and admired those who could—so I thought without a hair of doubt that Milt's judgment was superior to mine and I strove mightily to sculpt those raw "distortions" in my own makeup so they could live up to the more authoritarian standard he set. It was a strange war I was living out in myself after I began digging Klonsky's ideas, a war between my powerful instincts which led in many directions and his even more powerful reasoning abilities which compressed the world to the space between his hairline and the bridge of his nose. Here was a man and a mind I admired unqualifiedly and from whom I learned with the greed of a saved-up lifetime of unanswered questions, whom I loved, who I knew was more profound and valuable than myself under the eye of God—so I tried like a fiend to lace my molten wildness into the forms he upheld. This was not only so I could know and be "the truth" as a writing-man who had a massive hunger for a giant ultimate greatness (I turned the face of Ambition white so murderous was my lust!), but also—down deep in the most human cry of my machine—so I could, by virtue of the holy mathematics I thought Klonsky would provide me with, cut in half or to zero my perpetual inner suffering, hurts, confusion, the dreadful globe of consciousness I wore on top of my neck. In other words: "You shall know the truth and it will set you free," and K. was and spoke more truth than I had ever heard before, so I tried to heave the most fundamental baggage of me off my shoulders and open-armed embrace the very Christ of Truth I believed my friend stood for. It was—this need and effort of mine—ultimately to be against the character, the reason-for-being, of my particular self but I tried, I tried, I tried, and so grateful and romantic and tearfully kidlike was I in my fantasies that I used to imagine a showdown scene of some sort in which I dedicatedly gave up my life for my friend. And, dig, I was already then a published writer, not a nut, and yet so powerful was my need of finding and being "truth" and being made whole through Klonsky's teaching that it took precedence over everything. Religion, the spirit of life and not the sensations which up to then had ecstatically gassed me and (in the guise of "style" and "beauty," especially in words) been my substitute for the less obvious lightning which underscores all of human life, had been shown to me by a buddy who was also the closest thing to a model of mortality that my raw heart and brain had ever had the mixed luck to mold itself on.

3

I can back up Klonsky's objective weight and influence on the New York literary scene by pointing out that at the time I first knew him I wasn't alone in being literally soul-struck by his rare qualities. Others who also used him as a standard of excellence included his old friend from Brooklyn, the writer Anatole Broyard, my ex-girlfriend Connie (who would beard people in the Village, including the present *New Yorker* poet-poetry editor Howard Moss, and back them against Whelan's as she preached Klonsky's "genius") and even the much older poet-critic Allen Tate, who told me in the summer of 1959 on Cape Cod that Milt had left a lasting impression on him after a brief two months they spent together at the writer's colony in Cummington, Massachusetts, in 1942 when K. was a bare nineteen-and-a-half. Cocktail glass in hand while the breeze blew off the pond in Wellfleet at an outdoor party at the summer home of historian Arthur Schlesinger, Jr., Tate kept asking me questions about what Klonsky was up to. Tate's questions were strong, direct, wanting answers, and he wouldn't let up as I tried to duck the issue with a ginny, let's-have-a-good-time grin on my face. The reason I dodged giving full value to Tate's questions was that I was peeved, as I always was after I had become a fairly "known" writer, to have Klonsky the magnet of conversation instead of myself; but underneath the momentary bite of jealousy and the goofy gin-grin I was gratified that without realizing it Tate was reinforcing what I had always felt about my extraordinary friend—and Tate both thirty years older than Klonsky and myself and also, as you'll remember, the great ex-pal and critical explainer of our most brilliant modern American poet, Hart Crane: additional proof to me that he was an A-1 spotter of poetic horseflesh and knew as I knew that Milt belonged in the very first brigade. It was a vindication from an unexpected source in an unexpected place—the boozy giggles of women sexing the air, the sun darkening over Slough Pond and the twilight breeze swirling Tate's thin hair as he sharply spoke of Klonsky's analysis of Marvell's "The Garden" above the drone of sixty summer-hedonists—if any vindication was needed of what I always knew to be true of Klonsky and an answer to the skeptical or jealous cracks that I sometimes heard about Milt in the angry boil of New York intellectual-literary life.

As I got to know Klonsky better in the beginning 1945–1947 period—and don't forget the relationship has gone on for fifteen years—certain things I had barely sensed at the start became more pronounced. He was much hipper than I was, a word and attitude just feeling its way toward the light at that time but true just the same. From the age of fourteen on he had known pot-smokers, painters, swinging young musicians, fast-moving operators of one kind or another, and they helped leather his young skin and sleek his ideas. I saw that Milt combined the outward toughness of the streets—specifically, the teeming unprivate be-quick-witted-or-be-suckered streets of the Bronx and later Brooklyn—with a fine, mystical, extraordinarily sophisticated mind. Pure as a star fathoms deep inside his wickedly complex mental machinery, he came on with a veteran's knowing-ness, the bite to his thoughts was as stinging as iodine, he had been taught and schooled and skilled in New York's ultramodern lifeshop and the techniques of irony, double-meaning, deception, feint, twist, turn, were as native to him as the alleys he had dodged down as a metropolitan kid. Klonsky was ancient stuff in comparison to my Tom Wolfean green exuberance and naivete; not only had the concrete streets and the tricky heels that scarred them toughened and compressed my friend's outlook—and these streets, these New York forms were long to glow in Klonsky's mind as materials for a brilliant poetic vision—but his mind had also been sharpened and seasoned by personal acquaintance at a very early age with extremely brainy Jewish radical-intellectuals (one or both of his parents was socialist) and later on with such avantgarde wheels as W.H. Auden, Tate, Delmore Schwartz, Marianne Moore, etc. All of this plus his reading (the Bible, Milton, Shakespeare, in addition to the contemporary mind-punishers I listed before, literally every literary landmark you can think of plus the most difficult philosophers with special loving attention to metaphysicians) had submerged him much more deeply and gravely into adult life than myself. Recognition of this soon overwhelmed me, I was diminished intellectually to the size of a dime, and naturally I got on board this new brain-train as soon as I could and forced myself to read many of the same books—even though they didn't particularly rock me in many cases—and tried to expand my own broad but essentially nearby tastes.

You see, I had always thought I was going to be a novelist (from about fifteen on), not a philosopher, not a poet, not an omniscient intellectual type who does graduate work here and Marxes it up there and Freuds everywhere and achieves passing livingroom glory while making his genuine bread working for some committee. My interest was keen and insatiable for modern narrative of all kinds and I particularly dug the American scene (my scene!) and gobbled up novels by the shelf-full from Dreiser and Edith Wharton to the present. I was and still am in love with the American experience, which I identified with myself, my life, and Klonsky's more exquisite kicks with the English metaphysical and French symbolist poets was at first totally alien to me—impressive but distant. But I plugged through the new books and new thoughts with Milt as my grudging guide and tightlipped teacher (he was more consumed by his own vision than in wanting the ego-boost of imposing his thoughts on me, it was I who plucked this whole self-educational scheme out of him), always trying to relate this new dimension of literary experience to my maddened interest in the naturalistic, seeable, graspable, "real" contemporary U.S. world that excited all the glands within me. Even at the time that my idolatry of Milt was at its highest I never had any doubt about giving up my own way of writing or trying to become a poet, or doing anything to resist the savage thrills that *only* the present-tense U.S. scene was able to give me as writer and person. I was pliable and appreciative of ways of looking at life other than my own but central to my being was my own destiny as a writer, even at the cost of the pain I once thought I could shed with Milt's mighty formula; Klonsky understood and had faith in this daemon of my own and so was able to give me with unaccustomed straightforwardness the overflow of his closely-guarded inner thoughts. Without a doubt he thought I often suffered from what skin-divers call "rhapsody of the deep" right here on land, but he respected this drive and need of my own, I could tell this with certainty from the beginning.

By asking many questions—the ancient device of the novelist-type, who is usually bugged as sheer human with a mammoth curiosity—I sucked in and pieced together the background of Milt's life for very personal basic reasons. Primary was the whole Jewish problem which used to murder me blind both as man and writer; I know from experience that my swinging non-Jewish friends, occasional girlfriends, even detractors, feel this whole Jew business comes out of left field, is a private obsession, in today's new interscrewing world where the name and rank you carry means nothing compared to what you can lay down.

But I would lie to myself and to you if I said that my life has not been conditioned by my enormous wrestling with this historical mountain on my back; by this I simply mean that when I set out to hurl myself into the America I loved through my imagination, as a would-be novelist, it would always come to me in the black of the soul that perhaps I was trying to run out on my fate or responsibility as a *Juden*, that maybe I was trying to embrace so fully the American cosmos in order to wipe out the "Oy vey" self-sneeringness, awfulness, shameness, strangeness, which had vomited all over my psyche after I got my first dose of lipsmacking anti-kike contempt. I only knew the curse of the Yiddish tag not the joy (if any exists—O send me the word, Lord!), because having been orphaned, bounced from home to home, taught no heritage except what I learned in newspapers, Hitler-raving newsreels, tough-guy U.S. fiction and chalk-scrawls in the street I couldn't imagine any balm for this filthy trick played on me. I had only crawling shame and no pride whatsoever in being Jewish, had my beak clipped at age seventeen (a pioneering practice then among Jews with loot and now a widespread staple in every self-respecting, face-hating Jewish suburb), had turned my back and ear on the Yiddish spoken at my Grandma's, refused a bar mitzvah out of contempt, bawled my eyes red a 100 times for having been "chosen"—you can have it, baby, yes you Liz Taylor and you Sammy Davis!—and during the age seventeen to twenty-one period had more than once pretended I was a clean-cut (you should see the way even mature Jews admire that word, you justly peed-off ex-White Protestant dissenters!) gentile boy. I know I was driven into psychiatry like so many young American Jews by my inability to handle this hell-coal of identity, but I found—or was in the process of finding out during this time when I met Klonsky—that psychiatry could not magically change who you were or at least who *I* was. What almost sobbed in me was the obsessive thought that I would never be able to participate completely, unself-consciously, naturally, in this great expanse of land and myth over here, that the unwanted Yiddle brand would label me forever a lousy outsider in the eyes of my countrymen, that I who loved America would be prevented always from truly knowing my love and therefore being able to sing her tremendous raucous song with word-pictures I had been minting in my imagination since 1939. What many critics and readers have not yet understood is that the kid who wanted to be an American novelist in 1938 or 1939 wanted to be an *explorer*, his imagination had been whetted crazily by the explorations of Lewis, Dreiser, Wolfe, Faulkner, Anderson, Hemingway, Steinbeck into the *experience* of the vast land, the entire unconscious meaning and drive of the American novel at that time was that it was uncovering—writer by writer by writer—the pricelessly real human scene that lay buried to all but the new prose-men who were truly surveying the continent for the first time. You must be able to see how this could fire the particular kind of imagination it took to want to be one of the new American novelist-explorers, how the potential novelist was smitten with the argot, color, dynamism, pace, smell, big-truck feel of the continent—and how the young hebe who had drunk all of this starspangled juice into his veins and wanted to live it and be it would burn triply because he felt in moments of acutest doubt that he could never legitimately be *of* it. Here I was consumed by the voice and landscape and (be truthful!) *romance* of roaring-drunk modern America—and, believe me, this is what has motivated your major U.S. "realistic" novelists of our period, the fact that their imaginations or fantasy-lives saw actual beauty and meaning in the giant, seemingly meaningless, even ugly reality of our daily life here—and I felt that because I was that Christ-killing, communistic, hand-talking, loan-sharking, ikey-kikey walking toilet known as Jew (the cultural reasons for this hatred and contempt were unimportant: bigotry, shmigotry, who cared what the thousand traceable causes were when the less-than-human reality was all that counted!), I would be forever shut out of this violent paradise. I got down in my psyche and impotently prayed to be different, I cursed the walls of my flesh for freezing me into a living advertisement of what seemed to disgust the majority of Americans (yes, you ancient Jews forgive me and you 1960 U.S. umpires call it as you see it!) and worst of all I felt I had been kidding the heart out of myself in thinking I could justly write of the broad America. What real right did I have to sing its wop-lifted steel or paint its electric-eyed face or show the golden music in the fresh-corn voice of a midwestern drum majorette as if I were a downhome Wolfe or Whitman or my beloved Dreiser? Wasn't I just another Walter Winchell–type Jew who wrapped himself in the flag precisely because he was shivering out in the fucking cold? These were awful question marks that perforated my being and I desperately suspended final answers as I writhed around hunting for ways out of my psychic trap.

Therefore when I met Milt, dug him, watched the way he handled his Jewishness it was as if I had a thousand eyes that literally ferreted into his being and background in order to try and pluck out his secret for myself. By this I mean that he didn't seem to operate under the sense of Yiddish shame and inferiority that crippled not only myself but so many of the middle-class Jewish kids who came from roughly my own uptown environment. I later found out that Klonsky was gravely concerned with his heritage, had backed it up and fortified it with his reading in the Bible and with the thoughts of innumerable Jewish mystics from antiquity to the present, but in the sheerly secular everyday world of street and eat and movie-going jazz-listening he was not bugged in the same way I was. He acted like a man, not someone castrated and squirming because of their racial unease, and the more I thought about the unconscious pride and soldierliness he showed in ordinary life the more I was disgusted by my own sliced roots. Each of us typified to me two different kinds of big-city Jewish boy. I noticed that Milt and several of the other Brooklyn (for that's where he spent most of his formative years) Jewish intellectuals on the Village scene were much more ballsy and less superficially "sensitive"—especially about the Yiddle theme—than the Central Park West Jewish boys in whose aura and style I was formed. This observation bit deep into my own personal hangup and I had to trace it out in my mind with almost fanatical exactitude in order to try and free myself of the knife of self-inflicted pain which I plunged repeatedly into my being.

In case you don't know the snob setup or social hierarchy of New York Jewish life it was always assumed in the environment that clamped its teeth into my youthful jelly that life-successful Jews would live comfortably in fashionable Manhattan (before the suburb kick became as significant as it is today) while their social and financial inferiors would crawl it out in the Bronx or Brooklyn. I had been money-sheltered before my parents died on me as a 10-year-old, had gone to the usual Indian-name summer camp in Maine and later to a Jewish prep school in Harrison, New York; and because of insulated experience I had always thought—like practically all the kids from my background, which in New York was the Central Park West-West End Avenue area from the 60's to the 90's but could just as well have been Jamaica Plain or Newton Center outside of Boston, or South Orange in New Jersey, or Squirrel Hill in Pittsburgh, any of the well-hedged Jewish communities strung throughout the country—that Bronx and Brooklyn Jews were dirty, loud, vulgar, *mockyish*, all the things their upper-middle-class brethren tried to put behind them. ("White Jews," I once heard a half-joking lady hipster who had nervoused her way out of the Lower East Side swarm say about my relatives when she met me in their West 86th St., 20-story fortress.) But I found when I hit the Village in the early 1940s—and had it pounded home to me in the case of Klonsky—that the young Jewish swingers who had gone to CCNY or Brooklyn College (where Milt went before doing graduate work at Columbia) were on the whole much smarter, shrewder, wiser-neurotic, startlingly at home with abstract thought—carrying the real nail-chewed freight of life, ye manicured Temple Emanu-El solace-salesmen!—than their crewcut counterparts who had made it at Princeton or Harvard or the University of Pennsylvania. Even as I write this I can remember as if a closet had burst open the innumerable college-type fantasies that held middle- and upper-middle-class Jewish teenagers in thrall during highschool, the Yale banners on the wall, the clothes selected with a serious *Esquire* eye, the fraternity dreams (passionately acted out in the mind), the whole banging joy of "going to school out of town." You see we were Americanized first, we Jews with money, and everything American was greedily eaten into our lifestreams until we literally pissed style, detail, USA-knowhow—jesus, how we West 86th St. F. Seymour Fitzgeraldbergs modeled ourselves on the dukely gentiles who had set the cool out-of-town university style!

It came to me as I watched Klonsky and later a dozen more Brooklyn and Bronx hipsters dealing-and-wheeling their way to dominance on the Village scene—and I truly mean dominance, with ass, with prestige, with man-to-man and man-to-chick superiority which spoke for itself—that we who had come from all the uptowns and suburbs across the land had originally weakened our manhood in order to "get in," to be white Anglo-Saxon imitations, and we bled so much more easily and bitterly than these mental street-fighters who had been nourished on drives more exciting than getting into Yale. Compared to the J-boys my own age who had Ivy Leagued-it or gone to any of the second-rate rich boy's schools out of town—yes my old Pi Lambda Phi buddies! the football game and the Saturday night big-name-band dance, the amateurish quarter-screw with the New Rochelle import in the back seat of the Chrysler convertible, the grotesque wasted dribble of Jack Daniels (at $7.30 a bottle!) along the white oxford button-down shirt collar, the crushed orchid still pinned on the shoulder of Miss Fay Noren (formerly Nussbaum)'s formal as she vomits in the approved, glamorous, God-it-was-a-wild-weekend style—compared to that frantic and no-where ritual I found many more new ideas and much more mental determination and stature in these Brooklyn-Bronx-Avenue A cats who had slitted their contemptuous way past a cornball Exeter-type smoothness to a real subway-grasp of contemporary reality. These unashamed (because they couldn't help it), often bitterly slanted and harsh-talking Jewish boys knew chicks without Cole Porter romanticization and could throw a mature lay in the sunlight as well as the Scotch-dripping hi-fied dark—Klonsky himself made 16-year-old time under the boardwalks of Coney Island and Brighton Beach—knew the tough classics instead of the latest Salinger or Hemingway or Graham Greene confection, knew the sharp outlines and brick anatomy of human life in the twentieth (and last! it often seemed) century instead of some wistful-schmaltzy sentimentalization of it. I found this observation to hold true time and again as I struggled with my own Yiddish self-consciousness: namely that I was more drawn mentally and emotionally to Jews with poorish, boorish, crude, rude, radical, intellectually-sharpshooting backgrounds than to those custom-tailored kinsmen of mine who rumbaed feverishly above the scene in some chic dream of "good living" on one side of Central Park or the other.

Getting back to Milt he came from roughly the kind of environment I once put down, growing up in the Brighton Beach section of Brooklyn, and as I said looking on first glance to my uptown-snobbed eyes like a hood or con-man—and containing in that vault about his eyes what seemed to me practically the fucking scroll of English literature and the high peaks of Western thought. It was a fascinating, dangerous, aggressive combination of opposites back in medieval 1945 when I first fell in with Klonsky; having a precedent in certain modern Parisian poets fathered by Baudelaire and Rimbaud, although I didn't know it at the time, and now of course much more prevalent on the beat or hipster scene where you can't move 10 blocks in New York or Frisco or New Orleans without seeing rough hewn or furtive or unshaven guys (and girl equivalents) who will stun the pants off you by their hip immediacy of perception—"Lightning to read by, yeah!" a strange cat muttered to me at the corner of University and 9th Street three days ago while we were waiting for the traffic light to break and the summer sky rumbled forth a few choice flares—who will quote Melville out of the side of their lip-chewed mouths, smoke pot, dig Monk, get a genuine big charge out of de Kooning's paintings and the rest. Klonsky in other words was a New Style, a new type of literary-man to my square, collegiate, ultraromantic eyes when I first felt his hooded devil-gaze back there in the courtyard of 224 Sullivan Street, and even now in 1960 that the cut of his angle to life no longer draws so much blood from others and his counterparts stylistically speaking have popped up everywhere, I still see him as the integrator of the once-opposites of toughness vs. literacy, snarl vs. beauty, making-out vs. delicacy—use the entire churchly nineteenth-century vocabulary and reverse it and you'll understand me—but at a deeper level than when he first undermined my corny middle-class images of taste and heroism.

With time, these truly crazy last 15 years, this original fascination of mine with Klonsky's surface uniqueness slowly shed itself for the deeper qualities that resided within the man. Again and again—in his apartment on Sullivan Street, then Morton Street, now West 4th Street, or at a party or on the street or in a tense jam with any of the hotheaded intellectuals and hipsters or wild "Fuck you!"–screaming chicks whom we knew in common—I was struck by the man's Roman courage, independence and always that profound sense of measuring the worth of objects and words without being carried away or yet losing the jaguar-spring of his vitality. He was durable, I realized through that decade-and-a-half when we'd be grooving after a great pot night and join together like old buddies or then again when we'd be formal, icy and estranged because one had trod on the other's being. Yes durable, as well put together as the finest timepiece and mentally as lean and muscular as an athlete. But beyond his wiremesh diaphragm, that tight sifting brain that could weed out falsehood and rhetoric with the unerring instinct of a terrier and make him the equal of any scientist or businessman I had ever met in his sheer assessment of reality, lay that brilliant poetic instrument-panel of a mind which created before one's eyes idea-designs and thought-organizations that had no precedent. Klonsky, as I've said, was not a Romantic poet or man, his first true loves had been the metaphysical poet-hipsters of the seventeenth century like Donne and Marvell, and he scorned like a war veteran a lyricism that was not contained in an idea like tit in brassiere. But this very sense of *control* gave added thrust to his utterances, there was no waste, and when you were walking or jiving with him and heard him throw out this verbal steel that his mind manufactured in its ceaseless Pittsburgh foundry you were aced, man, it went through you like a blade, its concentrated truth created a standard from which you could no more squirm or dodge than JC from his cross. "It is impossible to speak the truth so as to be understood without being believed," said Blake or Zola and it was true of Milt—by the route of his imagination he seized on the inevitable and it left your heart numb as he tore down the supports of the world and rebuilt it by the cunning and inspiration of his vision. I am ashamed now, in the hour of showdown, that I can remember few of his exact quotes, that the years and the electric shock treatments I had to be slugged with during my season of so-called flip have knocked out the lines that drilled me to the core, even if I can't produce exact evidence like a lawyer I know that the reality has to seep through to you, that I have grasped and will grasp enough high moments of the extraordinariness of Milt to build an arch of testimony if not the graven tablet of profundity that his contribution calls for.

Klonsky as I watched him through the years was a man who bore a heavy burden—heavier than mine and my friends.' In the midst of the innumerable endless intellectual discussions, raving fights that all of us hip young New York writers would have either at Isaac Rosenfeld's pad or Herbie Poster's when he was living with the now-Evelyn Murray—the yelling, sharp, sometimes hysterical bomb-throwing that would put a livingroom on fire with the Russian-Yiddish intensity that flamed in each of our overbearing egos—Klonsky would always have the tragic forbearance of a wiseman at least 120 years older than the rest of us. The whole feeling was eerie because not only was he younger than the older writers who threw their whole weight of emotional knottedness into the fray, he was grooving, he was fucking more, he was in their eyes the jazzy kid with a chick under each arm, there was nothing in the slightest Lionel Trillingish about him, it didn't seem to fit that he could be a goddamn saint when he had all this going for him! And yet by precept, by example, by knowing when to button his lip and when to stiffen up like Little Caesar his invisible mental and spiritual metronome dominated those living rooms of 15 years ago and set the beat that got into the very balls of all of us who were on that scene. Why, this cool mother was effortlessly putting us down at our own great-writer-geniusy trade and reducing to mere cartoons our private dreams of storming the turf of Joyce and Yeats and all that jive, there was too much perfection even in his apt silences for the ambitious blood to tolerate! And yet I always thought as I made my way home after a night watching Milt in action and then watching him abruptly cut out of a smokefilled, Trotskyish-type livingroom for *real* action—while the rest of us brainy cripples sat on and on reshaping the world in words until the words became a meaningless sexless hum in our tired ears and on our aching mouths— that his friends and mine had no idea of the extent and depth at which he lived and which allowed him such wisdom, guts, nerve, such jet-flight above our shrinking little empires of personal ego and pride. If ever there was a cat *alone*, not melodramatically, sobbingly, literarily, showily, but ice-locked in a moonscape beyond our knowledge and performance it was Milt—I thought that and think it still. "I once thought I was the messiah," he told me half-ironically once in 1950 while we were walking around the Circle in Washington Square, and even though his voice had its special irony-dripping tone there was enough truth in it to bring one up short. Suppose it was true? I thought, suppose I was indeed hanging out and digging the new crop of Washington Square chicks with the Son of God come down again and I was one of the new apostles? I got the mortal shivers as I heard Milt bite out his words that day because I knew how different he was from the other highbrow writers I shmoozed with along the 8th Street route or at parties, there was an intangible and humbling mystery about his goddamn perfection, he literally *could* be a new swinging Christ whose holy knowledge was concealed by street-crust because of blushing shame at his immortal responsibility. I realize how nutty this can seem if I say it cold and factually now, and yet you must understand that Klonsky's entire orientation was metaphysical, religious, "the poet must think with nothing less than the mind of God" he once told me, and all of this was handled by him without an ounce of personal display or the gross egotism that would normally make you suspicious of someone's coming on in a superpretentious way. Milt had this unswerving chastity or purity of intellect which always gave "soul" to his most casual observations—gave character, actuality, reality, none of the wordy bullshit that big-mouthed writers so easily fall into—and it always took the edge off his metropolitan wiseguyism, even when the latter unwittingly burned its way into the blisters and soft spots that most of us were helplessly studded with. Once you realized the atonal scale he played on it came like the rush of the sun that there was no deceit in this strange man. He *never* whored to an audience, chicks excepted, no matter what the stakes or the occasion; never dimpled his speech, unbuttoned himself, apologized, retreated, or dodged the implications of words or action. He was not above lying with foxiness for a specific goal or remaining stonily silent. But when he spoke he said what he had to say with clarity and economy, he shot down the target of his thought with the swiftness and proportionateness of an arrow, not with sadism, psychological peculiarities (saying one thing and meaning another) or any of the extracurricular gimmicks that even the keenest people we know dress their talk with. What it all boiled down to was that of all the writers of my own generation whom I had the opportunity to meet, talk with, buddy with, clash with or even just appreciate through their work—and this includes Mailer, Kerouac, Ginsberg, Bill Goyen, Broyard, Brossard, Jim Jones, Baldwin, all the 35-to-40 hotshots who are blowing my generation's sound in print—Milt to me was always pre-eminent, the Number One boy country-wide, the living, human, ultrahuman soul with by far the greatest potential and a man I loved in an unqualified and admiring sense until for the fulfillment of my own personality and "career" I had to assert my own independence and almost break with him along the way. But that comes later.

4

In the climate we all make it in, the age of suspicion, put-down, sneer, needle, it's almost inevitable that a swinging person is going to probe himself for the hidden motivations in the way he acts, makes his little scenes. Introspection is

the private playground of every brain around, there's no escaping it, and especially in New York where psychiatry has gotten such an incredible play is there a
used condom of doubt that drags down every full-hearted gesture into the subway
mire of the psyche's triple-dealing. Face it, man—nothing is safe in our world
from the meanest interpretation, nothing is pure or uncomplex, nothing but
nothing escapes from the enlarged vocabulary of analysis that our quick and
unhappy minds grind out for sheer dissonant sport. Therefore when I once spoke
admiringly of Klonsky to an outspoken chick painter who was a friend of mine
she said that it sounded like a "faggot scene" to her and rightly or wrongly I was
thrown for a skipped-beat loss by this interpretation. I tried to explain to her that
as a writer, a guy fanatically engrossed (at that time) and even dedicated to the
entire literary pursuit, I was especially appreciative of Milt because his language
and thought—his articulation of the very cosmos, as I heard it—were the rarest I
had ever run into. She said this was a rationalization, that I loved the man
himself in an under-the-sheets, fruity, cock-twining way and used the other as a
covering for this love. I cut it off there in a fiery inner rage and didn't try to argue
my way through her thorns and up the hill to the mountaintop I knew was there;
but afterwards, when I was alone, I was obviously forced in the privacy of my
mind to try and cope with this hurting surgery into my masculine pride and
come up with an answer as tough as the truth. If it were genuine faggotry I would
have to concede it because I turned myself inside out in those days in my slavery
to truth, my pride was more invested in what I thought was reality than in
stooping to save face. You must keep in mind that I had wanted to be a "great
writer" and not a star in a Sutton Place living room—listen to the innocence of a
young stud's choices!—and I would have defiantly confessed to murder let alone
cocksucking if I truly thought that Ibsen and Tolstoy and the rest of the heavenly
lions would approve. My moral snobbery was pinned high to courage and
honesty, and even though I felt fear and shame at my weaknesses and vul-
nerabilities I would at that time hurl them into society itself, blurt them right out
rather than hide them even though it meant sweating through the follow-up
cycle of anxiety because I felt it was necessary to upholding the fearless hero-
writer's role as I imagined it. But I realized when I came down and thought
coolly that I wasn't alone in loving Klonsky, and this helped undo the faggot knot
which this chick had glibly twisted around me. I had seen the same quality of
love for Milt in Connie, in Anatole Broyard, in various girls whom Milt had
been making it with, and I finally came to the conclusion that the human
qualities which inspire love resided within him—quite apart from me. This was
not physical love on my part (which I suppose is the way the defensive modern
cat immediately thinks when someone calls him on his *masculinity*, so bugged
are we by what bad or embarrassing thing of ours might be showing to the world).
But if it were physical—and I've had only one actual, lowdown homosexual bout
in a long if erratic apprenticeship to flesh—I would have felt forced, as I've said,
to own up to it and pay my dues.

Yet this was not Klonsky's kick (so far as I had ever known) nor mine, and the love I and others had for him came in awed response to the unique and often seemingly divine beauty of his mind and soul. I began to understand the deeper I thought about it that Klonsky had become a sort of underground institution in Village and New York literary life and that my close relationship with him was only one of a number he had with other eager-beaver young strivers (guys and girls both) who came nuzzling close to the shrine to lap up this supernal insight that my friend effortlessly gave out. This realization in no way lessened my appreciation or made me jealous—and I wasn't above such emotions, like yourself—because I felt from the beginning with Milt that I was in the presence of a man who had really major gifts; comparable in potentiality to a Sigmund Freud or a Joyce or an Einstein and I'm not laying it on even a sixteenth-of-an-inch, and that these ultimately belonged to the world rather than to any single needy individual who latched close to him. Yet it's true that I thought of him as my special buddy and winced when his interest in me wasn't returned with the love and respect—or was it more truly naked selfishness, my brutal wanting to suck his brain dry?—that I poured onto him. (I remember once in 1955 how I fidgeted all afternoon waiting to get Milt's judgment on a book review of mine on Thomas Wolfe's letters that had been turned down by the *Hudson Review* and how when I came into his apartment on Morton Street to get the trusted come-at-4 P.M. word he was sitting with three high hipsters talking of nooky and had forgotten to read my piece and how I grabbed it with a frozen smile on my face and did the cold exit routine.) But even then, smarting from this indifference in my own thinskinned way, I knew in my core that Klonsky could belong to no one person, that it demeaned his being for me or anyone to try and play footsy with it in some trueblue boy-scout dream of blood-brother friendship, that he had to swing where all his engines took him and fly right through our hearts and love if need be because he was surveying one *wild* fucking blue. Or so I thought—and still think.

As I watched Milton closely during the years of our thickest friendship I saw him silently groaning under the blackest weights of anyone I knew. His loneliness had been trebled by his sense of responsibility, the heavyweight pillar of his imagination stood upright in a galactic night all its own without any of the consolations that lesser dreamers could comfort themselves with. As a man as well as a poet-mind Klonsky had privately dared, challenged and even whipped by the might of his ideas the best figures of his time—to hear him speak of Auden, Yeats, Joyce, Kafka, Beckett, was to hear an equal, a Shelley plain, and the maturity of his comments swept away the champagne bubbles of romance that I sprayed on literature and revealed the steel soul of the cat I championed in all its mortal gravity. There could be no way out for him except by doing work of the same acknowledged stature, he had committed himself by word and action to the league of the "immortals" and he was self-condemned to the isolation and only half-thereness that "immortality" demands of men and women who live in time. There was no childish competitiveness on the part of Klonsky vis-à-vis these stern figures, it was not to test himself in the ring of literature that he braved or broke the standards erected by these twentieth-century culture heroes (like my friend Mailer, who puts courage above reality) but rather it was because he had truly been born with a special line hooked into the inner switchboard of existence, was haunted by what he heard—"Time is a sin!" he once burst out to me in that extraordinary way that made abstract concepts real as your hand—like a religious Poe and possessed a *spiritual* life so grave and proportionate that only the superbest adult utterance could do it justice.

It was precisely by virtue of this deeper and finer insight that Milt was alone, untouchable after all was said or done, a hip Moses locked on his own Sinai who had to bring those commandments down to the terra (as the good Lord Buckley calls it) via his typewriter or the whole thing, life itself, his life in particular, all things that have meaning and value, would be just one big "hipe" (fake), to use a word he had picked up off the snarling cement of the big town. I saw him embattled in this way, quiet about the enormous confrontation that awaited him in literature, the sleek ships of thought gliding ceaselessly in his mind beneath the controlled surface he showed to the outside world. Those of us who loved and admired him—Anatole Broyard and myself, Delmore Schwartz before he went totally into his paranoid bag, to name only three among two dozen who had the literary sensitivity to appreciate what a great horseman into the unknown this dark villain could be—expected tremendous things of our boy and I'm sure he did of himself, very justly. But the pressure on the guy was fierce, always present though unspoken, and I in particular bugged him almost daily about what he was working on and always got an almost virginal, evasive answer—as if I were trying to rape him of his treasure. Unlike the rest of us self-infatuated literary giants on the downtown scene Milt never spoke about his work or inmost thoughts in public, would've bled internally rather than use the work-bit as a gambit at parties, didn't once spill his guts for a momentary psychological or cunt triumph (although it's conceivable and understandable to me that in the night-stillness of his apartment he used his literary weapon to awe down a skirt and get at the morsel). He carried the undissolvable lump of his being intact wherever he went, the boil never broke, he was never wet or rhetorical or easy in any way towards himself or others and I knew from the small-talk of mutual friends of ours that he excited the same sort of curiosity in others as to what he was carrying around in that locked safe-deposit box.

But he was in heavy trouble—had been since the day I first met him although I didn't know it until 10 years later—and it was this that he knew before the rest of us I am now convinced. Geared to poetry, having a potentially mighty and sure poetic vision that had been reinforced by the most intensive reading and chanting (he was no closet poet, when we were high he raised his voice to the reach of his mind and the blind world around me became ignited with light and blessed mental music!). Milt nevertheless was so perfectionist and self-critical that he refused to risk himself upon the page until he could bring forth a cathedral work. He had let trickle out a few poems in the ultraclassy literary mags since the age of 19, but these—subtle, tricky, indirect stabs at his great target which to my mind were not fully committed and were deliberately soaked in the "inwit" and chinese-box effects he knew so brilliantly from his intellectual immersion in seventeenth-century English verse—weren't the major part of his output. Only his own head was the private spectator at his greatest work, witnessing and ultimately rejecting the unfinished feats of poetry that his creative monster threw up for inspection. Instead, to make bread, to keep writing until he congealed sufficiently unto himself to attempt his extraordinary poetic bid, he wrote "excellent" prose for *Commentary* and one or two other academic highbrow outfits—prose on the Village, Brighton Beach, money-changing in the Paris ghetto (he had met the all-time Yiddish caricature there in a hook-nosed beret during six or seven months spent abroad), etc. This prose was and is fine of its kind, superior in its choice of language and gravity but not quite the kind of stunning and grand expression I had expected of him. In the area of prose—which in a kind of rough simple way I always separated from poetry—I had strong self-confidence and a definite point of view, since I had been writing and publishing sentences from my second year in high school on. When Klonsky invaded my terrain so to speak, splashed around in the same common trough of communication in which I felt myself an easy and knowing pro, I tried to see the literary greatness that I knew to be in the man glow through but found myself carping because he was doing his work in the same medium that had always been swimming-water to me. I suspended judgment, always waiting for the time when he would switch to his native poetic vision or what I conceived as such. But it came only haltingly, in droplets, and it was then that I slowly understood that the enormous expectations we lovers had of him plus his own terrible high standards—"Klonsky was a polished poet at 17," Anatole Broyard once told me with something close to awe, which I well understood because Broyard meant precociously adult, aware, responsible, heavyweight as well as polished—had made him fearful that he might never bring off what he seemed fated by his unique combination of brains and soul to do.

1960

7.
The Kerouac Legacy

I met Kerouac only twice, both for brief periods of not more than 15 minutes, and communication between us was abrupt and unreal. What I wrote about the man and writer was the result of feeling, experience and legwork, not friendship. The hippies-Yippies have replaced the beats today, but they are the logical and expanded second wave; when their history is written it will all point back unerringly to the homemade anarchistic breakthrough of the Beat Generation— the dropouts, communes, drugs, beards, hair, handcrafts, meditation, etc. I owe my own turn-on as a writer who had been coldshouldered by my quasi-academic peers of the Cerebral Generation to the revivifying power of the beats and I can testify in court if need be to the actuality of the beat messianic excitement. Behind it, in my judgment, was the principal catalytic figure of Kerouac; today Ginsberg and Burroughs get a much bigger and better press and are highly respected by the university intellectuals whereas Kerouac is regarded very fishily as a simple-minded athletic type run amok. It might even be that his final value will have been primarily inspirational: but if this is so, it was extensive beyond current awareness and I am enormously glad that I sweated my way through this overlong and slightly obsessive piece, even incurring Kerouac's oblique anger (via letter) at the less flattering questions I raised about the future of his work. Both of us were in a touchy situation because my article served as the introduction to Desolation Angels (1965) when his reputation in New York was charred and uncertain after mere vogue-followers had deserted for yet a new substitute penis in the search for thrills. Jan Cremer, post-beat, pre-Provo, cockeyed kid and terrifyingly cool manipulator of his own destiny, stands astride the two very separate possibilities of pop celebrity and uniquely independent writer-painter. He would like to be a fantasy figure, "a world idol" as he puts it looking you right in the eye without a smile, a rough combination of Bobby Kennedy and Yevtushenko and Cassius Clay (as he told me in 1966—see how quickly his images have become ghosts!); his idea of selfdivinity can drive you crazy; and yet I admire both his unusual poise and his courage but have no certainty about which direction he will take. My hunch is that he will be determined by circumstances and therefore become an

88

avantgarde showbusiness symptom of his time rather than the disturbing prophet I truly feel in him. It is almost an arrow pointing the way our times have changed that my own involvements, and those of our shattered American world, have developed in the last decade from Jack Kerouac (who returned to womblike Lowell, Massachusetts, and shucked off every relationship with his own Beat Generation) to Eldridge Cleaver and Abbie Hoffman. Jan Cremer fascinates me because he made a unique individual play out of what would later become hippie materials, cashing in on the style of the young culture outlaws who are now a new world-class, but Cleaver and Hoffman have each in their own way joined the Youth Revolution to socialist-anarchist motors that have taken them into the crumbling center of America. They are leaders—a powerful word on the New Left these days—and young men and women stand behind their words with action. Beats, Provos, Black Panthers, Yippies: what strange names for literature but then what else is literature right now but the eruption of the outraged spirit in language? Dig it while I give and take with these men who project to me more than themselves, who summon up a new quality of experience that grips me and causes me to work out on the most basic level of my own life.

All of us with nerve have played God on occasion, but when was the last time you created a generation? Two weeks ago maybe? Or instead did you just rush to your psychiatrist and plead with him to cool you down because you were scared of thinking such fantastic-sick-delusory-taboo-grandiose thoughts? The latter seems more reasonable if less glamorous; I've chickened out the same way.

But Jack Kerouac singlehandedly created the Beat Generation. Although Allen Ginsberg, Gregory Corso and William Burroughs brought their separate and cumulative "madness" to the yeasty phenomenon of the BG (and you will find them in *Desolation Angels* under the names of Irwin Garden, Raphael Urso and Bull Hubbard), it was Kerouac who was the Unifying Principle by virtue of a unique combination of elements. A little boy tucked into the frame of a resourceful and independent man, a scholarly Christian-mystic-Buddhist who dug Charlie Parker and Miles Davis and ice-cream, a sentimental, apolitical American smalltowner who nevertheless meditated on the universe itself like Thoreau before him, Jack Kerouac threw a loop over an area of experience that had previously been disunited and gave it meaning and continuity. The significant thing about Kerouac's creation of the Beat Generation, what made it valid and spontaneous enough to leave a lasting wrinkle on history and memorialize his name, was that there was nothing calculated or phony about the triumph of his style. He and his friends in the mid to late 50s, before and while the beat flame was at its hottest, were merely living harder and more extensively than any of their articulate American counterparts. One of the minor characters in *Angels*, an Asian Studies teacher out on the Coast, says at an outdoor party that the core of Buddhism is simply "knowing as many different people as you can," and certainly this distinguished Kerouac and his boys with a bang.

They zoomed around this and other countries (San Francisco, Mexico City, Tangier, Paris, London, back to New York, out to Denver, yeah!) with a speed, spirit and fierce enthusiasm "to dig everything" that ridiculed the self-protective ploys engaged in by the majority of young American writers at the time. This is not to say that Kerouac, Ginsberg, Corso and Burroughs didn't have individual equals and perhaps even superiors among their homegrown literary brothers; men like Salinger, Robert Lowell, Mailer, Joseph Heller, James Jones, Styron, Baldwin, etc., were beholden to no one in their ambition and thrust of individual points of view, but that is exactly what each remained—individual. The beats, on the other hand, and Jack Kerouac in particular, evolved a *community* among themselves that included and respected individual rocketry but nevertheless tried to orchestrate it with the needs of a group; the group or the gang, like society in miniature, was at least as important as its most glittering stars—in fact you might say it was a constellation of stars who swung in the same orbit and gave mutual light—and this differentiated the beat invasion of our literature from the work of unrelated individuals conducting solo flights that had little in common.

It can be argued that the practice of art is a crucial individual effort reserved for adults and that the beats brought a streetgang cop-fear and incestuousness into their magazines, poetry and prose that barred the door against reality and turned craft into an orgy of self-justification. As time recedes from the high point of the Beat Generation spree, roughly 1957–1961, such a perspectivelike approach seems fairly sane and reasonable; from our present distance much of the beat racket and messianic activity can look like a psychotics' picnic spiked with bombersized dexies. Now that the BG has broken up—and it has become dispersed less than 10 years after its truly spontaneous eruption, with its members for the most part going their separate existential ways—a lot of the dizzy excitement of the earlier period (recorded in *Desolation Angels* and in most of Kerouac's novels since *On the Road*) can be seen as exaggerated, hysterical, foolish and held together with a postadolescent red ribbon that will cause some of its early apostles to giggle with embarrassment as the rugged road of age and arthritis overtakes them.

But there was much more to the beats, and to Kerouac himself, than a list of excesses, "worship of primitivism" (a sniffy phrase introduced by the critic Norman Podhoretz), crazy lurches from North Beach to the Village, a go-go-go jazzedup movie that when viewed with moral self-righteousness can seem like a cute little benzedream of anarchy come true. This more or less cliched picture, especially when contrasted with the "Dare I eat a peach?" self-consciousness practiced in both the universities and the influential big-little magazines like the *Partisan* and *Kenyon Reviews*, was however a real part of a beat insurrection; they were in revolt against a prevailing cerebral-formalist temper that had shut them out of literary existence, as it had hundreds of other young writers in the America of the late 40s and 50s, and the ton of experience and imagery that had been suppressed by the critical policemen of post-Eliot U.S. letters came to the surface like a toilet explosion. The first joy of the beat writers when they made their assault was to prance on the tits of the forbidden, shout the "antirational"—what a dreary amount of rational Thou Shalt Nots had been forced down their brains like castor oil—exult in the antimetrical, rejoice in the incantatory, act out every bastard shape and form that testified to an Imagination which had been imprisoned by graduate-school wardens who laid down the laws for A Significant Mid-Twentieth-Century American Literature.

One should therefore first regard the insane playfulness, deliberate infantilism, nutty haikus, naked stripteases, free-form chants and literary war dances of the beats as a tremendous lift of conscience, a much-needed *release* from an authoritarian inhibiting-and-punishing intellectual climate that had succeeded in intimidating honest American writing. But the writer's need to blurt his soul is ultimately the most determined of all and will only tolerate interference to a moderate point; when the critic-teachers presume to become lawgivers they ultimately lose their power by trying to take away the manhood (or womanhood) of others. By reason of personality, a large and open mind, a deceptively obsessive literary background coupled with the romantic American good looks of a movie swinger, Jack Kerouac became the image and catalyst of this Freedom Movement and set in motion a genuinely new style that pierced to the motorcycle seat of his contemporaries' feelings because it expressed mutual experience that had been hushed up or considered improper for literature. The birth of a style is always a fascinating occasion because it represents a radical shift in outlook and values; even if time proves that Kerouac's style is too slight to withstand the successive grandslams of fashion that lie in wait, and if he should go down in the record books as primarily a pep pill rather than an accomplished master of his own experience (and we will examine these alternatives as we dig deeper into his work), it is shortsighted of anyone concerned with our time in America to minimize what Kerouac churned into light and put on flying wheels.

This last image is not inappropriate to his America and ours, inasmuch as he mythicized coast-to-coast restlessness in a zooming car in *On the Road* (1957) at the same time that he took our customary prose by its tail and whipped it as close to pure action as our jazzmen and painters were doing with their artforms. But Kerouac did even more than this: now in 1965, almost a decade after *Road*, we can see that he was probably the first important American novelist (along with Salinger) to create a true pop art as well. The roots of any innovator nourish themselves at deep, primary sources, and if we give a concentrated look at Kerouac's, the nature of his formative experience and the scope of his concern might surprise a number of prejudiced minds and awaken them to tardy recognition.

John (Jack) Kerouac, as every reader-participant of his work knows, was born in Lowell, Massachusetts, in 1922, a very much American kid but with a difference: he was of French-Canadian descent and the family (his father was a printer, interestingly enough) embraced the particularly parochial brand of Catholicism which observers have noted about that northern outpost of the Church. As far as WASP America went, Kerouac was almost as much of an Outsider as the radical-Jewish-homosexual Allen Ginsberg, the urchin-reform-school-Italian Gregory Corso and the junkie-homosexual-disgrace-of-a-good-family William Burroughs that he was later to team up with.

From his earliest years, apparently—and laced all through Kerouac's work—one sees an extreme tenderness toward animals, children, growing things, a kind of contemporary St. Francisism which occasionally becomes annoyingly gushy to dryer tastes; the sympathetic reader credits Kerouac with having genuine "saintly" forbearance as a human but also winces because of the religious-calendar prettiness in a work like *Visions of Gerard* (1963), the sincere and perhaps overly idealized elegy to a frail older brother who died during the writer's childhood. If Kerouac's feeling occasionally floods into a River of Tears it is nevertheless always present, buckets of it, and one is finally astonished by the enormous responsiveness of the man to seemingly everything that has ever happened to him—literally from birth to a minute ago.

As an Outsider, then, French Canadian, Catholic ("I am a Canuck, I could not speak English till I was 5 or 6, at 16 I spoke with a halting accent and was a big blue baby in school though varsity basketball later and if not for that no one would have noticed I could cope in any way with the world and would have been put in the madhouse for some kind of inadequacy. . ."), but with the features and build of an all-American prototype growing up in a solid New England manufacturing town, much of Kerouac's early life seems to have gone into fantasy and daydreams which he acted out. ("At the age of 11 I wrote whole little novels in nickel notebooks, also magazines in imitation of *Liberty Magazine* and kept extensive horse racing newspapers going.") He invented complicated games for himself, using the Outsider's solitude to create a world—many worlds, actually—modeled on the "real" one but extending it far beyond the dull-normal capacities of the other Lowell boys his own age. Games, daydreams, dreams themselves—his *Book of Dreams* (1961) is unique in our generation's written expression—fantasies and imaginative speculations are rife throughout all of Kerouac's grownup works; and the references all hearken back to his Lowell boyhood, to the characteristically American small-city details (Lowell had a population of 100,000 or less during Kerouac's childhood), and to what we can unblushingly call the American Idea, which the young Jack cultivated as only a yearning and physically vigorous dreamer can.

That is, as a Stranger, a first-generation American who couldn't speak the tongue until he was in knee pants, the history and raw beauty of the U.S. legend was more crucially important to his imagination than it was to the comparatively well-adjusted runnynoses who took their cokes and movies for granted and fatly basked in the taken-for-granted American customs and consumer goods that young Kerouac made into interior theatricals. It is impossible to forget that behind the 43-year-old Kerouac of today lies a wild total involvement in this country's folkways, history, small talk, visual delights, music and literature—especially the latter; Twain, Emily Dickinson, Melville, Sherwood Anderson, Whitman, Emerson, Hemingway, Saroyan, Thomas Wolfe, they were all gobbled up or at least tasted by him before his teens were over (along with a biography of Jack London that made him want to be an "adventurer"); he identified with his newfound literary fathers and grandfathers and apparently read omnivorously. As you'll see, this kind of immersion in the literature of his kinsmen—plunged into with the grateful passion that only the children of immigrants understand—was a necessity before he broke loose stylistically; he had to have sure knowledge and control of his medium after a long apprenticeship in order to chuck so much extraneous tradition in the basket when he finally found his own voice and risked its total rhythm and sound.

Around Kerouac's 17th year, we find him attending the somewhat posh Horace Mann School in upper Manhattan—the family had now moved to the Greater New York area with the onset of his father's fatal illness—and racking up a brilliant 92 point average. (His brightness by any standard confounds the careless "anti-intellectual" charges leveled at him by earnest Ethical Culture types.) Then in 1940 he entered Columbia University on a scholarship. Kerouac, so far as I know, never actually played varsity football for Columbia although he was on the squad until he broke his leg, and had been a flashy Gary Grayson–type halfback while at Horace Mann. He also never finished college, for World War II exploded after he had been there approximately two years; but during this period he did meet two important buddies and influences, William Burroughs and Allen Ginsberg, and it is interesting to keep in mind that the titles of both works which brought these men to public attention, *Naked Lunch* and *Howl* respectively, were coined by Kerouac, the verbal sorcerer. Burroughs was a spare, elegant, fiercely authentic junkie and occasional dilettante dabbler in crime, such as a holdup of a Turkish bath just for an André Gidean laugh, who earned his role of guru by having lived coolly and defiantly on the margin of society after being born into its social center—St. Louis's prominent Burroughs Adding Machine family and Harvard '36. His intelligence was acute, penetrating, impersonal and sweepingly bizarre. Young Ginsberg was a "visionary" oddball from Paterson, New Jersey—"I never thought he'd live to grow up," said hometowner William Carlos Williams about him—the son of a minor poet and a suffering crazy mother whom he has written beautifully about in *Kaddish* (1962), a radical, a Blakean, a dreamy smiling Jewish Fauvist, and one can picture the three of them bouncing ideas off each other during apocalyptic Morningside Heights nights just after America got sucked into the war.

. . . Jack Kerouac's French Canadian-Catholic-Yankee arc was widened to compassionately include non-participating acceptance of the homosexuality of his literary pals, association with interesting criminals and prostitutes, drugs,

Manhattan freakishness of every kind, including those crazy forays with Ginsberg, Herbert Huncke (ex-con, drugman and recent writer), Burroughs and Neal Cassady (Dean Moriarty of *On the Road*) into the hustling life of Times Square. An artist of originality, such as Kerouac, is compounded of many layers, his capacity for experience is always widening, his instinct for friends and lovers is based on what he can learn as well as brute personal need; one feels that Kerouac was expanding in all directions at this time, reading Blake, Rimbaud, Dostoevsky, Joyce, Baudelaire, Céline and the Buddhists now in addition to his groovy American word-slingers, beginning to write poetry (perhaps with Ginsberg's enthusiastic encouragement), painting, becoming in other words the many-sided phenomenon he would have to become in order to escape easy definition and inspire the deep affection of such a variety of heterogeneous people as he eventually did.

When WWII finally did come, Kerouac signed on as a merchant seaman and sailed to arctic Greenland on the ill-fated S.S. Dorchester, now famous for the four chaplains who gave up their lives during a U-boat sinking near Iceland, but he had been called to Navy boot camp just before that fatal 1943 sailing. After a comparatively short duty in the Navy, Kerouac was discharged as "schizoid personality," a primitive mental description not very different from the way a number of his fellow writers were bracketed by a service unable to handle their double and triple vision. Now he was to be on his own (except for his boyishly obsessive devotion to his mother, as his patient readers know only too well) for the rest of the race. After the Navy, the remainder of the war was spent as a merchant seaman sailing the North Atlantic again; then, in rough order, came a year under the G.I. Bill at Manhattan's New School for Social Research, the completion of his first novel, hoboing and hitchhiking across the United States and Mexico, and the growing attachment for San Francisco as the first port of call after he came down from his perch on top of the Washington State mountains as a fire-watcher.

I can remember the word being passed around in New York in the late 40s that "another Thomas Wolfe, a roaring boy named Kerouac, ever hear of him?" was loose on the scene (and I can also remember the shaft of jealousy that shot through me upon hearing this). But the significant thing was that in addition to hard, I-won't-be-stopped writing during these crucial years—and this extra gland was to make Kerouac stand out from all the other first novelists clogging the city—he had an uncanny gift for winging right along toward new experience; he was the first vocal member of a postwar breed, the Beat Transcontinental American, for in New York he numbered among his friends (and happily shook up) such writers as Burroughs, Ginsberg, Corso, John Clellon Holmes (who has a coolly memorable portrait of him in *Go*) as well as jazz musicians, painters, hippies, while on the Coast he had equally strong currents going with Neal Cassady—"the discovery of a style of my own based on spontaneous get-with-it came after reading the marvelous free narrative letters of Neal Cassady"—and the poets Philip Whalen, Gary Snyder, Peter Orlovsky (Simon Darlovsky in this book and Ginsberg's loyal buddy), Philip Lamantia, Robert Duncan, John Montgomery and others.

Absorbing the life for his work by scatting around the country, Kerouac was also feeding scores of people by his presence, enthusiastically daring the poets to wail, the painters to paint, little magazines to get started (*Big Table*, 1960–1961, was named by him for its brief but significant career) and in the simplest sense being the human pivot for an improvised sub-society of artists, writers and young poetic-religious idealists alienated from our sapping materialistic culture. It doesn't seem exaggerated to say that Kerouac by his superior capacity for involvement with "his generation" unified surprising numbers of underground Americans who would probably have remained lonely shadows but for his special brand of charisma. And Transcontinental though Kerouac was, the West Coast, and the Frisco area in particular, were to prove culturally more ready for him than the East.

California looks toward the Orient; its young intellectuals and truth-seekers are far more open to untraditional and experimental concepts than their counterparts in the New York and New England cultural fortresses, and it was to be no accident that the beat chariot fueled up in S.F. and then rolled from west to east in the late 50s rather than the other way around. But more specifically for our knowledge of Kerouac, it was on the Coast, especially from Frisco north to the high Washington State mountains, that climate and geography allowed his *Dharma Bums* (1958) to combine a natural outdoorsy way of life with the Buddhist precepts and speculations that play a very consistent part in all of Kerouac's writing and especially in *Desolation Angels*. In this propitious environment Kerouac found a number of kindred neo-Buddhist, antimaterialist, gently anarchistic young Americans whom he would never have come upon in New York, Boston or Philadelphia; they discussed and brooded upon philosophy and religion with him (informally, but seriously) and brought—all of them together, with Kerouac the popularizer—a new literary-religious possibility into the *content* of the American novel that anticipated more technical studies of Zen and presaged a shift in the intellectual world from a closed science-oriented outlook to a more existential approach. This is not to imply that Kerouac is an original thinker in any technical philosophical sense, although every artist who makes an impact uses his brain as well as his feelings; Kerouac's originality lay in his instinct for where the vital action lay and in his enormously nimble, speed-championship ability to report the state of the contemporary beat soul (not unlike Hemingway in *The Sun Also Rises* some 35 years earlier).

Before Kerouac appropriated San Francisco and the West Coast, the buzz that had been heard in New York publishing circles about this word-high natureboy came to a climax in 1950 with the publication of his first novel, *The Town and the City*. From the title you can tell that he was still under the influence of Thomas Wolfe—*The Web and the Rock, Of Time and the River*, etc.—and although his ear for recording the speech of his contemporaries is already intimidating in its fullness of recall and high fidelity of detail and cadence, the book remains a preliminary trial run for the work to come. In it are the nutty humor, the Times Square hallucinated montage scenes, fresh and affectionate sketches of beats-to-be, intimate descriptions of marijuana highs and bedbuggy East Side pads, but at the age of 28 Kerouac was still writing in the bag of the traditional realistic American novel and had not yet sprung the balls that were to move him into the light. Kerouac himself has referred to *Town* as a "novel novel," something at least in part madeup and synthetic, i.e., *fictional*. He has also told us that the book took three years to write and rewrite.

But by 1951, a short year after its publication, we know that he was already beginning to swing out with his own method-philosophy of composition. It took another seven years—with the printing of *On the Road*, and even then readers were shielded from Kerouac's stylistic innovations by the orthodox Viking Press editing job done on the book—for that sound and style to reach the public; but Allen Ginsberg has told us in the introduction to *Howl* (1956) that Kerouac "spit forth intelligence into 11 books written in half the number of years (1951-1956)"—*On the Road* (1957), *The Subterraneans* (1958), *The Dharma Bums* (1958), *Maggie Cassidy* (1959), *Dr. Sax* (1959), *Mexico City Blues* (1959), *Visions of Cody* (1960), *Book of Dreams* (1961), *Visions of Gerard* (1963), *San Francisco Blues* (unpublished) and *Wake Up* (unpublished). The dates in parenthesis refer to the year the books were issued. At the age of 29 Kerouac suddenly made his breakthrough in a phenomenal burst of energy and found the way to tell his particular story with its freeing sentence-spurts that were to make him the one and only "crazy Catholic mystic" hotrodder of American prose.

This style, as in that of any truly significant writer, was hardly a surface mannerism but rather the ultimate expression of a radical conviction that had to incarnate itself in the language he used, the rhythm with which he used it and the unbuttoned punctuation that freed the headlong drive of his superior energy. He had invented what Ginsberg called, a trifle fancily, "a spontaneous bop prosody," which meant that Kerouac had evolved through experience and self-revelation a firm technique which could now be backed up ideologically.

Its essentials were this: Kerouac would "sketch from memory" a "definite image-object" more or less as a painter would work on a still-life; this "sketching" necessitated an "undisturbed flow from the mind of idea-words," comparable to a jazz soloist blowing freely; there would be "no periods separating sentence-structures already arbitrarily riddled by false colons and timid commas;" in place of the conventional period would be "vigorous space dashes separating rhetorical breathing," again just as a jazzman draws breath between phrases; there would be no "selectivity" of expression, but instead the free association of the mind into "limitless seas" of thought; the writer has to "satisfy himself first," after which the "reader can't fail to receive a telepathic shock" by virtue of the same psychological "laws" operating in his own mind; there could be "no pause" in composition, "no revisions" (except for errors of fact) since nothing is ultimately incomprehensible or "muddy" that "runs in time;" the motto of this kind of prose was to be "speak now or forever hold your peace"—putting the writer on a true existential spot; and finally, the writing was to be done "without consciousness," in a Yeatsian semitrance if possible, allowing the unconscious to "admit" in uninhibited and therefore "necessarily modern language" what overly conscious art would normally censor.

Kerouac had leapt to these insights about Action Writing almost 15 years ago—before he sat down to gun his way through *Road*, which by his own statement was written in an incredible three weeks. (*The Subterraneans*, which contains some of his most intense and indeed beautiful word-sperm, was written in three days and nights with the aid of bennies and/or dex.) Whether or not the readers of *Desolation Angels*— or contemporary American writers in general— embrace the ideas in Kerouac's Instant Literature manual, their relevance for this dungareed Roman candle is unquestionably valid. The kind of experience that sent him, and of which he personally was a torrid part, had a blistering pace-discontinuity-hecticness-promiscuity-lunge-evanescence that begged for a receptacle geared to catch it on the fly. At the time of Kerouac's greatest productivity in the early 50s, the humpedly meditated and intellectually cautious manner of the "great" university English departments and the big literary quarterlies was the dominant, intimidating mode so far as "serious" prose went; I know from my own experience that many young writers without Kerouac's determination to go all the way were castrated by their fear of defying standards then thought to be unimpeachable. So tied up were these standards with status, position in the intellectual community, even "sanity" in its most extensive sense, that writers who thumbed their nose or being at them had to risk everything from the categorization of simple duncehood to being called a lunatic. But Kerouac, "a born virtuoso and lover of language," as Henry Miller accurately pointed out, was literarily confident enough to realize—with the loyalty of a genuine pioneer to his actual inner life—that he would have to turn his back on the Eliot-Trilling-Older Generation dicta and risk contempt in order to keep the faith with reality as *he* knew it. Obviously this takes artistic dedication, courage, enormous capacity for work, indifference to the criticism which always hurts, an almost fanatical sense of necessity—all the guts that have always made the real art of one generation strikingly different from the preceding one, however "goofy" or unfamiliar it looks and feels to those habituated to the past.

What many of Kerouac's almost paranoically suspicious critics refuse to take into account is the fundamental seriousness, but not *grimness*, of the man; his studious research into writer-seers as varied as Emily Dickinson, Rimbaud and

Joyce, the very heroic cream of the Names who rate humility and shining eyes from the brownnosing university play-it-safeniks; and his attempt to use what he has learned for the communication of fresh American experience that had no precise voice until he gave it one. This is not to say that he has entirely succeeded. It is too early, given Kerouac's ambition, for us to make that judgment; but we can lay out the body of his work, 14 published books, and at least make sense of what he has already achieved and also point out where he has perhaps overreached himself and gestured more with intention than fulfillment. As with any creative prose writer of major proportion—and I believe without doubt that Kerouac belongs on this scale for his and my generation—he is a social historian as well as a technical inventor, and his ultimate value to the future may very well lie in this area. No one in American prose before Kerouac, not even Hemingway, has written so authentically about an entirely new pocket of sensibility and attitude within the broad overcoat of society; especially one obsessed by art, sensations, self-investigation and ideas. Kerouac's characters (and he himself) are frantic young midcenturyites whose tastes and dreams were made out of the very novels, paintings, poems, movies and jazz created by an earlier Hemingway-Picasso-Hart Crane-Orson Welles-Lester Young network of pioneering hipsters. Nor are these warming modern names and what they stand for to Kerouac's gang treated with distant awe or any square worship of that sort; they are simply part of the climate in which the novelist and his characters live.

We ought to remember that the generation which came of age in the late 40s and mid 50s was the product of what had gone immediately before in the dramatization of the American imagination, just like Kerouac himself, and his-and-their occasional romanticization of the stars who lighted the way was not essentially different from what you can find in any graduate school—only emotionally truer and less concerned with appearances. So credit the King of the Beats with having the eyes and ears to do justice to an unacknowledged new American Hall of Fame that was the inevitable result of our country's increasing awareness of the message of modernity, but remained unrepresented in fiction until Kerouac hiply used it for his subject matter. Yet art is more than literal social history, so that if Kerouac is a novelist-historian in the sense of James T. Farrell, F. Scott Fitzgerald or the early Hemingway, he like them must show the soul of his matter in the form; the artist-writer's lovely duty is to materialize what he is writing about in a shape indivisible from its content ("a poem should not mean but be").

It therefore would have been naive and ridiculous for Kerouac to write about his jittery, neurotic, drug-taking, auto-racing, poetry-chanting, bop-digging, zen-squatting crew in a manner like John Updike or even John O'Hara; he had to duplicate in his prose that curious combination of agitation and rapture that streamed like a pennant from the lives of his boys and girls; and it is my belief that precisely here he stepped out in front by coining a prose inseparable from the existence it records, riffing out a total experience containing fact, color, rhythm, scene, sound—roll 'em!—and all bound up in one organic package that baffles easy imitation. In this sense art has always been more than its reduction to a platform—and it is interesting (in a nonjudgmental sense) that Allen Ginsberg and John Clellon Holmes have always been more articulate beat ideologists than Kerouac, who has always squirmed out of any programmatic statements about his "mission" because it was ultimately to be found in the work rather than a Town Hall debate. Except for that machinegun typewriter in his lap—or head!—he was seemingly deaf and dumb or reckless ("I want God to show me His face") and bizarre as a public spokesman; simply because this was not his job, and any effort to reduce the totality of experience communicated in his books would have seemed to him, like Faulkner, a falsification and a soapbox stunt rather than a recreation—which is where the true power of Kerouac and narrative art itself comes clean. As Gilbert Sorrentino has pointed out, Kerouac accurately intuited our time's boredom with the "psychological novel" and invented an Indianapolis Speedway narrative style that comes right out of Defoe—Defoe with a super-charged motor, if you will.

If Kerouac's books are then to be the final test, and if the writing itself must support the entire weight of his bid—as I believe it must—has he (1) made his work equal its theory? and (2) will the writing finally merit the high claims its author obviously has for it? To begin with, we should consider the cumulative architecture of all his books since *On the Road*, because in a published statement made in 1962 Kerouac said: "My work comprises one vast book like Proust's except that my remembrances are written on the run instead of afterwards in a sickbed. . . . The whole thing forms one enormous comedy, seen through the eyes of poor Ti Jean (me), otherwise known as Jack Duluoz, the world of raging action and folly and also of gentle sweetness seen through the keyhole of his eye."

Let's try to break this down. Kerouac regards his work as highly autobio-graphical—which it obviously is, with only the most transparent disguises of people's names making it "fictional"—and a decade after the beginning of his windmill production he has found an analogy for it in *Remembrance of Things Past*. Proust's massive spiderweb, however, gets its form from a fantastically complicated recapturing of the past, whereas Kerouac's novels are all present-tense sprints which are barely hooked together by the presence of the "I" (Kerouac) and the hundreds of acquaintances who appear, disappear and reap-pear. In plain English, the books have only the loosest structure when taken as a whole, which doesn't at all invalidate what they say individually but makes the reference to Proust only partially true. In addition, the structure that Proust created to contain his experience was a tortuous and exquisitely articulated monolith, with each segment carefully and deviously fitted into the next, while the books of Kerouac's "Duluoz Legend" (his overall title for the series) are not necessarily dependent on those that have gone before except chronologically. Esthetically and philosophically, then, the form of Proust's giant book is much more deeply tricky, with the structure following from his Bergsonian ideas about Time and embodying them; Kerouac, whose innovations are challenging in their own right and need no apology, has clearly not conceived a structure as original as Proust's. As a progressing work, his "Legend" is Proustian only in the omniscience of the "I," and the "I" 's fidelity to what has been experienced, but it does not add to its meaning with each new book—that meaning is clearly evident with each single novel and only grows spatially with additions instead of unfolding, as does Proust's. Finally, the reference to Proust's work seems very much an afterthought with Kerouac rather than a plan that had been strategically worked out from the start.

If structurally the "Duluoz Legend" is much less cohesive and prearranged than the reference to Proust implies, what about the prose itself? I believe that it is in the actual writing that Kerouac has made his most exciting contribution; no one else writing in America at this time has achieved a rhythm as close to jazz, action, the actual speed of the mind and the reality of a nationwide scene that has been lived by thousands of us between the ages of 17 and 45. Kerouac, no matter how "eccentric" some might think him as a writer, is really the Big Daddy of jukebox-universal hip life in our accelerated U.S.A. His sentences or lines— and they are more important in his work than paragraphs, chapters or even separate books, since all the latter are just extensions in time and space of the original catlike immediacy of response—are pure mental reflexes to each moment that dots our daily experience. Because of Kerouac's nonstop interior participation in the present, these mental impulses flash and chirp with a brightly felt directness that allows no moss whatsoever to settle between the perception and the act of communication. Almost 10 years before the "vulgar" immediacy of Pop Art showed us the astounding environment we actually live in—targeted our sight on a close-up of mad Americana that had been excluded from the older generation's comparatively heavy Abstract Expressionism—Kerouac was happily Popping our prose into a flexible flyer of flawless observation, exactness of detail, brand-names, ice-cream colors, the movie-comedy confusion of a Sunday afternoon jam session, the spooky delight of reading *Dr. Jekyll and Mr. Hyde* in the woods of Big Sur, all sorts of incongruously charming and touching aspects of reality that were too slender and evanescent to have gotten into our heavyweight literature before.

The unadorned strength of the prose lay in the fact that no detail was too odd or tiny or inhuman to escape Kerouac's remarkably quick and unbored eye; and because of his compulsive-spontaneous method of composition he was able to trap actuality as it happened—the literal preciousness of the moment—where other writers would have become weary at the mere thought of how to handle it all. Such strength coupled with humorous delicacy, and made gut-curdlingly real by the "cosmic" sadness especially in evidence in *Desolation Angels*, cannot be disregarded by anyone seriously concerned with how our writing is going to envelop new experience: "If it has been lived or thought it will one day become literature," said Emile Zola. Kerouac's influence as a writer is already far more widespread than is yet acknowledged or even fully appreciated, so extensive has its reach been; Ginsberg, Frank O'Hara, LeRoi Jones, folksinger-poet Bob Dylan, Hubert Selby, John Rechy, even Mailer, John Clellon Holmes, Lawrence Ferlinghetti and myself are only some of his opposite numbers who have learned how to get closer to their own rendering of experience specifically because of Kerouac's freedom of language, "punctuation" (the etiquette of traditional English as opposed to American) and, in the fullest sense, his literary imagination.

Yet this same prose reveals itself as well to be at times little-boyish, thread-barely naked (so that you want to wrap a blanket around both it and its creator), cute-surrealistic-collegiate, often reading more like breathless short telegraphic takes than "writing" as we are accustomed to the meaning of the word. This is the risk—that the spontaneity is only paper-deep and can be blown away by a stiff new cultural wind. Since there is no "character" or "plot" development in the old-fashioned sense, only an accretion of details—like this—with the voice of the narrator increasingly taking on the tones of speech rather than literature—so that it might have been taped instead of written—just as Jack taped four chapters of *Visions of Cody*—the words have a funny lightness—like feathers or kids' paper airplanes—they trip along like pony hoofs—no deep impression left on the page—with a kind of comicstrip simplification—everything impatiently kissed on the surface—but is experience only that which we can see right off?

To be realistic, Kerouac's writings can seem like nonwriting compared to our steelier literary products; he has dared all on a challengingly frank, committed, unweaseling rhythmic fling that can get dangerously close to verbal onanism rather than our conception of fundamental novel-writing. The books themselves often seem like sustained underwater feats rather than "works" in the customary, thought-out, wrought sense. You get the impression that they landed between covers only by accident and that if you removed the endpapers that hold them together they would fly away like clouds; so light and meringuelike is their texture, so fluid and unincised their words, so *casual* their conception of art that they seem doomed for extinction the moment after they are set down.

I find it inevitable, even for admirers, to seriously entertain the possibility that Kerouac's work will not outlive the man and his period; already he has told us all his secrets and apparently bored—by the uninhibited exposure of his soul—readers who have no special sympathy for his rucksack fucksack romanticism. And yet this is the risk he has taken; the general reader to whom he has romantically exhibited his genuine being is as merciless as the rolling years, as uncharitable as winter, as restless and fickle as the stomach of a millionaire. One cannot help but think, poor Jack, poor Ti Jean, to have flung his innermost flower into the crass hopper of public taste and the need for cannibalistic kicks! My personal belief is this: whatever is monotonous, indulgent or false in Kerouac's prose will be skinned alive by sharp-eyed cynics who wait with itching blades for prey as helplessly unprotected as this author is apparently condemned (and has chosen) to be. Kerouac has been flayed before and will be again; it is his god-damned fate. But I also believe that the best of his work will endure because it is too honestly made with the thread of actual life to cheapen with age. It would not surprise me in the least to have his brave and unbelligerently up-yours style become the most authentic prose record of our screwy neo-adolescent era, appreciated more as time makes its seeming eccentricities acceptable rather than now when it is still indigestible to the prejudiced middle-class mind.

In subtle and unexpected ways, haunted by the juvenile ghosts of his childhood as he might be and therefore unnerving even his fondest intellectual admirers, I think Kerouac is one of the more *intelligent* men of his time. But if the immediate past has been personally difficult for him—and you will see just how painful it has been, both in *Desolation Angels* and in *Big Sur* (1962)—there is little to say that the future will be easier. He is a most vulnerable guy; his literary personality and content invite even more barbs, which wound an already heavily black-and-blued spirit; but the resilient and gentle nub of his being—whose motto is Acceptance, Peace, Forgiveness, indeed Luv—is stronger than one would have suspected, given his sensitivity. And for this resource of his wilderness-stubborn Canuck nature all who feel indebted to the man and his work are grateful.

The danger now confronting Kerouac, and it looms large, is one of repetition. He can add another dozen hardcover-bound spurts to his "Duluoz Legend" and they will be as individually valid as their predecessors, but unless he deepens, enlarges or changes his pace they will only add medals to an accomplishment already achieved—they will not advance his talent vertically or scale the new meanings that a man of his capacity should take on. In fact one hopes, with a kind of fierce pride in Kerouac that is shared by all of us who were purged by his esthetic Declaration of Independence, that time itself will use up and exhaust his "Duluoz Legend" and that he will then go on to other literary odysseys which he alone can initiate.

Desolation Angels is concerned with Beat Generation events of 1956 and 1957, just before the publication of *On the Road*. You will immediately recognize the scene and its place in the Duluoz-Kerouac autobiography. The first half of the book was completed in Mexico City in October of 1956 and "typed up" in 1957; the second half, entitled *Passing Through*, wasn't written until 1961 although chronologically it follows on the heels of the first. Throughout both sections the overwhelming *leitmotiv* is one of "sorrowful peace," of "passing through" the void of this world as gently and kindly as one can, to await a "golden eternity" on the other side of mortality. This humility and tenderness toward a suffering existence has always been in Kerouac, although sometimes defensively shielded, but when the Jack of real life and the hero of his books has been choked by experience beyond the point of endurance, the repressed priest and "Buddha" (as Allen Ginsberg valentined him) in his ancient bones comes to the fore. All through *Angels*, before and after its scenes of celebration, mayhem, desperation, sheer fizz and bubble, there is the need for retreat and contemplation; and when this occurs, comes the tragic note of resignation—manly, worldly-wise, based on the just knowledge of other historic pilgrimages either intuited by Kerouac or read by him or both—which in recent books has become characteristic of this Old Young Martyred Cocksman.

Let no one be deceived. "I am the man, I suffered, I was there," wrote Mr. Whitman, and only an educated fool—as Mahalia Jackson says—or a chronic sneerer would withhold the same claim for Kerouac. His mysticism and religious yearning are (whether you or I like it or not) finally ineradicable from his personality. In this book he gives both qualities full sweep, the mood is elegiacal, occasionally flirting with the maudlin and Romantically Damned, but revolving always around the essential isolation and travail that imperfect beings like ourselves must cope with daily. If critics were to give grades for Humanity, Kerouac would snare pure As each time out; his outcries and sobbing chants into the human night are unphony, to me at least unarguable. They personalize his use of the novel-form to an extreme degree, in which it becomes the vehicle for his need and takes on the intimacy of a private letter made public; but Kerouac's pain (and joy) becomes his reader's because it is cleaner in feeling than the comparatively hedged and echoed emotions we bring to it with our what's-the-percentage "adult" philosophy.

Like Winston Churchill—admittedly a weird comparison, but even more weirdly pertinent—Kerouac has both made and written the history in which he played the leading role. The uniqueness of his position in our often synthetic and contrived New York publishing house "literature" of the 60s speaks for itself and is in no immediate danger of duplication. If it goes unhonored or is belittled by literary journalists who are not likely to make a contribution to reality themselves, the pimples of pettiness are not hard to spot; Kerouac, singled out by the genie of contemporary fate to do and be something that was given to absolutely no one else of this time and place, can no longer be toppled by any single individual. The image he geysered into being was higher, brighter, quicker, funkier and sweeter than that of any American brother his age who tried barreling down the central highway of experience in this country during the last decade.

But the route has now been covered. Jack has shown us the neon rainbow in the oil slick; made us hear the bop trumpets blowing in West Coast spade heaven; gotten us high on Buddha and Christ; pumped his life into ours and dressed our minds in the multicolored image of his own. He has, in my opinion, conclusively done his work in this phase of his very special career. And I hope for the sake of the love we all hold for him that he will use those spooky powers given to all Lowell, Massachusetts, Rimbaudian halfbacks and transform his expression into yet another aspect of himself. For I think he is fast approaching an unequal balance—giving more than he is taking in. Two-way communication is fading because during the last 10 years he taught us what he knows, put his thought-pictures into our brains, and now we can either anticipate him or read him too transparently. I sincerely believe the time has come for Kerouac to submerge like Sonny Rollins—who quit the music scene, took a trip to Atlantis, came back newer than before—and pull a consummate switch as an artist; since he is a cat with at least nine lives, one of which has become an intimate buddy to literally thousands of people of our mutual generation and which we will carry with us to oblivion or old age, I am almost certain he can turn on a new and greater sound if he hears the need in our ears and sees us parched for a new vision. He is too much a part of all of us not to look and listen to our mid-60s plight; to hear him speak—and it's a voice that has *penetrated* a larger number of us than any other of this exact time and place, trust my reportorial accuracy regardless of what you may think of my taste—just turn the page and tune in.

1965

8.
Who's Afraid of *The New Yorker* Now?

My rebellion against the dead stylistic authority of the New Yorker was a necessity, as it later was for Tom Wolfe and eight-tenths of the strident new writers who are twirling our heads around; I had worked for the magazine as both a larking reporter and "ideaman" in my early 20s before I was fired for the double sin of chewing gum in Katherine White's face and forgetting to zip my pants after a quick No. 1 (read: an arrogant Joosh boy and not toilet-trained to boot); but it was only when I was editing a magazine myself, Nugget, from 1961–1965 during my earnest make-it-or-perish pilgrimage back into the bowels of the uptown world, that I felt the impetus to put down on paper my thoughts about what had been the most influential magazine of my time. I lost at least one friend there (Lillian Ross) as a result, and this pained me and still does. But it seemed to me urgent to attempt this deflation of what had become in my scheme of values a reactionary publication. More important, to line up this piece with my notions of total engagement, I was cutting off a possible market by my attack and in turn hoping that my article by some unlikely curve of fate would open the eyes of the advertising agencies that feed the New Yorker on the basis of what it has been, not what it is. In other words, I wanted to hit them esthetically, morally and financially; if writing in this country is to be the significant act it can be, it must radiate out into every sector of a given situation and carry with it the sting and consequences of real action. Significant writers today are not trying to change the world abstractly but concretely, naming names, quoting money prices, deals, what so-and-so had for lunch and what his cardiogram says, committing themselves totally to a specific piece in every conceivable sense so that a result can issue from the union of art and journalism. There can no longer be any acceptable separation of the economic success of a magazine or publishing house from its taste and moral stance; and no serious writer can blot out his responsibility to actually try and sabotage the economy of a communications setup that he finds noxious rather than healthy. Literary criticism must then become life-action and pose a threat that goes past the livingroom and into the kitchen or bedroom, wherever the vital motor is located. If the attacking writer is ridiculed and dismissed, that is his

105

risk; but writing about cultural institutions which is not concerned with going all the way—literally attempting to change or uproot them, from their very use of language to the quality of the private lives of their stockholders—will never make a fly's dent on the actual reality. I see a coming total journalism in this area which will embarrass you out of every secret you've ever hidden, and if your role is public and cultural, be prepared for the worst because a generation much beater than I was will stop at nothing in the exposure of what they see as immoral shit. I consider this inevitable and necessary to the extension of literature as genuine action.

1

There used to be a time, let me tell the younger generation, when *The New Yorker* had sting, when its latest short story was discussed all over town, when any self-respecting intellectual or chic-ster had to take a stand in relation to it. Out of curiosity and deadly habit I picked up the October 28 issue to see what kind of a review the new Albee play got, and John McCarten's sad, inadequate, slightly snotty two columns only confirmed what an increasing number of friends of mine—and myself—have thought:

Unless there is a revolution on 43rd Street, and it isn't likely, *The New Yorker* as we have known it has had it as a cultural force.

No matter how many irrelevant if statusy pieces *The New Yorker* publishes in the near future by W. H. Auden, Edmund Wilson, Anthony Eden or Mary McCarthy, the magazine has become middleaged, safe and increasingly divorced from the action. The Albee review, by old retainer McCarten, brought this home with a forcefulness that to me illuminates in one lightning-flare all the stale attitudes and plump-bellied complacency that has overtaken this once great magazine. The review, if you've read it (and even if you haven't you can imagine it), is pleasant reading because McCarten—following in the footsteps of the finest *New Yorker* staff writers—uses a combination of the spoken and written language with that deceptive ease which comes from an admiration and imitation of *informal style.* That, I think, will be *The New Yorker's* greatest contribution to sophistication and the country's style at large when, in the dim future, the score is added up and the final judgment made.

McCarten is only the last of a long line of expert Ears, men who wrote the language with absolute attention to all of its nuances as they heard it spoken and who delighted in the precious art of fitting words together. Before McCarten came Joe Mitchell, Wolcott Gibbs, John McNulty, St. Clair McKelway, E. B. White, Geoffrey Hellman, names upon names who fifty years from today, with slight exceptions, might all be taken for the same person—or the same person in different moods. Taste plus a literal shudder at being pretentious lay at the bottom of the creation of *New Yorker* style; and beneath this was, of course, the dominant figure of Harold Ross with his maniacal punctiliousness, but even more important, with his native American journalist's fear of being European or thickly, densely highbrow and hence a fraud. One cannot capsulize with justice the many fine points that went into the making of New Yorker style—and anyone who had the experience of working there during the magazine's frontrunning days can tell of the incredible painstaking care and obsessiveness that neuroticized the very air—but even using broad strokes to rough in the picture you can justly reduce *The New Yorker* world to one acute element: style.

So stylish was *The New Yorker's* image of itself that (as can be seen in the numberless "Profiles" written by anonymous human machines who almost reduced art to science) the concern with appropriateness became overrefined to the point where style itself was devalued as brassy display and the article that "writes itself" was substituted as the high point of journalistic suavity. Never had a magazine in this country devoted such theatrical care to the subtleties of communication, carefulness, tact, finally draining the spirit of its staff down to the microscopic beauty of a properly placed comma and ultimately paralyzing them in static detail and self-conscious poise, the original ideal of perfection having become in the late 50s and now 60s a perversion instead of a furthering of the journalist's duty to render reality.

But McCarten's review of *Who's Afraid of Virginia Woolf?* is pivotal in a much more crucial sense than yet touched upon because it unwittingly reveals the fear of the new that has threatened *The New Yorker* as an institution and its fine craftsmen as men and women—as egos who had Position and are now foundering in the wave of "barbarism" that has overwhelmed their values. Even during the heyday of intellectual snobbery as canonized by the *Partisan* and *Kenyon Reviews* during the 40s, *The New Yorker* felt eminently protected, sure of itself, because the underlying axis of the magazine was always journalistic, concrete, and it excelled with the tangible as did no competitor. Harold Ross or his heir William Shawn might not understand or enjoy James Joyce or even Picasso, being expert newsmen first and artistic dilettantes second, but their roots in the American experience were unquestioned, ruggedly sustained by the journalist's reliance on facts and the exciting job of putting out a tough-minded but lightly handled organism every week. This security can no longer exist at *The New Yorker*; inroads were made by the selective inclusion of the eminent highbrows into its pages (Dwight Macdonald, Wilson, Delmore Schwartz, Roethke, Rosenberg, Marianne Moore, etc.), and while once they just decorated the cake devised by Chef Ross, who was always suspicious of them, at this point they brought with them an ill wind of disturbing thought. With the eclecticism of the assured and wealthy, *The New Yorker* thought it could head into the future with literary self-esteem protected by this dressing of accepted intellectuals, who threatened only with words, but it was unprepared for the burst of new values crouched barely behind these older, more hypocritically courteous men— hypocritical only in that while they were in as deadly earnest as the young baby-throwing Albees, Ginsbergs and John Cages they spoke in the university-groomed, buttoned-down manner of their period and therefore could pass as white.

It is the new wave, in every sense, that has cast *The New Yorker* adrift from every familiar mooring and turned it, out of defensiveness, into a castrated and even reactionary publication. As we read it now, there is more crass life and inventiveness in the advertising than in the body copy; from the middle of the magazine to the end you will come upon pages with 5 and ½ inches' width of advertising to 3 of writing, and the painful thing to anyone in the business is the fact that the writing wastes even the petty amount of space it can still command because of the echo of the old colloquial style, using its now trivial diction and informalities to fill up precious space instead of revolutionizing the style to fit the reality. Magazines live in the world, and no one who understands the bitter economics of magazine publishing would fault a publication for having the beautiful cushion of heavy advertising to rest on; *The New Yorker* earned its present wealth the hard way, and one's professional respect goes out to it on the business level because without revenues you either perish or distort yourself; but the fairyland of four-color advertising and its layout, makeup, zing, thrill, even slickness, from the middle to the back of *The New Yorker* shames the lack of superior life in the editorial copy and makes the irony of this demise of brilliance that much more pitiable. Just recall the stories of Ross not allowing the advertising people even to walk on the editorial floor; and now *they* have the power, not only because they bring in the gelt, but because they are negotiating the basic energy and flashy fantasies that brighten our eyes when we pick up the magazine. Soon they will truly control *The New Yorker*, blunt its last edge; and the usurpation will be just, because these men are as determined as Ross's breed and are not kidding themselves in their huckster role, while the diehard editorial neoclassicists, the punctuation castratos who have gone to bed with commas for a quarter of a century, are living in a world that no longer exists.

I said above that what I take to be the descent of *The New Yorker* into an advertising showcase is pitiable, and you could only feel that way if you once worked there—as did William Gaddis, Truman Capote, Chandler Brossard, myself, a whole busload of interesting writers now pushing 40—or if you were susceptible to the tremendous superegolike authority that the magazine exerted on the liveliest young literary types and tastebuds in the 40s. But the emotion opposite to pity is contempt, and it is in this vein that I would like to conclude. Contempt, viciousness, snottiness, the reduction of your foe to absurdity, enormous distance between you and the thing talked about, dirty fun—all these things come out of fear, and it was fear that John McCarten demonstrated in his review of the new Albee play. Fear is not a pleasant emotion to witness, but it is even worse when it is disguised with pseudo-wisecracks which leave your reader bewildered as to why you don't attempt to get into the muscle of what you're discussing. The Albee play (which I haven't yet seen), and what Mr. Albee represents, seems to me an almost too-perfect symbol of everything that is wrong with *The New Yorker*, and I would like to trace it through.

This was Edward Albee's first play uptown, the city had been buzzing all summer long with news of the impending event—news, mind you, that once *The New Yorker* when it believed in its title would have eaten up and happily passed along to its readers—and everyone hip to this town's temperature knew that this was more than just another play. It was a dramatic story from a variety of angles: the marginal man pitted against the Big Street, the fact that Albee had never faced the "test" of a full evening-length play, the question of whether the tone of the times was really ripe for a savagely fragile avantgardist to hold his own in the hardnose world of unions and box-office, the fact that here was no European import but one of our very own (so slender, so few) who was going out to bait the killers of the dream. Much was riding on this debut, quite apart from the line-by-line merits of *Who's Afraid of Virginia Woolf?* and John McCarten withdrew from the entire excitement of the occasion, treated it with the coolness of catatonia, put it down (which in itself is immaterial) in terms that don't apply, and brought off the most pathetic crack of the week in weaseling out of mature criticism with the words "a vulgar mishmash." What Irishman is kidding what Jew, and haven't we all come a long way from the vulgar potato famines, eh John?

It is not McCarten as an individual alone who is intended to bear the brunt of this obituary; it is McCarten as the representative—the very able representative, by the way—of an entire editorial way of life that has passed its peak and is descending as ungracefully as every real power does when the true gism gives out. This is not to say that *The New Yorker* will not coast with the already established winners for a decade or more and fur the minds of its readers with the warm feel of occasional mink; sporadic excellent pieces, their value on the literary exchange having been appraised long in advance, will no doubt tastefully appear and momentarily restore faith to the worried parishioners; but the virility, adventurousness, connection with the living tissue of your audience can only be restored by rebirth. This is not about to happen in the near future and could only occur after the present *New Yorker* trust fades away and 20 years hence stirs the fires of someone who buys the title and is then animated, directed, by the legend of a memorable past joined with a love of the living present.

That love—today a savoring of horror because we have had to live with it, a true delectation of the dislocated age we inhabit, an elastic and surreal response to cruelty and ugliness instead of the desperate and unreal attempt to duck its existence—is absent in the very motor of the present-day *New Yorker*. Its creators are overaged, overinsulated; the truly gorgeous notion of style which they gave to America has invisibly changed into a new style which they are afraid of and don't understand. The magazine is merely cruising now, because it has no place to go except to stay afloat and collect the reward for endurance. But every now and then you'll run across one of its pop-gun artists, like John McCarten, firing away as in the good old days, and then all of a sudden you'll feel embarrassed for the man because he is such a goddamned fool and is so proud of it. . . .

Good night, sweet sheet.

2

James Baldwin's remarkably direct, shocking, uncensored confrontation of white American ignorance in the November 17th *New Yorker* has been singled out as evidence that my obituary on this magazine, for being grossly removed from the reality we all know, was premature. But the freshness of Baldwin's article graphically illustrates how desperately in need *The New Yorker* is of genuine communication, if it is to justify itself, and how unreal its normal posture looks in relation to only one (the Negro issue) of the radical metamorphoses that are transpiring before our contemporary American eyes. Baldwin is one of the very few Negro writers ever to publish in *The New Yorker*, perhaps the only one, and while his appearance there represents a loosening of the perfumed barrier, it also reaffirms *The New Yorker*'s sense of security in identifying itself with a name and an issue that have already been accepted by ashamed white liberals rather than daring to initiate any troubling thoughts of its own.

From a magazine point of view, it is realistic to keep in mind that Baldwin is publishing his views in *Esquire, Playboy, The New York Times Magazine, Harper's, Nugget*, etc., as well as *The New Yorker*. He has suddenly become one of the most pertinent voices of the day because only he, so far, can truly humanize and illuminate the ugly guilt felt by his noncolored countrymen and therefore no magazine editor—whether of *The New Yorker* or *Seventeen*—is insensitive to his tremendous value as a bridge between alien camps. (With increased awareness of his unique position Baldwin has become ever more forceful in his role, to the point where in his *New Yorker* article—conscious of his genteel new audience—he echoes his thunder long after felling every neces-sary tree, and can't resist threatening his characteristically vulnerable, femalized-psychiatrized readership with murder for their timid deceits in relation to his own manly suffering: It was perhaps irresistible in the surroundings, and had them groveling for a week until the next cocktail party, but even Baldwin's mature and fulfilled voice can't entirely sustain the overdramatized burden of avenging prophet which is now permitting his prose to embrace every discursive thought as though it were flame.)

It is not *The New Yorker* who should be naively congratulated on running an outspoken piece by the leading Negro literary spokesman in the U.S. today, valid and blistering as "Letter from a Region in My Mind" was. Both Baldwin and the magazine can be seen as frankly exploiting each other, he for a platform and top-billing right in the hushed center of the Ivy League White Protestant psyche, they for a variety of smart reasons: "courage," prestige, news-value, the hard fact that any article on the Negro is today an automatic circulation-booster, plus genuine open-mouthed admiration of Baldwin and what he stands for in contrast to their own inhibition and lack of editorial conviction. It is hardly possible that William Shawn and the upper echelon who run the present-day *New Yorker* are truly blind and deaf to the new realities that have overtaken most lives—they must get drunk or high with their Negro help on occasion even if they don't ball with them—but so long has the magazine's esthetic been based on a class-oriented sense of repression that one can visualize the sense of shock and love with which Baldwin's warning of vengeance was received. My God, they must have thought when the manuscript was handed around, what new life in even this threat of death! And yet it is bitterly ironic that the acceptance of such new actuality can only be made real to certain self-guarded sensibilities when the knife-point is testing the throat. In the issue of the Negro, and of his eloquent star champion Mr. Baldwin, *The New Yorker* was no doubt succulently willing to yield its white-on-white pages because it sensed a mightier force that could buoy it up and inseminate its jellied blood with meaning; but rather than this being any creative credit to the magazine, it is—in the cold light of editorial values—more probable to read it as a confession of the absence of a positive viewpoint of its own and the desire to spread its legs and offer its body (Baldwin's piece ran 85 pages, advertising-garnished though most of them were) to a genuine infidel at its papier-mâché gates in return for the vicarious life it could extract from even a potential executioner.

Publication of the isolated Baldwin manifesto does not represent consistent *New Yorker* policy in the sense that Dorothy Parker, Shaw, O'Hara, McNulty, Perelman and the other minor masters once did—or even as the unlikely stablemates Salinger, Macdonald, Liebling and young Rev. Updike do today—and it is in the lack of cohesiveness that one can see the waning of a definite spirit, and the attempt to substitute plastic surgery for honest limbs and a tangible soul. It has been said in explanation that *The New Yorker* was young and gay when the world was such, and became calculated and grey when history demanded a realistic change of heart; but the world was ancient and agonized long before *The New Yorker* brightened it with a vivacity that might have owed its external froth to the collegiate 20s, but certainly won its unique life because of the gleam in Harold Ross's dry eye.

Style changes of necessity and any magazine, person, attitude minted in the 20s would have to shed its particular glitter when time rusted it or else be laughed into bankruptcy; no one criticizes *The New Yorker* for not being consistent to the short skirt under which it was so nonchalantly conceived, but for the weekly proof that it has been unable to integrate its youth into its middleage with the same integrity. It may well be, as the wise bores tell us, that values narrow with the years and that it is asking too much to ask *The New Yorker* to bite into life with the same tang that enabled it to grow into its present juiceless imitation of itself. If that is so, then let's pity the dull swindle of age which parades as maturity and write it off as still another hypocrisy dripped onto this insultingly miseducated generation; but *The New Yorker* is too incestuously facesaving to ever healthily admit that its needle no longer bites the flab of its own time, that in function it has become a cover-to-cover tranquilizer precisely for that "little old lady from Dubuque" who, it used to purr, would be horrified by it.

You cannot say, nor was it ever the intention here, that *The New Yorker* doesn't publish valuable or exciting pieces that appear almost as spasmodically as an old movie star's erection: sure they do—Salinger; Macdonald (most effective probably when restrained by space); Liebling (but no longer food or boxing, the vein having been worked dry and repeated because of the magazine's shortsighted encouragement); Tynan when he wrote for them; used warhorse O'Hara still on occasion (although they run him much too often for maximum mileage, apparently out of fear of offending); Wilson when he's not being pedestrianly dated or hopelessly touting old pals like Morley Callaghan and Dawn Powell; J. F. Powers when not being too ultracool about the Catholic world he carries in his pocket; Lillian Ross when in classic form; the neat and deftly written capsule book reviews, isolated treats. But what *The New Yorker* and its trancelike reflex buyers shut from consciousness is that you have to pick through a weekly issue like a private eye, to spot the article/story that contains the life, and junk the rest; it's a page-by-page fliptease for which you pay 35¢ and often as not the one redeeming piece—and how often is there more than one?—isn't there.

The mounting piles of unread synthetic *New Yorkers* in the livingrooms of time-squeezed real New Yorkers declares the anachronism of three-fifths of their editorial matter to a city speedster, and makes one realize that the pace and interests of the magazine—the boring tempest-in-a-tulip fiction, the spinsterishly detailed articles—have been muffled like the rationale of Exurbia itself. "Out here in the hinterland," writes Professor Warren French of Kansas State University to me, "we are still interested in Manhattan itself—its life still excites us— but I am sure no one at *The New Yorker* knows how bored we are with accounts of how tough it is to camp out in a $40,000 chateau in Fairfield County. Such an editorial environment goes well with *Silent Spring*, one of the last really exciting things to appear in *The New Yorker*, but one which has nothing to do with the city at all and is another evidence of the concerns of Exurbia."

Exurbia, suburbia, or Thurbier, the decline of *The New Yorker* can really be seen in the loss of that very fashionableness which, after all else was said, this magazine always felt snugly in about and therefore genially indifferent to intellectual criticism. Fashion, though it be mocked by bushy minds on the fringe of events, is a visible image of where the sharpest point of interest is in any given period, and fashion-setters can be defined as those so sensitive to the daily life of their time that they can feel its pulse long before thicker skins know that one even exists. When country-boy Ross was intuitively turned on to the Algonquin crowd (Parker, Kaufman, Marc Connelly, Benchley, F. P. A., Auntie Woolcott, etc.), whose unpremeditated sophistication in the pages of the infant *New Yorker* gave encouragement to less extroverted and more subtle talents, a chain-reaction of unparalleled goodies was set in motion that caught the flavor and sharply defined the metropolitan stance of the time.

As close as a nose-hair to its day, the magazine anticipated and created style because it was a totally jumping headquarters for the cleverest wits on the scene—everyone who was anyone wanted to get into the act—and from approximately the early 30s to the mid 50s so phenomenal was *The New Yorker's* cultural influence that it imposed its character on nothing less than the American conception of the humorous essay, cartoon, "casual" piece, short story, and ultimately revolutionized magazine journalism in this country with its original reportage. Not one uptown New York book publisher was immune to its salty taste (Simon & Schuster almost made an entire career out of eagerly publishing the magazine between hardcovers every three months), practically every newspaperman throughout the country hoarded dumb misprints to submit and read it with glee, in fact every human communications-medium in the days before the present deluge was literally groomed and conditioned by this tart arbiter of How To Say It Right.

But such genuine power can be said to have ended at least eight years ago—as the uneasy giant of American experience hoisted the window on hungry new life that demanded its own appropriate tongue—just when *The New Yorker* began to scoop in sweet advertising money in that recurring failure of U.S. cultural success: namely, starve with a patched elite audience while putting down your exciting opening notes, then clean up on the masses with a pat formularization of your once-hot magic, and by all means con yourself as you bank the winnings until you're inseparable from the new audience and love your own corn like the farmers who lap it up. Money is power, yes, and *The New Yorker* is now sloshing in green where once it held its threadbare Princeton clothes on high with a hidden safety-pin and laughed; but money-power is common compared to the beam of an original idea which can be mirrored endlessly, or the shape of a new look which can change our vision, or the pace of a new rhythm which can quicken our sense of time and therefore alter the significance of events.

The subtle, enormous influence *The New Yorker* once had in these intangible areas, to the extent of intimately shaping the cream of an American generation now in their 50s, has painfully shrunken because thousands of a new young generation—bulging, bursting, bopping and rocketing at every mental seam— find nothing for themselves but incomprehension or condescending miniaturization in the wrinkle-free *New Yorker* existence salon. "I first discovered that something was amiss," continues Professor French in his letter, "when I found (I was then at the ill-fated University of Florida) that the handful of alert students we had were not reading *The New Yorker* any more as my handful of friends had when we haunted the Ivy League some 20 years ago. *The New Yorker* meant nothing to them, and I was astonished at this, since it had meant so very much to me and others in the dim past. I began to see, however, that *The New Yorker* just really had nothing for them."

In other words, the interest, fascination and identification with the liveliest aspects of one's time and place—that which Ross gave *The New Yorker* with the unappeasable sniffer of a great newshound—has given way to the imitation of such life, primarily because of the intolerable petrification of the magazine's conventions, and the "fashion" that it now robes itself in has inevitably become that of the *ancien régime.* The format of a magazine can be a candid indication of its soul, even more than the editorial matter, and the obvious fact known to practiced eyes in the trade is that the predictable *New Yorker* look—as literally mechanical as the Automat—dissipates joy and buries brilliance within its monotonous sameness. One issue looks, feels and smells like the next, and weekly they add to the undisturbed pyre on the hippest coffee-tables in town because the alert, nervous, multiple-eyed contemporary is psychologically unable to confront an experience so static that it depresses him before he begins. What does it matter if Harold Rosenberg writes penetratingly about painting when his copy is set as excitingly as an actuarial report, discouraging visual imagination at the very moment he is trying to cultivate your mind's eye? The sharpest rollicking pieces by Liebling, Macdonald, West, even almost Salinger, slip by the meshes of the brain into week-later oblivion because of the convictionless regularity of the format, as smooth and faceless as a robot factory. At one time this makeup and typeface spoke coolness, self-effacement, modesty, taste, but all it means now—contrasted with the competition from bold, jazzy four-color ads that bring with them the booming materialism of the outside world—is a deliberate absence of identity that has become as artificial as any outmoded virtue that no longer serves its purpose. Rather than proving any superiority to the lush commercial jungle that now overhangs its tidy garden, *The New Yorker's* uninventive and vapid format is almost a caricature of the standard psychoanalytic insight about rigidity of form being a defense against new experience.

If *The New Yorker* is esthetically reactionary—and the time has long passed when you can snoot the visual as applied to a magazine, or anything else, in this aggressively all-conscious era—it is improbable to expect the magazine's implicit liberalism to be anything more than a moral gesture to another phantom defleshed by history and therefore made kiddie-safe. From what we know Ross was apolitical, a 20s toughie cynicized by Menckenism but possessed of enough confident moxie to editorially transcend politics in the sparkling play of the Manhattan world he loved so much; however, with the ascension to the editorship by Shawn, backed up by the Whites (Katherine and E.B.) and the other policymakers, a gloved New Deal hand showed itself which grips the magazine to this day. But instead of being a vote for progress any more than *The New Yorker's* assembly-line format or archly repressed fiction, this "liberalism" tiptoeingly pitches an effete advocacy of justice which can get wet over the death of Mrs. Roosevelt and small dogs, but conveniently ignores the irony of humaneness of feeling based on the luxury of power. It would never occur to *The New Yorker's* desk-liberalism that its fineness of empathy is an empty vanity, practiced to assuage its impotence in the face of a reality that asks for illumination and action rather than melodious consolation. But like the possession-weary segment of America it has come to represent, this exhausted innovator reclines on the thornless cushion of a passé humanitarianism, without once demonstrating the independence to peer into the revolt which threatens the validity of liberal ideology in our day: namely, that the majority of contemporary humanity can no longer afford to be humane in a mannerly charade of the urgent problems confronting them, and the sensitive hand extended in brotherhood—as in the "serious" lead essays in "The Talk of the Town"—is foolish to expect reciprocity when its manicured good will proceeds from a refinement of the obvious, rather than from the investigation of what has not yet been defined and demands to be. The liberal kindness that emanates from *The New Yorker's* editorial voice has all the power of a canary used to its cage, and unsurprisingly wants to immure its reader like itself, never caring to acknowledge the elementary insight of contemporary Christianity that kindness must be radical today if it is intended as a responsible point of view and not a hollow social grace.

If there was ever an illustration that for our day the liberal conscience is fast becoming the compromised conscience, a better specimen than *The New Yorker* could hardly be found: Preaching an outworn union of fine moral discrimination and epicureanism, it nevertheless buttresses its ooo-la-la conceits with nakedly materialistic and undiscriminating lures from the hardassed manipulators of American commercial taste. As the world shoves its genuine leering face into the pages of the magazine, not in the editorial niceties but in the encroachingly covetous advertisements, *The New Yorker's* conspiracy against reality suddenly takes on the willed perversity of a porcelain thumb stubbornly thrust in the bloodshot eye of the truth. And as the outer world grows increasingly more barbarous in its honest appetites—sexual, political, psychological, sensational— this once-peer is helplessly thrown into static silhouette against the greater energies that dominate it. It is now becoming the passive well-coifed little queen of rough-trade cultural forces that have surpassed it in vigor, wit, pertinence, rhythm, design, excitement, surprise, illumination and self-belief.

To preserve the fiction held by its now largely conventional-minded, easily buffaloed public (and the loser-be-fucked ad agencies) that it is a unique, classy, razzmatazz leader, *The New Yorker* must become increasingly eclectic under the rationalizing flag of its buttery liberalism, scurrying to pluck the safely best from here and there and feed it into the cold jaws of its machine format. But unlike magazines which began with such an opportunistic policy and owe their being and style to precisely their callous lack of belief, *The New Yorker* assumed every jewel of its rare life from its spirit. When it rationalizes that, as it is already cautiously doing out of cynical necessity because it fluffed the challenge of imaginatively redefining its purpose and character in a new America that demands publications which penetrate it with the stinging voice of the accelerated present—stretching its now rubber conscience to include tokens of radical chic* and impressiveness on top but not at the bottom where it counts—it will finally become indistinguishable from any other superslick magazine. As a matter of fact, and this sentence to anyone my age who was once in love is hard to write, it already has.

1962, 1970

---

*The term "radical chic" was coined by Seymour Krim in this expansion of this article originally written for *the Village Voice*. The first part of the article, without the term, appeared in the November 8, 1962 issue of the *Voice*. The expanded piece, adding the discussion of James Baldwin's article "The Fire Next Time" which included the term "radical chic," first appeared in *Shake it for the World, Smartass* in January, 1970. In June, 1970 Tom Wolfe used the phrase as the title for his famous essay about Leonard Bernstein in *New York* magazine and also incorporated it into the title of his collection, *Radical Chic & Mau-Mauing the Flak Catchers*, published by Farrar, Straus and Giroux later that same year.

9.
The Newspaper As Literature/
Literature As Leadership

On October 30, 1966 (but it could have been tomorrow), the late *New York World Journal Tribune* carried a page-one story by Jimmy Breslin from Fairfield, California, that told of the arrival at the Travis Air Force Base of four dead Marines from Vietnam. Breslin gave a closeup of exactly what happened as the four aluminum boxes were lifted off the transport plane that brought them in and were taken by covered truck to a mortuary on the air force base. He told how the cold northern California night-wind spun the tags on the metal coffins, how they were trucked in darkness behind the terminal where 165 new soldiers were about to fly off to the same place from where the bodies had come, and how the human remains of these dead Marines—called "H.R." in military shorthand—were gingerly handled by the embarrassed personnel in the mortuary:

> "Lift easy," one of them said. "Yeah, lift very easy," another one said. . . . The airmen brought the other three cases in and now the four dead Marines were side by side on the wooden rack. "There is nothing inside these boxes, just human remains," one of the airmen said. "Inside they got a rest for the head and then just an empty box," another one said.

Breslin tells us that on each aluminum box was stenciled, "RETURN TO USAF MORTUARY TSN RVN," and in the last paragraph of his 1800-word story he explains that this "meant when the bodies of the four Marines were taken out of the cases, the cases should be put on a plane and returned to Tan Son Nhut in the Republic of Vietnam, so that the cases could be used again."

In that flat, open, deceptive (Gertrude Stein and Ernest Hemingway are stretched out in those "cases," repetitively tolled three times along with the dead Marines) and yet completely practical tone of voice, Breslin gave a picture of contemporary reality that went beyond the particular Sunday story he had written. By sticking entirely to the facts and selecting them with a prose artist's touch—the art in Breslin's shrewd hands being to underplay details packed with emotional consequence and by flattening them allow their intrinsic value to float clear—he forced his readers to experience larger meanings than the return of

117

four men, or parts of them, from Vietnam. The simple details themselves, without any evidence of strain on Breslin's part (naturalness is his big trump card as a persuader), became symbolic of the technological impersonality demanded by war in the 60s; of how men who were alive 24 hours before on distant soil became converted into neatly packaged meat sent home in the wink of a mechanical eye; of how the quick and utilitarian techniques for transporting and disposing of this meat becomes the foreground of a story about death today and makes the luxury of sentiment ridiculous; of how the living try to adjust to the rapid businesslike logistics of human annihilation and the only act of baffled mourning allowed them is to handle a sealed aluminum box gently.

For all they knew there could be dirty underwear in it, so weird, abstract, numbing to the emotions and mind is the way boisterous young bucks fly out from this West Coast terminal and quickly fly back as souls of aluminum.

All this and more can be legitimately read into Breslin's story, and yet he did not have time to calculate all the echoes set up by what he had written; working under a deadline for a daily paper, with his piece due in New York by roughly 5 P.M. on Saturday evening (October 29th) at the latest, he had to write as well as he possibly could about an event dissolving in front of his eyes—like a sharpshooter on the run. (Actually, I heard later from Dick Schaap that Breslin had tried this particular story before and been dissatisfied with it; this was his second run on it, according to Schaap; but since every story a good newspaperman writes is different, like a jazzman cutting several versions of the same tune out of an excess of spirit, it is not unfair to the existential reality of this story's composition to see it as a totally fresh shot out of Breslin's typewriter.)

The details enumerated earlier, with the actual names of the personnel on the air force base to be spelled correctly, the right numbers on the transport plane and the insignia on the mortuary to be set down so accurately that they could stand up in a court of law, constituted his materials. With this data plus the intake of his senses he had to build a story with a purpose and build it quickly; unlike a "pure" fiction writer he could not convert the four dead Marines into 24 to dramatize the scene—although an air force major in the story is actually quoted as saying that there were three separate shipments of aluminum boxes that day—nor could he alter the shape of the terminal or the number of planes parked out in front ready to fly newcomers to the combat area. (For the record there were two commercial airliners supplied by TWA and Pan American ready to do this unpublicized chore, with a third air force transport plane assigned to carry the equipment.)

But within the circumscribed reality of this particular story, without violating facts that could be checked by others and would be hotly scrutinized by those who had actually been on the air force base that night, Breslin had to write, rewrite, twist, carve his piece. If he wrote it in a West Coast motel room after covering the story, as is likely, he probably had no more than three hours to do approximately 10 wide-margin double-spaced pages. (Most metropolitan newspapermen triple-space on four stapled sheets of copy paper with carbons in between known as "books;" the triple-spacing is to allow for editing and the extra sheets go to various desks; Breslin's double-spacing on one single piece of copy paper at a time indicates the weight he can throw around any New York newspaper office except the *Times*.) Typing in clean bursts with an aggressiveness and intensity that doesn't appear in the copy, surrounded by hot, visibly smoking coffee, smoldering cigarettes, his 7½-by-5-inch wire-ringed National notebook and a nearby telephone which he might have used half a dozen times to fill in tiny chinks of information—Breslin has the personal style of a boom-boom MGM supernewspaperman, but each of these props is active in itself or tends to create a rhythm of action—he had to see into this story with his own experience-cum-feelers and find the precise way for rendering a new event that had never crossed his consciousness before in all its fine relationships. Each story is totally new to the newspaperman or truthteller-on-the-run, even if he has taken a quick bite out of it before; each time he "covers" or "goes out on the street" he is faced with unique combinations of history, large or small, and the only way he can confront an event that he can't wholly anticipate or control is by his technique and finally his depth of perception.

Breslin's depth as a writer (and he can also be shallow and obvious) reveals itself in the quiet line-by-line way in which he places the significant small detail and the entirely believable, telling quote: "We don't pick them up like freight," one of the defensive airmen tells him in the mortuary that "had white walls and no windows and a heavy air conditioning unit hanging from the ceiling." (Notice how he relies on the "and" to both keep his sentence moving and deal out the necessary facts without pausing; the device can get mechanical—and when a Breslin story fails it can be flatter than stale beer—but what Gertrude Stein and Hemingway never realized was how handy their simplified English would become for journalists who cram sentences to the teeth with fact and are always looking for the most painless way to do the job.)

As a columnist, Breslin is permitted to use the "I" whenever he wants since the very idea of having a column is based upon owning a big "I;" but his best or at least most serious stories direct attention to the scene itself—four dead Marines, a Greenwich Village firehouse that lost half a dozen men in a building cave-in, the night at the New York Hilton when Rockefeller heard that he'd won the governorship for the third time; the more important the event, the less Breslin will inject himself, although he has written totally knockout *New York* magazine feature stories in the first person that gain their freshness from his willingness to bat out the literal truth about his drinking, rages, tyranny over neighbors-wife-and-family, bad debts, etc. These stories almost never fail to entertain because they shout with honesty of emotion and are never self-conscious. Breslin inherits the old-fashioned newspaper code of suspicion for intellectuals and intellectuality—which has been melting in the last several years with his support of liberal and vaguely avantgarde causes—but the virtue of his show-me-I'm-from-Queens stance, at least in the first-person pieces, is that it keeps him earthy, tangible, solid and finally modest in a way that a writer who took his mortal being more heavily could not be. Breslin's comparative spiritual modesty as well as his narrow-mindedness and occasional noisy rant seems the direct result of his Irish Catholic upbringing, which puts an unquestioned God cleanly above man and permits Breslin to be easy in print about himself because he is not trying to save the world.

From his point of view it would probably be blasphemous and even more important—to that knowing street-urchin eye—inexpressibly stupid.

But if this 37-year-old Babe Ruth, Jr., of the cityroom is ultimately easier to take and "puts a cheaper price on his ass" (to Pete Hamill the key to snapping newspaper prose) than other first-person blabbers whose confessions appear in Important Books, there is nothing shy about the writing ego that went into "4 Bodies At Midnight," the headline for his dead Marine story. Here, disdaining to use the first person because it would have shown a lack of "class" (to which Breslin is as sensitive as Frank Sinatra—both gangster buffs), he had to project his feelings through the dead kids and the situation itself and did not let himself offer an opinion. In other words, he had to write a *short story* as formal as the kind taught in any fiction class, except his was about people with actual dogtag numbers and a real place still doing its ugly work today. By an unexpected evolution—or is it a revolution?—the American realistic short story from Stephen Crane to post–John O'Hara has now been inherited by the imaginative newspaperman, like Breslin, and all the independent probing of reality that the best native literary artists of the past have achieved can now be tried by a creative reporter without undue sweat.

Not only is there no longer any pretense involved (pretense in the sense that so-called "fine" writing was once a world apart, in a *book*, while newspaper prose was supposed "to line somebody's birdcage" in Hamill's words), there is a definite advantage to the newspaperman in recreating reality if he uses every conceivable literary avenue open to him; for his job, depending on the intensity of his sense of mission, is to penetrate ever more deeply into the truth of every story—and this can only be done if he has the instruments of language, narrative knowhow, character-development, etc., that until now have always been associated with fiction. ("Every technique of fiction is now available to us," Tom Wolfe said recently. And if Breslin is currently the Kid Ruth of the New Journalism, Wolfe is certainly its ultraflashy-smooth Ted Williams. Wolfe goes on to say: "Stream-of-consciousness and subjective truth is the next breakthrough. Gay Talese's article in *Esquire* in 1958, 'Joe Louis At 50,' is a classic in this direction; Truman Capote, who in my opinion is not a first-rate writer, was only doing in *In Cold Blood* what Talese had done six or seven years before.")

Perhaps there was a time, really, truly, down in the belly, when fiction in America shed more light on the outlook of a generation than nonfiction; but today the application of fictional and avantgarde prose techniques to the actual scene before us seems much more crucially necessary. When Breslin wrote his story about the silent flight of four statistics from Asia to California he was telling us things about the America that each of us must confront on our own—this real-unreal country and each of our lives in it being bound up with a strange war, monsterlike technology, guilt over the death of these four young guys, secret happiness that we escaped their fate, bewilderment toward the future. He was reporting to us from the outer perimeter of our own coolly murderous time, expanding through the clarity of his writing skill our knowledge of what is *actually going on* in places we can't possibly get to but which all add up to our sense of fateful identity as a people.

If for some reason he had written this same story as a fictional sketch—changing names, location, inflating or "working up" the tone while he disguised the specifics as so many unimaginative novelists do for no significant purpose except self-protection—would he have achieved anything more? The question, admittedly loaded, answers itself. Not only with this kind of story would he have added nothing to the central mood that justly shakes up the reader after finishing it, fictionalizing what was as rich as fiction in his mind to begin with would have disgraced the reality of what he saw. The punch of his story lies in its actuality; although Breslin has a reputation in New York newspaper circles of occasionally "piping" or making up quotes that fit a situation or clinch a scene, this can only be done in a small part and in itself is sometimes an act of courage. To put quotes in the mouths of living people is a more audacious act of the imagination than to invent words for people who have never existed, especially when the writer knows these quotes will be read by the participants and he will be judged for it.

Breslin's story *gains* its impact precisely because it is not made up; it can be checked; and it was written out of that dual responsibility which rides the writer-reporter as it doesn't the totally free "creative writer," namely factual justice to his material and yet equal pride in the literary possibilities offered by his imagination. He is playing the most potentially dangerous game of all, writing about real, observable, aftermath-ridden life situations; and yet—to the extent that he is a writer equal in skill and ambition to the best novelists—he has to invest this living material with every bit of his artistic sense, his concern for language, mood, nuance, insight, suspense, moral value. And if he is a genuine first-rate writer, on a par with any who have put their signature on this ruptured time, he has to illuminate the material with his own needle-sharp angle of vision—"material" which is people who are very much alive, nameable, often prominent, people whom he will meet again as a vulnerable man himself caught up in the crosscurrents of contemporary U.S. life.

The reporter-writer does not have the freedom that the old-fashioned novelist or short story writer had and still has. He is hemmed in by his awareness of the living characters who make up the cast of each new story. If he wants to satirize them, make them pathetic, select a fact or describe a gesture that will perhaps show them up as frauds he has to be aware (and is soon made aware!) that there will be a kickback right in the psychic breadbasket. There is a resiliency between what he writes and the public, and if he takes risks either imaginative or moral he does not do it in a vacuum or in the eye of posterity; he is bound to be reacted to with a bang in the present. This means that in the case of a Breslin, Tom Wolfe, Pete Hamill—as well as Murray Kempton and Ralph J. Gleason, the two older pillars of the New Journalism—the literary imagination that each possesses is not allowed the freewheeling of a writer who is not called daily to the bar of justice for his work.

Breslin's artistic imagination in the dead Marine story had to function within the framework of the air base, the number of caskets, the name of the community that houses the base, all the tough facts that constitute the skeleton of every reporter's story; in addition, he had to cope with the intangible human element that hangs over every scrap of type that appears in a newspaper with a byline attached to it. Will he get punched in the mouth after the story appears? Has he wounded someone unintentionally or seriously fucked them up? Is there a possibility of inaccuracy that will backfire and embarrass not only himself and his newspaper but the precarious balance of the event involved? Within this network running from potential anxiety to real outward danger to hardheaded responsibility for the factual truth, Breslin or any feeling newspaperman tries his creative chutzpah to its limit in order to extract the most he possibly can from a fleeting set of circumstances that will never come again.

Until quite recently it was customarily thought that the place for high imagination in contemporary prose writing was in fiction—but is this the kind of writing that is most significant today for the helplessly involved reader who is in a state of flux trying to relate his life to the world? When Establishment book critics say that there are no major novelists of the American 60s comparable to the Hemingway-Fitzgerald-Wolfe-Faulkner combine, they mean that none stand as solid and sharply cut against the waving backdrop of the shapeless age we inhabit. But these men, in spite of the bookish glamour attached to their names, were in the most radical sense *reporters* whose subject matter and vision was too hot or subtle or complicated or violent or lyrical or intractable or challenging for the massmedia of their period. They had to make up their own stories, based on what they observed and felt, and publish them as loners who leanly stood for personal integrity and subjective truth in opposition to the superficial "objective" journalism of their day. The exclusion of the deeper half of reality by oldtime journalism was very much at the bottom of the mystique of the American Novel as it has been sentimentalized in our time—that only in this medium could the real down-and-dirty story of the country and the nature of its people be told. If you were a prose writer, there was almost a necessity to work in the form of fiction 20 or 30 years ago because only through it could you "tell" more than you could in journalism; by inventing characters with madeup names, put in imagined situations, you could reveal more about being a modern American than in any other way.

But why should the necessities of the 20s, 30s and 40s (although the fictional necessity was already fading by the end of the war) be right for today? The talk in New York about newspapermen like Breslin, Wolfe, Hamill, the perennial Kempton, Ralph J. Gleason of the *San Francisco Chronicle,* and after that journalists who write for weekly or monthly publications like Nat Hentoff, Jack Newfield ("the immediacy of TV has created the opening for this kind of writing"), John Wilcock, Allan Katzman, Richard Goldstein, Gay Talese, Barbara Long, Michael C. D. Macdonald, Gail Sheehy, Brian O'Doherty, Paul Krassner, Sid Bernard, Gene Lees, Lawrence Lipton, Saul Maloff, Jack Kroll, Warren Hincle, Roger Kahn, Albert Goldman, etc., is where the immediate interest and excitement lies. The freshness of these writers, first the daily newspapermen, then the weekly journalists, then the monthly essayists and social observers—include here half-time novelists like Paul Goodman, Harvey Swados, Mailer, Susan Sontag, John Clellon Holmes—is that they are using the eyes and ears that American novelists used 30 years ago upon a uniformly fantastic public reality that millions of people must cope with daily. A current of appreciation flows between their audience and what they have to say; they are "needed" in an acute, shit-cutting way that novelists no longer seem to be, if only because of the time-gap between real action out on the streets and fiction; it is only when the novelist gives us a deeper vision of this evidence before our eyes—like Heller with *Catch-22* or Selby with *Last Exit to Brooklyn*—that the naked individual imagination seems as pertinent as it once was, because it extends our understanding.

With present law what it is, Selby and Heller would have been jailed or murdered by their unforgiving subjects if they wrote their true names and deeds in the same way that they fictionalized them. And John Barth might be expelled from the human race (or at least his university professorship) for his view of it. But in 1967 that is the only practical justification for "fictionalizing"—if it says something that can't possibly be said otherwise. And with the accelerating frankness and freedom of expression that journalists demand today—they are perhaps the most disciplined literary rebels of our time because of their mature sense of fact, the moral radar because they are situated out in front and become the alerted senses for the rest of us—how much *has* to be fictionalized? Reality itself has become so extravagant in its contradictions, absurdities, violence, speed of change, science-fictional technology, weirdness and constant unfamiliarity, that just to match what is with accuracy takes the conscientious reporter into the realms of the Unknown—into what used to be called "the world of the imagination."

And yet *that* is the wild world we all live in today when we just try to play it straight.

If living itself often seems more and more like a nonstop LSD trip—"illogical, surrealistic, and mad" as the 50-year-old Ralph Gleason keeps saying in his nuttily misnamed "On The Town" column in the *San Francisco Chronicle*—what fertile new truths can most fiction writers tell us about a reality that has far outraced them at their own game? How can they compete with the absurd and startling authorship of each new hour? It becomes a diminished echo, the average serious good novel today; but the average sharp piece of New Journalism can at present never become an echo because it keeps moving into this new universe of unreality and exposing it with the zest that Sinclair Lewis once used to tear the hide off Main Street. A new generation of authority-suspicious newspapermen can only take so much repression and traditional burying of what they know to be true before ripping up cliches in the face of a new scene; no one is in the professional position to see and communicate as much as the daily reporter, and yet up to now he has been handcuffed by the much-used and abused journalistic slogan, "good taste," which until the 60s left the most alive writing in a U.S. newspaper story on the copydesk floor. If I am covering a story about a Washington politician found dead in a screw-a-minute 43d St. hotel with a spade hooker, and I want to write about it truthfully, I have to mention details that would have offended my mother and father (dead these 35 years) because emotionally they couldn't handle this information. Newspapers, geared to the broadest readership of all publications, used to cater to people like my mother and father and yours, and such stories—prostitution, miscegenation, homosexuality, suicide, psychosis among well-known people, etc.—were edited or whitewashed so that the middle-class public could continue its hypocritical idealism in spite of facts which were quite different.

Then, during the first 40 years of this century in America, it was only a minority of the fiction writers, playwrights (practically none before O'Neill) and poets among the users of words who broke this conspiracy of public lying and attempted to show things for what they were. There was a pragmatic reason for our Stephen Cranes, Dreisers, O'Neills, Djuna Barneses, Faulkners, Hemingways. They were necessary if one wanted to know how creatures like oneself actually lived, suffered and died. Hollywood, slick magazines, radio—as well as newspapers—demanded by their cynical manufacture of safe good cheer, Protestant wish-fulfillment and the cleaning-up of evidence that a few brave maniacs of hairy expression take up the burden for all.

But this neat division between purity and compromise doesn't exist any longer—obviously. The current generation brought up under the huge umbrella of the massmedia doesn't despise the sellout aspects of the bigtime action as we 40-and-over puritans did because of our conditioning. As McLuhan suggests, the massmedia are an extension of the rock generation's nervous system— newspapers, movies, TV, radio, records, tapes, every device of communication which reaches millions of people—and it is inconceivable that they are going to romanticize (as we did) the power of a "fine" novel that sells 1500 copies in the wake of the communications hurricane on which they were suckled. No, they want to make it in the public media that this country since World War II has revved up to such a colossal pitch; but they want to do it on the terms that the former generation once thought of only for poetry, novels and serious plays— with total integrity; and right now a struggle for power is going on between the technicians who invented and the advertisers who capitalized on these octopal massmediums and the young visionaries (who might have been novelists 30 years ago) presently using them as hotlines of communication. But it is still the Word, written, spoken, sung, the very Word that has been the most significant instrument for men throughout history, it is that Word as conveyor of reality which is at the heart of this tug of war and through which a new and broader conception of literature is being shaped.

Does the book-reverencing literary critic or any other stubborn protector of the unsacred past realize that Lord Buckley, Lenny Bruce and Mort Sahl, Joan Baez, Buffy St. Marie and Bob Dylan, users of pop forms like nightclub comedy and folkrock preaching, have cut into the serious American literary man's ground by using the massmedia to make knifing comment of needed immediacy?

And does the Harvard doctor of letters recognize that a Jimmy Breslin or Pete Hamill, two cocky Irish parochial-school boys off the greater New York streets, are using that traditional literary doormat, the newspaper, to get to reality-through-language much more quickly than is done through books?

Sure they do; but they don't know quite how to handle it.

As you doubtless know, Matthew Arnold called 19th-century journalism "literature [written] in a hurry," a famous phrase that until now has reflected the sense of utilitarianism and literary inferiority felt by most journalists when they compared themselves to "writers." In Manhattan newspaper (and weekly magazine) shops you'll find veterans who spit on their work and automatically say that the importance of today's newspaper is to provide the wrapper for a smelly flounder tomorrow. The movie-portraits are for real, folks: no one is more snottily and superficially cynical about both reality and writing than the oldtime, ex-alcoholic, security-obsessed newspaper granddad whom you'll run into on the overnight rewrite desk of a New York paper. He drools about Mencken or Hemingway or James Gould Cozzens, but it never crosses his mind that he could have done comparable work within the limits of his own job; from his point of view newspapering is merely Grinding It Out under the humbling restrictions of time, space, subject matter and childishly basic English; he thinks newspaper work "ruins your prose" and any idea that every story—even an obituary—can be interpreted, shaded, significantly woven, carrying a human center and an implicit judgment on experience, has long since been shut out in the empty night of unthought while granddad figures out new ways to pad the overtime sheet.

But this hard-guy-with-soul-of-mush attitude, this fatalistic acceptance and sneering embrace of the Grub Street rhythm of newspapering, is the dying style of a generation who looked at literature through the intimidated eyes of being "hacks," as they saw themselves, or "clerks of fact" as Pete Hamill has beautifully put it; self-mocking errand boys without a grain of conviction, carrying into print the latest fart of some celebrity of politics, entertainment or high (low) finance and being embittered because the Name was up there in lights that they helped plug in while they were condemned to doing whitecollar porter work in the cityroom. Traditionally, the average cityside newspaperman was a machine, a phone-bully, a sidewalk-buttonholer, a privacy-invader, a freebie-collector and not a writer at all—he had a formula for processing his information (much of it dumped on him by publicity men) and was not encouraged to depart from it. It is no wonder at all that the combination of what he saw—and the reporter has entré into every doorway of life without exception if he chooses to use it—coupled with the injunction not to express it produced that style of the Big Sneer which gave him his uniqueness as an American type. But underneath the cocked fedora and the rest of the so-called glamor crust you could find a man who thought of himself as a failure by the worldly standards pounded into his being by his work—money, achievement and status.

Newspaper offices were known in the trade as being comfortable, in-the-know flophouses where losers came to trickle out their lives; alcoholics floated on the assurance of seniority granted them by the once-righteous power of the American Newspaper Guild and those who weren't alcoholics floated just the same, notching up Army-style credits and cautious little nesteggs against the last winter of enfeeblement and the final smirk. The idea that they might be frontrunners snaring and interpreting reality as it broke before their eyes would have been a joke to the majority of these putdown experts who envied the stars on the world stage that they covered, but never conceived that they themselves were in the position to make history and not merely record it.

But this lock on the imagination of the old cigar-chewing bigots—and their young imitators who snipe and curse at easy targets to prove that they are really in The Business—in no way deterred the balling sense of opportunity felt by a nuclear-goosed generation of newcomers now in their 30s (Breslin, Wolfe, Hamill, Gay Talese, Alfred G. Aronowitz, Dick Schaap, Eliot Fremont-Smith, Larry Merchant, Kenneth Gross, Vincent Canby, Mike Royko, Nicholas von Hoffman, etc.) and the two intransigent standouts 49 and 50 respectively (Murray Kempton and Ralph J. Gleason), who realized in differing ways what could be done within the dulling graveyard of a newspaper. Certainly there had been great inspirations in the profession only recently dead or played out: Heywood Broun (admired by Gleason), Westbrook Pegler (ditto for Kempton, Hamill and Wolfe in spite of W.P.'s politics), H. L. Mencken ("a favorite," Wolfe), Damon Runyon, Jimmy Cannon and even Walter Winchell (the last two hugely appreciated by Hamill for their language and Cannon in particular for his jazzy literary flair). But most of these older writers, however superpro in the daily journalism of their day, hit their high moments with the "crusading" approach that has been the essence of the American newspaper religion since Lincoln Steffens. If the large majority of professional reporters and editors of news have developed a protective sneer to cope with the stuffed urinal of human avarice, weakness and folly into which they've been dunked, the minority of newsmen whose names stand out from the past have always had their moral indignation heightened and made sharply eloquent by what they've been exposed to.

It commands one's respect, this unique kind of moral courage, and it is central to the old-fashioned idea of the press as watchdog to the community—more often a capped-tooth watchdog, unfortunately—but it is not at the heart of the style that lies waiting for the total reporters of the immediate future. This new style or revolution in reportorial values—which can be seen in varying part in Breslin (the novelistic fullness of his recreation of reality); Wolfe (the rhythmic montage of disjointed contemporary phenomena); Hamill (sophisticated realism which brings an urban snarl to bear on the absurdity of what he covers); Kempton (an elegance of mind and irony trained on the soiled collar of events); Gleason (his unkidding notion that the world today is insane and his enthusiastic tubthumping for popular avantgardists who can cut a path to the future)—goes far beyond the public role of pointing a finger at specific fraud or deceit, which has usually been the American journalist's finest hour from Steffens to Pegler. It rather points the finger at Self (both the writer's and the reader's) in relation to the World Out There; it concerns the *whole man*—the acting out in print, as Hamill intuitively senses on certain stories, of the subjective being as it collides with objective happenings. A good example would be the vulgarity and possibly the evil of Johnson's 1966 Asian tour as seen through Hamill's personal eyes (". . . a non-event") and then communicated to a public of half a million or more people through the *New York Post*. If the New Journalist is the outrider for news of reality itself—since we live in an age where the interaction between public events and private response is becoming the whole mortal show for everyone, the anonymous as well as the notorious, all of whom live under the threat of each new day's surprises—then it should be clear why the specific villain-baiting of a Pegler or, occasionally, Kempton is a cowboy-and-Indians game compared to the infinity of inner and outer space that the newspaperman has now inherited. When the New Journalist goes out to cover a story today he is handling nothing less than the time in which he lives; no matter how trivial his story, if his frame of reference is broad as well as acute, he can bring to bear upon it his own fate as a riddled modern man and relate it to the similarly riddled lives of his readers. It is no longer the mere formal outlines of an experience that we expect from a Breslin, Wolfe or Hamill, but its entire quality, overtones and undertones, in a word the "saturation reporting" (Wolfe's phrase) that we used to get from novelists but now need daily to understand the untrustworthy world in which our own small destinies are being negotiated.

This need to know our fate may be more intense than ever before—the "officialese" of which Orwell contemptuously spoke has grown thicker and demands immediate translation if men's minds are not to be permanently blown by impenetrable doubletalk—but the literary elite in this country has long shied away from American journalism in its crass or bulldog-edition actuality. Truman Capote, upon the publication of *In Cold Blood*, took great strenuous pains to distinguish what he was doing (and did very fastidiously well) from what the unelegant New Journalists were attempting to do every day on cheaper paper; their stuff was "just journalism," while his was "Art," dig?

But was it art in the most profound sense, which entails great risk, a new point of view, and above all the conviction to change the world to your way of seeing?

With the division of literary labor between the truck-drivers and the high princes of words—so common in our country for the last 25 or 30 years—the university, the abstract novel (Barth, Hawkes, Sontag, etc.) and literary theory have claimed the more refined or at least better-trained minds while it has been left to the guy next door to wade into the enormous literary problem of trying to tell the whole truth in the newspapers. Wolfe, 36, is a Yale Ph.D. in American Studies—true; but Breslin, Hamill and Gleason never graduated from college (Hamill, the 32-year-old whizkid, never even finished highschool) and Kempton apprenticed for what is currently the most mandarin style in daily journalism by being a grubby assistant labor reporter. These men learned by writing under the pinched code, the brutal deadlines and the unflinching pragmatism that characterizes all newspaper work; now—suddenly—the literary doors of their profession have been kicked wider open than at any time in the past and they have been catapulted into becoming spokesmen whose role and responsibility to truth has grown enormously. It is not unfair to say that as writers they are more pertinent to this time of permanent crisis than eight- or nine-tenths of the straight literary figures who read them regularly every afternoon and then patronize them in the evening over cocktails.

And yet—if one could undo years of aloofness, fear, luxurious introspection, sheltered alienation, university tenure, all the proud and wanly smiling snobbery that went with being a Serious American Writer of this period just ending—what better place for truly significant prose than the daily newspaper? Why shouldn't it seem the most logical place in the world for writers who teethed on fictional naturalism-realism to test their concepts of reality upon alive characters and report their findings to a huge captive audience that has to listen merely to get the news? More than that, the journalistic stakes are a thousand times greater than in the past because of the immediate reverberation of an original statement today: if Harrison Salisbury shook up the Washington power machine with his *Times* reports of the U.S. bombing of Hanoi, and William Manchester threw a gritty bomb into national Democratic politics with his imaginative and yet factual portrait of *The Death of a President*, consider the power that our most eminent prose writers could finally wield in their own country by being the most sensitive conductors for news, the transmitters of verbal reality for the nation.

Power is not to be despised in a culture that uses it like America; and writers, too long the weak and easily seduced stepsisters of the national family, are not to be condemned for craving it; when H. L. Mencken said of this country and Poe, "They let him die like a cat up an alley," he was merely concretizing the hatred that literary artists have always felt in this society toward a citizenry that has found them ornamental rather than basic. But what could possibly be more basic than this generation's Poes and Melvilles (or Ray Bradburys and Saul Bellows) applying their vision of existence to news as it breaks, reading individual values into what is now a mechanical UPI report, interviewing Johnson as candidly as Brady photographed Lincoln, finally breaking out of the profound isolation of their heads and gambling their point of view on its involvement with events? News has *become* reality for millions in this Age of Journalism; but what if this reality—a mine disaster, a nuclear test under the Atlantic, the death of Ann Sheridan, a Harlem riot—were to be both accurately and originally reported at the very moment that it happened (not three months later in *Esquire*) by an Ellison or Kerouac or Jean Stafford?

Suppose, in other words, that our very understanding of what is news was to be overturned by coverage that made uncommon human sense as well as giving the facts, and that our information was no longer flat and closed but fully dimensional and open—as open and revealing and meaningful as the writer could make it by pouring his spirit into a union with the event? Have you ever stopped to think what could happen to the programmed newspaper reader if the finest literary talent was used to illuminate even the most perfunctory one-paragraph auto accident out on the street, how the closed or small mind would be jolted by a recognition of the mutual dependence of all our beings if a writer who cared interposed the warm hands of his typewriter between the cold statistic and fact-numbed heads?

The "symbolic action" that literary artists have frustratedly contented themselves with in a book would take a radical turn into monumental real action if they could dominate the sources of news, not only in the press, but in the fields of spoken literature as well—radio and TV. To be novelistically engaged with one's time in the manner of the early Malraux, Koestler and Camus is an undeniably great modern primitive example; but now there is a real chance that the masses' version of truth, of what is, of reality itself, can be revolutionized if men and women of proven artistic vision step down from their rickety subjective towers of private being into the communal ego-socialism of daily journalism. The artificial split between literature and journalism has never seemed more beside the point as the human race staggers into the last third of the 20th century not really knowing if it will survive or what kind of freaky mutation it will become. If such encompassing self-doubt has eaten into the race, isn't it inevitable that it has affected literature as well, that the so-called transiency of journalism is no greater than the seeming irrelevance of most literature today? The step from a Jimmy Breslin "up" to Robert Lowell is no longer the giant step that it might once have been when newspapermen stood in awe of honest-to-gawd writers; the best of the New Journalists are already writers equal in their way to any of their generation; but the step from Robert Lowell "down" to a Jimmy Breslin has implications that go beyond writing to the possibility of the artist affecting the reaction to events themselves by shaping the significance of daily reality with his own hand. Since the New Journalists have gone like pilgrims to literature to learn the techniques for being faithful to all that they alone are in a position to see, and sweat daily to give added dimension, nuance, perspective and insight to their stories, let once-mighty literature swallow its whitefaced pride and give its mythic propensity to jouralism—the *de facto* literature of our time.

If this seems like a special curving of the truth, consider the fact that at least 30 underground weekly and biweekly newspapers—from such respectable rebels as the *Village Voice* and the Los Angeles *Free Press* to the latest *Rat* and *Oracle*—have sprung up like bayonets in the last 10 (especially the last five) years out of the same soil that once produced little magazines. Why have they replaced their toy tiger literary counterparts, or if not entirely replaced them at least been the strongest force for "new," "different," "anti-Establishment" writing in the last decade? Because (in essence) it is only by usurping the public sources of news or actuality itself—and newspapers more than any other publications have always been the official version of reality, the standard of sanity, the middle-class scale of justice—that fedup young writer-journalists can advance a totally liberated view of the contemporary scene which challenges the entire range of assumed belief. A strictly imaginative work, with no literal frame of reference outside the author's mind, can be evaded today by a defensive reader who claims it has no relevance for him; but how can any reader evade a typical L. A. *Free Press* story about two cops who were found stashing marijuana for themselves which they had confiscated from some young hippies during a bust?

If the 20s were the supreme time of technical experimentation and overthrow in literature, the 60s are the comparably radical decade for the revolution in human values and the breakout in personal lifestyle; it is no longer the pure "literary" expression of the private mind that grabs most of us, but rather the unspoken public declaration of the most hidden energies of individual being that have been crouching in the shadowed doorways of our society. Artists, and especially literary artists, have in the American past been the belligerent walking illustrations of a totally free individualism because they would have suffocated without it; now an entire generation of longhaired Flower Children (to use one of their fast-changing names) has taken over what were essentially the anti-authority attitudes of bohemia and the artist; and the significant word-artist himself—with exceptions like Allen Ginsberg, Mailer, Bobby Dylan, bruised but embracing Jewish sprinters who can identify more easily with change than their more stolid gentile brethren—has stood uncomfortably tight in the face of the very journalistic-pop forms where he is most vitally needed.

For the last two centuries the "artist" has been the martyred holy man of secular life (van Gogh's ear, Nietzsche's insanity, Rimbaud's cancer, Kafka's tortured mental maze, Melville's polar isolation, the list of hell's angels is endless) whose vision of perfection ate into existence long after he was wiped out of the race as a blot on his generation. This was the reverse fairytale formula, that the genuine artist be despised or misunderstood during his lifetime and then haunt men forever from the untouchable penthouse of his grave. Anyone who presumed to be an artist took ironic comfort from the grotesque set of ground-rules laid down over the last 150 or so years and prepared himself for misery with his work as his only blessing. The contemporary artist knew too much about the lives of his bitched breed in the past to expect anything different for himself; "silence, exile and cunning," as defiant Jimmy Joyce put it, were his strategems, his work was the goal, and death was his friend because they lived on such close bedroom terms until the work was done. This, in a bitter nutshell, was the diagram of most outstanding literary artists' earthly existences.

But the world has changed and the diagram must change also.

The lonely dedication of the artist pursuing his chimera no longer impresses us the same way it once did; it is a still-shot from the past, as out of style as a silent movie; mankind's survival itself, mentally as well as bodily, morally as well as materially, hopefully as well as horribly, seems much more crucial as we survey the climate of emergency that clobbers each heart and soul alive right now. The "heroic" suffering and victimization that once distinguished the artist's life has now become the property of everyman-everywoman in this bleak Beckett playlet called Existence, 1967. The neurotic torments that once clung to the artist as to a lover are now democratically spread among the race at large. In other words, the artist's lot has now become the human predicament, they are one, and any artist worth the name must now attempt to solve the riddle of the world because there is no longer any other theme worthy of him. But if his torment is now shared by mankind at large, his imagination and the ability to make it tangible are still his alone until every human alive learns the trick of converting pain into fame; and they have not yet been used upon the mass-communication techniques (journalism in all its forms) that dominate this period as he has formerly used them on traditional stuff like clay, canvas and book.

Art, the most independently truthful form of human expression, was not made to hang on a wall or hide in a page but rather to show duller eyes a more radical and truer version of the life slipping through each generation's hands. For it to speak today—rather than be spoken about and not experienced at full volume—it has ready and waiting for it the outlets of press and electronic journalism; and on the reading-listening-looking end it has for the first time in history a mass audience of millions of individuals milling about in noisy desperation, confused, nihilistic, disgusted with political leadership, laughing at formal religion, looking for jet-age prophets from Tim Leary to Bobby Kennedy who will lead them to the promised land.

But modern literature and art has always been both more truthful and more accurate in its views of the contemporary crisis than any charismatic personality who flits across the headlines.

It has been the most penetrating and significant use of the imagination known to us.

Isn't the time ready for its potential to explode into the center of society via the journalism that has become literature for the majority, so that the human animal may finally know what the "landmine" (the word is Isaac Babel's) of great writing can do when it is hooked up to presidents, governments, prices, power, murder and every variety of antiparadise that clubs us daily? What is art for, from Shakespeare to Terry Southern, if not to transform the world by example? And if Camus is coming to be recognized as much as a spiritual leader as a rare, exalted writer, why can't we begin to see that the word-artist in action in this time *is* the new spiritual leader by virtue of the technological wings that carry what he says?

Jimmy Breslin, cute anti-intellectual that he can be, nevertheless once wrote a disgusted WJT[*] column about the misuse and abuse of language by a machine politician who had the indifferent arrogance to run for office when he could barely speak intelligibly. Norman Mailer wrote an equivalent piece about the prose of LBJ. What they were saying is that language is the clearest indication of being in this time and that they as writers were by their own words superior to the individuals they were writing about. But the implications extend beyond Breslin, Mailer or any single individual; what it seems to mean practically speaking is that articulate leadership has been thrust upon the writer in the authority-empty vacuum of this period; and the most effective way for it to reveal itself is in the mirror of the daily press where the intelligence and sensibility of the writer-artist can carve the very news of the world each day into a revelation that will in turn *act* upon history instead of merely reflect it. What else but actuality itself—and

---

[*]*World Journal Tribune*—Ed.

what is "news" in our time but actuality compressed to a boil?—is worthy of the revolutionary insight that the literary artist has always lined his work with but until now has never had the chance to impose upon the literalness of events? It is no longer just a technical literary question of "fiction" vs. "nonfiction"; the essential issue that creative writers are now faced with is whether the literary-artistic imagination is to be effective in creating a new view of reality that does not shrink the potentialities of being alive in the 20th century or whether it is to be wasted on a pen-pusher's slavish copying of a life which is no longer tolerable according to the deepest needs of men.

If writers of the highest rank were to invade journalism as did E. E. Cummings, James Agee and Albert Camus—and if multimedia journalists are in fact the current "arbiters of reality" (the phrase was first used by a reporter on the *New York Times* about his own paper)—then it is inevitable that the original point of view of the creative writer trained upon people and events in the news has to open new possibilities in every newspaper reader's concept of the real and hence in himself. We writers, in other words, now have the long-sought-for opportunity to basically influence men's conception of the present and therefore the immediate future on a *mass scale* if we are not too proud or frail to enter into the race for moral and ideological power through our daily work in the massmedia. If we show our gossamer stuff in the day-to-day terms that the majority of people understand—pitting our skill and insight and freshness of seeing against the raw acts of this time that make up the news and undermining today's brute reality by our verbal projection of a greater one—there is nothing that can stop our long-postponed hunger for ultimate justice and beauty here and now from becoming a radical force in the life-game. If you agree with me that art is the only untainted vision of truth that can be made demonstrable to all, and if we demonstrate it upon the daily happenings of this time in the journalistic forms that capsulize authenticity for the terse minds of modern men, how can we dodge the fact that we have an alchemic dream with our grasp—the transmutation of base everyday matter into the poem of life?

We may well be on the doorstep of that necessary leap into the future when the world itself is literally governed by art, or truth made manifest, because there is nowhere else to turn and everywhere to go.

1967

10.
Joan Blondell: The Last
of the Great Troupers Teaches Sadness
to the Literary Kid

Joan Blondell was the straight shooter of all time; but unlike the rewards that are supposed to come to individuals who are honest, forthright, spunky and just, she was a very scared and lonely woman when I knew her in the New York 60s.

Not that she ever weakened for a moment and let a tear fall from one of those giant eyes. That wasn't her style. But her life was narrow and barren, from what I could see of it (what I was permitted to see of it), and it was a crushing kind of education for me. God knows what I had been expecting, but look into your own fantasies about the classic movie stars—are there any left?—and then drive a pound of nails through the dream.

Let me start at the beginning. On September 30, 1960, my friend Peggy Boyesen—now a senior editor at Harcourt Brace Jovanovich under the name of Peggy Brooks—toddled me along to a star party for the failed play *Crazy October*. James Leo Herlihy had written the play and tossed the party in his West 14th St. apartment in order to pay his dues to Blondell, Tallulah Bankhead and Estelle Winwood, all of whom had gone down with this script. Tennessee Williams was also there when we walked in, and I realized I was being exposed to something like the insides of a jewel box of American theatrical celebrities.

But the jewel box proved to be a quiet dud. Williams didn't talk and stuffed himself with hors d'oeuvres. Winwood I never got to meet. And the great Tallulah seemed shrunken and wasted, perfunctorily shaking my hand as if it were a cold fish while she sat there attended by two or three homosexual courtiers. It was only when I landed on a couch on the other side of the room and got a grin from a famous face so familiar I couldn't place it, that I realized here was Joan Blondell. Terrific! "Who are you?" she asked, like a normal human being, and soon we were going at it a mile a minute.

Blondell was then 51 or 54, depending on which obit you read (the *Times* had her born in 1909, the *News* and *Post* in 1906), and she looked pretty good if not sensational. Her eyes and breasts had always been her most arresting features and time had done nothing to blunt their electric zap; but the rest of her looked as if it might have been through a wringer and then gently pressed for the occasion. Yet

134

her voice was throaty and tinkled, her eyes danced with amusement, she was game (or seemed to be) for whatever lay around the corner, and in about an hour I bundled Peggy and Joan out the door and we walked the four or five blocks down to El Faro on Greenwich Street. I was as proud as a little strutting drum major. I didn't know then that Blondell had probably been hiding in the house for a week before this cocktail party, that she was starved for simple humanity and yet desperately unprepared for it.

Anyway, that's the way I became her friend for a short time. And the reason I have the date down with such assurance is that somewhere during dinner (paella and white wine, if memory serves) I met my buddy John Benson Brooks in the john and he asked me who the redheaded chick was. Not Blondell, mind you, but my friend Peg. I thought that was the height of style. Needless to say, I introduced them when I stepped out into the night to put Blondell in a cab, and before too long I heard they were a tight couple and then married. Peggy Brooks will never forget September 30, 1960, for sure.

The myth-hugging romantic in me wishes I could tell you the same pretty story about Blondell and myself, and have every would-be star-fucker hang his or her tongue out for an envious moment, but it wasn't to be that way. Please don't get the wrong idea. Even though there was an age gap between us of 13 to 16 years—depending on which newspaper you trust, or don't—I wanted very much to go to bed with her. It would have been great status and, even more important, the very physical incarnation of every erotic fantasy we've all had about screwing the fountainhead of sexuality. To my helpless generation there was nothing conceivably hotter than Hollywood star pussy, and Blondell had slung that marvelous ass and those fantastic breasts around long enough on celluloid to enter every straight American male's mental nightlife.

But there was something removed and even burnt-out about Blondell's response to men when I got to know her. Except for the gentle parody of courtship we sometimes played out on her terrace—dancing to Guy Lombardo's recording of "Stars Fell on Alabama," her saying "You're dreamy" (a line from a film, to please me) and lightly brush-kissing with grins—there was never any chance we would make it. Even if she had felt free enough to want to, as I later learned, she would have been painfully inhibited by the recent scars on her back, which she had collected in Santa Monica by backing through a glass door while bringing a lunch tray to her grandchildren.

But let me get back to the scenario. We exchanged phone numbers that first night and she made it plain that she'd enjoy an unpressured friendship with "my very own intellectual" (I had just edited an anthology of Beat Generation writing). She had rented a big apartment on Sutton Place when she thought the Herlihy play was going into Broadway—it closed out of town—and that was where I always visited her.

The apartment was a lonely, high-priced barn, made even emptier by the three dogs who skittered and scampered like little spoiled brats across the uncarpeted floors. Blondell fed them the best filet mignon, was constantly worrying about them over the phone to the vet, compulsively picked them up and kissed them, showed them off with such gushiness that it wasn't hard to see them as substitute children. Her real children were grown up by then, the son by her first marriage to cameraman George Barnes and the daughter by Dick Powell. In fact she was a grandmother, but the dogs were her only family in New York. Sometimes I thought they were her only friends.

She wanted very much to be outgoing with a new person like myself—even when I asked her the most cornball questions, she was the soul of tolerance—but she was awkward as a spinster. Here was this gal who had embodied the breezy, wisecracking sexpot until it became a national trademark, offering me champagne, Brazilian chocolates (neither of which she touched) and goodies I've since forgotten as if she was afraid I'd stick my coat on and run unless she knocked herself out. It was incredible to me that she didn't realize it was my honor to be there, not hers to try and please me. I later found out she had a tremendous inferiority complex towards anyone she considered literate—she had never finished high school and a genuine college graduate could make her stutter—and for years had been studying from a reading list given to her by Jack Goodman, a now-dead Simon and Schuster editor. (Not unlike that other self-punishing Hollywood lady, Sheila Graham, who humbly studied the reading list Scott Fitzgerald gave her as if it were the Bible.)

Not only was this insecurity or shame based on her lack of formal education, I slowly began to feel it was physical as well. "I had the biggest tits on Broadway when I was 16," she once said with a curl to her lips, as if she had gotten her early jobs because she was a freak. In other words, she was ebulliently assy and sassy in front of footlights or camera, but once she was off, this overwhelming vulnerability overtook her. It wasn't helped by the scores of people who used her, from the New York cop who near-raped her in the late '20s and originally damaged her back by throwing her to a concrete floor, to even a so-called good guy like me who pumped her like crazy. I couldn't resist, no writer could when faced with walking history like Blondell.

What was Dick Powell like? Crosby? Gable? Judy Garland? Bette Davis? Did she really have an affair with sportswriter Jimmy Cannon? (Pete Hamill, when Cannon was dying some years later, told me that "at least Jimmy had a beautiful woman like Joan Blondell in his arms.") Super-producer Mike Todd, her last husband? Come on Joanie, let's dish!

Blondell was at her genial and relaxed best in this kind of third degree. She undoubtedly thought my curiosity naive, and had been pumped this way a thousand times before by grips and bartenders and all the ordinary working stiffs who naturally gravitated to some ineffable gum-chewing democracy in that spirit, but she had faith in her judgment. When it came to show business of any kind, she carried the values that her vaudeville dad had inculcated from the first days she had gone on stage with Edward Blondell & Co. at age five. Besides, "dish" was her favorite verb—she had taught it to me—and I knew she couldn't resist. It meant really getting down with people and life, but never slinging dirt for its own sake.

This is Blondell in her own words on the questions I threw her: Dick Powell was a hick from Kansas whose god was money. Crosby was a "gentleman" who ran cool to cold. Gable was a cuddly bear with a little bad breath. Garland was the most splendid dame she knew in Hollywood and the one she most identified with, witty and poignant. (She had picked up some telling words from Jack Goodman's book list, kid yourself not if I've led you to believe she was all Runyonesque thumbs in the mouth.) Davis was the worker and strategist supreme among the female stars of her day. She never so much as laid a vamp on Jimmy Cannon, it was all PR stuff to make the columns. Mike Todd was a fascinating character who had a tremendous erotic hold on her and also scared her out of their marriage with his murderous jealousy. Eddie Fisher (later to marry Liz Taylor after Todd left her a widow) was Todd's gunsel, in the same sense that Elisha Cook Jr. was Sidney Greenstreet's in *The Maltese Falcon*.

Straight as a dime she was, even in an age of inflation. "I was always a one-man woman," she said. "I never cheated." I later found out that her mother, Kathryn, drove her beloved ex-clown dad to the edge all their married life by picking up good-looking men in all the towns they played. This must have counted heavily with Joan. Now, when I knew her, she not only didn't cheat, the only men in her life (apart from myself) were some of Tallulah's leftover gay boys who told her amusing stories and occasionally did petit point on some of her livingroom chairs at enormous prices. She respected talent and was glad to pay it.

The last memory I have of Blondell before she gave up the Sutton Place barn to go back to the Coast was one late morning when I came up to have coffee. Wearing a kimono (the looser the garment, the easier on her damaged back), she was on the phone to L.A. trying to pin down a new movie role. She needed the money, she told me, even though the part was a stereotype that brought up her puke juices. "Yes," she was saying into the mouthpiece, "will you please leave a message that Joan Blondell, the actress, called. Mr. Fiegleman has my number."

Not Joan Blondell. Not Miss Joan Blondell. Not *the* Joan Blondell. But Joan Blondell, the actress, who respects you, and respects Mr. Fiegleman, and has a job to do even if life hasn't turned out the way we all once hoped it should.

1980

11.
My Sister, Joyce Brothers

I once spooked Dr. Joyce Brothers, the most formidable JAP (Jewish American Princess) in the country, and she has haunted my life ever since in revenge. I know she'll never stop until I do her justice.

When I call the Weather Bureau, they plug Dr. Joyce after the temperature and tell me I'll find hope if I call 936-4444 ("Hello, I'm Dr. Joyce Brothers: Medically speaking, there is no such thing as a nervous breakdown."). When I grab my *New York Post* fix each noon, there on page 24 is "America's foremost psychologist" smiling up at me like a tireless light bulb. When I teach one night a week at Columbia, it is in a building only two doors away from where Dr. J. was a psychology assistant, 1948–1952.

And when I won $1638 during a Vegas gambling weekend in the mid 1970s, I spread the money out on the bed of the same Ramada Inn room where Brothers was to be robbed of $220 at gunpoint, then briefly locked in the same john where I exultantly drank cognac under the shower. I found this out later.

I can't get away from Joyce Brothers, either as man, American, writer, reader, viewer, listener, thinker, feeler. For more than 10 years I have lived her life almost as if it were my own to try to understand her and understand myself. We symbolize opposite poles of New York Jewish need and intensity that practically led to civil war when we met, yet there was bitter, grudging respect on each side. Let me tell you what I mean.

Where I was orphaned and rebellious at age 10 in Washington Heights, Joyce Diane Bauer grew up in Queens the shining apple of her lawyer-parents' eyes (both Morris and Estelle Bauer were successful attorneys). And where I was expelled from DeWitt Clinton HS for publishing a dirty-word lit magazine called *expression* and at 17 had to kiss ass for readmission, Joyce Bauer was graduating from Far Rockaway HS with the best marks in her class. While I was flunking out of the U. of North Carolina and drifting through the WWII years proud, defiant and dreamy as a poem, Dr. Joyce was getting her B.S. from Cornell at 20. No poetic license for this cool cookie!

138

At 22, she had already wrapped up in marriage the indisputable target of every ambitious JAP—Dr. Milton Brothers, boy intern. At 23, she had her M.A. from Columbia in experimental psychology ("An Analysis of the Enzyme Activity of the Conditioned Salivary Response in Human Subjects"). At 26, her Ph.D. ("An Experimental Investigation of Avoidance, Anxiety and Escape Behavior in Humans as Measured by Action Potentials in Muscles"). At 28, Dr. Joyce became nationally known by winning top prize on the first leg of the $64,000 Question, telling 20 million viewers that "*cestus*" was the name of the leather glove worn by ancient Roman boxers.

That was the same year I cracked like an eggshell and watched Dr. J. bring down the house from a folding wooden chair in Bellevue. I was wearing a white robe, like a fighter, the subject that finally brought her a total of $134,000 after she had memorized the *Ring Encyclopedia* and watched every "Great Fight of the Century."

I patched myself together, dreams intact but scarred with vinegar, while Dr. Joyce quickly converted her victory into an avalanche of radio and pop psychology shows, a *Good Housekeeping* column ("make your marriage a love affair") and a syndicated newspaper column, and bought Milty a practice. "I was supposed to be a 'Joseph' and not a 'Joyce'—my parents were expecting a boy," she told Joe Wershba of the *Post*. "So to some extent I've been trying to prove I'm better than a Joseph. I'm enormously organized."

Your reporter was not enormously organized. I was passionate, raw, nose-thumbing, bourgeois-baiting, hoping to turn America on its ear with words shot from a cannon, but Joyce Brothers and I needed each other like uptight brother and sister. The mass audience and status I snubbed but couldn't live without led me to her. The mass-ier audience and money and fame she loved without shame led her to me. Here is the way it happened.

On a managing editor's gamble, I had become a counter-culture general assignment reporter for the respectable *New York Herald Tribune* before it sank. I wrote handcuffed but light and sassy pieces that Dr. Joyce clipped in her Yorkville apartment and filed in her famous yellow-and-white metal cabinets. (She has filed the world in those cabinets.) I could be useful to her, although I didn't know it. She, in turn, was to become my lifeline to keeping my name in uptown print. She didn't know that, either.

The *Trib* suddenly collapsed one Tuesday in the late '60s. Two days later Seymour Peck of the Sunday *Times* telegraphed me at home to do a feature on her for the Arts & Leisure section. "She's made for you," he said when I called him. I agreed. What a plum, this little "Dr." Goody Two-Shoes who was prostituting the honor of the unknown soldiers of science, who had groomed her, so she could have a signed photo in the window of Lindy's Broadway deli! The only member of the American Psychology Association who was "repped" by General Artists Corp., which said in the handout Peck gave me for background:

"She looks like Loretta Young, walks like Marilyn Monroe and talks like Dr. Freud." I rubbed my hands while setting up the interview with a perfumed NBC publicity eunuch.

But I knew in a flash, when I first saw Joyce walking toward me on the second floor of 30 Rockefeller Plaza, that this was not going to work out the way I had fantasized. It was as if we had seen into each other's secret hearts before saying a word. The air was charged with invisible bayonets: tall man vs. tiny woman, Village intellectual vs. Madison Avenue money player, hired gun vs. the network darling. "Hiya, Doc," said two jaunty announcers coming from their stint in the next-door studio, as we stood there hypocritically shaking hands, and I couldn't help notice the way she beamed.

You want to be loved, don't you, Dr. Joyce? I thought, never once conceding that I wanted exactly the same response for my smartass image as she did for her comforting one. My calculating, note-taking eye saw her left hand tremble slightly as she semi-disguised the hornrims she was holding while we struggled for something to say, waiting for the elevator. I wouldn't acknowledge that my hand was shaking also as I lit a smoke.

We squared off in the well-known NBC coffee shop, Greentrees, my notepaper on the Formica table. Dr. Joyce frozen-faced in the outfit that had become her trademark: light blue blouse, skirt and eentsy blue loafers to match her eyes (which were now staring unflinchingly past the enemy). I plunged right in, driven by my pounding pulses.

What was a behavioral psychologist like herself doing handing out psychotherapy over the airwaves? Why had a reputable scientist with a Columbia Ph.D. shaved a year off her age in every public printout? (*Who's Who* lists her as born October 20, 1928; her typewritten Ph. D. thesis, which I had had in these very hands in the Columbia Psych Library, says in her own words that her birthdate is October 20, 1927.)

Why did she cheapen her credibility by, among other things, playing foil to Johnny Carson? And now that Charles Van Doren and Teddy Nadler had come clean, surely as one adult to another she could admit she got at least an inch of help on the *$64,000 Question?*

Dr. Joyce looked down at her coffee, three of four delicate beads of perspiration sprouting on her upper lip. ("Studies show that sweat prepares animals to cope with danger," she once wrote. "Diet, pace yourself, keep an emotional diary.") This is the gist of what she said in that small, unwavering, adolescent-girl voice:

"Johnny is very gentle with me on his show. I respect and like him. At 12 I lied about my age to get a counselor job in a camp for problem children. I don't consider it a sin if there's a legitimate purpose behind it. In this case the ability to reach many people in a youth-obsessed culture where I could conceivably be penalized for my age. I've always been interested in people, even when I did lab work. A tremendous amount of material in the field of psychology is being researched and developed. It's my purpose to take this new understanding and bring it in clear form to the average person.

"Yes, my training was essentially in experimental psychology (you call it behavioral), but I will never offer advice that has not been susceptible to verification. I definitely wanted the fame and fun and money of this new world of mass communication. But I never received the hint of an answer as a contestant, it was completely and utterly honest, they even tried to squeeze me off the show and failed! I get 2000 letters a week and try to read each one. When I'm given a problem, I refer to the psychological research, boil down the language, give a layman's answer. I've spent as much as 15 hours preparing for a 15-minute show, I've rewritten a page as much as 16 times."

Then she looked up at me, the shadow of a tear fleeting across her pale blue eyes: "You're out to do a hatchet job."

"Not so. My questions just hold a mirror up to your contradictions."

"No, you have contempt for me," she said quietly. She looked down at the cold coffee and said that when the *Trib* collapsed she had called the city room and tried to get my number. She had read my stuff and wanted me to work with her on a "sound but light-hearted" follow-up to her first book, *10 Days to a Successful Memory*, since she was not really a writer. But obviously that was a mistake, she now saw.

Dr. Joyce left a dollar on the table and stood up, all five feet of her ("Experts agree that a smaller girl has an easier time of it, people are usually more protective"), saying that if I needed more information her assistant would give it to me. Then she walked out of the coffee shop. Not like Marilyn Monroe, but like a small, determined woman who has just learned that her dog has been run over and she has to cope.

I tore up my yellow-paper notes and 10 minutes later was at the *Times* building on West 43rd St, grimly taking the elevator (no armed guard at the desk in those days) and walking right over to where Seymour Peck sat in shirtsleeves.

"I can't do the Brothers," I said, slapping down the packet of background clips he'd given me. "You don't have to pay me a cent." (He paid me in full.)

"Take it easy, Seymour No. 2." Our little joke. "What happened?"

"She's obviously a fraud," I said, "but I can't undress her in public. It's too goddamned cruel. You have to get somebody else."

He calmly nodded without quite understanding, the intuition of a good editor, and I found myself glowing with rosy-cheeked blood at the lie. Sure Dr. Joyce was a high-ego powerhouse who loved the spotlight, just like a certain small-time writer I knew, but I also knew in my gut that she had never once dipped beneath her scrupulous code in this new league. I might detest the skin-deep seriousness of the media game she accepted without a murmur, but not her. She had worked harder and more conscientiously than I ever had, for all my anti-Establishment thunder, and I knew she had never really harmed anyone with her capsules of informed common sense. She was also enough of a 'street' psychologist to have seen through me like a shot.

A decade has rolled by, I've been too proud to write Joyce Brothers and tell her the truth about that meeting: that she is my straight, smart JAP sister who has survived on a rougher track than I could ever play on and once caught her smartass brother with his juvenile, scarlet-envy pants down. Straights and non-straights can never be totally at ease together. But I think now Dr. J. will give me some peace, even when I bump into her in every crazy corner of this new 24-hour, total communications world she helped create: "Studies show if you're the kind of person who makes others uneasy, people will like you better if you do something clumsy like spill your drink, trip over the rug, enter a room with a smudge on your face."

Yes, sweetheart, next time!

1980

12.
How I Hated London Before I Got to Like It a Lot and Then Had to Go Away

A lot of the hallucinated, pounding, chase-novel tension leaks out of a New Yorker when he bravely thumbs his nose goodbye to the Bitch of Manhattan and comes to stitch himself together in the great sanitarium city of London. I've been stitching for more than a year. My sleep is more pastoral, my mind less in fuming little pieces, and I brutally put myself down for not making the move earlier. But being a New York American is a special street-prince illness, massman's version of the royal hemophilia. You're the frigging top, baby, you've said to yourself for almost half a century, and you carry this snotty bacillus deep in the imperial blood wherever you lug that critical and sour self of yours. You take the New York disease with you like bad breath and blow it indifferently in the face of everything new and at first it spoils you for every other city on the globe, I mean without exception.

You enter a strange town, as I did London, and observe the quaint customs as if you were looking at a zoo. Let's see what you've got, you funny-looking squares! That's about the level of every New York hipster's approach if you were to perch inside his quick slick trick brain. He/she may disguise it with a gas attack of democratic enthusiasm, "Gee, boy, shit, what a city you've got!" but underneath the charitable pep you're dealing with the worst of city snobs. Never forget it.

Although I was glad I had left America, felt like a hero to finally remove my mouth from New York's silver tit, I couldn't bear London for the first three months I was there. It made a murderer out of me in my heart. Let me start at the bottom, if that's the correct name for it, and work my way up, or at least around. Without a girlfriend but with crisp new pounds from my cellophane Rockefeller Center Money Kit crackling away in my crisp new duds, I couldn't even get laid properly. Aging strippers demanded overpriced, Jersey City–tasting champagne as a token of esteem to their sagging chests and spreading hams and £20 in front as a down payment for possible action. Checking later with other horny, uprooted Manhattanites—after, by the way, I was gratefully shacked up with a soulful Italian girl out of Australia—I found that my early troubles were

143

typical. Swinging London is a cold nasty fish when it comes to buying the kind of adult body-love that lonely travelers need to cool themselves out and stop spinning around on the monster escalators of culture-shock. Badly advertised London doesn't give a damn.

But the lack of a bird to coo for me, even momentarily and for a price, was only the keenest, the most piercing, of my early London blues. Everything followed from that cold void. The traffic seemed to me insane. Yes, big foolish hunks of steel and chrome roar around like bully robots in the States, but they don't whip down curbs like tracer bullets making you dance for your life and do stop at clearly designated red lights with grumbling resignation. Their traffic lights seemed to me miles apart. Pedestrian crossing-zones were as clear as Greek. A mild prescription from a New York doctor couldn't be filled. I went through the most towering agonies about whether to call a brother writer, just another damn heavy-drinking, sex-warped scribbler, Lord so-and-so or use his first name. The calculated servility of shop people made me want to shake them into self-respect. Cockney, such a camp to every third-rate actor in the States, "Gor, where's me bleedin' upper-plite, Kite?" was just about as charming as a drill on a rotten tooth.

You've got the picture! The famous city of London was a foreign, as in alien, and constantly irritating place for me in the beginning. I was in a 24-hour sweat—money, manners, traffic, pubs, peculiar-tasting cigarettes, unfindable streets, they all conspired to drive me up the crumbling walls of this sad historical dump of a city. Everything looked, tasted, and felt seedy after the hard-edge diamond sidewalks of my high-pressure town. On the twelfth bitter week I felt that the suicidal London drear (a combination of chill, damp skies the gray color of a public men's room) was going to entomb me, too, in some new version of being buried alive unless I got my trembling spirit out of there in a hurry. I didn't leave America to die like a used condom floating down an indifferent London gutter, decorated by a couple of orange peels and the greasy newspaper-cone that held a pathetic fish-and-chips dinner for a big swinger who earned £13 a week selling newspapers at the Camden North Line stop. My life and my country had been too sensational in every sense for this kind of poor, mean, colorless, small-time draining of the rank gorgeous blood I had brought with me. Corrupted that blood might be; but it wasn't yet watery and sniveling.

Thank god for what was left of my rotten American money. I got out on BOAC, right down to Málaga, lusting for my season in the sun like a disgusted priest heading for the nearest whorehouse. Except for my mates there (Alan Ross, C.P. Snow, Katey Carver, Harvey and Anna Lockwood Matusow, Mike Zwerin), London could go right on shitting icicles until it became part of the polar cap, some anthropological relic better left to Ph.D.s than men. Rafaella flew out to join me as soon as she had tied up some intricate spaghetti ends to our London life. Together we knocked around Spain for four months—almost five for me, she having left in grim, soundless tears on Christmas Eve from the Madrid train station for Paris—congratulating ourselves, even when we were ultimately stoned into sunburned zombies by the sameness of everything, that we were down in pleasure's country and not smelling that vicious, characteristic stuff they wash the Tube down with every night. *España!* Cheap brandy, cheap lodging, incredibly inexpensive pros if you can't make it with your woman, as I couldn't with Raf for a terrible time, when I memorialized Jack Kerouac's sudden death with a weekend in Barcelona. A straightforward Valencia girl blew the very cream out of my soul in that big sex plant down near the Barcelona waterfront while Rafaella picked up a young dude from Iceland and my darling got her needs taken care of some other way. These chic modern relationships, you know.

I was recoiling from London, from the dark gloomy sad London in me before I ever knew there was such a place to match human hopelessness, and I lapped up the hot, selfish life of the Costa del Sol like a smirking bargain-hunter. I even did my thing at the typewriter with some regularity as each day followed in the sandaled footsteps of the one before, pouring the hurts of my impotent relationship with Raf into the machine in the best Yanqui working-neurotic tradition. And the Lord said, Ye shall work, Yank, and thus does uptight Yank keep his eyes from the abyss! But Rafaella was sinuous, playful, cosmopolitan, human, stylish, spontaneous, she had contempt for a love (mine) that substituted an Olivetti Studio 45 machine for the real thing, she had bitterness and blues centuries older and deeper than mine for this wiseassed American salesman who talked such gold into her coral ear and came up with brass and lies in the pinch. She despised my fear of women, my fear of giving myself to a woman for all my American animalism, she told me as we grimly hustled her bags onto the train for Paris, but she was lonely in this terrible world as I was lonely and, oh, darling, take care, I'll write as soon as I get back to London, yes, you too, darling, I'll be back after the new year a better man, I swear to you! We didn't kiss.

I wasn't even sure I was going back to that piss-gray and frigid city (although I had to) and to this heavyhearted love affair, but after one night of spinning around like a narcissistic top, fantasying how I would sweep all of sensuous Barcelona into my selfish dripping loins and at least take from women like the true groovy monster I was, even if I couldn't give—after all of this, I lay my swelled and smoking head on its Hotel Manila pillowcase for hours, days, at a time smiling like a child and weeping softly to myself as I cuddled a special delivery letter from Raf telling of the little hovel she had gotten for us both to try again in out in Blackheath. Both of us knew long distance it was now a kind of black-humor fairytale, this little first-floor garret stuck out at the ass-end of town, our tormented relationship (she laughed with pity at my sticklike "Buchenwald legs," I bled each time her dainty upper lip shot back with laughter and revealed its harsh red wall of North Italian gum), my returning for an uncertain three weeks at most to a city and miserly state of mind that turned me white with despair before I was to fly out, back to New York.

Raf had put newspapers over the windows to keep out the cold when I trudged up the hill from the British Rail station to this godforsaken little hole in this third-rate London "outlying district"—and there we were, face to face again, irony and hope creasing our mouths and eyes as we threw ourselves upon the other with desperate murmurs from deep inside. This almost freezing little room, decorated with beautiful prints that my Raf had picked up in London for a song, was quite a comedown from our former Eaton Terrace basement suite with its ferocious landlady (friend of mine from the States who had turned into Madame Formidable when she got hold of some property) and menacing hot-water boiler. But it wasn't going to be for long, I told myself with the fear that Raf could see right into my foul brain. God only knew what was going to happen to us, Raf knew that, she was no fool, but I had to be in London for the publication of my first book here (*Views of a Nearsighted Cannoneer*, Alan Ross Ltd.) and that would be the end of it. The fact that a super-john New Yorker was living in a hick London back-door that no one ever heard of, with scrubby, miserable country all around, freezing in the dead of winter with a rebuking Italian girl he didn't even know was alive six months before, was just a little more unmerry English death-gas as far as I was concerned. I was prepared to numb my way through it all until I flew out of this depressing winter urinal of a land and a life.

But a peculiar thing began to happen while I was killing time. I started to enjoy walking around my new quiet neighborhood out in the boondocks. This wasn't the jostling frantic King's Road or even one of those shabby/genteel urban poverty pockets where my spirits fell through to the sidewalk. This was a pretty solid setup without being overbearing or stiff-collar, and the voices in the air, the damn trees themselves, were modest and cheerful. You see London differently when you get on the edges of it, pardon me, you see Londoners differently, and even though we were technically a mile or two outside the city gates, I was really being given a last chance to see how these decent, peculiar people live without whining or stage effects in small little communities.

In my head I began to see a hundred, a thousand, five thousand, separate communities which really give London its character, not one big howling blur like my native race track streets. I started kibitizing—talking—with the local druggist (they call him chemist), grocer, newsdealer, all of them, and I liked the familiar red-nosed faces and badly dyed toups I began to see every day in the shops. Community. Palaver. Natural square rhythms. Perhaps even a reflection of myself in other unpretty but lived-in faces if I could ever really settle down. My high-speed Manhattan psyche began to deaccelerate, not the drugged other-worldliness of southern Spain, but more like a smallish city outside of Portland, Maine. I got my business done with a minimum of hysteria, even mended some of the easier flesh wounds with Rafaella. The days were real and uncomplicated and the nights clean with our desperate passion. The time came for my flight to that violent movie city across the water and I was sad, uncertain, not knowing what would happen. Raf thought I would never be back. I didn't know. We actually walked hand-in-hand on the endless black heath itself before I caught the bus to Heathrow. Jesus! Others thought it was Desolation City, this three quarters of a mile of nothingness, but we thought it was our own rare turf, the scene of our strongest chapter, the possibility of an ongoing life together that didn't explode each evening into sulk and savagery because it was pinned to the earth in such a bare, everlasting way. We kissed and held on for dear life out on the heath, Raf and I, London and I. And then I was gone. Into my neurotic New York jumpsuit and hissing for home.

But not for long.

That thrust towards some kind of peace, that hope for a honey-flowing exit out of the trap of our arid selves and into each other that Raf and I could taste if not sustain, the sweet calming tricks played on my metabolism that I had felt in the nourishing gloom of Blackheath, made my two and a half weeks back with the Bitch of Manhattan an unreal high. I had to milk the Bitch of money, just my small share of that green fuel that carries us through the world these days, and then I was on my global own, a small-time Hamlet with decisions crowding down around his brain—would I head this way or that? I still hadn't given London my pledge in blood, oh no, human love and the setting in which it can swing are one thing, one damn beautiful thing my Better Self agrees, but I had 40-odd years of solo flying on my chart and the first thought always when things got too question-marked was to hop in my dreammobile and cut out for some new pole where I could vibrate all alone. The fact that these vibrations usually turn into shudders within a week is a secret I've kept from myself like a trained spy. But as soon as the inevitable New York cop barked at me for smoking in the 72nd St. subway station, as soon as my oldest pal put me down for the unmanly length of my London hairdo, as secretaries and big-shots began yammering at me over the hysterical Manhattan telephone wires while I tried to siphon off my green fuel, I knew that some exotic foreign bug had gotten into me and eaten away practically all of that ridiculous sense of superiority which I had originally brought to Europe.

London, you amused old fart, move over! I was coming back.

I had funneled enough of the green into my tank to last for another six months before I had to scuffle. And I still had enough long-odds hope that the combination of London peace and peaceful pussy would cement me to the one woman, bring an ice pack to my Manhattan-made fevers, allow me to breathe regularly enough to expand my mental chest and crack what I now believe was an unnaturally cramped, frozen, narrow inner landscape. My chopmeat-raw human animal wanted to graze and feed in urban meadow, not shoot down back alleys with the pounding feet of urban nightmare echoing in the heartless block behind me. Brothers, I was tired of running, even when I was standing still.

I came back to London for the third time as tame as a pussy cat, ready to be grateful for what it was, for what it could give me just by being itself, not what I wanted it to be. That's the terrible mistake that most New York, in fact American, wiseguys make the first time—they want a London that fits their Cinema 16 image, their literary image, Sherlock Holmes screwing Fannie Hill in a polished hansom cab while the driver touches his cap and says deferentially, "Right on, sir," and they grow sour when they don't exactly find it. The only way for an American of spirit to make it in London is to let the spooky serpentine ambience of the place, its coils upon coils of hidden streets and overlooked souls, grow upon you slowly, inevitably, powerfully; if you rush it you're finished, and yet what is our stateside contribution to this world but the essence of speed, energy, and bright white stabbing light? Only an accident or a heart attack will let us really know dark and shabby London. Only a need deeper than our tastes, habits, bolting abbreviated rhythms—yes, only the need to live will make you a fan, everything else says, Hit the road, Jack! I wanted to live for a change.

Blackheath was just a little too far out of reach to have an occasional night in London before the bloody transport shuts down at 11:30, and so Rafaella had nabbed another underdog place for us in Kennington, on the wrong side of the Thames. I cursed it even more than I did Blackheath as I lugged my bags up that dripping, prole staircase to our dismal room, and I also felt right at home with a crooked smile blooming on my knowing face. Here she was, my darksouled but loyal wop, capable of castrating me, betraying me, but never of indifference, and here was a racial stew of a district with blacks and Chinese and all the other secret survivors of Angloland keeping their bonfires of the heart lit on the garbage-strewn shores south of London Bridge. Elegant slob that I am, I felt like a contented bum in this mixture of the Lower East Side and San Francisco, peoplewise, with enough stunted greenery around to keep the ethnic recipe fairly unexplosive.

And so unchic Kennington, of all places, not Kensington, not South Kensington, has been my base of operations ever since the early spring of 1970 as I fight to stay on here in a London that I now have deep feelings for. It takes me a big 10 minutes to get into the Haymarket, pick up my mail at the American Express, and then fan out into the city itself for whatever foolishness I have to do that day. It's also a good work retreat for a word merchant, cheap, quiet (apart from the 250-pound docker who clumps in the room above me—actually nice, steady clumps once you get used to them), and it gives me a painful insight into the economic underside of London life. I started at the top in Evelyn Waugh territory on Eaton Terrace, slid down to the solid, frumpy H. G. Wells attached-house number out in Blackheath, and now I was in Poverty City along with Orwell in nicely stinking Kennington.

It sharpened my view of all London. Once you look past the tarnished medals and the fraying braid of this town, you can see hundreds upon hundreds of thousands of people surviving so close to the knuckle that they're afraid to flex their hands American style. Panic would set in if they aped their big swinging reckless brothers doing that nonstop acrobatic act across the waters. Men and women and little half-pints over here earn approximately one half of what they would on the other side at the same job. Sandwiches are thinner, drinks smaller, paper is skimpier and breaks under a load of groceries if you forget your sweet little faggot shopping bag. Even newsprint is tinier and I squint like a feeb over the afternoon editions.

There is a reminiscent air of the Depression 30s everywhere once you get away from the minority of posh sections, which my countrymen tend to cluster in out of laziness and ignorance and too much of the gelt. Crime and grayness seem to be everywhere compared to where I come from. Some of this has to do with the way the watery northern light hits, but much of it is the result of age and time and this is the part that is hardest for a New Yorker and an American to get used to. I come from a city, even more a society that is shiny and new. Without thinking twice about it in our well-wired robot heads, we expect and usually get super-performance from our gadgets. If we don't, we line them up against the wall of the General Motors Building in Detroit—autos, toasters, computers, tanks, stereos, cardiograph machines—and we shoot them without pity. Efficiency is our Second Self, even our Zen Buddhists want a toilet that will flush away the turds of life, but the extent to which we are obsessed by machines who love other machines can never be known until we leave the States and walk smack into rust and bathroom-floor overflow. It shakes us to the last washer in our chrome kidneys.

Your London, my London, is amateurish and a tool-and-diemaker's vaudeville show by comparison. I now feel like a fucking saint at my cool with phone calls that don't get through, power and personnel failures at the local tube station, the sputtering black-out of the traffic light at the corner—the technological lot, you might call it. But it's good for the Yank to be forced into being a saint for a year or two during an otherwise unsaintly, bulling, demanding, jet-hopping, mustard-smeared, immediate-gratification kind of life that has rotted up half the world in its fat rush to everywhere and nowhere. Now after 13 months I've slowed down to try and pace my monster to London's vulnerable human scale instead of the King Kong cities which made savage would-be giants out of my generation in the States. I walk where in New York I'd take a cab to practically toot around the corner, I breathe where in the same N.Y. I'd be resentful that I wasn't strapped into a portable Pulmotor. I look at the flowers and even stop to smell them as if they were women, which they are, whereas in my hard-drive city they're usually a cellophane item behind a plate-glass window. I enjoy the kids poking a football in the park and don't see them as midget gangsters with my suspicious, probing, bloodshot Manhattan eyes.

London, I've stretched out to meet you on your own terms, this is what I'm saying, and goddamnit I like it—I need it—I respect it—the absence of that whipping psychic pressure, of being Dr. Uptight, the fact that you leave me alone to do what I want to do when I want to do it. America and I make large-gestured rhetoric out of the idea of individual freedom, desperate and unhappy countries along with their citizens strenuously try to jack themselves up with language as loose as the gut on an outdated tennis racket, but I've actually found more of it here in your dark and cruddy bosom than I ever found at home. Nobody really seems to give a particular damn what you wear, who or what it is that's hanging on your arm, where you're going in that smeared rainy weather— up to the Victoria Sporting Club to gamble away your pittance from the State, down to the American Embassy to protest godknowswhat, or even out to Essex to take a pastoral LSD trip as Raf and I did, swinging with the birds as we flew over the treetops of this world and then floating down with parachute-softness on the greenest grass this side of paradise. Stoned in London! I've done it in New York, L.A., Mexico City, Frisco too, but I think inconspicuous doping is sweeter and less paranoid in this big accepting ocean of a city than in those tight quivering hippie pincushion towns where the wrong move squirts blood. Who needs it? when the point of a good inner-space trip is warmth, peace, health and the great triumphant unlimbering of the secret self, all of which London whispers to the contorted Yank without changing the expression of its official chin-strap bobbie face. Bugger all, says the Face, just don't get caught.

But I don't want to send out the false signal that London is doing its London thing on another fog-bound planet, removed from all the static that flickers daily along the wires that tie the global village into a sweaty knot. True, London stands alone on its huge, spindly, quaint dinosaur legs, but it's also defenseless to a lot of culture-shock batted across the Atlantic from my own Yankee Stadium. It seems to this Londoner-by-graft, closely watching as I have the election of Heath, your growing headaches with color, traffic, hard stuff (heroin, coke), muggings, etc., that everything that happens in my country, my hometown, happens here inside of three years on a smaller but equally consistent scale. In fact, if I'd had this theory working when Heath-Nixon handed Mr. Wilson that unexpected belt to the prime ministerial jaw and took their government on its waltz down Tory Lane I might have picked up a nice bit of change at one of their turf accountant shops.

But assuming what I say is true, that there's a two- or three-year time lag between patterns that emerge in the States and then surface here, I'd much rather face these broadsides in London, diluted, shaved and showered, robbed of their manic violence, than take them full-blast upon my heaving native streets. And I speak not only for myself. In the coming decade I know they'll see hordes of fleeing Americans crowding into this big shapeless union suit of a city, fumbling and cursing the old fly-buttons, but saying a small prayer that they can stop the ringing in their ears from all those sirens declaring the birth of a new, violent Electronic Man in the U.S.A.

As I tap out these last words with my six-month reprieve just about up, news comes from the States that I've been hired to teach for a year in a Midwest college with a salary too real for me to pass up. So I've lost my fight to stay on here indefinitely. Perhaps I would have lost no matter what I did. You can't entirely turn your back on your homeland even if it lets you down in the existential pinch—it's yourn, as we say. Rafaella and I don't know what to do, her coolness to America, her proud scorn at my cowardice in returning, our unhappy sex life, our overwhelming dependence on each other—it will go down to the last uncertain moment at the airline ticket counter, I know it! I tell my girl that if she doesn't come with me I'll be back at the first midterm break and she turns away, disbelieving: That clanking monster over there has devoured another victim, she thinks. But I will be back, with Raf on my arm in her new Iowa City sport dress and me in my jazzy all-American loafers and Farmer Brown suspenders; or to find her here in the December shadows and claim her for our own special lifetime of loving misery.

London, hear this: Your city was slow to get to me, ha ha, that's slipping it to you gently, but when it did it opened up buried yearnings for another kind of life and I won't be speeding home as quite the same man who left with an adventurer's feather slapped in his cap in the spring of '69. I'll be looking over my shoulder like a startled visionary at what I've left behind.

1970

13.
Son of Laughing Boy

The last clear, definite, stamped, everlasting picture of Peter LaFarge that I hold in my brain has him in cowboy drag slouching down the steps of a small with-it (*Times Book Review* people, actors) restaurant in the West 40s, tears oozing down his cheeks from the contact lenses he thought would make him look like Randolph Scott forever stalking Laredo. Peter and I hadn't spoken for about two years on this January noontime in 1965 and I just noted him out of the corner of my own pragmatic, Kissinger-lensed (I was wearing hornrims at the time) specs and said to myself a little self-righteously but with a pang in my heart that I'd never admit: You poor fucking star-shooter. You think this masquerade can go on forever. Well, baby, it can't. Nay.

You see, I was putting him down for being a masquerader and telling myself like some kind of tough Jewish Calvinist that he was going to pay, thou must pay the wages of Freudian sin, for his defiant narcissism and street-stardom, and by Christ he did pay because less than six months later he was dead and the sense of psychiatric realism that the bad years had drilled into me checked off self-satisfaction when I heard the news. I wasn't glad Pete was dead; I was glad I had been right, because both of us had been in pursuit of American reality, the final purpose of our competition, and now it was clear with one of us morgue-meat and the other not that I had won the right to trust my judgment about art in America, about trying to pound out some values in a time absolutely without them for those of us trying to carve our personalities on the media landscape.

Yet there was something fantastically, challengingly beautiful as well as doomed about Peter's bid to become his own impossible hero. He had come out of the Southwest, the son of Oliver LaFarge, the Harvard man who had brought the Navajo into American life with *Laughing Boy* in 1930. I later found out, as did everyone who knew Peter, that he never got on with his Great White Father. And Jim Nash, the underground reporter-poet of violent American losers like Neal Cassady and Willard Motley and now Peter, tells me that he was practically a non-son after the old man birthed him and in fact named him Oliver, Jr. with a cool, arrogant eye for the future of his little carbon copy which included a New England church school and Harvard.

But it didn't work out that way. Oliver, a steel spring of a man with priests and four generations of American gentleman-artists lining his genes, lost his brilliant tautness after *Laughing Boy* and could only plot life with inspiration over a bottle. His Pulitzer Prize novel locked and froze his imagination and he never duplicated it again. He left his puling namesake and his eastern horsey-set wife (Wanden Matthews) and remarried into exotic Spanish stock down in Santa Fe. There he stayed until World War II, pacing the plaza with his unexpressed obsessions like Ahab, the proud and sterile don of Southwest fiction.

Oliver, Jr. was flung to his mother and then his ranchman-stepfather, growing up on the latter's spread in Colorado, a sickly kid who was almost the perfect, introspective, high-nerved offspring of transplanted New York—Boston elitists, which is just about what Oliver, Sr. and Wanden were when they let their hair down in the Southwest in the late 1920s. But take those high, frail nerves and wire them to such reality symbols as horses, water holes, rodeos, cowboys, Indians, that whole other America waiting across the mountains, and you can begin to see what Oliver, Jr. was becoming. And somewhere along those hot deserts of the Southwest, drunk on dago red after a Young Riders Only rodeo, gunning a fast adolescent car, sharing precocious marijuana with a surprised Navajo gas-station attendant and then wildly ripping out the pages of one of his father's books, Oliver, Jr. threw away his given name and thumbed his nose at his birthright and became Peter LaFarge. Pete.

I had love for Pete LaFarge and, although I couldn't admit it at the time, it was probably what we call homosexual love, granted that I never consciously wanted to rim his asshole with a fine feathery tongue. I would have turned vicious at the thought, or white as the ghost of my guilt, and so would Pete with his machismo cowboy front. Both of us wanted to tongue the girls—what else?—but for a while we grooved on each other's company to the point of love and perhaps we should have used those tongues on each other, where would have been the shame? Pete was beautiful to the eye and ear in many ways—shoulders, torso, teeth, straight-arrow bearing, his voice strong, modulated, like the scent of flowers on the wind; his speaking voice that is, although he did actually put it semi-together as a composer/folksinger on a bigger scale than just my appreciation of him as a man and had a brief, clouded success in the big pop music league for two or so years. His most famous tune, to get ahead of my story, was the ballad of "Ira Hayes," which Johnny Cash recorded down in Nashville with a stoned Peter standing by; this was a very strong moment for Pete, buddying with Cash, staying at his house for the record date, Cash honoring him by deferring to Pete on the arrangement. But even though Pete cut about four records of his own and threatened to crash the scene nationally, it was not as a singer so much as a rare aristocratic kind of rebel cowboy that we got to know him in the Village in late 1959. He had just come to town, or more accurately just emerged onto my scene after uncertainly bouncing around on the Upper West Side trying to find his New York legs. He and his very shy, very plain first wife finally found a nice, roomy apartment on Christopher Street not very far from where the Lion's Head and the 55 Club now are, near Sheridan Square, and it was from this headquarters that Pete began to make his downtown play as a new kind of bohemian personality-pitcher.

It was rough-cut Jack Micheline, the ex-beat poet—*I want to run up to children/And kiss them/But there is too much noise/Men kill each other*—who introduced me to him half a block from where I live and then swept on his lonely corkscrew way down the Second Avenue night. Pete and I got off immediately, mentally, emotionally, rhythmically: dope-music-rap all night long and grabbing breakfast at Ratner's before falling out exhausted and happy in our separate beds and separate lives—two spiritual orphan-boys reaching for each other's warming fires. He was a melody man in the warm, sweet tones he gave out, softly musical in all of his tall, slightly awkward, Abe Lincolnish gestures, telling me of a world where the unfamiliar names of Woody Guthrie, Cisco Houston, Bob Dylan, Cynthia Gooding, were spoken with all of the involvement that I gave to the more international names of Camus and Orwell and Henry Miller. I naturally thought there was something smalltown hicky about him when he began to talk writing because, being the son of a well-known novelist, he was aggressive/defensive about his prose tastes at the beginning, all of which seemed to spin around Steinbeck, Jack London, and his father. But it soon became clear that poetry was a much purer love with him, English verse and English verse drama, ballads; and prose was too strangulated with his emotions towards his father for him to have a clear bead on it.

But once he trusted you, and he was as suspicious as a fawn behind that butch, roll-your-own, lanky Linc pose, he opened up like a total melon—plasmic, juicy, vulnerable as pussy-flesh—to all the knowledge you had and he didn't, and he supped on it like a starving man. I was starved for something else, the knowledge and experience of American human nature radically different from my own nasal, city brand. And here it was flowing out of the wild-cactus Southwest right into my gray Manhattan, into my need for so much more than Manhattan, and we fed each other in deep and secret ways that brought smiles of fulfillment to both our shining faces. It was a pure ball each time we got together.

When we first met, I was putting together a classy (Ginsberg, Kerouac, Di Prima, O'Hara) beatnik section for the third-rate raunch magazine, *Swank*, and Pete, his head foaming with Beat Generation cliches that pained me when I heard them because they were not his, his experience, his voice, his language as they were then ours, Pete as I say gave me a poem for the blue-papered section (to distinguish it from the nipples and the How-to-Get-Laid articles). Bang! Slogans vanished, Beat Gen. mouthiness slid away from his writing voice and out came a clean spare little cry about poor actors failing in New York, "Shakespeare's lightning flickering in their mouths" as they literally fainted from lack of food. It was a miniature thing but terrific. Then several months later I bludgeoned Bill Ward and Harriet Sohmers into publishing one hunk of a Southwest verse drama of Pete's in the *Provincetown Review*, the literary saloon that behaved like a magazine for my East Village-in-winter, P-town-in-summer roughneck gang. Pete's voice belled out in print—naive, clear, anachronistic— as if Billy the Kid had had his training in Sherwood Forest with Robin Hood's boys and pulled tough-guy stickups with "sire" and "yclept" instead of the right words. Pete's were virginal on the page compared to our down and dirty, knowing English. Pete's were those of a gifted amateur, but one you never stopped rooting for because of the sweet, dark, authentic presence of the man himself; yet I knew then he would never make it as a writer in the old-fashioned word-meant-for-the-eye sense, and that he didn't have the broad spine of the real playwright who powers through mobs of emotion to a single goal, but I also knew I could never tell him this. He was as emotionally frail as a sheet of the thinnest glass and you could imagine it popping like crazy under any sudden heat.

Pete, I later, slowly found out, had been a temperamental, high-throned, I'll-be-a-star-or-nothing young actor when he first hit New York—in many pioneering if wasted ways he was the typical mirage-kid of our time, the Boy Who Wants It All, having been, in mounting order, rodeo rider, actor, playwright, director, poet, finally folkbard, almost everything his father-stung, ambition-stung imagination could come up with. But in a much more disturbing sense he was a life-actor, glowing star of his own sidewalk drama, and he anticipated by at least 10 years the combined street theaters of cruelty and absurdity that we are all now involved in; where swaggering strangers either want to knock you down for money reasons or more subtly, even more unnervingly, blaze their power fantasies into your unprotected eye with threatening, psychedelic clothing and satanic charms and above all the dancing field of force of the new freak lifestyle that dares everyone to wing out in public as far as they can imagine—or be canceled out as certified voyagers on Spaceship Earth.

Pete was a tormented swinger long before we knew the rules of the new game, in fact a tormented swinger, not in the fading Sinatra-Concord Hotel sense, but in the need to swing out on a psychic trapeze before any audience of strangers. He never bellowed out on the street like the share of high poets I have known and have even been on festive New York summer nights, booming lines off the 3 A.M. buildings. None of that *La Bohème* playing-around for him. Instead, he walked confidently through the crowded Village streets like a determined high priest, except that he was dressed like Tom Mix or much later on, the Phantom of the Opera, something chilling that I will get to as the plot thickens. He was humorless and proud when living his part in public and filled me with uncomfortable awe and angry, thinskinned feelings of cowardice the first time I walked by his side along Sheridan Square when he was doing his cowboy number. This wildman was asking for New York ridicule, I thought, wondering if we could avoid the inevitable fight when the cracks from the sidewalk jockeys began, but Pete had his audience buffaloed, respectful, hushed, almost as if he had stepped out of *El Topo* and was putting Christ-in-chaps magic on them, zap zap zap. And yet the bitter funny thing was that just at this time, about six months after he had surfaced downtown, word had begun to trickle back to the Village that he had been a bad, incompetent rider during his brief workout on the rodeo circuit. Almost, you understand, as if he didn't deserve to lope around in them Marlboro Man duds even as show. Some obscure thread of justification was cut when we heard this news and I felt one more clamp in my lip as to what I could speak to Pete about.

Another odd thing we heard, one that helped to add to Pete's intangible spookiness, that aura of unreality or extrareality that flickered around the solid, arm-punching meatiness of him, was that some of the real cowboys he rode with in those southwestern bucking contests and even later in Madison Square Garden thought that he was an Indian and not a white man at all. Since his pedigree was whiter than white and he had taught himself to hate that advantage—although every now and then I thought I saw the flare of Social Register pride flush through the prole-ethnic image he was into—Peter must have secretly enjoyed to the hilt the rumor down in Colorado/Arizona/New Mexico that he was a true son of the tomahawk. He could by nature play either role: He had the tall, muscular, battered body of the cowboy and the straight black hair and olive-skinned face of what could be an Indian. And in that fanatical imagination—not his deep emotional needs, which I thought were pretty simple and silently crying out for ease from pain, but in the techniques he devised to cover those gaping needs—the double impersonation of being both the Lone Ranger and Tonto must have given him devil-chuckles for days and days.

The cowboy part of the ripoff against "four generations of New England gentleman-artists" was Pete's dirty-nailed, common-man finger up tradition, as I read it, but being taken for a Navajo in Colorado or New Mexico was the final hysterical laugh in his cruel war with his father. LaFarge, Sr. had created genuine Indians in the pages of *Laughing Boy* a year before Pete hit the planet in 1931, the first and perhaps the only American paleface to do so in this century, but the last thing he wanted was a son of his own cast in that funky image. It's been said that the older LaFarge made notes on the Indians he wrote about from a proper distance, like a cartoon of the Harvard anthropologist that he actually was when he first came to the Southwest in the 20s. But that when Pete in his confused late teens sought him out in Santa Fe there was competition and spite between them, with the degraded Indians as the prize, because the son insisted on getting deliberately close.

As I said earlier, Pete smoked grass with them, split firewater, brought some young Indian kids "home," almost as if to throw this taboo intimacy in his father's lean, fastidious face. The only writer in the country who could make the modern fate of the Indian very real to middle-class Americans 40 years ago had never been able to relax in their presence, apparently. It seems to me that Pete took pleasure in taunting his father this way, if he couldn't win the old man's approval—a poor student, a fuckup on the range, a hundred creative projects begun and dropped in the usual teenage overambition syndrome—he could twist fear or at least respect out of Senior High & Mighty. But he failed miserably in that Oedipal bid as well. Oliver LaFarge kicked his son out of his house and told him to keep away from *his* Indians, that he didn't know red beans about them, that he was screwing up their already stunted and alienated lives.

This pitiable contest, which took place in the late 40s, more or less severed relations between father and son until after I knew him, when humble bids for approval would pass via airmail from Pete to his father and short semi-civil replies would come back. Pete even sent his father a copy of my 1960 anthology, *The Beats,* and told me with strange pride (in the light of his bitching about his father when we got high or drank and were loose, not strange at all when you put the key word ambivalence in the lock again) that the old cold sachem thought it was O.K. I couldn't have cared less. I was so absorbed in my own literary skull at this point that I had indifference ranging to mild contempt for whatever Oliver LaFarge might think. But I was struck to the point of wonder by the almost childlike reverence Pete still had for his father's opinions, and courteously accepted the bare compliment because it meant so much to my friend.

It now occurs to me that if I had made fun of it Pete might actually have tried to do me in.

I had not yet read *Laughing Boy*—how many of you present-tense addicts out there have?—and Oliver LaFarge was just a name to me that I thought had been permanently covered over by the silent earthquakes of time, never realizing that time-past is an illusion waiting to be cracked by neglected life doing pushups in the shadows so that it will be strong and wiry when its moment comes again. No really valid thing in our past can ever unmake itself, sayeth the preacher-man in me today—it only waits to spring forward when new time is ripe for it, as it now is for Injuns, Old Man LaFarge, hopefully even Pete himself. That old American story of a primary injustice (deballing of the redskin), then "success" in bringing it to the conscience of the nation (*Laughing Boy*), then the young snots of the latest generation (Pete) sneering at the gallant struggles of the recent past, then the father bewildered by a reevaluation he can't understand and a disrespect that makes him doubt the value of his life and work, then the son finally admitting that he has his father in him and the father bowing his imperial head to the reality that he too is in his wild son. . . .

For in 1961, Pete, already becoming as manic as the city of Nueva York itself, flying so crookedly high on uppers to match the new pace in his life (working at his desk for 12 hours in a row writing songs and then dashing over to Gerde's Folk City to try them out, still trying to finish his play, chasing little girl folkniks) that he was barely able to cut his one and only Columbia album, got his father to write the liner notes. "It still bewilders me to have this turn up in the family," says Oliver LaFarge on the sleeve of *Peter LaFarge*, "but it's a proud bewilderment." And just as the father lent his pen to the hoped-for glory and redemption of his wayward son, and then yielded up his own life in 1963, so Pete in turn gave up part of his remaining two years after that to some kind of penance for Oliver. They were locked into this guilt/expiation thing together, like sculpture.

But back to 1961. John Hammond almost wouldn't release that first record because of its raggedness and unprofessionalism, especially sore since he had backed Pete against the advice of more computerized Columbia heads; and Peter's name was close to being mud now in the high tubular skyscrapers in midtown because he came to his sessions unprepared, drunk, drugged, already strapped hard into the cockpit of that speedway trip of million-dollar death which was ultimately to crash him into his own wall and burn him up. As he got closer to the hot lights and big money I didn't see too much of him, and when I did, the old sweetness was there but also a kind of impatience with what he thought was my amateur standing and my amateur understanding of image power. He would no longer feel comfortable discussing the philosophical problem that had united us deeply at the beginning: namely how to use our egos in the world, as voices, in a way that was justified by the substance of what we were selling. Truth was no longer a contemporary word for Pete compared to success. Yet he was not getting the success, either, in that italicized sense that to him was the only authentic American criterion. Columbia fired him flat out after the album and he became the lost child of little-league Folkways Records. He must have thought that I would judge him as he judged himself, by those neon standards, because he rarely called me now (and then always at 2 or 3 A.M. in a barbiturate fog) and I felt it hard to call him because the warm, giving side had hardened into a kind of bigtime loser's ice and there was no way for me to reach what was left of his wild, pure heart.

As Jim Nash has told it to me, Peter was in the Kettle of Fish on Macdougal Street when someone phoned in the radio news of his father's death. Without saying a word, he left the bar which was our own 60s Village equivalent of Eugene O'Neill's 1915 Hell Hole at 6th Ave. & W. 4th St. and disappeared into the Canadian woods to confront himself like Zarathustra in the fastness of the German Alps. After a couple of weeks Pete came back illusorily cleansed and sobered and started something called the Federation of Indian Rights. The idea was to raise cash to help the first American people fight legal battles and publicize their endless humiliations; but the folkniks he counted on to support him either suspected a con in the soul of Pious Pete or were too mesmerized by the growing money and celebrity possibilities of protest music to sacrifice anything real for one of its major sources. It was probably a combination of things, but whatever the reasons, Pete's possibly noble gesture died a slow death of disinterest and cynicism.

He got a confirmation of the spiritual void out there which was later to blossom into the full-fanged paranoia that I encountered in our last meeting. But even granting the cruel spurning he got, I'm forced, now, to question his motives in founding this Good Guy organization, as I believe everyone who knew him in New York then must do. Was it an emotional identification with Oliver, Sr.'s life-obsession now that he was dead and no longer to be feared, a passionate son's We instead of a fragmented Me against the bigots who wanted a Whites Only democracy? Was it Pete's own sincere concern with the banging-around that the Indians always seemed to be taking, already demonstrated by his cutting lyrics in the ballad of "Ira Hayes," or was it that self-serving exploitation of a fashionable underdog idea that always makes the motives of performers (especially those not quite making it) seem fishy to the less vocal?

I think, finally, that it was for real. But a "movement without organization is as good as a bowel movement," to quote the late Saul Alinsky, and my friend could hardly organize his trips to the john at this point. Whatever the dream or even the scheme in Pete's head, it all disintegrated into waste and personal shame like so many of his grand gestures. Pete was a man drowning day by day in contradictions. For example, he was a lovely hit-or-miss poet and even prose writer (" . . . *they covered their eyes, turning wallward, shoving the vision into small heaps in the corner . . .*") but he never really built on it the way serious poets and prosemen I know take charge of their talent. He was an inflamed would-be playwright, but it was more Colorado boy-loner dreams of "fantastic new Broadway hit" that blew his mind rather than necessity or dedication. He wanted to be a hundred marvelous shimmering things in the air, in other words, but in the end he was forced back to his bones like all of us.

His were folk music and song, where in spite of the fatherly boosting he got from Josh White and other kind, older players, he was not a pure first-rater—although Pete Seeger has said that some of his songs will live—and, even more than composing and singing, a new kind of desperate pop-cowboy style as a person. It was in this unique and fated personal presence of his, the then-bizarre western outfit worn like Madison Avenue silk, the soft, insinuating, mellifluous voice, the romantic bearing, the odd courtesies of southern-type gentleman and rugged cowpoke combined, the dark-blood Indian overtones I've spoken of, the warm eagerness of his response to everything that was new and unfamiliar without his griming himself with the dirty work of study and immersion—it was in the fluid combination of the man's elements that he lives in my mind like a wronged prince. Even now, eight years later, it's very damn hard for me to think he is dead, truly disintegrated as matter, no more ever.

Isn't the death and voidness of one who has been close to us an indication of the coming death and voidness of ourselves, their going an amputation of a piece of me or you that goes to dust with them? Come back, LaFarge, and keep me alive, you prick!

Pete's life was a terrible mess before he tossed it all in the garbage and quietly wiped his spectral hands, but I've learned that it's out of messes, the messiest lives, half-lives, wasted lives, that the future usually gets its leads. The impossibility of Pete's human situation, that fierce need to look and act like his own kind of southwestern superstar when his beaten body (a boiler-room explosion while doing navy draft duty, left-ear deafness, thrown and stomped by horses) and mind needed simpler, more basic approval, well, that spangled reach of his fantasy becomes purified now that the flesh has dropped away from the spirit and what we can see is the integrity of his imagination. I almost called it the integrity of his romanticism, but that word has become such a put-down and smells with such condescension towards its owner that it no longer seems to do proper justice to the sacrificial victim of impossible hopes. Yet it fits. Pete was important because he was so wrapped up in his bandana myth that he became it totally, frighteningly, something that is easier to accept now than when he was alive and you were nervously waiting for what was going to unfurl next.

In fact his values were as mangled as that entire American entertainment world he longed to star in during the late 50s and early 60s, that juvenile paradise where the comicbook virtues that a kid like Pete thought should be his, Manliness, Independence, Courage, Fightin' for the Underdog, etc., don't laugh, were exaggerated beyond belief and trailed huge money-tags in the bargain. In other words, be a righteous hero and be paid a million Cadillac-purring bucks for it too! It was a fantasy of pop heroism which became a disaster for those who tried to live it out as did Peter.

But whether or not Pete was a willful guzzler of ego-flattering illusions about righting wrongs with your guitar and your profile and your cowboy workshirt and being paid off in bags of gold for being a media saint, it was the extremes he went to in order to try and make these toy dreams real that carries through the years like some proud Cherokee lance. He was nothing if not consistent in his terrible efforts to live up to his mental picture of how a mod hero should come on—to look like his booted ideal, dress like it, behave like it—and the rigidity, the self-punishing discipline that must have gone on in that eerie head, is impressive even now when we take street masqueraders in stride.

Who else did I know who was so serious about unreality, so soldierlike in the pursuit of phantoms that would otherwise have cracked up in laughter everyone who knew him? No one, there was no single person like Pete in this royal madness to be a High Chaparral superman except, perhaps, another, earlier me who had paraded the streets with plastic-surgeoned nose held high and tears squinching out of *my* contact lenses, a walking work of stilted art unable to bear the lower-case reality until—watch out!—it all broke apart for me 18 big years ago and I traded in my *übermensch* for something approximating earthsize in a couple of funny farms.

But Pete never did. Never would. Can we say then, in a double voice, you shmuck, and also more power to you, forever and forever more power to you, sweet shmuck, because legend comes from such misery? Even when he was going under towards the end, and had become a true textbook paranoid like his much more sophisticated but still brother Village-poet, brother tragic-poet, Delmore Schwartz, there was no lessening of the intense seriousness with which he took his mission. The very last time I saw him to talk with was by accident, awkward after we had gone our separate ways those past several years—no clash, just drifting back to what our essential private selves had been before that joyous clasp of mutuality—like ex-marrieds who stumble on each other in the rain. We almost crashed head-on on Second Avenue a few blocks from my apartment, Pete now dressed in that black Phantom of the Opera cape I mentioned earlier and also seeming to hold a small club or cane under its folds. And while I was still in light shock from the sheer unexpectedness of seeing him he started telling me with twisted mouth, not stopping, that the Mafia in New York was keeping his folksongs off the jukebox, that there probably was a contract out on him because he was man enough to buck the corrupt record Establishment. I just nodded my head like a dummy, unnerved in more ways than one.

Although Pete never knew it and probably would not have cared if he did, I had been keeping tabs on him through the *Village Voice*, which was running small ads every month about a series of Town Hall concerts he was giving. I had thought with grudging admiration that he was still socking it to the people no matter what kind of personal hassles he was having, and when I saw him on the street this was the first thought waiting to be shaped into speech before he rolled right over it into his own obsession. It was never spoken in his lifetime. I was later told, after he was dead, that these concerts were like a vanity press arrangement: Pete would hire the hall himself and hope to recoup on admissions. But he was soon heavily in debt because even his "friends" in the tight folk-metaphysic fraternity didn't show up after a while since our boy was so tripped out he'd forget the lyrics halfway through his own songs; and now here he was on Second Avenue and St. Marks Place in the middle of the beggars muttering into my face about Eyetalian (literally) mobsters out to get him. Not a single word as to what I'd been up to these last couple of years.

I invited him home for a joint or a drink or a cup of coffee, take your choice, Peter, and he sat in the chair next to my unused fireplace still wearing the Lon Chaney cape, with that brutish hunk of wood resting in his lap, and turning hard in the eyes when I tried to josh him out of the Mafia movie he was playing. What made this particular bit of insanity more heartbreaking than the others I had seen was that you could visualize a vulnerable little Colorado kid way back in the 30s eating up tales of big-city underworld murders, *The Shadow, Dime Detective,* eyes growing wide with terrified delight. And now all of this sinister penny-thriller stuff had swept the sense out of his head and replaced it with the monsters he had always wanted to believe in.

I think we get furious at the self-willed falsification of reality because it's really such a snotty insult to our own endless labors to understand this inky spot we've all been put on, because it spits and craps on all the hard work we've put into our own lives. Come back! you cry out in your own way to the mind making a mockery of simple checkable facts, it's not true what you're saying. But Pete LaFarge was riding his own runaway mustang in my small one-room pad that he had once been so relaxed in, laughed in, sang in; there was silent rage glowing at my jokes, "Pete, believe me, Carlo Gambino has other things to think about than offing you," and then like that slow awakening you have to fire in a room I felt the real presence of physical danger.

I stopped talking. I mumbled, which was shameful in a man past 40, a throwback to adolescent fear. He stood up tall as a young god, drew the cape close with his left hand while the right one held the sweated club underneath it, shot me a look of contempt, and limped out the door on that one built-up boot I always forgot about but which a novelist friend (Alan Kapelner), who knew him too, assures me was there. You see, Peter was crippled in many small ways but was determined to disguise each of them because the way he appeared to others—acceptance, praise, O worship me, you unperceiving people, because I am truly good and holy—was confirmation to him of what he longed to be. Away from others, he to himself, in those writhing minutes before the Nembutals knocked him into sleep perhaps, there must often have been that feeling of "profound nothingness" which caused my French contemporary Nathalie Sarraute to invent that ice-cold phrase for so many of us these days.

Pete exited from my real life that day except for the one last glimpse of the Broadway cowboy I used for openers. But every now and then his name would pop up in the papers—frantic attempts to revive the Town Hall series, a flop concert to publicize the floundering Federation of Indian Rights—and I remember the sense of betrayal I felt that newspapers I later actually worked for as a personal journalist (the *Herald Tribune, New York Post*) would give space to a man who was so self-destructive and now near to being out of control. Yes, poor fucker Pete was being jerked around by imaginary demons all right, but my indignant jealousy at seeing his name and face in print is proof of how even those of us on the scene who claim we are compassionate can drop our dignity like pants in front of the toilet and squat down like dogs in the howling lust for public recognition.

Pete was in serious trouble, dislocated, thrashing the last waters of his life, probably beyond help, but trying in the only honest way he knew to sing and perform his way out of hell. And all that I, an ex-lover if only in the sense I described, could do for him was to resent his name in the papers because I thought he was unworthy of it compared to myself. To be even blunter about it, my thinking went like this: Hadn't I struggled to knit my flying brains into one and stamp principle for myself out of night-wind and despair, and was the *Trib* or *Post* giving me the attention as a fresh voice with the word that they tossed to this kamikaze destroyer of what was real?

Yes—pretty shitty, isn't it, but true, that decent men and women on the media make in our nutsy America wish broken-spirit failure to their friends ("It's hate, envy and malice that drive the artist on"—James Jones), co-sufferers, those they once loved, because they too are caught up in that desperate race to make their private egos into public headlines and measure their worth by how widely they are known. Although I was older than Pete and should have been cooler because I knew from experience what a shuck a few scattershot items in the paper or on the air were, how quickly forgotten, I cursed my haunted friend because he was getting notoriety I wanted for myself. If I meet him in heaven or some other easy place as yet without a name, believe it, I will softly kiss his ass and wash his feet with my fund of earned tears and suck his cock as gently as a maiden and make a lot of it up to him somehow. I think we'll both be relaxed then, no longer going bananas inside the American fame machine, and then we can really find out why we found each other exciting and truthful men at our best.

According to Jim Nash again, Pete and his new foreign-born wife (I never met her but she was in the folk-world too) gave a housewarming party at their unpaid-for garden apartment on the Upper East Side a few weeks before he died and not one person came because he was so frantic, scary now, and perhaps they knew he already had his stamped ticket for the happy hunting ground and were afraid he would pull them down to the mounds too. It's hard for me to believe that Ramblin' Jack Elliott, the Brooklyn Jewish cowboy singer who was as loyal to Pete as a brother during these last years, wouldn't show up—but he may have been out of town hustling. I knew nothing about all of this at the time, of course, we were just New York memories to each other now ("Oh yeah, I used to hang out with that dude years ago") as, in separate parts of the city, we scrounged for our lives as artists and people.

And then one day as I was taking my monthly slumming trip in the *Daily News*, the only paper in Manhattan that carried a real story because it feels and acts 10 years younger after each violent death, there was the news that Pete couldn't stand it anymore and had opted out by using the contents of a night table next to his bed which contained a couple of syringes, Nembutals, whiskey, and some other things not immediately identifiable. There was also some poetic writing, as I remember, which didn't make the paper because it couldn't be deciphered. And that was it. The end of a life that had once been as close to me as my own, and was now as separate and complete as a folk tale that holds within itself much that is important and sad about a people.

1973

14.
For My Brothers and Sisters
in the Failure Business*

We are all victims of the imagination in this country. The American Dream may sometimes seem like a dirty joke these days, but it was internalized long ago by our fevered little minds and it remains to haunt us as we fumble with the unglamorous pennies of life during the illusionless middle years. At 51, believe it or not, or believe it and pity me if you are young and swift, I still don't know truly "what I want to be." I've published several serious books. I rate an inch in *Who's Who in America*. I teach at a so-called respected university. But in that profuse upstairs delicatessen of mine I'm as open to every wild possibility as I was at 13, although even I know that the chances of acting them out diminish with each heartbeat.

One life was never quite enough for what I had in mind.

At 50 my father was as built-in as a concrete foundation and at 55 he was crushed out of existence by the superstructure of his life. I have no superstructure except possibly in my head. I literally live alone with my fierce dreams, and my possessions are few. My father knew where he stood or thought he did, having

---

*America to me was and is the dream of my life. I cannot separate my private self from it. I have become a pessimist because I live in a time so hard on people, including me, that I sometimes wish I hadn't been born into all this. Not only to spare me more bum trips but to free me from my knowledge of other people's situations. I have never really learned how to live. I improvise—and fuck up anyway. But through it all I owe so unfathomably much of whatever I am to being American that I couldn't conceive of my being alive in any other dress. It is what I want. Yes. I think the time must come soon if mankind is going to find life possible when this romance with country has to be junked for the sake of everyone else. This world is made up of individuals—what my friend at the liquor store, Vinnie Porrazzo, calls God's children—not separate governments. But until we become a state equal to every other one, I want to be a decent patriot; maybe afterwards, too, on a smaller scale. That's all I've ever really wanted. I'm homesick for that sweet land of liberty and not only the pursuit of happiness but the fulfillment of it. Not to die for my country, I've already done it too often, but to live for it. Oh, I'll tell you, I'll make a mean mother of a patriot. I want America to know this kid was here.—S.K.

164

originally come from an iron-cross Europe, but I only know that I stand on today with a silent prayer that tomorrow will bring to me my revelation and miraculize me.

That's because I come from America, which has to be the classic, ultimate, then-they-broke-the-mold incubator of not knowing who you are until you find out. I have never really found out and I expect what remains of my life to be one long search party for the final me. I don't kid myself that I'm alone in this, hardly, and I don't really think that the great day will ever come when I hold a finished me in my fist and say here you are, congratulations. I'm talking primarily about the expression of that me in the world, the shape it takes, the profile it zings out, the "work" it does.

You may sometimes think everyone lives in the crotch of the pleasure principle these days except you, but you have company, friend. I live under the same pressures you do. It is still your work or role that finally gives you your definition in our society, and the thousands upon thousands of people who I believe are like me are those who have never found the professional skin to fit the riot in their souls. Many never will. I think what I have to say here will speak for some of their secret life and for that other sad America you don't hear too much about. This isn't presumption so much as a voice of scars and stars talking. I've lived it and will probably go on living it until they take away my hotdog.

Consider (as the noble Dickens used to say about just such a lad as I) a boy at the turn of the 30s growing up in this land without parents, discipline, any religion to speak of, yet with a famished need that almost unconsciously filled the vacuum where the solid family heart should be, the dizzying spectacle of his senses. America was my carnival at an earlier age than most and I wanted to be everything in it that turned me on, like a youth bouncing around crazed on a boardwalk. I mean literally everything. I was as unanchored a kid as you can conceive of, an open fuse-box of blind yearning, and out of what I now assume was unimaginable loneliness and human hunger I greedily tried on the personalities of every type on the national scene as picked up through newspapers, magazines, movies, radio, and just nosing around.

And what a juicy parade through any inexperienced and wildly applauding mind America was then, what a nonstop variety show of heroes, adventurers, fabulous kinds of human beings to hook on to if you were totally on your own without any guidance and looking for your star in a society that almost drove you batty with desire. In my earnest role-playing the philosophical tramp and the cool millionaire-playboy were second nature to me, as were the style and stance of ballplayers, barnstorming pilots, polar explorers, radio personalities (how can I ever forget you, gorgeous-voiced Ted Husing?), generals, bridge-building engineers, treasure-hunters, crooners, inventors. I wanted to be and actually was Glenn Cunningham, Joe E. Penner, Kid Chocolate, Chandu the Magician, Eugene O'Neill, a Gangbuster. If you're old enough, tick off the names of the rotogravure big-shots of the time and see Seymour impersonating them in his private magic theater. And later on when I had lost my adolescent shame and knew myself to be a freak of the imagination, even wallowed in it, I identified with women like Amelia Earhart and even the hot ripe early pinup girl, Iris Adrian, and transvestited my mind to see the world through their long lashes and tough lace. Democracy means democracy of the fantasy life, too, there are no cops crouching in the corridors of the brain. Dr. Freud's superego hasn't been able to pull its old country rank over here, even though it's tried like a mother, or should I say a father?

But my point is this: what a great fitting-room for experimentation, a huge sci-fi lab for making the self you wanted, America was for those of us who needed models, forms, shapes we could throw ourselves into. Obviously, everyone from my generation didn't chuck caution out the window even if they felt the lure, as I did, of a new make-your-own-lifesize-man era. Some of my more realistic contemporaries narrowed it all down early and became the comparative successes they are today. Whether it's making a lot of money selling scrap in a junkyard (Ed Feinberg) or writing thrillers for connoisseurs of kinkiness (Patricia Highsmith), they all had to focus clearly, work hard. As traps and frustrations of 51 close down around me, with all the small defects and petty hurts that sometimes seem to choke away all thoughts of the unique Homeric journey of the inner person in America, everyone's inner person, I salute them for achieving some of what they wanted. Nobody gets it all. But I salute anyone in this bewildering dreamland of a nation who has managed to cut through the wilderness of tangled trails to some definite cabin of achievement and reward.

Yet those of us who have never really nailed it down, who have charged through life from enthusiasm to enthusiasm, from new project to new project, even from personality-revolution to personality-revolution, have a secret also. I'm sorry to say it isn't the kind that desperate people can use to improve themselves, like those ads in the newspaper. Sadly enough, it *is* the kind that people in my seven-league but very leaky boots often take to psychiatrists, hoping to simplify their experience because they can't cope with the murderous tangle of it. But for those of us who have lived through each twist and turn, the psychiatry sessions, the occasional abyss, the endless review of our lives to see where we went wrong, and then come to see our natures as strange and special manifestations of a time and place that will never come again, there is a wonder in it that almost makes up for the beating we are beginning to take at the hands of the professional heavyweight world.

Our secret is that we still have an epic longing to be more than what we are, to multiply ourselves, to integrate all the identities and action-fantasies we have experienced, above all to keep experimenting with our lives all the way to Forest Lawn to see how much we can make real out of that prolific American Dream machine within. Let me say it plainly: Our true projects have finally been ourselves. It's as if we had taken literally the old cornball Land of Opportunity slogan and incorporated it into the pit of the being instead of the space around us; and fallen so much in love with the ongoing excitement of becoming, even the illusion of becoming, that our pants often fall down and reveal our dirty skivvies and skinny legs. The laughter hurts, believe me, but it doesn't stop us for very long. We were hooked early.

What it comes down to is that the America of the pioneer has been made subjective by us. The endless rolling back of the frontier goes on within our heads all the time. We are the updated Daniel Boones of American inner-space. Each of our lives, for those of us in this countrywide fraternity, seems to us a novel or a play or a movie in itself, draining our energy but then at other moments lifting us up to spectacular highs, yet always moving, the big wagon-train of great new possibilities always crushing on. The fact that all of this is private doesn't make it any less real. What it does do is make us ache with hopelessness at times as to how to find a vocation for this private super-adventure serial out on the streets of life.

I know for a fact that I wanted to become a novelist in my teens just so that I could be all these different personalities and events that it was physically impossible for me to be any other way. As a matter of fact, I feel that the writing of the realistic/romantic novel in America (and they were usually one and the same, with the hairy details just used to tack down the sweep of imagination) came out of these basic human needs to transcend the one body and temperament you were born with in order to mingle imaginatively with a cast of thousands that could only exist in a monster-country like ours. Others wanted to become actors for much the same reason, to impersonate all the people they could not be, but in my case I wanted to compose the script itself so that I could participate in the minds as well as the outward actions of characters who were all extensions of myself and my own mad love affair with the fabulous diversity of this society.

I never accepted the discipline or, finally, the belief in a pure fiction separate from myself and never became the marvelous novelist of my teenage ambition. But I was an inward one, just as so many young kids today shoot movies in their heads with themselves as the leading character. I think it was just an accident of history that made me good at words instead of the sounds and pictures which are the newest language, but I feel little superiority at being able to pitch a word or two compared to those like myself in other ways who are tongue-tied. What unites us all is that we never knew except in bits and pieces how to find a total expression, appreciated by our peers, in which we could deliver ourselves of all the huge and contradictory desires we felt within. The country was too rich and confusing for us to want to be one thing at the expense of another. We were the victims of our enormous appreciation of it all.

Even though, with words coming easily to me, I began in my 20s that long string of never totally satisfying jobs as Office of War Information rewrite man, assistant pulp editor, motion-picture publicity writer, motion-picture script reader, book reviewer, finally editor of a magazine, I was always looking past them. When I heard a great black blues singer, I wanted to incorporate that sound in me and even tried singing in Greenwich Village. When I saw a handsome movie star close up, I thought that was my birthright also and went to a plastic surgeon to try and make me look more like this example of male beauty. When I had saturated myself with the brilliant records of Lenny Bruce and Lord Buckley, I thought that I too should improvise in a nightclub and even played a small engagement in the Midwest to painfully act this dream out. Whatever I saw that was good in others and which I didn't possess, I tried literally to add to my nature, graft on to the living flesh. It seemed to me, and I'm sure to those like me who haven't yet spoken, that American society was essentially a launching pad for the endless development of the Self.

We cared more about trying to enlarge and extend the boundaries of being what we were, of demonically sucking all of the country's possibilities into ourselves, than we did about perfecting a single craft or profession. As I've said, it was a beautiful, breathless eagerness for all the life we could hold inside, packed layer on layer like a bulging quart container of ice cream. Granted that in a way it was the most rank kind of selfishness and self-absorption, yet this too was forecast and made part of the national inheritance in 1870 when Walt Whitman chanted, "One's-self I sing—a simple, separate person; yet utter the word Democratic, the word En-Masse." That's what this democracy was for us, a huge supermarket of mass man where we could take a piece here and a piece there to make our personalities for ourselves instead of putting up with what was given at the beginning.

But this lovely idea became for some of us a tragedy, or at least a terrible confusion that wasn't counted on at the beginning. When do you stop making a personality? When do you stop fantasizing an endless you and try to make it with what you've got? The answer is never, really. You keep adding and subtracting from that creation which is yourself until the last moment. Once begun, it is not a habit that can be given up easily. Some people who started off this risky life-game with high hopes found that after a while they were unable to live with the self they began with and unable to come close to the self, or selves, they desired to be. They live in pain, and some are no longer living at all, having found it too bitter to take.

In my own case, because of the fluency with words, I was able to express my own longings and desires with personal statements in print as the years went by, and thus I wasn't as completely frustrated as those other dreamers I know who have run the gamut of jobs and flings at movies, writing, dancing, politics, and yet have never found a home to match their imaginations. Simply put, they never found a form to contain them, or have only caught it momentarily, and then it was gone.

During my 20s and 30s, even into my 40s, it was exhilarating to learn and be involved at this and then that steaming source—the *Partisan Review* brigade of radical intellectuals, then the Beat Generation, then a wonderful fling at daily newspaper reporting on the New York *Herald Tribune*, then the breakthrough (to my mind) of the New Journalism. I was confident as are all American nomads of the jeweled highways of the imagination that there would be a sudden confluence of all the roads at some fated point and then I would put it all together with a gorgeous thunderclap. No soap. Actually all of this *can* conceivably happen, but the mathematics are against you as time goes on. Yet time is just that factor we don't want to hear about until it elbows us in the nose.

We know all along that time is squeezing us into a corner while we mentally rocket to each new star that flares across our sky, and yet we can't help ourselves. We forget that our contemporaries are building up wealth of one kind or another, reputations, consistency, credit in the world, and that it counts for more as age settles down around all of us, the very age we have denied or ignored. In a way, those of us who have lived higher in the mind than on the sidewalk making and revising our salad of possibilities have stayed younger than we should have. We have even been sealed off from our own image as it's seen by others.

Yet each one of us sooner or later gets the elbow that reminds us that the "real world" we have postponed making a deal with, in fact played with like Chaplin kicking the globe around in *The Great Dictator*, has been evaluating us with a different set of standards than the ones we have been applying to ourselves. If we have been snotty towards ordinary success, proud and mysterious as we followed the inner light, even making thoughtless cracks about those who settle for little, then the day always comes when our own inability to put it all together is seen by another who wants to cut us down to size and our lives suddenly explode in our faces. . . .

I was living in Europe at the time, where the attitude towards personal success and failure is much less of a real distinction than over here because of the evenhanded wounds of recent history. Everyone was badly hurt by the war. Even today one man or woman's fate counts for less than some kind of minimum well-being for masses of people who are trapped by political and economic circumstances beyond their control and must learn to live, cheerfully if possible, without much hope for large personal triumphs. It is a relief for Americans who come from a society that glorifies individual achievement to the aching and breaking point to live over there for a while, and try to recuperate from the American heat in a different psychological climate. In fact many of our permanent expatriates are just the kind of people I have been talking about all through this communication, a band who have never found themselves by our official standards and perhaps never will, but who can live more at peace beyond our shores with less money and less strain than at home.

I, too, had been unkinked in this easier, we're-all-fucked-together-so-let's-make-the-best-of-it environment, self-lulled into thinking I was as rich and potential a human gold mine as I always believed—as all of us in my camp want to believe—when the dirty American word "failure" winged its way across the water and hit me where it hurts. . . . It suddenly and brutally defined to me the price I had paid for my bid to be everything that proposed itself to my imagination. Maybe I never had a choice, and would have been an uncertain performer at whatever I did, but my decision to aim at the stars had been a conscious one and this was the way it was being weighed on the common man's do-it-or-shut-up scale. . . .

But if you are a proud, searching "failure" in this society, and we can take ironic comfort in the fact that there are hundreds of thousands of us, then it is smart and honorable to know what you attempted and why you are now vulnerable to the body blows of those who once saw you robed in the glow of your vision and now only see an unmade bed and a few unwashed cups on the bare wooden table of a gray day. What we usually refuse to acknowledge in our increasingly defensive posture is that we chose our royal inner trip out of an excess of blind faith, out of a reach beyond what we might have had if our desires had been less grandiose. I can't really criticize this, I think it is inherent in the American mystique to want to go all the way to the limit of your imagination, but if we are straight about it we must accept that we are in large part responsible for the jam we are now in.

In my own situation I know only too well that from childhood and adolescence on I clutched at the habit of dreaming up a glittering future, always, instead of putting my head down and slugging my way through the present. I must confess that in an almost reflexive sense I still find myself doing this childish number, as do so many of those other poor lovely romantics who are like me. It's a primitive method so native to us by now that it is part of us. What was once a psychological choice when we were young, in other words, has now become for many of us a habit as hard to kick as junk. The handy magic of relying on the future, on tomorrow, to knit together all the parts of a self that we hoarded up for a lifetime can't be stopped at this late date, or won't be stopped, because our frame of mind was always that of a long-odds gambler. One day it would all pay off. But for most of us, I'm afraid that day will never come—the original hopes, their extravagant range and spaciousness, and yes, their lack of specific clarity and specific definition, were beyond translation into deed. They dramatized our lives for a good long while and then turned slightly sour when people began to ask for proof.

For a minority, and I still believe this, the special form they seek to pull it all together will unexpectedly click into place after years of turning the key this way and that. And as for myself, I am lucky I guess in that I can write about this very phenomenon that I live while others who experience it just as toughly, maybe even more so, are without the words to tell you what they have gone through.

Maybe that is my "revelation," the final "me," my purpose in the schemelessness of things after looking so strenuously in all directions and being so discontented with what I can apparently do without strain.

But this is a poor second to what I wanted and I will never be satisfied with sketching my own portrait and that of those like me when it was action we finally craved, after all those dress rehearsals in the mind, and not self-analysis. America worked on us too hard, when you get right down to it. We imaginatively lived out all the mythic possibilities, all the personal turn-on of practically superhuman accomplishment, stimulated by the fables of the media. We were the perfect big-eyed consumers of this country's four-color ad to the universe, wanting to be one tempting thing and then another and ending up, most of us, with little but the sadly smiling hope that time would somehow solve our situation. When I've been brave, I've told my friends who share my plight that this is no longer a true possibility to hang on to. Time will most likely repeat itself. We will most likely repeat ourselves. Most of my friends agree, with that hard twinkle in the eye that unites all of us who have earned it.

But you cannot separate us from the deepest promise of the country as it was lived within by very sensitive poets without a tongue, so to speak, and perhaps the ultimate failure of the country. This last is not an easy thing to say, even in a time in which America-baiting is the rage. Like most of us in the failure business, I am, we are, patriots so outrageously old-fashioned that we incorporated the spirit of the country in our very heads, took literally its every invitation to the greatest kind of self-fulfillment ever known. There's something beautiful about being an American sucker, even if you pay for it with tears and worse. We were millionaires of the spirit for at least 20 adult years before we felt the lowering of the boom, and in the last analysis it is the spirit, the attitude within, a quality of soul, that this country has to offer to history much more than its tangible steel and the bright blood too often accompanying it. . . .

1974

15.
Notes Towards My Death*

Richard Gehman died last week in a Lancaster, Pennsylvania, hospital at the age of 50. I think it was the booze destroying his liver, although the *Times* as usual supplied none of the details. They'll give a minute account of a Republican caucus in Albany that means nothing to me, but when it comes to death they become as prim as a girl I used to know who fornicated me but refused to get undressed in my presence.

Perhaps the name Richard Gehman means nothing to you. Life is changing so quickly today that it's sometimes hard to remember if your loud dead uncle's first name was Lou or Harry. But to a good-sized handful of us in New York, Dick (The Factory) Gehman was something of a star figure at one time. He was one of the highest paid and most prolific commercial magazine writers in the country during the 50s and very early 60s. He went through at least four wives, fathered nine children, hurtled from coast to coast with pieces burning in five typewriters at the same time.

He used to show us the inch-long calluses on his typing fingers as proof of his fanatic industry. We laughed at him, those of us who remained in Lilliputian Village high on esthetic dreams and scrounging out a penny a word for the little magazines, but we were impressed by his productivity and lifestyle even when we said he wrote crap for money. He influenced my actual life. His second wife,

---

*One by one the people I know—older, just a shade older, on a par with me (Bob Reisner), even younger (Leonard Shecter, Hal Sharlatt)—are dying off each day with unfinished business written on their faces. We all get tagged that way even though I hope to make it a match worth your admission ticket. But I, too, am waiting crouched in the line with the grin that any contender wears when he knows he's going to get it. I even think I know how. But this knowledge or this nerve means nothing, really, except to me; death was never moved by a good performance. No matter how good or bad I might be at the crucial moment it will not bring back the sweet/smart people of my generation who offered me love, beauty, money, faith, sex, charm, knowledge, understanding. I took it for granted then; I thought it was coming to me, that I was special. Now I'm trying to pay some of it back before I get still.— S.K.

after their separation, became the most important person in my own life for several years before I tried to crown her with a Little League baseball bat during a jealous rage. She married someone else soon after that, for which I can hardly blame her.

And as late as 1970, long after we had been out of touch, Gehman was responsible for getting me a teaching job at the University of Iowa when I was down and out in London. He had read something I'd written and by surprise letter to American Express told me who to contact at the Writers Workshop in Iowa City in order to nail down a sweet $12,000 a year for not too much work.

In other words, Gehman was a generous man who affected a number of lives in spite of the transiency of his writing and the swagger of his days and now he is blotto. As I said, I believe it was alcohol that killed him as it did Jack Kerouac, another whirlwind, whose death leaped up at me out of the back page of the *International Herald Tribune* when I was in Barcelona in October of 1969. That was a shocker too, as were the suicide of Diane Arbus, the OD of Lenny Bruce, the stopped heart of Tom Murray, one of the funniest New York men I have ever rolled on the floor for.

I knew Bruce the least, but all of these people were almost exactly my age and now I am thinking of death too. I'm not thinking of it in an immediate sense, so don't look for a paragraph or two in the *Times* next week which will omit the best details, but I am wondering in a steady way how it will come to me. What shape will the bastard take? How will I feel when I know it's on me if I'm given that last thin dime of consciousness?

I don't find thinking this way morbid. I find it essential in view of what has unexpectedly happened to some of my more exciting contemporaries. Besides, it suits my sense of subjective drama and my vile curiosity. I have always claimed I had that third eye, cool and unfazed, which can look upon one's own disasters as objectively as it looked at the face of a mountain or a burn victim and now I am applying it to my own death.

First, I don't think I'll die a "natural" death because I'm not sure there are any left. Any unwilled human death today is unnatural. We find the idea unacceptable compared to the amount we give to stay alive from Monday to Monday. All that energy and foxiness spent for nothing? Death is too simplistic to be natural anymore. Even a long illness, in that favorite veiled phrase of the *Times* obituary page, is no longer a natural death to our minds. It is a wrong death. Too many possible outs come to the imagination of even the dying person to make him go philosophically into that dark night.

I maintain that every death today is violent. That is the nature of human death in our time, whether it's splattered all over TV or remains invisible to all but the unbelieving consciousness of the victim, and that is the death I am traveling towards. But what kind of violent death? Yes, that is the question.

Suicide is always a live possibility, although I have successfully fought its lures all my adult life. Yet I was born under its sign—my mother hurled herself from a

Washington Heights roof when I was 10—and I understand its appeal. I even once wrote an essay in its defense. In fact I dedicated the last book I wrote to three bohemian night-riders who went down this way.

The methods for saying goodbye to all this are more stylish and less painful now than in my poor mother's day and I don't discount them. The Nembutals that I occasionally take to dope me for needed sleep sit in the medicine chest like a loaded pistol. The grease would be my 90-proof Wodka Wyborowa, a tough Polish brew, and in a couple of hours I would hear the angels singing. At the very least, I wouldn't hear the screaming in the streets, in the headlines, in my own conscience because of a helpless implication in personal and public agonies that I can't control or cure.

Yet I don't think that's the way it will be. It's too convenient, in spite of the relief it brought to friends of mine like Anky Larrabee, William Poster, Beverly Kenny, Weldon Kees, and Peter LaFarge. I think my lumps will be sterner, a matching of my temperament by the physical force that will destroy me. By this I mean that if I get it from a speeding car or a high-powered truck, it will be because I was careless, stupidly proud, defiant of reality, too paralyzed by fear to function in the streets, etc., etc. My death, I believe, will be a meeting of the naked inner man with his true measurer in the world of fatal fact.

Even if I die by chance, an air conditioner falling from a window, a United Airlines 727 crumpling at 30,000 feet, a dumb police bullet ricocheting off a building and into my head, I still think the needs that led me to that sidewalk or into that airplane were mine alone and not yours. But I don't expect to go by so-called chance when there are so many more logical possibilities. Murder, for example, is something that most of us who came out of the middle class enjoyed from a distance in the media and never once thought of in relation to our own tender white meat.

I think of it now. When I'm stoned or drunk, I'm outspoken, especially in touchy areas where I seem to feel that it's cowardly for a writer and intellectual to back down. This might once have been met only with an invitation to fight with one's fists. Young male writers, the majority of them poets, have in fact challenged me in the last few years, and so far I've been successful in not getting another nose-job. I've been able to defuse most of them without getting too much dirt on my self-respect.

But I've been lucky to deal with amateurs. What about the violence nuts cruising the streets of America, whether they're possessed secret messiahs or TV repairmen or both? No one is fighting fair anymore because it's no longer an important concept. A black friend of mine in Harlem wouldn't mind seeing me get my ass kicked because he thinks I'm Jewish-spoiled. Not wiped out, mind you, just chastened. But he's a friend.

The little hunchback who lives next door to him, and buys the Panther paper, is not a friend. He wouldn't mind getting a cheap thrill seeing some righteous big-mouth like me take the blade.

So, given a passionate or overt personality like mine, murder is something that I can't pass off on the movies, not with the mood of strangers ("a nation of strangers," is what my poet friend H.L. Van Brunt calls America) being what it is today. I always wanted to call them countrymen, or friends, and I can see myself slightly loaded in some New York or Chicago tavern mouthing those Whitmanesque words while some zombie pumps bullets into my middleaged flab. I fall to the floor like a B movie with the hand of brotherhood outstretched and this countryman spits in my helpless face. Fadeout.

Yes, all of this could happen and I'll be keenly curious all the way to D-day to know how it will finally come, but my real hunch on the matter is that I will just be wrecked out, like most of us. I can feel it coming, that slow, inevitable ungluing of the organs under the terrible stress that grinds our days. For four months the little finger on my left hand has felt like it's in a coma, probably the Carpal-Tunnel Syndrome according to a dermatologist friend of mine speculating while he writes me a free prescription for Dexamyl. Sure I'll get it checked— as soon as I get my hemorrhoids clipped. There's money, you know, and time, the Time-Money Syndrome, that keeps falling further and further behind while these breakdowns on different parts of the front keep sending out their signals.

You can patch these things up for a while. I'm aware of that; Band-Aids and make-dos of one kind or another are beginning to hang down almost every side of me. But I feel that I can't have led the life I have inside, in my mind and emotions, without having it reflected in the meat. The ride I've taken has been down the third rail, the current has been boiling my vitals ever since I've been about 13, and something's got to give. I don't know how much longer the basic equipment will stand up, although I observe little rips and tears with a certain amount of philosophic pleasure.

It confirms my sense of the overall stress situation, of the necessary relationship between the living spirit and the blackened suit of flesh that is burnt out by the heat within it.

What I expect to happen is that the further I push towards my limit as a human, and I don't mean anything abstract but just simple foot on the gas trying to reach some kind of local destination through the worst traffic jam in history, the further will my body and brain be butchered until a bloody equation is reached. There will be a togetherness between my statement as a man and my death as a thing. I will die piece by piece as I struggle to make myself whole.

My best moments, to continue this prophecy that I think is just, will come as I am being ripped apart ("He said it was like a thousand pounds of cut glass in his chest"—A.C. Spectorsky's wife to me after his first heart attack) for having lived hard, or merely for having lived. That's the way it will happen, I think. My death will be bad news to what's left of me but I will then have married my fate so utterly that only I will know the rightness of that last, paid-for breath while one or two people cry for what they see. For godsakes, don't.

1972

16.
Chaos
New York/Moving Out*

. . . .But we know there's no peace for us, who's kidding who?, we were not meant for evenness, AllState ain't going to make things easy for us, it's combustion in the head and in the motor that guns us forward! Get rid of the fuel, we sometimes cry at night, I'll take the horse and buggy, lovey, but it's not to be, you know that!

Sure, hordes of young men/femmers countrywide are moving back to that little old shack in Red River, New Mexico and Custer, South Dakota—just a one-holer for that thrilling 3 A.M. pee!—bless them for it, friends, new beginnings, Make It Now cried Ez the Pound!, but they can't oblit the machine in all that Eden-type green ground, Massey-Ferguson will sell them a power mower before they're through! And even if they do, a new America full of hydrosolar dreams will spring from the springs and valleys, the same high-tech show all over again, believe it dear people, fate is on us like a kid sailor's tattoo!

OK, agreed, we're not all sweety honey dears, I guess, but we're dear to each other because we got no one else to cling to, I've got to stand up for a truth or two in the jungle of our confusion and bring it back to you! Not everyone's truth, I know it, but mine in relation to you, strictly off the cuff, just like a '50s ad lib, dig it former great radio private-eye Howard Duff! Cuff-shooter, hipshooter, Manhattan Wild West truth-roper—yes, Elmo, even occasional degenerate doper!—I'm not making no pitch for spontaneity at the expense of thought, I'm just trying for a different kind of thought, thought kicking off thought like a Chinese popping New Year's down on Pell Street!

This excerpt from his unpublished book-length prose poem was chosen by Seymour Krim for this volume. It is also included in the slightly longer excerpt recorded in 1984 by the American Audio Prose Library, Inc.—Ed.

Hell, if I'm for real you can stop right here—OK, stop!—when the phone rings, do your thing, and pick me right up again without a snit, sock right back in, ain't no sin! It's just the never-ending thought-trip of our anxieties, goddamn Heinz's 57 beautiful varieties, a bronco ride in the midst of shambles—a beat as we dance on them cut-glass brambles!—oh we need a whoop to take us through these days, demand it, damn it! For years we've calculated our lives, thought them out, but I tell you that's not enough, we have to shout them out too, oh nuts! just fingerpop to the beat and it'll get you through, got to trust your boogiewoogie Jew!

Art as psychotherapy, why not?, bop poetry for American screwups, why not?, jazzmatazz for patriotic schizos, why the hell not?, all those things we once thought impure for art, well they're not impure for us! Where do you think art cometh from if not the deepest rhythms that keep us going, those sweet sweet sounds that feed us on our daily rounds? Motors, rotors, teletypes clicking with fingerlicking electronic joy—how many dudes from my gang entered the newspaper game just to hear that teletype sing, ear cocked in that little cage past the cityroom?—but you don't have to be a teletype-boogie freak to catch a ride on this here train, I mean it Mrs. Hollywood widow of Claude Rains! This train as old dustbowl Woody Guthrie used to twang it is your train, my train, everybody's ride-'em-high train!, and your engineer got to keep it oiled and rolling through the night, let's travel far and travel light!

But we all know there's no hot trains no more, no Silver Flyers in the American head no more, yet there sure are lots of train men hanging 'round those groovy bars and coffee parlors in engineer boots and red suspenders, the hope lives on even while the cars are gathering rust off in some siding in the dust! That's because it's outdoor lantern-swinging stuff, isn't it?, the old frontier romance—Thanksgiving giblets, yessiree Grandma, and squaring the dance!—not like a Lockheed SR-71 flying above the old sun, all sheathed-up and tubed for speed, yeah it's all getting swift-on-swift and the Great Train Caper is part of that dying past, face it folks: little we once had now seems to last! Watch it recede right before our staggered eyes, that past of ours, "just like a dream," isn't it cruelly so? But we carry it right along in our mental wallets with some snatch of a '30s song—"They're having a heat wave, a tropical seat wave!"—fight for some kind of continuity, America give me my annuity on the life I lived before!, before tomorrow sweeps us all away into this weird new day!

Oh the country is going fast these days, it's going to go faster, we all know it and can't slow it no way, Pam tells me she's been speeding for three days and living off ice-cream and moving furniture! Speed indeed! we were the kids who loved it from the start, Indy-500, Lindy-up-in-the-blue, Sir Malcolm Campbell out on them Salt Lake Flats, Glenn Cunningham churning that 4:04 mile, and now it's all a laugh with Pam and the other newies turning on with reds and greenies that blow Sir Malc away into the cornball state of yesterday! We know it's getting quicker, the course is getting whirlier, the memories of our slow track fade while we go booming faster paster those sonic signposts, look at me team, I'm flying! Is it only weepers and sentimentalists who look back at the family album?, is it a drag for you to view your foreign past as it's not for me?, do you want to fly now and amnesiac the rest?, I don't blame you! Our memories sometimes feel as if they came from another life, nickel telephones—those Nedick's doggies too!—10 cent cigars, quarter lipsticks, that big Zenith radio sitting like a shrine, did we really live that life or was it someone else we heard about? Ah nutserooni, Father Andrew A. Rooney, it's all smoking so fast that we've forgotten our own minds, they're smeared with print and TeeVee and Aunt Sue reading her Bible at the kitchen table in Newark 40 years ago, who can separate the fact from fiction?, it's all tumbled together in some slick actor's diction!

Yes, sure, agreed, decreed!, it's not us alone, the whole plant's speeding like that Friday night bar-fight bleeding in the St. Vince emergency room, but we were the mod pioneers numero uno, we were the first to scream hallelujah on the seats of the human rollercoaster, snap to the pop of a Westinghouse toaster! Have our noggins been pounded into weirdo pumpkins by the America that has passed through and behind our eyes?, are we on the inner ropes, folks?, are we using them like Ali?—champ of the American ropes, making them bounce for him!—and forgetting all the Corbetts and Jersey Joe Braddocks that came before unless that Guinness Book of Records is strapped in our hands? Have we been so swamped, gutted, bomberood, electroshocked, yeah discount-house schlocked! by all that's happened to us in the last 50 years—by what's happened to me in the last 53!—that we can no longer chart it out, have to dive in brave from day-to-day, just as I'm diving in brave from minute-to-minute, OK? Sure, historians go back and sort it out for us—such and such happened when whuch and whuch did so and so, it surely did, kids!—but I'm talking about the historian in each one of us, the memory-boy/memory-girl buried in the big confused American adult, how tiny all those snapshots of tennis foursomes and Maine summer camps and your Pittsburgh girlfriend of 18 years ago now seem in the gaudy color show that creams our eyes!

Try it, you'll like it, they told us about America from the start, and we ate the wh-o-o-o-le thing, but Alka Seltzer won't save us now, not just because I'm a Bromo Man and an Aqua Velva fellow who loves The Great New Bottle! Pour it on is all we can say back to our land—go to it, Daddy Uncle Sam! oh slurp it on, more Alka, more promo in your Bromo, Mighty Dog Is Pure Beef, more GE, NBC, drown us in it BBD&O's Fred Winnett!, so we can be the special monsters we were meant to be! Do you really think that we can call a halt? At this late dateroo? No way, ofay, and all you darktown strutters too, why even if they leveled "free trade" off and found one product for 15 out of sweet reason's sake—saned up out society, Dennis Moriarity!—do you think that we could shake the fever from our bones in one puny generation? We're used to being bomberood, not from the skies but in the eyes, the ears, the goddamn rears, you know how they bomb us down and how we love it—at least live with it as hunger for the senses no matter how the mind and heart protest!

Come on, admit it, we're war-lovers of the commercial fronts, how we know them jingles, soundtracks—Burma Shave, Electric Burma Shave!—like connoisseurs of crap, stamp-collectors of sheeit, the socialist part of our heads putting it down and the capitalist side putting it up! Sweated in the pits of band-studios, sound-chambers we are even if we never played a lick, product and music and snickering participation go hand-in-hand in the land we invented—hail to our achievements, buddies, and never say it doesn't belong to you! We could have seceded from our world long ago, somehow, some way, if it didn't suit that burble in the blood that Geritols us onward, PalmOliveward, you brand-name pilgrims you! This is our dream we made, not theirs, not China's, not old Roosh, our own Indian Penny dream Mr. & Mrs. Clean!, and if we don't live with it, try to live with it, who will, who can? Yes, it's gotten out of hand—take that paw away from your genital, you secret freakos mine, it won't run away!—and now it's broken loose everywhere, the world's own moorings are shot to blazes, we were just the first national crazies and now we're trying to come down when our fate, I tell you, is to move yet further up and out!

Peace on a planet—name your choice, Ms. *Astrology Today* buff Janet!—when we get there, maybe, but never down here, dear! Oh it must sound like Hell, Inc. to all you Burpee seed planters and tenders out there, when all you want is calm and a little rain for your cucumbers and a J & B before dinner and an "Odd Couple" rerun later on! Sure, you can have it for an hour, perhaps a day, even six months, a year, but then some high-cheekboned ex–Erasmus Hall High School tight end hungering in the Scarsdale bushes is going to rape your bank account and steal your wife—you were tired of her anyway, and she of you, but would never admit it to yourselves!—and trash your Tudor home and you'll be out on your no-trespass street raving at the stars with your .38 in one hand and a clump of hair in the other, torn from your very own Mr. Joe's Realweave scalp-job! Ah, believe me, I'm not out to make your life miserable by my pictures—Breughel was a pattycake compared to our gruesome Instamatics!—I wish you all the happiness that's possible in our American whirl, but think you kid yourself if you still romance your head with dreams of order and growing old nice-nice in this shifting mirage we call our U.S. life!

Didn't Marynia Farnham, my last psychoshmiko doc—you had competition, Hymie!—quit East 28th St. for New Hampshire and the barren joys of working with state loonies because she was hitting 70 and friends of hers were getting mugged while parking wheelchairs in front of Mozart Lincoln Center concerts? She was safe up there last time I saw her on Whipple Hill, watched out for by a husky farmer down the road, but the whiskey bottles were lined up on her trolley to get her through the days and nights of age, no psychoanalytic blandishments for Marynia as she views the ripped pattern of her American past, better a shot-glass blast from old Jack Daniels! I hope you're still swinging on that Whipple Hill gate, Doc, still owe you $673 and watch the *Times* obits to see if my debt is canceled out—we're all money-crazed louts, I'm no different, and it'll all be settled four years from now when I come back to bury you on this line!—but she has no illusions about the creak of time in our youngman's/youngwoman's playpen! She'll fade with Reason and Bourbon feeding each other as she views the Manhattan monster from Whipple Hill, glad to have escaped—sorry not to have been gently raped but too brittle to afford the pleasure!—yet never dreaming for a minute that this rugged riot of a land had something easier for the daughters of the pioneers! She knew violence in my own unconscious let alone the city streets, and when she cuts out to meet her dead hubby, Freud and Jung in that Doctor's Convention on high she'll have no Future of an Illusion clouding her 20/20 eyes!

Yes sir, I mean those of you hardliners who pray a Republican Party triumph of Law and Order for your backyard roses' glory—and I've got nothing against you Repubs, I loved Willkie for humane's well as maybe homo reasons, I even love the straight-spined charm and nasal snip of my Vassary spinster landlord!— are exalting prettiness above the destiny of our fluid, screw-it landscape, surely it's more a ramscape bucking towards an unknown future! Never still, it won't ever freeze itself into Greek-type columns over here, American Roman's out, it's all disorder and half-born and the buzzing gnats of doubt no matter how many screens and barbed wire fences we put up to shut them, stomp them out!

"Don't you want to get a piece of land for your old age?" old buddy Chandler asked me after he bought that strip out in Amagansett, and I knew—just like you!—the reality behind his question, his wiped-out old man, the years without a proper home, oh I know, I've lived it too, but I want to possess the country and not just no strip! Possess it in the head at least, listen I'm not above a hunk, hardly, only that strips and nips of land waver before my eyes with scenes of people dynamiting them with their emotions—I see no peace, I'm saying, even on Long Island! Sure we burn for peace, yearn for peace, even those earth-colored blower-uppers from Porto Rico to Alaska eventually want it on virile terms—peace, shalom, you white-faced bums!—but could you go on deducting for that Manhattan Hanover Retirement Fund if you knew it would never come, hmmm? Well, better go on deducting for its own sweet sake—or do it for the memory of Veronica Lake!—because it will never come to the likes of us, I dearly don't see how! Yes, a down payment may be a kind of peace, a steel door to block a ripoff to your lifetime's treasure, no knife-jobs on your street this week, no shadows fleeing across your roofs cradling that 9-inch Sony, that will be your peace—better embrace it, Stacy Keach! Peace, p-e-a-c-e, the fleece of adult living, the felt and satin for a bruis-ed heart, peace, god grant us—peace!, was never in the domestic cards for us! Peace meant cessation in our invisible horoscope, peace was stagnation and fat, peace was to take a sad expiring breath and work that garden with a glove while the world pounded by outside the window!

Hell yes, let war overseas become America's cardinal sin—slap it on the parish gates, ye feisty St. Louis Cardinals!—but inside the walls of Cannon City, U.S.A., it will phase down oh so slow, believe it, will only leave us when we change the name! Constructive violence—how's that?—constructive combustion, something on that order sort of and only inside such copouts which'll drive Padrone Ed Newman up the TeeVee cable at what he thinks is the corruption of our lingo will friction take another shape and form, maybe water-bagging the old dorm! But I am the voice of friction—if you can't handle it, dive into some snappy summer fiction!—you are the ear of friction, the line which is not corrugated with a sawtooth edge is bland as clear chicken soup to us, we love the thought of peace but not the texture!

See, I come from an older America full of a different kind of two-fisted, two-breasted terror and my idols then were guys like Georgie "Red" Wilson diving off the highboard at Camp Koda and Helena the Hot Toddy throwing bodylike lightning bolts to those open mouths at the Irving Place burlesque, highschool peckers rising like an enflamed prophet! Muscle and coordination were our gods, our kid imaginations were slashed with juicy red-nippled bods, peace was only welcome after panting war, not before! Danger and physicality for the boys—the most breathtaking zipzap joys!—sizzling lipstick and prancing tits for the gals, those were our iron standards, pals! And we who've endured from one America to another—hanging on like big-prize riders in the rodeo, you ain't throwing us Mr. Hoss!—carry that helpless lead that tails us down to another time, can't never be sunny-day kites again flying that limitless sublime! Who would've thought a hectic present-tenser like yours truly would one day search among the wrappers of his mind—old Spearmint throwaways, forgotten stowaways!—to make a path from then to now and take you with me, try to, for the sake of U.S. mapmaking! Oh look where we've come from, compatriotos, and smile at the vast unknown ahead—hey Vast Unknown, give us a little sweet head to keep us happy afore you scare us with those abominable snowmen who lie in wait! . . . .

17.
The 215,000 Word Habit:
Should I Give My Life to *The Times*?*

Excuse me while I put my *New York Times* aside and try to write this piece. It's now 8:35 in the evening, absolutely no baloney, although we used to use a shorter word, and I'm still working on Section B, page 4—"For Ferraro, Lost Friendships But Stronger Family," continued from page B1. I've already had my supper (broiled tilefish, little potatoes, bean salad, a glass of Boucheron blanc de blanc), not my *breakfast*, and I still have twenty pages of Section B to go plus Sections C and D. Let me not wring out the page count here—the real situation is monstrous enough—actually, the upcoming eighteen pages of Section B are nonreading materials, only classifieds. But what with hard news, features and reviews, tonight I still have forty-three pages to mow down before tomorrow begins in three hours and fifteen minutes and the same torment awaits me!

What's happened? What's going on? Was *The Times* always like this except we didn't notice—of course not, even I know that, but when did it start becoming pointedly pathological as a daily read? When did it really start getting out of hand for all but the professional human mice who spend their days in the stacks nibbling away at print? There's no exact telling when it passed over the line, but obviously it first began during the tenure of A. M. (Abe) Rosenthal as executive editor, 1977–1986. Rosenthal himself has said that he picked up new journalistic finger foods from that preppy innovator Clay Felker, when Clay was at the helm of *New York* magazine during the 1970s—before Mad Dog Rupert ate little Clay up and spat him out for jaw-strengthening exercises.

But what did Rosenthal pick up that has now made *The Times* into such a Frankenstein of unrestrained virtues, or did it turn into a noble glandular case for other reasons also? What we know is this: Rosenthal took from Felker all the magazine-type concepts he could newspaperize—things that Mr. Prep had originated as consumer service features, like The Passionate Shopper, The Underground Gourmet, Best Bets, How the Power Game Is Played, etc.—and

*Selected as a Notable Essay of 1988 for *Best American Essays 1989*. Edited by Geoffrey Wolff and Robert Atman. Introduction by Geoffrey Wolff (Boston: Ticknor & Fields, 1989).—Ed.

fleshed out (why? why?) what was already a portly paper. The answer to the mystifying question posed just now flashes in: yuppie readability, entertainment. If you're in print, why should the mags have it all in the Age of Plush and newspapers continue to trod the same old grim rut of who, what, when, where— how square! At the same time old shrewdie Abe was adding ice-cream colors to his paper's sober garb, that garb itself was also draping an increasingly voracious global waistline, until the weekday *Times* now averages around 215,000 words of hard copy, and Sunday's close to a million.

Two hundred and fifteen thousand words is what you're trying to grapple with every day; so am I, buddy, and it makes me want to cry at the torment that publisher Punch Sulzberger is inflicting on us. Could it be that Punch is one of those legendary "Jews without mercy," as some hard-liners of that beleaguered faith have been called? Is it necessary that a human newspaper be this size? But while you ponder that, keep in mind what an obsession, what a massive hanging goiter, the very thought of this great paper has become in the minds of its cringing readers. Just as I have my own forty-three unread pages of today's *Times* in escrow until I can gut out a first draft of this article—don't worry, I'll redeem those pages if it kills me before I permit my eyes to close tonight—so there must be untold thousands throughout this city (country?) who are fiercely trying to finish up before the new day arrives with its new 215,000-word responsibilities.

Few regular readers have the chutzpah to snub the paper entirely for a day, never doubting they will be punished in some mysterious way, yet few can get through it without psychic confusions about what to skip, whether to read on (onward!) at the expense of earning a living, vacuuming the rug, writing a letter to the phone company, etc. I kid you not, it's become a weird confrontation for many people, this *New York Times*, all of its sheer mass comprising nothing less than an alternate reality—but too fearfully much for people who don't want to devote their lives to it, as James Joyce asked his readers to do with his books.

Not only does *The Times* stagger its own readers with the enormous weight of humanity dumped on them every morning; things have reached the point where it has become America's number-one commissar of the real. If it doesn't appear in *The Times*, such is the unconscious reflex of the faithful, it isn't worthy of existence. To the extent that now it even reports on itself as a necessary source in the making of news. For example:

The day after I started flinging my own frail frame against this graven idol— the day that occurred three hours and fifteen minutes after the raw beginnings of this piece, a while back—the chesty confidence that holds power in place was exercised in full view without a hint of shame. Reporter Herbert Mitgang, doing a story on a new one-volume encyclopedia called *Chronicle of the 20th Century*, interviewed its editor in chief for no particular reason except that he had once been a managing editor of *The Times*. His name is Clifton Daniel and he is, incidentally, married to Harry Truman's daughter, so why not chuck him and his new brainchild a PR bone?

Fine, but then in the very same issue reporter Mitgang was himself interviewed by yet another *Times* reporter, Edwin McDowell, for writing a *New Yorker* magazine article (see how the old-boy network widens!) about American novelists who have been harassed by the Federal Bureau of Investigation. Reporter McDowell tells us the article was inspired by a book that Mitgang has put together called *Dangerous Dossiers: Exposing the Secret War Against America's Greatest Authors.* Did that end it? Not on your life. William H. Honan, until recently cultural editor of the newspaper, was then quoted by reporter McDowell as saying, ominously, "The New York Times was not aware of the article or book until today."

Ah, *The New York Times*! It quotes itself, it interviews itself, it sometimes seems to get confused with the world itself, which is reflected in the knit brows of the earnest—especially that flock of briefcase-carrying young women one sees on lower Manhattan buses, wrestling with the four windmill sections of you know what, too overpowered by duty to put the whole thing down for a minute and look out the window. But you just can't do that, it's like masturbation used to be for the current senior-citizen generation—God is watching.

I wouldn't dare say that *The Times* isn't the most incredible 30-cent buy in New York (a Snickers bar would have to come down 20 cents even to get in the running), but do dare say that it is at a perilous subjective cost. One can easily imagine actual madness and suicide resulting from an impossible attempt to read all of this newspaper every day, and I wouldn't be surprised if some CUNY social psychologist isn't already working on a grant proposal. If reality in our time has gotten out of hand—the new science of disorder, Chaos, can serve as a clue, correct?—then the newspaper has followed suit; but like the old naturalistic novel it has resorted to accretion of detail to keep up, rather than initiating a counterinsurgency against the flood.

There is a crisis at *The New York Times*, nor should my saying this make you guffaw when you look at the profit statement. If a reader feels that only by brilliant eye-editing (quick hop/skip here, forget this one, now should I plunge?) can he reach the last page without putting a sixty-foot trench in the middle of his day, something is gravely out of whack. Would it take a nuclear wipe-out to make *The Times* start all over again, lithe and quick? Is it crazily advisable to get even bigger and more impossible, an intimidatingly honored but unread monument, like William Gaddis's *J R* (National Book Award, 1976), totally cowing the reader with its vision of absolute coverage? Or is it obvious, as I concede it is, that this indefatigable machine of money, talent and heedless pride will continue on its way even when its desperate readers are cudgeling their brains, looking for a formula to cope? Even as a new day hints at its arrival in the predawn Eastern skies with Sections C and D of yesterday still barely skimmed? Is there to be no end to it, seriously, even unto eternity and beyond?

1988

18.
The CAT Scan of Our Era:
Actor
As Incarnation

Is this actually taking place? Is Chuck Wachtel really lecturing me that Robert De Niro has "greatness," as if 8 × 10 glossy performers truly existed on the same plane as writers, were worthy of the same exalted words that my gang used to use forty-nine years ago for D.H. Lawrence or even (the thought blushes, slightly) Clifford Odets? I look at Chuck with wonder. Why the immortal garlands for an acting-school putz who is actually the separately raised son of a real artist, my old tormented buddy Bob De Niro, who once floored me with a punch when I downgraded one of his paintings in the Village forties?

Why should a gourmet word-maven like young Chuck (*Joe the Engineer*, William Morrow) care about De Niro or Al Pacino or William Hurt or any of these overpriced replicators, duplicators, impersonators, when the names that formerly came from his lips attached to the word "great" were William Carlos Williams and Hubert Selby Jr.? Why?

But I know the answer even as I'm sending up these disingenuous smoke signals, so does everyone of my generation who almost half a century ago chose writing as the most heroic and venturesome act they could commit—we all know that the actor/performer has stolen the lightning! Yes, the "player," whom muttering writers for the past zillion years have usually treated like an infantile textbook case, your ultimate ditzy narcissist, has walked right into history with the authority of a new nose job. Media technology and "performing" (gawd!) go together, the perfect fit, and the hero-novelist under whose image our projection of ourselves flourished seems a dewy anachronism from the thirties.

The major American novelists of the new canon (Gass, Barth, Hawkes, Coover, etc.) are no longer known on the street corner, probably not even in the majority of classrooms at the local university, but that void has been filled by The Performer—the new galvanizing hero/-ine, the identifying magnet of the age. Even though the performer might be helpless without a script, He and She have become so magnified by the new technology that they've also become representatives of us all, hands down, no contest. Yes, exited poet Howard Moss, vanished essayist Milt Klonsky, lost prose jeweler Eli Waldron—fellow downtown votaries

185

at the Temple of the Word!—what a death grin you'd all come up with if I could tell you who now calls the shots for truth, sensitivity, perception, grandeur. Unbelievable, but it's the pretty boy and girl down the block who have grown past their highschool intimidation of the rest of us, have grown into valor at those outer edges we always assumed we owned—the dangerous, the existential, that naked self-exposure.

Can you believe it from (jayzus!) a player? Can you believe, further, that they now and for some time have snatched from literary celebrity the fires of legend? That sixty years after Gertrude Stein and Scott Fitzgerald, the latest dish about John Belushi's OD and David Bowie's androgyny and Stacy Keach's English jail-time is riveting precisely because these lives are more adventurous than that of the foul-mouthed poet at the end of the White Horse bar? The players and their cohorts are—I dread to say it—encountering more fresh human combinations, playing dangerously with more despair, more beauty, more money, more everything, than any other expressive segment of our society. Hoot if you want to, but isn't this the strange new meaning of avantgarde, being shot further out than the rest of us?

If the soaring American novelist of my young manhood has fallen into the automobile graveyard, and the bohemian poets and painters whom I knew wrote the final words on bourgeois defiance—Bodenheim, de Kooning, Kline, Delmore Schwartz, down to the kid ass-kickers like Ginsberg and Larry Rivers—it has remained for the (oh no!) actor to bring originality to the 1980s, where the nobler arts have repeated the story. Yes, like it or not, the actor worth the name makes new life out of life, Tom Signorelli breaking into my family phone call with the unwitting complicity of the New York Telephone Company because of an "emergency"—this time to tell me to see him in Mario Puzo's *The Sicilian*! What chutzpah. What wing-walking charm. Sure, it's a stunt; to the performer existence is pure show, and this may be the true CAT scan of our era in a way that professional thinkers are too desolated to accept.

What was inner for all the years of literary dominance is now being made outer. In a world as blindingly fast and forgettable as ours, truth is what can be seen and heard and sensualized. Look into the pit, friends: Admit that Samuel Beckett's one-volume trilogy, *Molloy, Malone Dies, The Unnamable*, will never get the "readers" it got as the theater piece *I'll Go On*, and that the recent seventeen-hour Bloomsday radio read of all of *Ulysses* was a rainfall to those who have never been able to get through the onslaught of print. Admit!

Is dramatization, and the almighty actor, then, going to be the externalized shorthand of life for the foreseeable future? I don't see how we can deny it, even while artifice drips from this vision like a false eyelash loaded with laboratory tears. Yes, our reality is now in the hands of professional showoffs, geniuses with no conviction except the culture of narcissism; but history has conspired to make them lightning rods. Did you say frightening clods? Play with my words any which way, the contemporary actor is now a metaphor for you and me, unlike the sequestered stars of yesteryear; and if we too wanted to be world class, we would stand up tall like Garrison Keillor and let the lights and music wash over us like a heavenly blow-job instead of cowering in the study. Face it: The word-makers now follow the trail of the players into the stardust mists of America, when once they would have fried them for breakfast.

Can you imagine intellectuals, friends of mine, teachers, essayists, lawyers, a shrink or two, actually buying books with titles like *From Mine to Thine* so they can "study" the ultimate narcissistic craft with an eye to crashing the movies as actors or, failing that, director/producers? Yet even as I howl at the joke I understand their humiliating need to cash in their lives, their professions, their self-respect. America, "the oldest modern country" (G. Stein), was still living up to its original clairvoyance when it unhesitatingly thrust Ronald Reagan into the White House with a roar from its unconscious—outta my way, movie critics who are blocking the future!

Does this mean, then, that those of us who have the old-fashioned brains and dash to write our own scripts, not just mouth them and prance and pirouette to chalk marks, must take a distant back seat to these darlings of first technology and then the world without going berserk? You've got it, luv. Oprah Winfrey knocks Joan Didion *and* May Swenson out of the box, Sean Penn devastates Derek Walcott, Arnold Schwarzenegger strides over print-shackled Hemingway as if Ernie were a bug. The true picture and sound of humanity in the late twentieth century is more than this pitiful black-and-white version I'm asking you to ingest right here, that's the message that's coming through, and it is being carried to the ends of the planet by the (who??) crusaders of velvet and plush.

Obvious question: Are such frail creatures up to the role of culture hero, not just getting it on for *Raiders of the Lost Ark* or *Crocodile Dundee* and triumphing over, say, the flu during the shoot, but bearing the image of humanity into the mysterious, roiling future? Yes, better believe it, such frail creatures must be up to it because history has picked this hour like a tolling bell and these once profile-obsessed mummers have been chosen to act out our own profile obsessions as well. It is no longer a question of who is worthy or unworthy to lead; the question is, always was, Who fits the needs of a new human tilt, who radiates the beams that once belonged to Byron, who has a special line from the back seat of that Mercedes to Mount Olympus?

The reward is no longer just immediate adoration if you're a member of the world's oldest gotta-be-loved-like-mad-or-I'll-perish profession. Although even that part of it symbolizes the mass yearning for approval of the age—a blending of hungers, you might say!—but the new kingdom of the player goes far beyond that. We have entered the era in which the rouged and primped purveyors of make-believe are now the world's embodiment of the Real Thing; the purveyors themselves are slowly beginning to think they are the Real Thing ("I've decided not to trust Gorbachev just yet"—Yves Montand), and in time it will be so acknowledged. Pity the poor writer or philosopher, scientist or composer, who still condescends to these unexpected icons—dare open your mouth and you will be lynched by the cry of sour grapes, envy, datedness, undignified lust for universality and all its perks.

Universality, all you Little League Goethes who thought it would be found in a book—how wrong we were.

1988

Index

189